MW01227448

EYE
OF THE CYCLOPS

Book One in the Eye of the Cyclops Series

CRAIG MAXWELL

Solaris Publishing, LLC
CRAIG MAXWELL
For all inquiries contact: Solarispublishing@outlook.com

Printed Worldwide
First Printing 2023
First Edition 2023

10 9 8 7 6 5 4 3 2 1

ISBN 979-8-9882646-0-6

Cover artist Oliviaprodesign fiverr.com

In Loving Memory
Roberta Maxwell
Aug 12, 1937- Nov 27, 2021
To my mother Roberta
My best friend. My Rock

You were my biggest supporter; you were my cheerleader and greatest champion. You were so excited and looking forward to reading this completed book. Well mom, here it is! Without you cheering me on this would not have become possible.
Thank you so much for supporting me when I felt this could not be done. I miss you so much mom, but my heart is full of joy knowing someday I will see you again in heaven.

Prologue

The smell of death permeated the air. Thousands of dead soldiers, men and women alike, littered the battlefield. Crimson rivers of blood flowed as swords, spears, arrows, bullets, and several other weapons of war met flesh and bone. Battle cries, shouts of anger, screams of agony rang across the plain. As the battle raged the sounds grew louder and louder in a mighty crescendo of pain and suffering.

Aldar Talon shouted commands as he, his sister Alana, and a battalion of soldiers ran into the fray. He gritted his teeth as his sword clashed with his opponents with a swift turn, and he thrust his blade into his foe's chest. He yanked his sword from the corpse's chest just in time. As another soldier charged him, Aldar dodged the attack and, before his enemy could recover, slashed the soldier across the throat.

Aldar Talon was a prince from a kingdom called Antillean, a beautiful land that had known peace for a thousand years. Unfortunately, all he could think about now was how to end this accursed war.

The prince was a muscular, clean-shaven forty-year-old man with hazel eyes, a straight nose, and a strong jaw. His armor was silver chain mail covered by a chest plate bearing his family crest and the blue-and-white banner of Antillean, which itself bore a mighty hawk with talons outstretched.

Alana, princess of Antillean, was strong and beautiful. She was thirty-seven and had a round face. She wore her silky brown hair in a long braid, and she wore the same armor and chain mail as her brother, instead of trousers she wore a knee-length battle dress. She was small in stature, and she used this to her advantage, as other soldiers underestimated her. She'd had to work hard to be allowed to fight in this war despite the objections of her father the king, Victor Talon. Together, she and Aldar fought and killed passionately for their kingdom's freedom.

"Look out!" Aldar yelled at her. Alana ducked just before a soldier could take off her head. She thrust her sword into the soldier's chest.

Aldar let out an angry curse as he continued to fight. *I almost lost her*, he thought. Before this war had started two months before, the Talon monarchy had known only peace—a peace that had been shattered by pain and death, thanks to the tyrant Xavier Pulsar, who had invaded their land. Xavier was the emperor of a kingdom known as Apollyon. He ruled his empire with an iron fist, and Apollyon was a land of despair and suffering.

Xavier's invasion had caught the Antillean people off guard, and he had captured several small towns on the southern fringe of Antillean, ransacking the villages and enslaving the townspeople. Why? Aldar was not sure; all he knew was that he had to beat the Apollyon army back out of Antillean. For a moment, he thought he saw Xavier sitting on top of a horse. *Enjoying himself, no doubt*, Aldar thought as he continued to fight.

~ ~ ~

Xavier Pulsar, an extraordinarily strong and muscular fifty years old, smiled broadly, folding his arms as he sat upon his black horse and watched Aldar and Alana fight. *Maybe I'll get lucky, and they will get themselves killed*, he thought, starting to chuckle. "The stupid fools! What kind of royalty charges headlong into battle?" Still, he did have to admit it was admirable, even if foolish.

Xavier had the brownish-olive skin that was typical of the Apollyon race. He also had a bald head, bumpy nose, and square jaw. His black eyes were piercing, and his unkempt beard and mustache were gray. Flames were tattooed like a crown across his forehead and decorated the length of his arms. On his chest, Xavier bore a tattoo of a man in chains being consumed by fire. This was the symbol of Xavier's empire and represented his favorite form of execution. All his tattoos were covered by black and red armor. The breastplate of his armor had the same symbol of the man consumed by fire.

Apollyon's emperor had nothing against the people of Antillean and had not wished to start a war, but he had little choice. Apollyon was in famine and was running out of resources. Although Xavier was a selfish ruler and had taken a lot from his people, hoarding nearly everything for himself, his army was loyal to him, for he fed them and treated them well. He knew that a happy army was a powerful weapon. Although ruthless, Xavier was also intelligent and had the support of some wealthy families that met his favor.

He also was paranoid and did not wish to lose his power, so he looked to Antillean, a land of wealth and prosperity—and an opportunity to extend his power. Although he did not long for war, he wished to conquer Antillean. To his surprise, Antillean had been able to quickly mount a resistance and stop his progress.

Xavier frowned as he watched another wave of his soldiers meet heavy resistance from the Antillean army. The sun was going to set soon, and he was starting to grow impatient. He watched, frustrated, as Aldar, Alana, and the rest of the Antillean army thwarted his attacks.

He noticed that Aldar was starting to show fatigue, and a diabolical thought came to him. He pondered for a moment, then shouted in a loud, gravelly voice, "Trumpeters, call for cease of battle!" A hundred trumpeters sounded a single blast all at once.

All combatants stopped fighting, for whenever an army sounded a single blast, it meant the head of that army wished to speak to the other ruler. Aldar wiped blood and sweat from his brow as he caught his breath.

A group of Apollyon soldiers cleared the way as Xavier Pulsar rode up to meet Aldar. "I must say, Aldar, it looks like you have had better days," Xavier said with a fiendish grin.

"What is that you want, Xavier? You can't tell me you stopped this battle to talk peace," Aldar replied.

Xavier let out a booming laugh. "You know me so well, Aldar. I know naught of peace; only the weak want peace."

"So, what in blazes do you want?" Aldar asked.

Xavier's smile broadened. "I wish to challenge you in a battle to the death."

Cheers arose from the Apollyon army, for all of them knew what an accomplished swordsman Xavier was. He had killed many people with his blade.

Xavier also knew what an accomplished swordsman Aldar Talon was. He waited for Aldar's answer with great anticipation, hoping the fool would accept this challenge.

Aldar stroked his chin in thought. "What are the terms for this challenge?" he asked.

Xavier chuckled. "Only this: one will live, the other will die, and the army of the loser will have lost their leader."

Alana put her hand on Aldar's shoulder. "Don't do it, brother. You have fought most of this battle; you are tired, but he is not. He will kill you to demoralize us."

Aldar smiled at his sister. "You are right, Alana, he is rested, and he will most certainly have the advantage." Xavier frowned in disappointment as Aldar continued, "But I cannot pass this opportunity up. I accept your challenge, Xavier."

Alana rolled her eyes as both armies let out a cheer. "I hope you know what you are doing, brother," she said as she put her hands on her hips, clearly annoyed.

Xavier's smile returned. "I am glad you have accepted. I was hoping your father had not raised a coward."

Aldar's face turned red. "You're right. Xavier. I am not a coward. You are," Aldar said, pointing an accusatory finger. Xavier's eyes widened with shock as Aldar continued, "You sit there all high and mighty on that horse. You just stay there watching as you send your soldiers to their deaths with no remorse. You do not care that your people are suffering, and you don't care about your army. You only care for yourself."

There was a moment of silence as tension started to rise. Xavier pursed his lips as he tried in vain to keep his composure. A great anger filled his heart as his eyes burned with rage. He shook his fist at Aldar. "I want you dead, you Antillean scum. It's too bad your father is too old to be here.

He could watch in horror as I take off your head and then hold it in the air and parade it around for all to see." Xavier dismounted, but he was so angry that he almost fell to the ground. He pulled his sword from his sheath, and it shook as his hands trembled. "No one insults me like that and lives," he snarled.

Aldar and Xavier walked toward each other. Xavier's eyes narrowed as Aldar approached. When they were six feet apart, they started to circle each other. Electricity filled the air, but all was silent, like the calm before a storm.

Aldar was calm and relaxed, while Xavier looked like he was ready to erupt like a volcano.

A scream burst from Xavier like a lion pouncing toward its prey, all his rage driving his attack.

Xavier swung his sword down to slice Aldar in half, but Aldar's sword swiped Xavier's sword aside, the clang echoing across the plain. Xavier let out a curse, then attacked again. Aldar again slapped Xavier's sword aside.

Xavier looked at Aldar, dumbfounded.

This time, Aldar attacked, catching Xavier off guard. Xavier barely managed to block the attack.

Both armies watched in silent amazement as their leaders fought, attacking and blocking each other. The dueling pair continued for several minutes as the evening sun began to set. Xavier could not believe it—he should have killed Aldar by now, but Aldar was still going strong even as Xavier's arms started to tire.

Xavier was starting to breathe heavily as exhaustion began to set in, but Aldar seemed not to be tired at all.

Xavier suddenly felt something he had thought he would never feel fear. Growing desperate, he doubled his efforts, attacking with all the strength he could muster.

Aldar backpedaled at this sudden furious attack.

Sensing his advantage, Xavier jumped back, dropping his sword, and pulled out a pistol he had hidden in his trousers. He cocked the hammer and pointed at Aldar before the prince could react.

They both paused for a second.

A smile spread across Aldar's face, and he started to laugh.

"Why do you find this so funny?" Xavier hissed.

"This is so typical of you, Xavier," Aldar said as he continued to laugh. "If you can't win, you cheat."

Xavier gritted his teeth and started to shake the pistol at Aldar, who said, "Before I die, I would like to address my army, if I may."

Xavier scowled at him. "I don't know why, but I will allow it."

"My soldiers, you have fought valiantly, and I am so very proud of you. My father would be proud of you as well. Alana, my dear sister, I am also proud of you. I know you can lead the Antillean army to victory." Then Aldar pointed his finger at Xavier. "So, upon my death, let the evidence speak for itself that the real coward is you."

Xavier screamed as he pulled the trigger.

The pistol did not fire.

Xavier looked at Aldar in horror, then dropped his pistol and reached for his sword, where it lay on the ground.

Seeing this unexpected advantage, Aldar attacked. As Xavier picked up his sword, he tried to block, but he was too late. The tip of Aldar's sword slashed across his face. Xavier screamed in agony and fell to his knees as his right eye flew out of its socket. Before Aldar could deal a finishing blow, an Apollyon soldier jumped in and blocked the attack.

All hell broke loose as both armies attacked. Aldar backpedaled at the onslaught of a horde of Apollyon soldiers that ran in and surrounded Xavier. They managed to get Xavier on his horse and a general yelled for retreat. The horns of the Apollyon army blasted the retreat call, and the Apollyon's turned and fled.

A cheer moved through the Antillean army as they started to pursue, but Aldar waved them back as he turned to watch a massive cloud of dust arise behind the fleeing Apollyon army. He looked back at his disappointed soldiers, knowing they wished to continue fighting, then looked across the battlefield. He was anguished by the sight of all the death, and a great sorrow filled his heart.

Aldar then climbed up onto a large rock, and the army cheered as he reached the top. He waved the cheers off, then addressed them. "You all did my father and your king proud today; however, today is not a day for celebration." He used his bloody sword to point all around him "Look at the death all around you. Today is a day of mourning." He felt a somber feeling arise in his army. "Many people died today, and families will be told that their sons and daughters will not be coming home.

"I don't know if Xavier Pulsar will survive his wound or not, but we must continue to be vigilant and defend Antillean to the end. I just pray this war will end soon. The sun is setting fast, and we must tend the wounded and take care of the dead."

"Your Majesty!" a healer shouted as Aldar finished speaking.

Aldar looked toward the calling healer, and horror filled his heart. "Alana!" he cried out. He ran to where she lay, blood running down her forehead. "Is she still alive?" he asked the healer with dread.

The healer frowned. "Barely, Your Majesty. She took a severe blow to the head. I will do what I can."

Aldar kneeled next to his sister and placed his hand on her forehead. A tear ran down his cheek. "You fought so hard to be here. Please live. Father will never forgive himself." He stood up to allow the healer to attend her. As he watched the other healers begin to tend the wounded, he then thought of his daughter Aurora, who adored her aunt Alana. "This will crush Aurora. Alana promised her she would return. Please let this war end soon," he prayed.

~ ~ ~

It was morning as twelve-year-old Aurora Talon walked down the hallway with her teacher, Bethany Dawn, walking beside her. Aurora, the oldest child of Aldar and Zena Talon, was an energetic and curious child. She wore her long red hair in a braid that reached the middle of her back. Aurora's oval face was freckled, with a pinched nose and mid-sized mouth below beautiful green eyes. She wore a royal-blue silk dress with white lace, accompanied by a tiara emblazoned with blue and white gems.

Aurora worried for her father and aunt as they defended their land, and she prayed that nothing bad would happen to them. Her aunt had promised they were going to pick berries when she returned.

Aurora had to deal with a more pressing fear at this moment, however. She looked up at Bethany, whom she loved more like a second mother than a teacher, the fear evident in her eyes. "Why must we see that statue? Mother says it's horrific to look at."

Bethany Dawn smiled at Aurora. She had been Aurora's teacher since the girl had turned seven. Bethany had run away from Xavier Pulsar's brutal slave pits and had been found, half dead, by Antillean soldiers just before the war started. They had brought her back to Antillean City, the capital of Antillean and the home of the Talon monarchy. She was one of many Apollyon slaves and immigrants who had made Antillean and the palace their home.

Bethany had eventually met the king and became his choice to teach Aurora. Now fifty-five years old, she was tall and skinny, with a square face, black eyes, and black hair streaked with gray. She had dark olive skin, which was slightly wrinkled, and always seemed to have a smile on her face. Bethany also laughed a lot. She had a witty sense of humor and told wonderful stories.

Today, Bethany wore a high-necked plain brown dress with black patterns. Bethany always wore high-necked dresses to conceal a brand on her neck—a ring of fire—which every Apollyon slave was forced to have. Aurora was generally curious about the brand, but Bethany talked little about her slave days because the memories brought her great sorrow.

Bethany took Aurora's hand gently. "It's okay, Aurora. No harm will come to us," she said reassuringly as they turned the corner of the palace. They walked down a long hall leading to a large chamber door, where a guard stood.

Aurora looked at the grand door. It was about twenty feet tall and bore the Talon crest.

The guard respectfully bowed. "Welcome, Young Majesty," he said with a smile. "Am I safe in assuming you have come to see the Eye of the Cyclops?" he asked.

When Aurora hesitated, Bethany spoke up. "Yes, she is. I thought it was about time she saw the Eye for herself."

The guard nodded approvingly as he turned and opened the door. "Enjoy, Your Majesty," he said with a grin.

Aurora peered nervously into the chamber but did not move. The chamber was huge and round, lit by wall sconces.

"Come, Aurora, you will be fine," Bethany said, coaxing the girl in.

In the middle of the room stood another guard. Aurora's eyes met his, and he bowed, saying, "Welcome to the Eye of the Cyclops."

Aurora looked up in amazement at the horrifying and grotesque statue of a cyclops. The cyclops was at least sixteen feet tall and was wearing a loincloth. It had huge, gnarled feet and large muscular legs. The cyclops's barrel-like muscular chest had scars across it, and veins popped out on the creature's thick neck. Its outstretched arms were muscular, and its hands had long, pointed fingernails.

The cyclops had a bald head with pointed ears, and its mouth was open, revealing its sharply pointed teeth. The creature had no nose, just two holes for nostrils. In its eye socket was a large reddish-orange orb that was dark and faded.

Aurora felt a chill run down her back.

Bethany pointed at the orb. "There it is, Aurora, the Eye of the Cyclops." She put her arm around the girl. "I know the statue is scary to look at, but it has an important story."

Aurora brightened. "You're going to tell me a story? I love it when you tell me stories."

"I know, but this is not just an ordinary story. It is horrifying but fascinating as well. Come, child, let us sit down." Bethany led Aurora to a bench facing the cyclops.

They sat down, and Aurora let her imagination take her away as Bethany spoke.

"This story begins at this very palace around a thousand years ago. Antillean was quite different back then and was ruled by a king named Ivan Albatross. He was a frail eighty-year-old man and was slowly losing his mind. He was bald on the top and had long scraggly white hair, a long-pointed nose, and a pointed chin. He had dark brown eyes, scraggly eyebrows, and a long, unkempt beard. He wore a torn purple robe and wore no shoes. He had a tarnished gold crown upon his head and smelled of urine and feces. To say the least, he was not very kingly. He had not always been this way, however; he was once a great leader and loved his people.

"That had changed twenty years earlier, when his only son, his daughter-in-law, and his two grandchildren died in a carriage accident. He and his wife, Alexandria, mourned the loss of their son and family. He had lost not only his son but also the heir to the throne, and Queen Alexandria was beyond childbearing years.

"Over the years, he started to neglect his people. He became cold and callous. The kingdom of Antillean was on the verge of economic collapse, and the people were on the verge of becoming impoverished.

"Then, just shy of her seventy-ninth birthday, Alexandria died. That was when the king finally grew mad and became increasingly erratic. The people of Antillean were suffering, and a rebellion formed against him. Sensing that his reign as king was in danger, he summoned one of his most trusted advisors, Cadmar. Cadmar was a middle-aged man with gray hair and black eyes. He was an evil mage who delved into powers no mortal man should have. The king entrusted Cadmar to come up with a device to protect his monarchy.

"Over the next several weeks, Cadmar and five other mages recovered a reddish-orange orb from a mine in the country of Avarlon, known today as Apollyon. Over several days, they called on the powers of darkness to infuse the orb. Over this time, a full-on rebellion had begun, and the people called for the king to lay down his crown. Even some of his army had turned to the rebellion. They were on the verge of civil war.

"Then a great battle began just outside the palace gates. The people were charging the palace. The few army men who were loyal to Ivan Albatross were on the verge of being run over. Cadmar finally came to the king with the magical orb. It's about time! The people are attacking!' the king snarled at Cadmar.

"Cadmar knelt in front of the king and held out the orb, saying, 'My apologies, Your Majesty.'

"Ivan grabbed the eye from Cadmar. The reddish-orange eye began to glow, and he felt a surge of power run through his veins. It startled him at first, but then he felt as though he were young again. It was intoxicating—no, it was *exhilarating*.

"As the rebelling crowd knocked down the palace gates, Cadmar was trying to explain how the eye worked, but somehow, Ivan knew what to do. Ivan lifted the eye above his head and began to chant. Suddenly, the blue sky turned a reddish-orange color as storm clouds rolled in. Lightning cracked the sky as the wind roared and a torrent of rain started to fall. A great earthquake shook the land, and the people began to panic.

"Ivan began to laugh maniacally as he harnessed the power of nature. He smiled with delight as the people ran away in terror. Over several weeks, he learned how to control the eye, and he murdered several thousands of Antillean people. The power of the eye possessed him. His eyes glowed orange-red and pulsed like burning flames as he became totally mad. Holding the eye over his head, the mad king could fly across the sky or appear out of thin air. With a loud command, he created fearsome cyclopes that ravaged the land, killing all those who opposed his power.

"Cadmar watched in horror as Ivan lost all sense of reality and slowly killed everyone, including his allies. Cadmar decided that he must steal the eye back and destroy it before Ivan could massacre any more people, so he and his mages attempted to blindside Ivan. But somehow, Ivan knew of their plan and was ready for them. Before they could attack, he held the eye above his head, and out of nowhere, the horrible cyclopes attacked the mages, ripping them apart and killing them unmercifully. With the mages' deaths, all knowledge of the creation of the eye was lost.

"Ivan felt invincible, like a god. 'I am Apollyon. I am immortal, a god, and destroyer of all who oppose me! he declared. He was also lonely, so he decided to do something unthinkable. He was going to bring his wife, Alexandria, back to life. Then he would bring his son and his family back as well, he decided. He laughed as lightning streaked across the sky.

"Late one evening, he called upon one of his servants, Tiban Talon, to exhume the body of the queen. Tiban was a twenty-five-year-old man with short sandy-brown hair and eyebrows and with hazel eyes in an oval face. He wore a brown ragged vest, trousers, and brown sandals. When he was approached by Ivan, Tiban refused to help until Ivan threatened to kill Tiban's wife and newborn child.

"Tiban, feeling ill as he approached the grave, said a prayer and then started to dig. After an hour, he had dug up the corpse. He apologized to the queen as he laid her decomposed body onto a stone slab. 'Shut up and back away, you scum,' Ivan commanded. Tiban bowed his head, then backed away in disgust at the terrible thing he had been forced to do. Ivan smiled broadly as he lifted the eye over his head. The eye glowed, as did the kings, as he commanded the queen to rise. The rotted corpse started to twitch. He shouted his command again, and the body began to shake. Ivan began to chuckle. He commanded again, this time lifting the eye as high as he could, holding it only by his fingertips and shouting at the top of his lungs for the queen to rise.

"He started to laugh loudly and uncontrollably as the sky grew suddenly dark and thunder shook the ground. The corpse shook violently. 'Come back to life, my love,' the king shouted in excitement.

"Suddenly, Tiban tackled Ivan from behind. Ivan let out a yelp as he fell hard to the ground. Ivan looked in horror as the eye clattered across the ground. 'No!' he cried.

"Tiban got to his feet as Ivan tried in vain to trip him. Tiban ran as fast as he could towards the eye. He stopped just short of it and looked down at it with terror. He did not know what to do. He was afraid to touch it for fear he would turn into the evil thing Ivan had become.

"Ivan then stood up and pulled a dagger from his robes. 'Foolish boy! You have no idea what the eye can do." It has power beyond your comprehension. Walk away now or I'll kill you.' Tiban looked at Ivan as the king approached with dagger in hand. Then he looked down to the eye.

"Tiban gritted his teeth, and Ivan's eyes grew large with shock as Tiban picked the eye up and trembled at the powerful surge he felt through his body. Tiban lifted the eye up in his hands and felt a wonderful euphoria. He felt like he could rule the world. He felt immortal. 'No!' he shouted. 'I will not let this evil take me.'

"Ivan let out a shriek and charged Tiban with his dagger in the air. Tiban chanted something, and a bolt of lightning shot out from the eye, striking Ivan in the chest. Ivan cried out in agony as his body shook violently, the bolt surging through his body. He then fell, limp, to the ground.

"Tiban set the eye on the ground and fell to his knees. 'How did I do that?' he wondered. He had somehow known what to say, and what he had wanted had happened. He looked at Ivan, whose face bore a horrible look of rage, but then the king's glowing orange-red eyes faded, and he lost all expression. Ivan's eyes closed forever.

"Tiban fell and lay on his back, exhaustion setting in. He could not believe what had just happened. He alone had stopped the evil king who had killed so many. This man who had claimed to be a god. This man was now dead. Tiban cried as a great relief washed over him.

"After several minutes, Tiban returned to his feet and reluctantly picked up the eye. With a command from him, all the cyclopes disappeared from the land and the sky cleared. Tiban dropped the eye to the ground, then took off his vest and used it as a sling to carry the eye, for he did not want to touch it again for fear it would make him mad as well.

"Word of Ivan's death spread across the land, and Tiban Talon became a hero. Soon afterward, he was crowned king of Antillean. His first command was for the eye to be destroyed. Unfortunately, no matter what they did, the eye seemed to be unbreakable, but Tiban did not give up hope.

"It was discovered that a special type of marble found deep in the mines of Antillean took the power from the eye when it met the eye, so King Tiban Talon commissioned several sculptors to create the cyclops statue you see here. It was his hope that the awful memory of the cyclopes would thwart any attempt to steal the eye. Finally, after several months, the statue was finished. With a smile on his face, King Tiban carefully placed the eye into the cyclops' eye socket. The light of the eye went dim, and all in attendance applauded. That is how the orb got its name, the *Eye of the Cyclops*.

"King Tiban posted four guards around the cyclops and two at the front door to make extra sure no one would attempt to steal the eye.

"Ivan Albatross and his wife are buried at the front gate of the palace. Their tombstone reads, 'Death comes to those who meddle with evil powers.'"

Aurora brought her hand to her chin in thought. "But, Bethany, I come in and out of this palace, and I have never seen any tombstone."

"Unfortunately, child, it has fallen into disrepair. Flowers and plants have reclaimed the grave. If you look hard next time, you can still see the tombstone. The writing is very faded, but it can still be read. Maybe later we can go out and see it together."

Aurora frowned as she noticed only one guard standing in front of the cyclops. "Why is there only one guard here instead of four" she asked.

Bethany smiled at her. "Tiban was one of the greatest great-grandfathers of your family line and was a brave hero who saved Antillean, but stories back then were exaggerated and much of this story is considered to be more of a legend these days. These guards are only here for ceremonial purposes, out of respect for the memory of Tiban Talon. The eye really has no power; it's just an ancient orb."

"Has anyone tried to remove the eye to see for sure?" Aurora asked.

"No, child, it is considered to be a memorial, and removing the eye would be disrespectful to the memory of Tiban Talon."

Aurora nodded in understanding, then noticed a package sitting next to Bethany "What is that?" she asked.

Bethany handed the package to Aurora. "A gift for you, my dear," she replied.

Aurora opened the package eagerly to find a book titled *The Eye of the Cyclops.*

Bethany put her hand on Aurora's shoulder. "It has everything in it that I told you about, and more."

Aurora wrapped her arms around Bethany. "Thank you, Bethany, for telling me this story, and thank you for the gift."

Bethany kissed Aurora on the forehead. "I know you love to read. Enjoy it."

Suddenly, they were interrupted by a soldier who walked in and said to the guard, "Hey, Jonathan, I just heard our company is going to join the war in three days."

"Thank the name of Tiban Talon," the guard replied. "I've been tired of just standing around here, doing nothing."

Aurora started to frown as she remembered that they were still at war. “Please protect Father and Aunt Alana, and please let this war end soon,” she prayed.

Part One

Legend of the Eye

Chapter One

The Rose of Apollyon

"Five years! This awful war has gone on for five full years. It is finally time for me to end it," Levi Eclipse muttered under his breath. "I am going to rid Apollyon of that demon and send him straight back to the underworld." The demon he was referring to was Xavier Pulsar.

Levi was an assassin posing as one of Xavier's personal liaisons for the past three years. Many were the times he had wished that Aldar Talon had successfully killed Emperor Pulsar. Now he hoped to do what Aldar had failed to accomplish, for Emperor Pulsar was bringing the people of Apollyon to their knees.

Because of his injury, Xavier Pulsar no longer fought in the war, instead spending most of his time in his palace, receiving messages of the war's progress. This had given Levi an enormous advantage. Over time, Levi observed all of Xavier Pulsar's movements and, despite its size, the layout of the palace.

The palace's massive towers, which jetted brilliantly toward the sky, were made of dark brick and many battlements. Scattered across the palace were ornate statues of gargoyles, dragons, grotesque monsters, and demons. Walls surrounded the palace with long walkways for the guards to walk and protect Xavier Pulsar. They towered over the city of Adaliah, the capital city, which lay in the middle of Apollyon.

Adaliah had been a beautiful city when it was known as Raina. Xavier had renamed the city Adaliah in memory of his dead sister. The city was slowly falling into decay and disrepair, and most of the people lived in poverty. Only a handful of families lived in luxury—the families that fell into Xavier Pulsar's favor. Even though the famine had ended two years previously and the lakes and rivers had returned, Apollyon still struggled.

Levi hoped to restore the land he loved to its former glory—before Emperor Pulsar had renamed it Apollyon—and for peace to reign.

Levi was a tall, thin, forty-nine-year-old man with brown eyes and balding gray hair. He had a long, thin face with a long nose, thin mouth, and round jaw, and he was clean-shaven. He wore a simple black uniform with red shirt, black vest and trousers, and black boots. Emblazoned on the front right side of his vest was the symbol of the man consumed by fire. His meager wages barely covered his needs. He was not impoverished but was not wealthy, either.

Levi thought of his wife and two children—a twenty-year-old son named Enoch and a daughter, Elaine, who had recently turned eighteen. He wanted a better life for them. He was tired of the oppression of Xavier's rule. Levi wanted to give his children a special gift, one they had never experienced: freedom. He also wanted to give this gift to his wife, Lana, who worked diligently to keep the Eclipse household going. He wanted to give this gift even at the cost of his life, for he knew the chances of his making it out alive were slim.

In case he was able to make it out of the palace on this day, however, he had Lana hiding outside the palace gates with two horses so they could make their escape. He had told her to take off without him if he was not back in an hour. Levi prayed that his plan would come to fruition, for the fate of Apollyon was on his shoulders. In just a few minutes, Xavier Pulsar was going to hold his weekly court with the commoners, and if all went well, Levi would be able to kill Xavier while the emperor was distracted.

Levi tried his best to look calm as he walked down the long, massive main hallway of the palace. The hallway, which was more than sixty feet wide, stretched several hundred feet. The stone walls of the hallway bore several wall sconces, as well as tapestries with the symbol of the man consumed by fire. The walls stretched to a massive arched ceiling fifty feet above the ground that was accented with gold and silver. The floor was marble with black and red streaks, and several pieces of furniture were spread through the hallway.

Levi passed several servants, handmaidens, and slaves. Many of them looked down in fear as they hurried to do their tasks. So far, everything was going without a hitch; all he had to do was nonchalantly walk to the entrance of the balcony of the throne room.

He stopped in his tracks when the entrance to the balcony was in sight. He held in a curse as he saw a familiar woman with shoulder-length black hair standing in front of the entryway. The woman, thirty years old, had dark brown eyes; a short, thin, nose, and a medium mouth set in an oval face. Her name was Pirena Solaris, and she was known as the Lady of Death.

No one was completely sure where she had come from, but she always called Emperor Pulsar uncle. What mattered now was that she was the emperor's personal assassin and general of the army's spy network. She had a scar on the left side of her neck from a scuffle with an Antillean soldier.

Pirena was a dangerous woman and had killed hundreds of people in the name of Xavier Pulsar. Next to Xavier Pulsar, she was the most feared person in Apollyon.

Today, Pirena was wearing black slippers and a black knee-length silk battle dress with the Apollyon symbol on the boddice. Two short swords in scabbards crisscrossed her back, and she was rumored to carry several small daggers in her sleeves and under her dress. As the Emperor's assassin, she was a master swordswoman and was proficient in hand-to-hand combat. She also was a master of disguise. It was said that she had once dressed as a rich heiress and once as a slave to get her quarry. She also was a thief and could sneak in and out of a building without detection.

She was the first woman and youngest person to attain the rank of general and ran the most disciplined branch of the Apollyon army. She was a strict disciplinarian and did not accept failure. The punishment she meted out for failure was quick, harsh, and sometimes deadly. Xavier Pulsar loved her dearly; in his eyes, she could do no wrong.

Pirena was fiercely loyal to the emperor, and if you were her target, it meant certain death. She killed with passion and had no mercy for her victims.

What is she doing here? Levi scowled. She had been away for several weeks. He paused for a moment. "Well, this will certainly complicate things," he muttered. "My chances of pulling this off have significantly dropped." He began walking toward her slowly.

Pirena turned her head toward him and gave him a devilish glare. Levi's heart skipped a beat as she yelled, "There you are!" He stopped and looked at her in terror, his blood running cold.

Pirena walked toward him. "Excuse me, Levi, I have a rat to drown," she said as she stormed passed him.

Relief washed over him as she headed toward Martin, head of palace security, who was walking several feet behind him. Martin, a tall, bald, lanky man wearing a black Apollyon uniform, had a look of horror in his eyes as Pirena screamed, "Security here is pathetic! I managed to sneak past several of your guards."

"Everything is all right, Pirena. Emperor Pulsar is just holding court with a bunch of worthless townspeople. There is no danger," Martin said with a trembling voice.

"All I got to say, if you don't do a better job and something happens to Uncle, it will be my blade severing your head."

Levi hurried to the entryway while Pirena continued to yell at Martin. The entryway door was locked. Fortunately, he had the key and unlocked the door before entering the staircase. He quietly shut and locked the door behind him, still hearing the voice of Pirena—now muffled—shouting.

He carefully walked up the stairs, trying to not make any noise or bring attention to anyone who might be nearby. He finally made it to the balcony overlooking the throne room. The balcony was massive, with red carpets and red upholstered seats, and it stood thirty feet above the throne room floor. It was reserved for the generals of the Apollyon army and the wealthy people who met Xavier's favor. Today it was empty, for, as

Martin had said, it was the common people's opportunity to hold court with the emperor. Because of this, the wall sconces were not lit and the balcony was dark. Levi hoped he would not be seen. He started to feel nervous as he crawled across the floor toward the railing. He reached under one of the seats to find that the dart gun was still where he had hidden it a week earlier.

Levi had made the gun himself. It was like a small pistol, with a special chamber, along with a mouthpiece on the back. He pulled a poisoned dart from his uniform pocket, making sure not to poke himself. He smiled as he put the deadly dart into the gun and blew air into the chamber. "One good well-placed shot, and that lout will be dead within a few minutes."

The gun and dart ready, Levi looked out at the throne room. It was massive; the stone walls reached a hundred feet tall. The arched ceilings were beautifully painted, showing the once-great city of Adaliah in all its former glory. The room was wide enough to fit a thousand people, and its floor was made of the same black-and-red-streaked marble of the hallway. Underneath the balcony was a massive entryway, and at the far end of the room on a raised platform sat the thrones of Emperor and Empress Pulsar. Both thrones were made of black iron and had red upholstery.

The stairway leading up to the platform was carpeted in black and red emblazoned with orange flames. Behind the thrones, on the wall hung a massive tapestry with the symbol of the man consumed by fire. Levi watched as Apollyon people make their way into the room from beneath him. On the far left was a massive door standing twenty feet high where Emperor Pulsar would make his entrance.

Levi heard the door underneath him close as the last of the people entered the throne room. "Come on, you filthy animals, gather together closely!" a soldier yelled at them. The crowd quietly did as they were told and slowly started to huddle close to one another. "Faster, worthless beasts!" the soldier yelled. The crowd then hurriedly fell into place, though some of them tumbled to the ground.

Levi shook his head. "These poor people, treated like animals. They come for help, and all they get is harassment."

Another soldier kicked one of the townspeople who had fallen. "Get up, idiot!" the soldier yelled.

After several minutes, things started to settle down and the crowd became silent. A great nervousness hung like a dark cloud across the room, like the people were on the verge of panic. In his perch, Levi sat hunched on the floor, feeling the anticipation of Xavier Pulsar's arrival almost overwhelming him. He could see that the crowd felt it too. It seemed like the air had been sucked out of the room and everyone held their breath.

Levi started to sweat anxiously. "When is he going to arrive?" Levi muttered to himself.

A loud gasp moved across the crowd as the doors to the left of the hall slowly opened. Then a man appeared, holding up a flag of Apollyon. The man, named Daniel Enigma, was Xavier's personal slave and often introduced the emperor. Enigma was a tall, middle-aged Apollyon man with a round face and long black scraggly hair. He had gray eyes and was unshaven. His nose was flat, and he was missing some teeth. He had suffered much punishment from Xavier Pulsar and had received several black eyes and broken noses through the years. He wore a black beret-like hat and simple black shirt and trousers.

That poor man did not deserve the fate he got, Levi thought. *Well, as soon as I kill Xavier, he will be free again, poor soul.*

"Hear ye, hear ye!" announced Daniel, breaking the silence. "Introducing the Rose of Apollyon, Empress Shiva Pulsar."

"What?" Levi almost shouted. She wasn't supposed to be there either. "What in the name of Apollyon is happening?" This day was not turning out at all as he had planned.

The crowd roared with excitement, for, unlike Xavier, Shiva was beloved. She was nothing like the emperor and did what she could to help the Apollyon people. Xavier rarely allowed her to come to court, primarily because she often tried to reason with him on behalf of the people. Xavier was a cruel ruler but loved Shiva very much and occasionally would listen to her. She was kind and compassionate, and the Apollyon people loved and respected her.

Shiva was known as the Rose of Apollyon because she was the most beautiful woman in Apollyon and perhaps the world. She was tall and had a perfectly shaped body. Her face was oval, and her long blonde hair reached her lower back. She had a baby-like pinched nose, oval jaw, and thin mouth. Her smooth olive skin had an almost copper-like tone, but her most beautiful feature was her amber eyes. At forty-four years old, she was more beautiful than most women who were half her age.

Today, the empress wore a golden crown in the shape of flames, and her long-sleeved scarlet dress bore orange and yellow flames. Upon her feet were scarlet slippers.

Although Levi wanted to kill Xavier, he did not wish to do it in front of Shiva, but he had no choice—this was his chance. He knew Shiva would be better off without that demon and she could rule the land at least until their son Maximus was ready.

The slave, Daniel, walked ahead of the empress, holding the flag high as six black-armored royal guards escorted her in. Shiva smiled and waved at the cheering crowd as she made her way up the stairs to stand in front of her throne. She turned to face the crowd and blew kisses at them before finally sitting down.

The crowd grew silent again as Daniel walked back to the door. All knew who was coming next.

As the emperor entered the doorway, Levi grinned. "Finally, my chance has come."

Chapter Two

Assassination

Daniel walked into the holding chamber with a smile on his face. He loved to have the honor of introducing Shiva. She was truly the people's empress, and he thought the world of her.

His smile quickly disappeared, and his fond feeling was replaced by fear and dread as Xavier Pulsar walked out of the shadows. Daniel tried his best not to quiver, for the sight of Xavier sent shivers down his spine.

While Shiva was the rose of Apollyon, Xavier was certainly the thorn. Daniel could never get used to the sight of him. Although the wound that Aldar inflicted on Xavier's face had healed a long time ago, it had left him with a horrific scar. Where his right eye had once been, the emperor now wore a glass eyeball colored red, with yellow flames in place of the iris. It would glint in the sunlight and, combined with Xavier's unkempt beard and real black eye, gave him a demonic look.

Despite his injury and being unable to fight, Xavier kept himself active and in spectacular shape. Today, he wore an open black vest that exposed his tattoo of the man consumed by fire. Along with this, he wore black trousers, black boots, and a sword in its scabbard. He gave Daniel a fiendish grin. "Well, dog, you did a good job introducing my wife. I assume you won't mess up my introduction?"

Daniel stuttered nervously, "Yes, Your Majesty—I mean no, Your Majesty! I mean, I won't mess up, Your Majesty."

Xavier let out a booming laugh and put his hand on Daniels's shoulder. "Daniel, you are so funny. I love it when you chatter like a buffoon."

"Yes, Your Majesty," Daniel said with a nervous laugh. "I will do my best to introduce you properly."

Xavier's smile disappeared, and he glared at Daniel. There was a long moment of awkward silence. Then Daniel jumped as Xavier yelled, "Well, you dog, what is taking you so long? Introduce me, already."

"Yes, Your Majesty! Right away, Your—"

"Move, you dog," Xavier said, cutting Daniel off.

Daniel almost fell as he ran to the entryway door. There, he stopped and took a deep breath. He stood tall and yelled, "Hear ye, hear ye! Introducing the Giver of Life, the Taker of Death, his Royal Majesty Emperor Pulsar!"

The crowd roared in a forced cheer, for if they did not cheer, it meant death.

Daniel walked out with the flag held high as six soldiers walked in front and six behind Xavier Pulsar.

Xavier walked out with his fist raised, his chest puffed out for all to see. He walked up the steps to the thrones, where he kissed Shiva and winked at her. She smiled back at him. Xavier then turned to the crowd and raised his fists in the air as the cheering reached a fever pitch. The crowd chanted, "Long live Emperor Pulsar! Long live Emperor Pulsar!"

As Daniel was putting the Apollyon flag in its holder, Xavier approached him. He slapped Daniel on the back, jolting the slave forward. "Good job, dog. I guess you get to eat today."

Daniel bowed. "Thank you, Your Majesty."

Xavier gave the slave a curt nod as he sat on his throne. He turned his attention to the cheering crowd and scowled at the sight of them. "Filthy vermin," he muttered to himself before waving the crowd to silence. "How dare you all come to my palace in rags. You are all dirty!" he shouted. The crowd shifted on their feet nervously as he continued. "You all smell like sewer rats. This is my home, and you come to me like this?" He spat on the floor in disgust. "Why in the name of Apollyon should I listen to your requests? I think I shall not."

"Ahem," Shiva said, grabbing his attention. When he met her eyes, she smiled at him. He rolled his eye in frustration, then stood up and approached her. "What is it, woman?" he whispered in her ear."

Shiva stopped smiling and looked at him sincerely. "Please have mercy on them, for they are poor and cannot afford good clothing or to bathe."

Xavier rolled his eye again but then smiled. "There's a reason I rarely allow you to come, but fine, I will listen to their pleas. I will do my best to ignore this insult for today." Shiva smiled again, and he returned to his throne, also smiling. "How in blazes does she do that?" he asked himself as he shook his head.

Once more addressing the crowd, he said, "I have changed my mind. I will give you this chance to redeem yourselves. However, remember, I am your ruler. I am the law. You only live your pathetic lives because I allow it." He turned to Daniel. "Now this worthless dog will explain the rules and procedures of this court."

Levi grew anxious as Daniel addressed the crowd. He looked down into the throne room floor in frustration. He needed Daniel to move out of the way. With Xavier moving back and forth to Shiva and then with Daniel standing in front of Xavier, Levi could not get a shot. It took Daniel forever to explain the rules, and Levi knew that the longer he waited, the greater the chance that he would be seen.

Xavier, watching Daniel as he addressed the crowd, let out a huge yawn. He hated holding court; it was so boring. He turned to Shiva and smiled at her, and she smiled back. *What a beautiful woman*, he thought, and his mind drifted back in time to twenty years before, when he had first fallen in love with her. He had just returned from a hunting trip and was to meet his most trusted friend and advisor, Nova Quasar. Nova had brought some slave traders from the land of Salonia who wished to make an accord with Apollyon.

It was a hot summer day as Xavier and his hunting party rode across the dirty streets of Adaliah. Trumpeters sounded their horns as his guards shouted, "Make way for the emperor!" People kneeled and shouted, "Long live the emperor!" while others scrambled to get out of the way of the charging entourage.

Sweat beaded on Xavier's forehead as they continued toward the palace. He smiled when it came into view, as he was looking forward to getting off his horse, taking a long bath, and drinking some chilled wine. Although his hunting trip had been successful, Xavier was tired and wanted to rest. Although his friend had worked hard on this meeting, Xavier decided he would postpone it. *Surely Nova would understand it would not hurt for the slave traders to wait until tomorrow,* he thought. *Besides, they are probably tired from their long journey as well,* he convinced himself as he reached the palace gates. He would have a grand feast that night, for the wild boar he had killed would make a fine meal, indeed.

The soldiers saluted him as they opened the gate to let him and his entourage through. As he made it through the gates, Xavier saw his friend and the slave traders in front of the palace entryway.

Nova smiled as Xavier rode up to them and came to a halt. Bowing his head, he said, "Welcome home, Your Majesty." Nova was forty-seven years old, tall, and handsome, with long blonde hair. He had a clean-shaven oval face, blue eyes, thin mouth, and average-size nose. He was wearing a black Apollyon officer's uniform, with medals on his left shoulder and the Apollyon symbol on the right.

Xavier's smile broadened as he got off his horse. "No need for the formalities, my friend. You know you can call me by my name."

Nova raised his head. "Sorry, Your Majesty—um . . . I mean Xavier," he said with laughter in his voice.

Xavier let out a booming laugh as he walked up and hugged Nova. "It has been a long time, my old friend. Glad you made it home safely," he said.

"As am I. It was a very long trip, and I am relieved to finally be home," Nova said. Nova turned to the two men standing behind him, saying, "These are the two men from Salonia I told you about."

The two men bowed. One of them said, "Pleased to finally meet you, Your Majesty." "Emperor Savage gives you his sincerest apologies for not being able to meet you in person." The two men wore black hooded robes, and Xavier could barely make out their faces. On the chest of their robes was the symbol of Salonia, a man with a hammer upraised to strike an anvil. The empire of Salonia was proud of its industry and of its suppliers of weapons, armor, and slaves.

Xavier nodded. "Give him my regards as well, and I hope to meet him soon."

The traders bowed again. "Yes, Your Majesty, we will let him know."

Nova looked at Xavier again. "I know you just returned from your trip. I am sure you are tired. You probably would like to freshen up before we meet."

Xavier gave Nova a sympathetic look. "About that, friend . . . I was thinking—" Xavier stopped in the middle of his sentence. He had seen in the background a beautiful young woman wearing a green silken dress. Xavier was completely mesmerized.

"Xavier, are you all right?" Nova said with a hint of concern, shaking Xavier out of his stupor. Then Nova noticed that Xavier had been looking at his daughter. "I am sorry, Xavier; I hope you do not mind I brought my daughter with me. I hope this will not be a problem. I haven't seen her for several months. She met me here to welcome me and join the meeting. I can send her home if you wish."

Xavier smiled. "I don't mind at all. She is your daughter; that makes her family. She is most welcome to join us."

Nova smiled back at Xavier, then spoke to his daughter. "Come, Shiva," he said, motioning to her. Xavier's smile broadened as she approached. "I know you two met a while ago when she was a child but let me reintroduce her. Xavier, this is my daughter Shiva."

Shiva bowed deeply. "It is a pleasure to see you again, Your Majesty."

Xavier nodded. “The pleasure is all mine,” he said. Shiva gave him a smile that sent shivers down his spine. She was beautiful. *What a sight to behold*, he thought.

Nova put his arm around Shiva’s shoulders. “She is the elder of my two daughters. She is eighteen. My other daughter, Shannon, is sixteen and unfortunately could not make it.”

Xavier pondered for a moment. Why had he not noticed Shiva before? How could he have overlooked such beauty?

Nova turned to the slave traders and apologized for the disruption.

The traders nodded. “We have families; we understand,” one of them replied.

Nova then addressed Xavier. “What were you going to say?”

“What do you mean?” Xavier asked.”

“You were in the middle of a sentence when you were distracted by Shiva.”

Xavier remembered that he was about to postpone the meeting until the next day. “I cannot remember what I was going to say; it must have not been important. I guess I am getting old,” he laughed.

Nova laughed along with him. “A sad but true fact, my friend,” Nova said.

Xavier then addressed the slave traders. “Where are my manners? Please, let us get out of the heat. Welcome to my palace. You will need to freshen up, as will I. Come on in. I will have my slaves bring you food and chilled wine.”

Two soldiers opened the massive doors of the palace, and Xavier led his guests into the grand hallway.

Nova gave a tour of the hallway to the traders as they continued to walk, but Xavier tuned him out. He could not stop staring at Shiva, who smiled back at him nervously.

The sight of her took his breath away. She walked straight and tall. She looked like royalty, the way she carried herself. Her long green silk dress flowed flawlessly as she walked down the hallway. Her amber eyes glowed like the twilight at the end of a summer day, and her rose-colored lips looked seductive. Her soft-looking skin had a perfect copper tan, and her lovely long blonde hair reached to the middle of her back. She was the most beautiful woman he had ever seen. In his eyes, she was perfect. *She is an angel—no, she is a goddess!* he thought.

Xavier returned to reality as he looked across to Shiva sitting next to him on her throne now twenty years later. He wished he were alone with her in their bedchamber, for now he wished to kiss her.

"Are you ready, Your Majesty?" Daniel asked, interrupting his thoughts. Xavier glared at him, and Daniel stepped back in fear.

Xavier sighed. "Yes, I am ready to proceed. Let's get it over with."

When Daniel bowed his head and nervously walked down the stairs, Levi thought, *Finally, my time has come.* He started to sweat nervously, unable to believe that after three years of preparation, he was finally going to kill the emperor. Levi struggled to steady himself as the butterflies in his stomach took wing. The anticipation was almost overwhelming as he put his gun on the railing and aimed it at Xavier's chest. *For freedom! For Apollyon!* he thought as he moved to pull the trigger.

"Look! Assassin on the balcony!" Pirena said, pointing at Levi.

Levi let out a curse as the room erupted into chaos. He had not seen Pirena standing next to the guards. In haste, he fired his dart gun.

The dart shot across the room, right at Xavier, but in the confusion, Shiva ran toward Xavier, right into the dart's path. She screamed in pain as the dart struck her side, and she stumbled forward.

Xavier caught her in his arms and laid her carefully on the floor, screaming at Daniel, "Get the healer! Make haste!" Daniel almost stumbled down the stairs as he ran down them and into the hallway.

Shiva cried in agony as Xavier pulled the dart out of her side and looked at it in horror. "A poison dart," he gasped. Xavier looked down at his rose and put his hand on her forehead. Cold sweat beaded on her brow. Her copper skin had turned an ashen gray, and her breathing had become labored. Xavier held her hand. "The healer will be here soon, my love," he said, trying to reassure her.

Shiva let out a gasp, then screamed in pain and started to shiver. "It hurts so bad," she said, tears rolling down her cheeks.

Xavier looked up. "Where in blazes is that healer? What is taking him so long?" he yelled.

"Xavier?" Shiva asked in a weak voice.

"What is it you want, my love?" Xavier asked, trying to keep the panic from his voice.

She squeezed his hand weakly. "Tell Maximus I love him."

"Don't talk that way," he said, more sharply than he had intended, then softened his voice. "You will be fine."

"Please," she pleaded. "I am dying; there's nothing that can be done. Please tell him."

Xavier hung his head, as the horrible reality of what she had said was true. "I promise. my love. my rose."

Shiva smiled at him. "Thank you," she said in a voice so weak that he could barely hear her.

Suddenly, she started to cough up blood and blood started to run out of her nose. She let out another gasp as her eyes fluttered and she started to shake violently. Her body seized up as she let out a last strained breath, then her eyes closed, and she went limp.

Xavier looked down at her in shock as Daniel ran up behind him. Daniel paused for a second to catch his breath. "The healer is on his—" Daniels's voice caught in his throat as he looked down at Shiva's corpse. He started to cry. "Shiva. My poor Shiva. She cannot be dead." He fell to his knees as tears streamed down his face.

Without warning, Xavier stood up and kicked him in the chest. Daniel gasped as the air was knocked out of him. Xavier kicked him again, this time in the side, and Daniel rolled down the stairs, hitting his head on the floor at the bottom. His head was swimming as he painfully rolled onto his back. Daniel heard footsteps coming down the stairs. His head cleared as he looked up at Xavier's face, and he shuddered, for there was a look of murder in Xavier's eye.

Xavier unsheathed his sword and held the point to Daniels's throat. "I told you to never call her Shiva again, only 'Your Majesty.' I should kill you now, you slow-moving slug. I wish I had never promised her I would not."

Rage filled Daniel's heart. "Go ahead, kill me. I want to die. Her Majesty is dead. It doesn't matter anymore. Kill me and be done with it, you cowardly cretin."

They were interrupted by Martin running up to Xavier. "I heard there was a commotion, Your Majesty. What happened?"

Xavier looked at Martin, his face burning with rage. He pointed his sword toward Shiva.

Martin's face went pale as he was gripped by realization of what had happened. He looked at Xavier with terror in his eyes.

"Because of you, my wife is dead, you incompetent, lazy, good-for-nothing sloth." Without warning, Xavier rammed his sword into Martin's chest.

Martin's eyes bulged in shock.

Blood splattered all over Xavier's face as he pulled the sword from Martin's chest. Martin's body fell, limp, to the floor. Xavier fell to his knees, smearing the blood across his face and letting out a blood-curdling scream.

After several silent minutes, the emperor got up and once again stared down at Daniel. "Get up!" he commanded.

Daniel slowly did as he was told, wobbling on his feet.

"I promised Shiva, I would never kill you, and in honor of her, I plan to keep it. A promise is a promise." He put his hand on Daniel's shoulder. "I know this has been a living hell for you, and I am sorry, but it is what it is." Xavier gave Daniel a long, hard look that was almost like respect. "Now get out of my sight," he said, pointing to the door.

"Yes, Your Majesty," Daniel said as he bowed the best he could. Then he hobbled out of the audience chamber.

Xavier yelled at the top of his lungs, "Someone find that assassin! I will make him wish his mother had never kissed his father."

Chapter Three

Murderer

Levi ran down the stairwell as fast as his feet could carry him, dropping the key as he reached the door. He got on his knees, frantically reaching for the key. After several seconds, he found it and unlocked the door. He scurried down the hallway, tears streaming down his face. Had that really happened? He could not believe it.

He had failed, and now Shiva was dead. Instead of saving Apollyon, he had just sealed its doom. He would forever be branded a murderer and the most hated man in the world. He had no idea what he was going to say when he reached Lana. He dreaded telling her what had just transpired. He prayed she would forgive him for this atrocity, for now, they would never be able to return to Apollyon. First, they must escape, and then he would tell her what had happened once they were far from the palace and in the woods. He just had to make it down the next hallway, to the door leading down to the sewers, and no one would find him.

He rounded the corner. Without warning, someone kicked him in the face. He fell hard on his back, staring up at the ceiling. Dazed and confused, he tried to sit up, but someone pushed him back to the floor.

He looked to see what was holding him down and saw a boot on his chest. As he looked up, two swords crossed against his throat. He looked into the eyes of Pirena Solaris, which were full of rage and hate.

"Murderer!" she screamed at him. "How dare you! You killed Aunt Shiva; you scum." She kicked him in the side. Levi howled in pain as he felt some of his ribs crack. "Did that hurt? Aw, too bad. You've only just begun to hurt."

Levi tried to catch his breath. "I'm sorry," he croaked.

"What do you mean, you're sorry?"

"I did not mean to kill her. I meant to kill the emperor."

Pirena snarled at him. "You try to kill Uncle, instead you kill Aunt Shiva, and you expect me to forgive you?" She slid her blades, so they barely broke the skin on his throat. "I should kill you now." Pulling her swords away, she commanded, "Pick him up and bind him."

Two soldiers Levi had not seen picked him up roughly, and he grunted in pain as they bound his hands.

Pirena spit in his face. "I will let Uncle kill you. I will enjoy watching you die slowly and painfully." Then she gave him a wicked grin. "Follow me to the Throne room," she commanded as she sheathed her swords, then led the way.

Levi groaned as the soldiers pushed and shoved him all the way there. As they entered the audience chamber, Levi watched—still in disbelief—Shiva's corpse being carried away. He then noticed Xavier facing away from him. The emperor seemed to be wiping his face with a bloody towel.

"Uncle, we caught the murderer," Pirena announced.

Xavier turned to face them and dropped the towel as his eyes widened in stunned shock. "Levi?"

Xavier stared at him for what seemed like an eternity. Then the emperor's face darkened, and he clenched his fists. "Why?" he asked.

Levi bowed his head. "I am sorry, Your Majesty. I did not mean to kill her; it was an accident."

Xavier shook his fist at Levi. "You're sorry? It was an accident. You didn't mean to kill her? I suppose you meant to kill me, didn't you, and you're sorry? I trusted you, and you try to kill me?" Storming to Levi, Xavier punched him in the stomach. Levi gasped and crumpled to the ground. "Oh, I'm sorry, Levi, that was an accident. I didn't mean to hurt you, but it's okay because I said I was sorry. Pick him up," Xavier demanded.

When the soldiers had lifted Levi back up, Xavier unsheathed his sword and held its tip to Levi's throat. "Who hired you to do this? Tell me and I may give you a merciful death."

"I did this on my own," Levi said.

"Don't lie to me, you vermin. Tell me who hired you. Tell me now!" Xavier screamed in rage.

"I told you, Your Majesty, I acted alone. This was my idea. No one hired me; this was my own doing."

"Liar!" Xavier pulled the sword back and thrust it toward Levi's throat but stopped an inch short.

Levi looked at the sword and then at Xavier in confusion.

Xavier sheathed his sword, his eyes brightening at the wonderful idea that had formed in his mind. "I met your wife a couple of times. Her name is Lana, if I'm not mistaken." Levi's eyes widened in horror as Xavier continued. "You also have a son. I think his name is Enoch—tall and strong young man, if I remember. Of course, your daughter, Elaine—beautiful young lady—she takes after her mother. Nice girl indeed." Xavier gave Levi a fiendish grin. "You love them with all your heart. They are your life."

"Your Majesty, please don't harm them! Lana and the children know nothing of this," Levi pleaded.

Xavier scowled at him. "Then tell me the truth. You will still die, but I will make them my slaves and they will be treated well. If you don't, I will kill them in front of you, and then I will kill you with the horror of watching them die still fresh in your mind. Now tell me, Levi, who hired you?"

"I tell you, Xavier, I acted alone."

Xavier punched Levi in the stomach again, and Levi again grunted as he bent over in pain.

"Do you think this is a joke, Levi? Do you think I will not kill your family? For the last time, who hired you?"

Levi struggled to catch his breath as he looked up at Xavier defiantly. "I said I acted on my own."

Xavier screamed as he punched Levi in the face. Levi fell unconscious on the floor. "Take this piece of dung to the dungeons and find his wife and children. Maybe they will talk."

As the soldiers dragged Levi across the floor toward the hallway, Pirena approached the emperor. She looked down at Martin's body. "Good, Uncle, you beat me to that lazy slob." Looking at Xavier, she saw the pain on his face. It was clear that he wanted to cry but could not and would not. He only stood in stunned silence.

Pirena moved closer to Xavier and started to cry. "Oh, Uncle, I am so sorry Aunt Shiva is dead, and it's not just Martin's fault; it is mine as well. I have failed you, Uncle. I saw Levi in the main hallway. I should have known I should have stopped him." She dropped to one knee and bowed her head. "Please kill me, Uncle. I deserve to die."

As Xavier put his hands on Pirena's shoulders and lifted her to her feet, Pirena braced herself for whatever punishment he would give. To her surprise, Xavier hugged her. "No, Pirena, this was not your fault. You had no way of knowing."

Pirena sobbed uncontrollably on his shoulder. "But I failed you! I'm your spy, your thief, your assassin—I should have seen this coming," she pleaded.

"You are not perfect. You can't be everywhere at all times. This was not your fault," Xavier told her, firmly but gently.

"But I am *supposed* to be perfect. I—"

Xavier put his finger on Pirena's lip and pulled back from her embrace. "Hush now. I will hear no more of this. It is not your fault."

When Pirena nodded at him hesitantly, he put his hands on her shoulders again and even managed a weak smile. "I know you are hurting, and you are mourning the loss of Aunt Shiva, but I need a favor of you."

Pirena smiled back at him. "I'll do anything, Uncle. Whatever you need me to do, I will do it."

"I know you will," he assured her. "I do not know if I will find out who hired Levi, so I need you to try your best to find out who. I want you to take your sorrow and your pain and turn them into anger to avenge your aunt. Find them for me, and we will make them pay dearly for what they have done."

A look of angry determination filled Pirena's face. "It will be done, Uncle. I will not stop until my dying breath."

Xavier's smile broadened. "That's my girl! Get angry let it be your guide." He kissed her on the forehead, then urged, "Now go, child, get started. Do your best. I love you," he added. "I must go as well, for I must tell Maximus that his mother is dead."

Pirena bowed solemnly, then turned and walked away.

Xavier looked around at the chamber, trying to process everything that had happened and wishing it were only a nightmare. He walked up the steps to Shiva's throne and put his hand on its arm. Her form was imprinted on the throne's cushions. Fury overtook his heart, and he started to shake. He shouted at the guards standing near him. "Have someone clean this bloody mess up!" Looking down at Martin's corpse, he demanded, "And cart this piece of trash out of my sight."

The guards scurried into frantic action as Xavier stomped down the steps to find his son.

Chapter Four

The Dungeon

Levi slowly opened his eyes as a sharp pain ran down his side. *Broken ribs*, he thought. He tried to touch his side but realized he was sitting down, and his hands were shackled to the floor. "Where am I?" he whispered, but then it dawned on him that he was in the dungeon. He looked around and saw a faint glow coming from a small, barred window in the wall above him. Otherwise, it was dark. A foul odor in his cell smelled of mold, urine, and feces. He started to shiver. The floor was cold and damp.

Over time, his eyes adjusted to the dark. He could see the bars of his cell mere feet from where he sat. The dungeon was the only place Levi had not scouted in his time at the palace. It was just as foul and revolting as he had imagined it. "Hello, anyone there?" he shouted. His voice echoed across the dungeon, mocking him. "I guess I must be in the solitary part of the dungeon," he muttered. He could not believe he was the only one there.

"So, I am alone." Suddenly, a rat scurried past his feet. "I guess not." He laughed until a sharp pain reminded him of his ribs. Then he wept for what he had done, killing Empress Shiva, the only hope for Apollyon. He worried for his children, for he had brought shame on his house and shame on them. He prayed that Lana had escaped and was safely heading to Antillean.

Levi's thoughts were interrupted by a faint sound in the distance that grew louder with every passing moment. It sounded like a woman yelling. When he recognized the familiar voice, anguish seized him, and he yelled his wife's name.

Through the bars of his cell, he saw a faint glow appear on the other side of the dungeon, revealing a hallway and three figures coming into view. Behind the three figures was another, a soldier holding a torch. Levi heard Lana scream, "Let go of me!" and he was finally able to see that her hands were bound and she—in between two soldiers—was one of the three figures.

She fought against the soldiers as they tried to drag her across the floor of the hallway. "Take it easy. No need to fight," said one of the soldiers holding her.

"For crying out loud, stop it," the other pleaded.

Lana screamed at them and continued to struggle as they took her to Levi's cell door. The soldier with the torch unlocked the door, and the other two tossed Lana in the cell. She hit the floor hard.

Now Levi could see that one of the soldiers who had been restraining Lana had a bloody nose. "You can have her," the soldier told him. "She punched me in the nose."

Lana turned her head toward the soldiers. "I hope I broke it," she snarled as the soldier unconsciously touched his nose.

"Come on, let's get out of here. She's a she-devil, she is."

Lana climbed to her feet and spat at them as they walked away. Then she turned to face Levi. The faint glow from the window revealed a fat lip and a black eye. Her long brown hair was askew, her blouse was tattered, and her skirts were torn. Levi looked at her in silent horror, and anger gripped him like a vice. "What in the name of Apollyon did they do to you? The cowards."

Lana turned away from him and started to sob, the light revealing that the back of her blouse was ripped. Levi could barely make out what appeared to be bloody welts on her back. "They whipped you?" He struggled against his bonds. "I will kill whoever did this to you. I will make them pay."

Lana ran over to sit beside him, putting her face against his chest and then starting to sob. Through her sobs, she began to tell him what had happened. "I tried to escape, my love. I heard a loud commotion and figured you were in trouble, so I turned my horse around to escape. I left your horse behind and tried to nonchalantly ride out of the city. I was almost at the city gates when I heard a loud clatter of hooves behind me. I turned my horse around to see a dozen soldiers on horseback galloping towards me. I heard someone yell, 'There she is!' I put my horse to a full gallop. There were too many of them, and they managed to surround me. A soldier hit me in the face and I fell off my horse. Then everything went dark."

Lana told him that she had been shaken awake, then tied and bound before being thrown on her stomach over the back of her horse. After several minutes, she had been pulled off the horse and dragged into Emperor Pulsar's apartments. The emperor had worn a look of pain and sorrow, but his expression had turned to one of anger as he had explained to her what had transpired.

Levi let out a groan. "Then you know, don't you?" he said.

"Yes, I do, my love. He told me you were spotted, about the poison dart and Shiva dying. He told me everything."

Levi turned his head away. "I am sorry, my love. I failed Apollyon, I failed our children, and I failed you. I was so stupid! I should have aborted the mission the moment I knew Pirena was there, that unholy wench. Look what has happened to you! This was my doing, and now you are going to suffer even more. Please forgive me."

Lana's sobs had stopped, and she smiled at him. "It was not your fault. Unfortunately, Shiva was at the wrong place at the wrong time."

"You were not there, woman. I practiced that shot a thousand times, and I killed her. She is dead because of me." He realized he was shouting at Lana, then let out a curse. "I am sorry, love," he said in a softer voice.

"It is all right; you are upset. I know you didn't mean to yell at me." Lana kissed him on the cheek.

"What else did they do to you?" Levi asked with great apprehension.

"I know this will make you upset, my love, but here is the rest of what happened to me." She told him how Emperor Pulsar had asked who had hired Levi. "She told him she had had no idea that Levi had planned to kill him and that she was in town to purchase flour and had no idea why she was being chased." The emperor had then slapped her across the face, calling her a liar and threatening to kill the children. "She still told him she had no idea," she added. Then Emperor Pulsar pointed to a hook hanging from the ceiling and had demanded that she be tied up and whipped.

"They had to untie her so they could bind her hands to the hook. That was when she punched that soldier in the nose." She had stomped the foot of the other soldier and tried to escape, punching yet another soldier in the face. "She made it to the door, but it was locked," she told him. That was when several soldiers had tackled her and tied her up.

A soldier had ripped the back of her blouse and started to whip her. "Oh, Levi, the pain was unbearable, but I didn't crack." Finally, Xavier had grabbed her and shaken her violently, continuing to tell her that he was going to kill their children. "Then he demanded I be brought here, and—well, here I am," she finished. Tears were streaming down her face again. She leaned into Levi. "I hope he doesn't find the children. Oh, I couldn't bear it if he does."

Levi kissed her forehead. "Do not fret, my love, they will be all right," he said, trying to reassure her. It was unfortunate that he could not even reassure himself. "They will escape Apollyon and will be free. Come now, rest on my shoulder, love, you need to sleep. You have been through a lot."

Lana nodded in silent agreement, and they sat in peaceful silence. Levi was about to drift off when a booming voice broke the silence.

"What a charming-looking couple." Levi and Lana jumped as a blinding spark lit the dungeon, showing them Xavier's grin as he lit his torch. The flickering light cast a horrifying shadow across his face, accentuating the fiendish grin. "So, Lana, you did know about this after all. Interesting indeed, and obviously your children know as well. It is amazing what you can find out when people think they are alone.

"Now your children will die, it is certain," the emperor told them. "You can't deny it, Levi, I heard you. They know, and I am going to find them, and I am going to kill them. I will put a price so high on their heads, the whole empire of Apollyon will search them out. Every stone will be turned; every cave will be explored; every tree will be climbed. There will be no escape."

"You will never find them, you son of a siren!" Levi roared at him. "They will escape, and you will never get a chance to kill them."

Xavier eyed Lana as he spoke to her husband. "That was a huge mistake, Levi. No one insults me and gets away with it."

"I am sorry, Your Majesty," Levi pleaded. "I am sorry I killed Empress Shiva."

"I am growing weary of your apologies, but perhaps my son will listen. Come over here, Maximus."

Levi's and Lana's eyes widened as a tall, dark figure walked into the torchlight. A fierce-looking Maximus Pulsar glared at them. He was nineteen years old and heir to the throne as Xavier and Shiva's only child. Maximus was a head taller than his father, and just as strong and muscular. His skin had the same bronze tone as his mother's, and his hair was short, black, and wavy. His mustache, neatly trimmed, sat between his bumpy nose and medium mouth. The younger Pulsar had a square face and cleft jaw, and black eyes that gave him an unnerving, piercing look. He was wearing black armor over black chainmail, the breastplate bearing the symbol of Apollyon.

Maximus clenched his fists as his lips moved into a snarl and he glared at them silently.

Levi, looking straight into Maximus's eyes, broke the tense silence. "I am sorry. I killed your mother. She was the only light in Apollyon, and I extinguished it. I am so sorry."

To Levi's surprise, Maximus started to laugh. "You're sorry? You kill my mother and you're sorry?" He continued to laugh.

Maximus grabbed the bars of the cell door and shook them violently. "You are a murderous coward, and you dare apologize?" He spat on the ground, "I want them dead, Father. They must pay for this atrocity. I want them to scream for mercy and we will not give it to them. I want them to suffer."

Xavier put his hand on his son's shoulder. "No worries. They will pay dearly for what they have done. First, we must find their children and we will kill them. They will suffer loss like we have. Then we will kill you," Xavier said, pointing at Levi and Lana. "You will die by fire—a fitting death."

Lana crawled to the cell door and pleaded, "Please, Your Majesty, I implore you, don't kill our children. Please have mercy."

"Your husband had no mercy on my rose, so why should I give them my mercy?" Xavier slammed his fist against the cell door. "Last chance—I will let them live if you tell me who hired Levi."

Lana looked at Xavier and said, "My husband tells the truth and I stand by what he says. No one hired him; this was our idea."

Xavier spat in her face. "They are as good as dead. In the meantime, I will find other ways to make you talk." Xavier pulled a pistol from his trousers and smiled at Maximus. "Ready for some fun?"

Maximus grinned. "I sure am, Father."

"Good." Xavier pointed his pistol at Lana's head. "Now tell me, Levi, who hired you?"

Levi licked his lips as sweat beaded on his brow. He looked at Lana, then Xavier, but said nothing.

Xavier changed the gun's aim from Lana's head to Levi's chest. "Okay, Lana, it is your turn to talk."

Lana stared at Xavier in defiant silence.

"My, what a stubborn couple they are! Oh well." Without warning, he aimed his pistol at Levi's leg and fired.

Levi cried out in agony as blood spurted from his leg. Lana rushed to his side and tried to stop the bleeding. Xavier and Maximus laughed in glee at the sight. "Do you want a turn?" Xavier asked as he reloaded the pistol.

"I would be delighted, Father," Maximus said, and Xavier handed him the pistol.

A clatter of footsteps interrupted them as a soldier holding a torch ran into sight and kneeled in front of Xavier. "Your Majesty, the mortician says that Shiva's body is ready, and he awaits your instructions."

Xavier's smile quickly faded away as he turned to Maximus. "I must go, my son. I will see you later."

"Father, I would like to go," Maximus protested.

"No, I must see your mother in private," Xavier replied. When Maximus frowned, he added, "No worries, son. I will send for you when I am done, and you can see your mother." Maximus nodded reluctantly, and Xavier told him, "In the meantime, you can vent your anger. Go ahead and shoot Levi in the other leg. Don't kill him, though. We need him to be alive to see his children die."

"Yes, Father. I will not kill the weasel, but I will make him pay."

Xavier nodded approvingly, then turned to the soldier and put his torch in a sconce on the wall, saying, "Lead the way," before following the soldier down the hallway.

Maximus paced back and forth like a hungry caged animal, staring at Levi and Lana as if they were his prey. Lana stood up and glared at Maximus defiantly. Maximus stopped and pointed the pistol at Levi.

"Oh, no, you don't," Lana said as she moved in front of Levi. "You will not be shooting my husband. If you are going to be shooting someone, it will have to be me."

"What are you doing, woman?" Levi protested.

Lana ignored him, continuing to glare at Maximus. For a long time, they simply stared at each other.

Finally, Maximus laughed. "You don't think I won't shoot you, witch? Think again." He pointed the pistol at her head.

Lana stood still, unflinching. "You plan on killing me? Wouldn't that make your father angry at you?"

“I don’t care!” he shouted, and the pistol started to shake.

“Have you ever killed anyone before?” Lana asked.

Maximus rolled his eyes. “Why are women so infuriating?” he snarled. “Fine, I will shoot you in the leg.”

Lana moved her left leg forward. “Please shoot this one. It is weaker than the other. “That way, I will be able to support myself with my good leg.”

Sweat beaded on Maximus’s forehead.

“Go ahead, Your Majesty. You wanted me to suffer, so here is your chance,” she prodded. Maximus moved the pistol to aim at her leg, his hands still trembling. Lana gave him a motherly smile. “Is there anything the matter, Your Majesty? You can shoot me in the right leg if you prefer.”

An animalistic rage filled Maximus’s eyes, and he pointed the pistol down the hallway and fired. He looked back at Lana, all rage gone from his eyes, then lowered his head. “Consider this my mercy,” he said quietly.

Lana bowed her head. “Thank you, Your Majesty, for your gracious mercy.”

“Don’t get used to it,” he said curtly, then grabbed the torch from the sconce on the wall and slowly walked down the hallway.

Levi and Lana watched Maximus walk away until he disappeared into the darkness. “You are a crazy woman, Lana Ann Eclipse, and I love you,” Levi said with all the strength he could muster.

She smiled at him. “Help untie me if you can, my love. I must tend to your wound.” She walked up to him. After several attempts, Levi was able to loosen her bonds with his teeth and she was free. Lana tore a piece of fabric from her skirts, and wrapped it around Levi’s wound. “I’m sorry I can give you nothing for the pain.”

Levi smiled. “Come lie with me again. Let us rest.”

Lana rested her head on his shoulder.

This time, they whispered in each other’s ears so anyone else who might be unable to hear what they said.

"How did you know Maximus wasn't going to shoot you?" Levi asked.

"I did not know for sure, my love. I know he is not as brutal as his father. Empress Shiva had a big impact on his life. I think when she was able, she taught him about kindness and compassion and tried her best to be a positive influence in his life. So, I challenged him in hope he had some of her compassion, and he did not shoot me."

Levi sighed, "And I destroyed that influence."

Lana scowled at him. "No more of that, it is what it is, and I will hear no more."

"I am sorry, my love."

"It is all right," she said. "Let us talk of the children. I pray they are all right."

Levi gave her his best smile. "They will be as soon as they make it into Antillean. They will be safe. King Talon is a compassionate man. Come, my love, let us rest."

Lana nodded, and soon, both were in dreamless sleep.

Chapter Five

Remembrance

Xavier Pulsar walked quickly down the hallway toward the mortuary. He stopped as he reached the door. He stood there for several minutes, dreading seeing what was on the other side. Then he took a deep breath and walked through the door. His heart skipped a beat. There she was, his love, his empress, his rose of Apollyon, lying on a stone table, looking like she was sleeping. She was wearing a white gown, and the crown of flames was still on her head.

Xavier walked up next to her. Even in death, she looked stunningly beautiful. He reached down and touched her hair, then gave her a kiss. Her cold lips were confirmation that she was dead, and a depressed, empty feeling took hold of Xavier. He could feel the great sadness preparing to consume him. "No!" he shouted, and the empty, sad feeling was replaced by rage. Xavier clenched his fists. They started to shake violently. "Why? Why? Why? How in the name of Apollyon did this happen? This cannot be. My rose is gone." He grabbed a mirror hanging on the wall and with all his strength smashed it to the ground.

The mortician, an old, balding man wearing a black uniform, ran into the room. "Your Majesty?" he asked, interrupting Xavier's tirade.

"What?" Xavier yelled at him.

The mortician shook in fear as he took a knee. "I am sorry for interrupting you, Your Majesty. I heard you come in, and all this noise." He paused for second. "I just wanted to make sure you were all right. My name is Benjamin, and I am here to serve you, Your Majesty. I am so sorry for your loss. Empress Pulsar will be dearly missed."

Xavier stood in silence, beginning to calm down. "You may rise," he commanded. Benjamin slowly rose, continuing to shake in fear. Xavier gave him a curt nod. "I would like to be alone with her a while. I will call you when I wish to talk."

The mortician bowed his head. “As Your Majesty commands. I will be in the back, and I will return when you call for me.” The mortician bowed his head one more time as he quickly walked out of the room.

Xavier looked at his bride again. This time, he smiled at her as memories flooded his mind. He remembered the long journey home after he was injured by Aldar Talon. His face had been covered in bandages and the pain in his face had been unbearable. He had felt every bump down the bone-jarring path and had wanted to kill the driver. How in blazes could a driver hit so many bumps in the road? By the time they had reached the palace, he was wishing he were dead and had been so weak that he had needed to be helped off the wagon. Finally, he had been in his bed and his personal healer had come to see his injury.

When the healer had taken off the bandages, he had gasped at the horrid cut and missing right eye. Despite being weak, Xavier had managed to grab the healer by his shirt and shake him violently. “What are you looking at?” He had pulled the healer closer. “Do I look like a monster? Am I repulsive?” He had let go of the healer as pain ran down his face; he had forgotten that it was painful to talk.

The healer had lain prostrate on the ground. “Forgive my transgression, Your Majesty. I meant no disrespect.”

“Now, Xavier, that is no way to treat someone who is trying to take care of you,” a sweet, familiar voice had called to him. Xavier had quickly covered his face with his hands, seeing Shiva out of the corner of his left eye. She had stood there in a gold and white laced dress, as beautiful and breathtaking as ever.

“Shiva, my love, I—ow!” he had yelled in pain.

“Please don’t talk, Xavier, it will just bring you pain,” she had said in a soothing voice. She had then smiled at the healer. “You may go now. Get a drink from the kitchens. I will call for you.” Once the healer had stood up, bowed, and gingerly walked out of the room, still shaking from the traumatic experience, Shiva had walked up to Xavier and stood by his side. “Come now, Xavier, there is no need to cover your face.”

Despite the pain, Xavier replied, "I am hideous. I—ow!" He yelped again.

"Please don't talk, Xavier. You are hurting yourself. Besides, you cannot hide your face from me forever." She had gently placed her soft hands on his rough, burly hands. He had desperately wanted to stop her but could not. When she pulled his hands away, Xavier had braced himself for the inevitable scream of terror. Her face had come into full view and a brief look of concern had filled her eyes, but then she had smiled.

Xavier had looked at her in shock, then smiled back. Pain had seized him again. "Ow!"

"Best not smile for a while, either." Shiva had chuckled, lifting his hand and kissing it. "Have no worry, for I am here, and I will take care of you." He had been about to protest when she put her finger to his lip. "Hush now, Xavier, please. No protests. I am going to take care of you." Then she winked at him. "I do not care if you are emperor of Apollyon or not; that is the way it is going to be."

Anger had rushed through him. No one told him what to do, and certainly no one shushed the emperor! Then he had looked at her angelic smile and all his anger had melted away. How could he be angry at her? He loved her with all his heart and soul and would do anything for her. He had put his hand on her cheek and managed to say, "I love you."

She had smiled and blown a kiss at him, and he had let her take care of him. She had fed him, bathed him, and dressed his wound. She had been there for him throughout his recovery. She had even given him updates from his highest general, Virion Nebula, whom he had assigned to run the war in his absence.

Finally, the day had come when he no longer needed the bandages, and his glass eye was placed in its socket. He could not believe how well Shiva had helped him, and he knew he certainly did not deserve the help she had given him. He could not understand how a woman who was so gentle and so kind would not run away from a barbarian such as he.

Xavier looked down at his dead bride, then took her hand in his and kissed it. "Thank you, my love. You gave me kindness and compassion; I only gave you sorrow and grief. I am sorry, my rose of Apollyon. I am sorry, for I am selfish and took your happiness away. I wish you were alive to hear me say this. I love you with all my heart. Please forgive me." He looked up and said loudly, "I wish to speak."

Benjamin walked in meekly. "Yes, Your majesty?"

An hour later, Xavier walked out of the mortuary door. A group of people were waiting in the hallway—servants, scribes, and liaisons. They all looked at him nervously and expectantly. "I need a decree to let the people know about the assassination attempt and what has happened to Empress Pulsar. I need to get in contact with General Nebula as soon as possible to let him know what has transpired. I need to contact King Talon as soon as contact can be made. I need someone to get my son so he can see his mother. Now make it happen," he commanded. Everyone in the hallway scattered to do their tasks. Xavier watched them scurry away, and soon, he was alone with only his thoughts to keep him company.

Chapter Six

A Meeting of the Monarchs

Victor Talon, King of Antillean, sat on his chair, his right hand knuckled under his chin on the conference table in front of him. He was deep in thought. Victor, seventy years old, was waiting to meet with his generals to talk about strategies and battle plans. He was an attractive man for his age, with short salt-and-pepper hair and short-trimmed beard and mustache along his square jaw. His nose was straight, his eyes hazel, and his lips thin. Upon his head he wore a gold crown engraved on the front with a hawk with its talons outstretched. The crown was adorned with blue gems. He wore a white silk shirt, blue silk trousers, blue silk slippers, and a blue cape embroidered with the same hawk. He also wore a ring with an engraved hawk.

Even though he was fit for a man his age, Victor was too old to fight in the war and it frustrated him to no end. He looked across the large room to where a painting of Tiban Talon was hung on the far wall. He stood up and walked to it. He studied it often. Even though he had never known his great ancestor, he would talk to the painting as though Tiban were alive in the room with him. "Oh, Tiban, I know you would know what to do. I could really use your counsel now."

Victor was tired. The war had taken its toll on him, its burden overwhelming. He did not want to fight a war; he wanted to spend his remaining years in peace. The war was agonizing for him, for he was the first ruler of Antillean in more than a thousand years to declare war, but he had had no choice, for Xavier Pulsar had been ransacking and destroying Antillean. Victor Talon loved his people, and it was up to him to serve and protect them. It pained him so to have so many of his countrymen and -women die.

Beyond that, the war angered him. Why had Xavier not asked for help? He would have been more than happy to help his neighbor. He would have helped feed the hungry people of Apollyon and given them hope for prosperity. Unfortunately, Xavier was a tyrant and thought only of himself, and because of his greed, the people of Antillean and Apollyon suffered. Five years after the start of the war, with several thousands of casualties on both sides, the war was in stalemate with no end in sight.

Several times, Victor had tried to negotiate peace with Xavier, but in vain. He wished he were younger; he wished he could do more. Victor felt useless as a king just sitting in his palace. He wanted to do more than have meetings with his generals and make battle plans; he wanted to fight. He pounded his fist on the table and ground his teeth, wishing Xavier were dead.

A knock on the conference door interrupted his thoughts. "Enter," he commanded.

A soldier entered the room. "Your Majesty, I have an urgent message for you. Emperor Pulsar wishes to speak to you."

"*He* wishes to speak to *me*?" King Talon asked in surprise. Xavier had never approached him. In all the times they had talked, King Talon had been the one who initiated the conference, not Xavier. This was strange, indeed. "Is everything getting set up?" he asked. When the soldier nodded, the king said, "Tell all who were to meet me that I'll be late and will be with them shortly."

The soldier bowed, murmuring, "Yes, Your Majesty," then left.

The king walked as quickly as he could to his meeting chamber. At the large wooden door with gold trim and a gold handle, he nodded at the two guards standing at the door. They bowed their heads as he opened the door and walked inside.

Violet Silverwood, his personal assistant and inventor, awaited him in the chamber. Violet, at fifty-three, had silver hair, blue eyes, and a hawklike nose. Today, she was wearing a long, flowing blue dress. She bowed her head. "Your Majesty, I have everything set up for you. Please take a seat; it will just take a few minutes, and everything will be ready."

Victor sat in a large oak chair. In front of him was a large crystal panel that Violet called a message cystallis. It was as tall as an average man and was at least the span of three large men. To the right of the king sat Violet, and in front of her was a large table bearing several cylindrical crystal knobs that she pushed and turned in different directions.

Victor had no idea how everything worked. Even after several explanations by Violet, he found it confusing. It had something to do with the sun and gravity or some odd things like that. It also powered several small portable cystallis machines for the battlefield. All he knew was that it worked at great expense and was used only in important situations. He waited with great anticipation, thoughts fluttering around his mind. *What does he want? This had better not be a waste of time.*

"Your Majesty, all is ready," Violet said, interrupting his thoughts.

The crystal panel started to glow, and an image slowly started to coalesce on the screen. Finally, Xavier appeared on the screen. Victor scowled; he had forgotten how hideous Xavier looked after Aldar had struck him in the face. Then Victor gave the emperor a curt nod. "Xavier, it has been a while since we last spoke."

"It's been almost a year, I think," Xavier replied, returning the same nod.

The two men sat in silence for several seconds before Victor finally broke the silence. "I must say I was pleasantly surprised when I was told you wished to speak to me. To what do I owe the pleasure of this conversation?"

Xavier frowned. "There certainly is no pleasure in this conversation, and I don't relish your company. However, given the situation I am in, I have no choice but to share what you call pleasantries."

Victor's face grew dark. "What in blazes is this? I am in no mood for your games."

"Have you nothing better to do than jest me? Is this a new twisted tactic you are trying to pull on me?"

"You must be getting desperate, and you are wasting my time, so unless you have anything important to say—" Victor stopped. It had just dawned on him that Xavier did not look angry. What did he mean by *given the situation he was in*? This was very strange indeed. Usually when Victor argued with him, he would shout back. Something was wrong.

"I do have something to say," Xavier said calmly. "My rose, my empress, Shiva, is dead."

Victor's eyes widened. He felt a cold chill run down his spine as the shock of what Xavier had said shook him to the core. He stared at Xavier. Was this a sick joke to throw him off? *No, he would never use Shiva as a ploy.* Victor saw the cold expressionless look on his face and knew the emperor was telling the truth.

"Well, Victor, do you have anything to say?" Xavier asked with a hint of irritation in his voice.

"I am so sorry for your loss. Shiva was a dear and loving woman. The world is a much darker place without her. What happened? I had not heard that she was ill. This is very unexpected and shocking."

Xavier folded his arms across his chest. "Shocking and unexpected, indeed. She was murdered."

"What monster would do such a thing? Shiva was a beloved woman," Victor said, feeling another wave of shock.

"It was an attempt on my life. The assassin was spotted, and the room erupted into chaos. The fool shot Shiva in the side with a poison dart. He meant to kill me, and he accidentally killed her—or so he claims."

"So, you captured the murderer?" Victor asked.

"Yes, we did, and it was one of my most trusted subjects. His name is Levi Eclipse. He was one of my personal liaisons and I thought I could trust him. I have him and his wife in the dungeon, where they await punishment, and I have my entire empire searching for his children."

"Why are you going after his children? Do you believe that they and his wife plotted this with him?"

Xavier pounded the arm of his chair with his fist. "Don't you dare ask how I serve my justice! He killed my wife, and he will pay dearly for it. It will cost him everything. I also know he did not act alone. I will find out who hired him, and they will pay dearly also.

"I don't think Levi and his wife will talk no matter what I do," he explained, "so I plan on executing them on the morrow. When I capture the children, I will make them talk. They are young and naïve; I will break them. Then I will execute them as well."

"But I don't think—"

"No," Xavier interrupted, "this is my justice. I don't care what you think of it. This is how I do things and the way it will be."

Victor sighed in exasperation. "Fine, do as you wish. I am sorry this happened. Is there anything I can do?"

"Yes, I need a cease in battle for at least a month in honor and memory of Shiva, if you are willing. I know it will take time to notify all our generals, but we can start the process right now."

"Of course, I can. I will let my generals know as soon as I can, and I will make my decrees known to the public. After the month is over, can we meet again? Maybe we could—"

"No," said Xavier, cutting him off a second time. "I wish not to talk peace with you. All I want to do is honor my rose, and nothing more. I will contact you a few days before the month is over so we can prepare to resume the war."

Victor sighed, his heart sinking. He had hoped that Xavier would reconsider the war. *But maybe he will change his mind before the month is done.* "So be it," he said in resignation. "Once again, I am sorry for your loss."

Xavier nodded and slowly disappeared, and the crystal screen faded into darkness. "Thank you, Violet," Victor said, nodding to her in appreciation. "Please do not repeat all that was said until I reveal this to the public."

Violet bowed her head. "As you command, Your Majesty. I will remain silent."

Victor smiled at her, then turned and exited the chamber.

Chapter Seven

A Meeting of the Generals

Victor Talon headed back to the conference room. He was not sure how to break the news to his generals and counsel. This was a bittersweet moment for him for he was to see his son, Aldar, who was back home on leave. Aldar had arrived two days before but had spent all the time with his family so Victor had not yet had a chance to see him. He had not seen Aldar in more than a year, and now he had to tell him this terrible news.

The king quickened his pace, reaching the door eagerly. A guard bowed his head and opened the door as he approached. A group of people stood up and bowed their heads as Victor entered, scanning the room for Aldar. His eyes met his son's. Aldar stood tall and proud in his Antillean general's uniform. "Come to me, Aldar, it has been too long," the king said.

Aldar rushed into his father's' arms, and they embraced for an extended period before finally letting go. "It has been a long time, Father."

"Much too long, son." Victor put his hand on his son's cheek and smiled at him. He noticed how old Aldar was looking. His son's face was weathered from months of war, and a touch of gray was intruding on Aldar's sandy brown hair. He frowned as he felt a touch of anger. *This war is taking a toll on my son as well*, he thought.

"Father?" Aldar asked.

Victor's smile returned, and he kissed Aldar on the forehead. "I just missed you so, is all. I prayed for you every day, that you would come home safely."

"Thanks to your prayers, for I have returned, albeit only for another week," Aldar replied.

Victor did his best not to frown again. "Please take a seat, son, for I have a lot to talk about." Aldar nodded and sat down next to his sister. A sense of pride filled Victor's heart at having his two children back together again. He knew that someday when he was dead and gone, the kingdom would be in good hands. He knew Aldar would be a great king, for Aldar had the honor, compassion, and determination to run this great nation.

Then there was Alana, his beautiful daughter, with her long, braided hair and silky blue dress. Because of the blow she had taken to the head, she was blind. It had pained him terribly when the healer had said she would never see again. To this day, he regretted allowing her to go to war.

Even though she had told him again and again that this was not his fault and that she was grateful that he had given her the opportunity to fight, he still blamed himself. She was a determined woman, and even though she could no longer see, her determination was strong as ever. She was always by his side, giving him advice and encouragement.

On Alana's other side sat Isaiah Phoenix, supreme general of the Antillean army. Isaiah was a sixty-year-old man, slightly heavyset and with balding gray hair. He had a round face, brown eyes, a stern mouth, a round double chin, and a large bulbous nose. He wore a blue-and-white general's uniform with several insignia and medals. The supreme general was a friend of Victor's and had served in the Antillean army long before the war. He commanded the war via his own personal message cystallis and traveled all over the land, making sure the army was running well. He just happened to be at the palace at the same time as Aldar.

In the other chairs sat other generals, scribes, and minor members of the king's counsel.

Victor frowned. Now that everyone was there, waiting for him, he did not know how to break the terrible news.

"Father, is everything all right? You are awfully quiet," Alana said.

That child is always there for me, the king thought. "No, Alana, unfortunately, I am not all right. I have very sad news. I just had a conversation with Emperor Pulsar. He contacted me to inform me that Shiva Pulsar is dead."

Looks of surprise, gasps of shock, and tears of sorrow filled the conference room as the news set in.

"How did this happen, Father?" Alana asked as a tear ran down her cheek.

Victor told them all that had transpired regarding the assassination attempt, including the poison dart. "I really hope Shiva did not suffer, poor girl, and their son now without his mother. What a tragedy." Victor shook his head.

"What does this mean now, Your Majesty? What is our next move in the war?" Isaiah asked with a stone-cold look on his face.

"Emperor Pulsar proposed to me that we have a one-month cease in battle in honor of Shiva. I suggested that we talk about peace. Xavier would have none of it and wants to resume the war after the month is over. I agreed to the cease in battle so he will have time for mourning and to prepare for Shiva's funeral. It is my hope and prayer that Emperor Pulsar will reconsider."

"Your Majesty, with all due respect, this might be a ploy by Emperor Pulsar," Isaiah said with doubt in his voice. "He may have had her hidden somewhere in his palace and faked her death."

"Now why in the world would Xavier do that? What advantage would this bring him?" Aldar asked.

"One month is plenty enough time to reorganize his army and attack Aldar. He could overrun us while our guard is down "Isaiah said.

Aldar shook his head. "Xavier is an untrustworthy tyrant, but he would never use Shiva as a ploy."

"Maybe, but I doubt it. Now that I think of it, I wouldn't put it past him to have killed her himself to do this," Isaiah said.

Aldar slammed his fist on the table, his face turning red with anger. "Are you mad? I know firsthand what an evil man he is. He does not care about his people, only himself and Shiva. She is truly the only one—and perhaps his son, Maximus—other than himself that he loves."

"Maybe we should—" Victor started, but Isaiah cut him off.

“Be that as it may, I still wouldn’t be surprised at all if this was a ploy.”

“Perhaps—” Victor started, but this time, Aldar cut him off.

“Didn’t you hear me, stubborn fool? There is no way Xavier would do that.”

“Fine!” Isaiah shouted. “If this is true, then we should attack. We could organize our armies, and while Xavier is distracted, we could attack with all our might.”

“I don’t think—” Victor started but was cut off yet again by Aldar.

“Do you think we are barbarians? Attack during a funeral? During a time of mourning? Come on, man, how can you be so cold and callous?”

“Gentlemen, we—” Victor started, but Isaiah cut him off.

“Xavier Pulsar would do the same. If, heaven forbid, Queen Talon should pass away and we had a funeral and a time of mourning, he would be knocking down our gates.”

Victor gave up trying to speak and instead rolled his eyes. He had forgotten that Aldar and Isaiah’s personalities clashed.

Aldar gave Isaiah an accusatory look. “If we did that to Xavier, we would be no different than he, and that would be a great shame. I could not live with myself, doing such an atrocious thing, and I don’t wish to be a hypocrite.

“Are you calling me a hypocrite? How dare you call me a hypocrite.”

Isaiah and Aldar stood and started to shout, hurling accusations and insults at each other.

“Enough!” came a strong, loud shriek.

The two generals stared at each other, then looked at Alana between them.

She slammed her fist on the table, standing. “What in blazes is wrong with you two?” She carefully turned herself from side to side to face them as best she could. “Do you two have no manners? You both are acting like little schoolchildren and making fools of yourselves.”

Aldar and Isaiah looked at her in stupefied surprise as she scolded them like a mother with two children fighting over their toys.

Victor smiled in satisfaction as she continued. "You two need to respect each other. You are both generals, so act like generals. Isaiah, I know you outrank Aldar, but remember he is also heir to the throne and deserves the utmost respect." Turning toward her brother, she added, "Aldar, even though you are heir to the throne, Isaiah outranks you and he deserves the utmost respect. Then there's the matter of your father and your king."

Aldar and Isaiah gave each other confused looks.

"Do you two realize Father was trying to talk? You two brainless idiots were so busy bickering and fighting, Father could not get a word in edgewise."

Aldar's and Isaiah's faces turned red in embarrassment.

"Father, do they look sufficiently embarrassed?" Alana asked.

"Yes, my dear, they most certainly do," Victor replied.

"Good, that is very satisfactory," Alana said to her father, then turned her head back and forth to address Aldar and Isaiah. "Well, do you two have anything to say to Father?" she asked impatiently.

Victor and Isaiah bowed their heads in shame. "I am sorry, Your Majesty," Isaiah said at the same time Aldar said, "Sorry, Father."

Victor steepled his fingers on the table for several seconds, then said, "You are forgiven. I know this war has been hard on us all and we are growing tired, but we must try to get along. Isaiah, I know you are passionate and have been working nonstop since the war began. You are my friend, and you are a great general. There is a reason that I made you supreme general. You are a no-nonsense man, and you only want what's best for the kingdom.

"However," he continued, "I must side with my son. There is no doubt in my mind that Emperor Pulsar speaks the truth. I know you want this war to be over—we all do—but I want to wait and see what happens.

I pray that Xavier will call an end to this senseless war. We all need to pray."

Everyone in the room nodded and voiced their agreement as Aldar and Isaiah went to sit back down. "Oh, no, you don't," Alana said, forestalling them. "You are not sitting down until you two shake hands and apologize."

"How did you know we were going to sit?" Isaiah asked incredulously.

"I may be blind, but my hearing works just fine."

Isaiah and Aldar gave Victor a pleading look, but Victor only grinned and shrugged his shoulders. Aldar and Isaiah rolled their eyes.

"Well? I don't hear anything. Are you going to apologize or not?"

Aldar and Isaiah clasped each other's hands and shook them vigorously as they apologized to one another.

"That is good." Alana smiled as Aldar and Isaiah as they went to take their seats, and Alana took hers.

"Now that that's resolved"—Victor chuckled as a slight laughter filled the room— "let us get to the business at hand. Isaiah, you must contact all the generals as soon as possible."

"Yes, Your Majesty," Isaiah said, bowing his head.

Victor made a gesture that included his scribes. "I need a decree made at once to inform the people what has transpired."

His scribes bowed their heads. "At once, Your Majesty," they said in unison.

Next, Victor turned his attention to Aldar. "Now, my son, I hear in two days your daughter might graduate sword-fighting school."

"Yes, Father." Aldar's face brightened and a smile returned to it.

"Well, your mother and I plan on seeing our lovely granddaughter graduate, so on that note, this meeting is adjourned."

Everyone stood up and bowed, then filtered out, leaving the king with his children. Victor put his arms around his son's and daughter's shoulders, then started to laugh.

"What is so funny, Father?" Aldar asked in confusion as they walked to the door.

"If Aurora fights like Alana used to, she will be hard to beat, and if she fights like Alana scolded you, she will be unstoppable."

They all started to laugh uncontrollably. Despite the news about Shiva, King Talon was happy to laugh with his children again.

Chapter Eight

The Rise of an Emperor

Xavier Pulsar walked down the long and dingy hallway with Maximus by his side, a large procession of soldiers and Daniel behind them. Today was the day justice was being served. Today, that traitor Levi and his wretched wife, Lana, were to be executed. *Death by fire—a fitting execution,* Xavier thought. He rubbed his hands together in excited anticipation. He could not wait to see them suffer. The only thing that would make this morning perfect would be having the traitor's children.

No matter. I will find them, and they will suffer the same fate as their parents, he thought, and a smile came to his face. "What a wonderful day, indeed. Are you ready, son?" When Maximus did not reply, Xavier said, "Did you not hear me?" He looked over to his son and saw Maximus turning his head as if to hide his face.

Without warning, Xavier stopped the procession. Everyone behind him almost stumbled over each other from the unexpected stop. Xavier glared at Maximus. "Face me, son." Maximus did not obey. "Do it now!" he shouted. Maximus jumped and turned to face him. Tears were streaming down his face.

Xavier's blood began to boil, and his face grew dark. He slapped Maximus across the face. "You cry? How dare you cry? You are the future emperor; you never cry."

Xavier grabbed Maximus by the shoulders and shook him hard. "What is the matter with you? An emperor is powerful, not weak. You are to be strong and merciless. A true emperor never cries, shows no mercy, and demands respect. You hear me? I do not want to ever see you cry again. Do you understand me?"

"Yes, Father, I do."

Xavier stopped shaking Maximus as a horrible memory filled his mind. He looked at his son, letting go of him, then looked away. "I am sorry, son. All this has been a long and terrible ordeal. I am tired and overwhelmed. I know this is hard, and we both miss your mother. I truly am sorry."

"It is all right, Father, I am sorry I cried," Maximus said, rubbing his shoulders.

"All is forgiven, then. Let us continue." Xavier started to walk. He slowed his pace as he looked over to his son and looked at his son's sword scabbard. In the scabbard was an old familiar sword with a bronze hilt and a red gem. It conjured up more memories—horrible memories. Memories he had thought he'd put away deep in the recesses of his mind.

Xavier was twelve years old, and his father, Killian, was teaching him how to sword fight when Xavier fell to the ground. "Get up, you weakling!" As Xavier slowly got back to his feet, Killian yelled, "Hurry up, you dog!" He slapped Xavier across the face. "Too slow! You are soft and weak. Get up faster—no, you should never fall."

Tears streamed down Xavier's face. Killian grabbed him by the shoulders and shook him hard. "You cry? How dare you cry? You are a worthless coward. How do you expect to be respected if you cry? A true emperor shows no weakness and demands respect. I never want to see you cry again; you hear me?"

Killian was a strong man, and tall, with thinning gray hair, black eyes, a long gray beard, and a gray mustache. His face and jaw were square, and he had a long thin nose and thin mouth. Upon his head, Killian wore a gold crown engraved with a sword with a copper hilt and red gem, the symbol of the nation of Avarlon, symbolizing peace and prosperity. Killian had used that sword in a battle to usurp an evil king. On this day, he also wore a brown shirt, gray trousers, brown slippers, and a gray cape also bearing the symbol of the sword.

Killian was a ruthless father, to say the least, though he had once been a kind and gentle man—until Xavier's younger sister had been born.

Xavier's mother, Valda, had died soon after giving birth to her and naming the girl Adaliah. Their father blamed Adaliah for their mother's death and never paid much attention to her.

When Killian was in public with the children, he would treat them nicely, so the people of Avarlon knew nothing of the abuse their king rained upon his children. The country had wealth that had not been seen in a generation. The land was a paradise, and the people respected and loved Killian. But Xavier hated him. For Killian, everything was about a perfect image, and he expected his children to be perfect.

Xavier was heir to the throne, and his father was especially hard on him. When Killian was displeased with Xavier, he would beat the boy. Xavier did what he could to protect his little sister, who was four years younger than him. When Adaliah made their father angry, Xavier would defend her and take more abuse.

A few years later, when Xavier was fifteen and Adaliah was eleven, he decided to go swimming in the river. Father had told them to stay away; they had had a lot of rain that summer and the river was swollen over its banks. It was an unusually hot day, and Xavier and Adaliah were miserable, so Xavier decided to go swimming despite his father's orders.

Adaliah was scared. "No, Xavier! Father will beat you again if you go."

"Oh, nonsense. Father is busy today. I'll be in and out and back long before Father comes back. Are you coming?"

Adaliah put her hands on her hips. "If you think I'm coming with you, you are sadly mistaken."

"Come on, sister, it will be fun. Don't tell me you're afraid."

"I am not!" she protested.

Finally, after much coaxing, she agreed to go with Xavier. They carefully snuck out of the palace and ran to the river.

Xavier could not understand what his father had been talking about. Sure, the river was up higher than usual, but it seemed to be calm enough. He and Adaliah laughed as they stepped in and stood splashing each other in ankle-deep water. "Come, let's dive in," Xavier suggested.

Adaliah looked out at the river and shuddered. "I'm not sure if that is a good idea."

Xavier sighed in exasperation. "Girls!" he sputtered at her. "Why are you such a chicken?"

"I am not a chicken!" Adaliah protested.

"All right, prove it," Xavier challenged her.

"Fine!" she shouted, scowling at him. "Try to keep up," she said. As she dived into the deeper water headfirst, she made a big splash, then disappeared under the surface.

Xavier stood and waited for her to resurface, but she did not. Then he heard a noise downriver. "Adaliah!" Xavier cried. She had traveled several feet downriver and was screaming and waving her hands in the air.

The current was taking her down the river fast. Xavier jumped in after her and, to his horror, realized that he was now in trouble as well. He swam as hard as he could against the current and finally managed to make it to the bank. "Adaliah!" he screamed at the top of his lungs, but there was no response. He frantically looked and ran up and down the river, but there was no sign of her.

After that, everything was a blur until nightfall, when he and his father held torches quietly as servants and townspeople ran up and down the river, trying to find Adaliah. Suddenly, a noise broke the silence. "I found her!" someone called.

Killian put his hand on Xavier's shoulder, preventing him from running to Adaliah. There was a great commotion, then there was once again silence. A man emerged from the crowd holding the limp, dead body of Adaliah. "I am sorry, Your Majesty, she is dead," the servant announced.

All the servants and townspeople who wore hats took them off, and a great sorrow filled the air. Xavier started to cry, sobbing uncontrollably. "My sister is gone and it's my fault!" he cried in anguish.

To his shock, his father hugged him. "It was an accident, my son. It's not your fault."

Xavier looked up at his father. Killian wore a sympathetic look on his face, but his eyes—his black, piercing, unnerving eyes—had murder in them. Terror filled Xavier's heart. He broke away and ran as fast as he could. In the distance, he heard his father tell the townspeople, "Xavier will be all right; the child just needs time alone."

Xavier ran into his room and grabbed what he could—some clothes, a knife, and supplies—then turned to run, planning to steal food from the kitchens, but he stopped in his tracks. In front of the door stood his father.

Xavier's blood ran cold as his father shut the door and snarled at him. "You are an abomination. I regret the day your mother gave birth to you. You are worthless. Now, because of you, your sister is dead. Even worse, you humiliated me. I told you never to cry again, and you did—in public, of all the places to cry. And you did it in front of people!" Killian pulled out his sword—the sword with the brass hilt and red gem.

Xavier pulled out his knife, and Killian laughed. "Do you really think you can kill me with that? I think not."

Xavier screamed as he charged his father, but before he could think, he was on the floor.

Xavier put his hand on his cheek, which was throbbing. Killian had kicked him in the face.

Killian straddled Xavier and held the point of his sword at Xavier's throat. "I should kill you, but I won't. I have an image to upkeep. I have decided it is time for me to have a new bride, and after we marry, she will bear me a son. He will be heir to the throne. I will tell the people that your sister's death was too much for you and you wish to abdicate the throne to your half-brother."

"But, Father—" Xavier protested.

"No!" Killian screamed at him. "It will be as I say. I will allow you to live here until the future emperor decides what to do with you. As for my relationship to you, when we are in public, I will acknowledge you;

however, when we are not, you are no longer my son. You are dead to me."

After that night, Killian married a wealthy lord's daughter. She became pregnant, but the son was stillborn. Soon after, she died. Xavier suspected that his father had poisoned her.

He then married his third wife, and she was barren, so Killian began to cheat on her to try to conceive a son. Devastated by his infidelity, Killian's third wife killed herself. Killian was infuriated. He finally considered adopting a son—anything to prevent Xavier from becoming emperor.

When Xavier caught wind of his father's plan, he decided that he had had enough. At twenty-five, Xavier was young and strong, and in the prime of his life. It was time to end this madness. It was time to kill his old man.

Killian was addressing all the wealthiest and most important people of Avarlon in his audience chamber. "I am pleased to tell you that—"

A commotion interrupted him, and then the doors of the audience chamber burst open. Xavier walked through them, two soldiers lying prone on the ground behind him.

The crowd moved out of Xavier's way. As he approached the throne, a dozen guards rushed up to him, surrounding him, swords drawn.

"Xavier, what is the meaning of this? How dare you interrupt this meeting. Well, what do you have to say for yourself?"

"Oh, I think you know, Father. You knew this day would come eventually."

"What on earth are you talking about?" Killian asked nervously.

Xavier pulled his sword from its sheath, then held it in the air in a salute. "I challenge you to a duel to the death, Father. I wish to depose you, and I will rule this land far better than you ever will. And I will be the greatest ruler this world has ever seen."

Killian looked abashed. "Why would you do that, son? I love you. I have taken care of you, and this is how you show your appreciation?"

"No, Father, you have not taken care of me. You never took care of Adaliah. You have beaten me and demoralized me and cared not at all about Adaliah." Xavier pointed his finger at his father. "You didn't even mourn her death. You blamed her for Mother's death, didn't you?"

Killian made no response, but his face grew dark, and his eyes widened as he started to tap his finger on the arm of his throne. "Well, Father, just admit it—you hated your daughter, you hate me, and you only care for yourself."

Instead of replying to his son, Killian addressed the crowd. "My sincerest apologies. It seems my wayward son needs to learn some manners."

The people in attendance started to laugh, and Xavier shook his fist at Killian. "Liar! You are a liar and a self-centered hypocrite, and I want you to die, filthy worm."

A collective gasp came from the guests in the throne room, and then all was silent, all eyes on Killian. The king stood up slowly, then clenched his fists and glared at Xavier with dark eyes.

Xavier smiled deviously, staring back at Killian with his own piercing eyes. Killian was taken aback, and a surprised look moved across his face; Xavier had always cowered under his glare before. But not this time. This time, his son stood tall and defiant.

Finally, Killian spoke, his voice a little higher than he intended. "You dare come here and threaten me?" He cleared his throat. "Do you realize what the punishment for threatening and insulting the emperor is?"

"Yes, Father, it means death," Xavier replied.

"And so, it shall be. Guards, take my insolent son to the dungeon."

As the soldiers slowly closed in on Xavier, he spoke. "What is the matter, Father? Are you afraid to fight me?"

When the soldiers grabbed Xavier and started to drag him out of the room, he raised his voice. "That's right, old man, you are afraid. You, the high and mighty emperor of Avarlon, afraid? The man who killed his way to the throne?" The soldiers almost had him to the door when Xavier shouted, "Coward! You are a coward."

"Enough!" Killian screamed. "Guards, unhand him." The guards gave Killian confused looks but did as they were told.

"You are a disgrace and a great disappointment. Come to the throne, my unworthy son," Killian snarled. Xavier did as he was told, walking up the steps up to the platform that the throne was upon. "You know what? I accept your challenge," Killian growled. More gasps of shock filled the room, and Killian raised his hand to the people. "Fear not, for I know what I am doing. I am going to kill this half-wit." He looked down at Xavier. "Your punishment is death, and it is I who will administer this punishment."

He then addressed the crowd. "You are all my witnesses today. I will show you all what a true and great emperor I am." He then called to his scribe, "Write this down. If I die today, I decree that Xavier Pulsar will be the new emperor. He will have all the rights and privileges of the emperor. All must obey his rule under punishment of death, so I decree."

Once he had written this, the scribe handed the document to Xavier, saying, "You must sign this.,"

Xavier grabbed the quill and eagerly signed the document. The scribe then handed the document to Killian, who he signed it, then dropped melted wax on the bottom of the document, where Killian stamped his seal.

"See, Xavier, I am not a coward. I have risked everything to prove what a great emperor I am."

Xavier laughed. "You are an idiot. I can't believe you agreed to this! Now I will show everyone what a fool you are. When I kill you, I shall hang this document over my bed so when I awake and when I go to sleep, I will be reminded of this glorious day. I shall display your sword there as well—a fitting reminder."

"I will also display this document for all to see Killian said. "I will hang your skull with it as well. Make room!" Killian commanded as he drew his sword. The crowd spread out to line the walls of the room, looking awed as Killian swished his sword.

Xavier slowly backed away to make room for Killian to reach the bottom of the stairs, and then they faced each other. They started to circle each other, and Killian smiled. "Prepare to die, my former son."

"Prepare yourself," Xavier replied, smiling back.

Without warning, Killian lunged. Xavier barely jumped out of the way, and Killian slapped the flat end of his sword against Xavier's behind. The crowd roared in laughter. "A fitting punishment before you die, don't you think?" Killian asked his son.

Xavier laughed it off as they circled once again. Killian lunged this time, but Xavier was ready and slapped Killian on the rear this time. Xavier roared with laughter. "A fitting punishment, don't you think, Father." *That stopped them laughing*, he thought.

Killian's eyes burned with rage from this humiliation, and he screamed as he charged Xavier. Their swords clashed and Xavier backpedaled from the onslaught. Then, to Killian's surprise, Xavier launched his own attack. Killian barely blocked the blows as he stumbled backward. He fell onto his back and rolled over to avoid Xavier's downward slashes. He used his own leg to knock Xavier's legs out from under him, knocking the younger man to the ground. Both men made their way back to their feet to cross swords again.

After several more minutes of fighting, Xavier started taunting Killian. "You're old, Father. You're getting tired, aren't you?" He could see the fatigue on his father's face as they moved up the steps toward the throne.

Xavier kicked Killian, and the older man crashed into the throne. Xavier thrust his sword at Killian's chest, but Killian dodged the attack and Xavier's sword got stuck in the throne. Xavier tried desperately to pull his sword free as his father charged, managing it just in time to block the attack.

Killian slashed his sword to take off Xavier's head. Xavier ducked in time. Seeing an opening, he kicked Killian in the chest. Killian fell off the platform and to the floor, landing hard on his back with a sickening crunch.

Killian tried to get to his feet, but he could not "I can't feel my legs!" he cried. His back was broken.

A shocked silence filled the room as Xavier walked down the steps and to his father. Killian, sword still in his hand, swung the sword in a vain attempt to stop his son, but Xavier slapped the sword from his hands, and it clattered across the floor.

Xavier walked over to the fallen sword and picked it up, holding it high for all to see as he let his own sword fall to the floor. All were silent, save for some who were crying. The people looked at Xavier, tears and shock on their faces. Xavier straddled his father and pointed the emperor's sword at Killian's throat.

Killian tried to pull at Xavier's legs but was too weak. He started to sob. "You are right, Xavier, I am a hypocrite. I beat you. I did blame Adaliah for your mother's death. I know it really wasn't her fault, but I missed your mother. Please don't kill me. You can still be emperor; just let me live," he pleaded, tears running down his cheeks.

Xavier looked down at his father expressionlessly, then pulled the sword away from Killian's throat. He held a finger up to his cheek as if considering what Killian had said. Killian watched him expectantly.

Suddenly, Xavier reached down and slapped Killian across the face. Killian howled in surprise.

"You cry, Father? How dare you cry? I thought you said an emperor shows no weakness. You're a pathetic, weak old man. You don't deserve my mercy. Now you lay here on the ground, and you cry." He once again pointed the sword at Killian's throat.

"Please, son, I am sorry."

"I cannot forgive, Father. Besides, even if I did forgive you, it would not matter; the decree we signed is law. It states that upon your death today, I will become emperor, so this is the only way, Father." Killian looked up at Xavier with pleading eyes. "Good-bye, Father."

Xavier plunged the sword into Killian's throat, and the older man was dead. Xavier yelled at the top of his lungs as he raised his bloody sword in victory for all to see. Then he set the sword on his father's chest, then picked up his own sword from where it lay on the floor and walked to the throne.

He sat on the throne, looked out at the shocked crowd, and smiled. He rather liked this view; he could get used to this. He pointed to Killian's—his own now, he reminded himself—scribe. "Come here and bring the decree with you." The trembling scribe did as he was told. Xavier held out his hand, and the scribe handed him the decree. "Stay here," the new emperor commanded, then addressed the crowd. "In accordance with the decree my father and I signed, I am your ruler." He spat on the floor and sneered at the nervous and trembling crowd. "You all laughed and mocked me. You thought this was an amusing joke." He let out a mocking laugh. "Look who is laughing now, you low-life worms. I should have you all killed."

He put his chin on his knuckled hand. "But alas, I was not the emperor when you mocked me, so I will forgive this transgression for today. However, if this ever happens again"—in one swift motion, he stood up and rammed his sword into the scribe's chest. The scribe gasped in shock and fell to the ground dead.

Xavier laughed. "Looks like I need a new scribe. Oh well, just a minor inconvenience."

He sat back down. "I am your ruler. I am Apollyon. I am destroyer of all who oppose me. My first decree as your new ruler is that this nation be called Apollyon in reminder of who I am. I also decree that this city be called Adaliah in memory of my sweet and lovely sister." He pointed at the commander of the soldiers. "Come to the steps and bring your soldiers with you." When the commander and the soldiers had done his bidding, Xavier demanded, "Now kneel and swear fealty to me."

The soldiers did as they were told and went down on one knee. “We are here to serve and obey, Your Majesty,” the commander declared and the soldiers echoing his words.

Xavier looked out at the people. “You all must do the same.” When the crowd only stood there with wide eyes, Xavier pounded the arms of his throne. “Do it now!” he screamed. The people stumbled over each other to fall to their knees and repeated what the soldiers had said. After they were done, the new emperor yelled impatiently, “Well, I am waiting!”

Everyone in the room started chanting, “Long live Emperor Pulsar! Long live Emperor Pulsar!”

“Your Majesty,” Daniel said, interrupting his thoughts. Xavier glared at Daniel, and the lesser man cowered under his stare.

That man is such a killjoy, Xavier thought. “What is it, Daniel?” he asked irritably.

“I—um . . . we are here. Are you ready for me to introduce you?”

Xavier had been so deep in thought that he had not realized they had arrived at their destination. They stood in front of a big round opening leading to his throne in a large open-air coliseum. Every seat was taken, and the crowd sat silently in anticipation of his entrance.

Xavier smiled at Daniel as he gestured toward the entrance. “Go ahead, Daniel.”

Chapter Nine

Consumed by Fire

Levi looked over the gate that led to the arena floor. He had seen that arena many times before, but this time was different. This time, he was not the spectator; he and Lana were the entertainment. He looked in awe at the number of people. There were thousands of them; every seat was taken. Many more stood in the top level.

Every available place was taken up, but an eerie silence permeated the air. All eyes were on the entryway to the throne.

Daniel appeared from the tunnel behind the throne and introduced Xavier and Maximus, and the people applauded them, a light, somber applause.

Xavier waved to the crowd as he and his son approached their seats, and then Maximus took his seat as Xavier waved the people to silence.

Levi could hear Xavier, as the emperor started to address the people. "Today we honor your empress, my best friend, my lover, my Rose of Apollyon, Shiva Pulsar. Today, justice will be served to those who were responsible for her death; they will be executed. She will be honored by their screams of pain and agony—death by fire, a fitting death. Their suffering will be a reminder of what happens to those who try to oppose the throne."

Levi saw Xavier point toward him and Lana as he commanded, "Bring out the condemned!" Levi looked at Lana, and she smiled as she took his arm.

"Come along, you two," a soldier commanded.

Levi and Lana emerged, Levi hobbling on his wounded leg and Lana helping support him, with a group of soldiers surrounding them. A great roar came from the crowd as rotten vegetables and fruits were thrown at them. "Murderer! Infidel! Wench! Harlot!" Other insults were hurled at them along with the rotten produce.

Levi and Lana looked around in awe at the outpouring of hatred, and then Levi hung his head. "Oh no, you don't," Lana scolded. "Lift up your head, my love. We will face this punishment together with our heads held high." Levi smiled at her and did as he was told as they made their way to the execution pyre, where two wooden poles with shackles on them were surrounded by kindling. Two soldiers, each holding two buckets of flammable liquid, stood at attention next to the pyre.

Levi and Lana turned to face Emperor Pulsar and Maximus, and the shouts and cries of anger reached a deafening pitch. Xavier waved the crowd into silence, then looked down at the condemned couple and spat. "Levi and Lana Eclipse, you disgust me! You are vile and repulsive creatures and are not worthy of living. You stand in front of me, my son, and this audience accused of killing the empress. Do you deny it?"

Levi stood as straight and tall as he could before speaking. "Your Majesty, I do not deny it. I killed her."

The crowd erupted again. "Let them die! Let them die!" they yelled in unison, hurling more items into the arena. Xavier held his hands with the palms up, moving them up and down slightly to encourage the crowd's outburst.

Finally, after several minutes, the people settled down and the emperor spoke again. "Levi, do you wish to address the people before you and Lana die?"

"Yes, Your Majesty, I wish to speak."

"Then speak your mind."

"People of Apollyon, words cannot describe how sorry I am that I killed your empress. She was the shining light of this great nation. She was this nation's hope, and I destroyed that hope." He looked at Maximus. "Maximus, I am sorry I killed your mother. She was a wonderful woman, and she was a great mother. You did not deserve what was handed to you." Finally, he looked at Xavier. "As far as you go, Your Majesty, I am sorry I killed Empress Shiva and not you. I wish you were dead."

Xavier's eye widened in surprise as Levi continued. "Shiva was the future, and I know she would lead this nation to prosperity. I know she would have taught Maximus to rule responsibly and would treat the Apollyon people with respect." A murmur moved around the crowd as Levi continued speaking to Xavier. "I can't believe I killed her. Because I killed her and not you, the future looks bleak. I—"

"Enough!" Xavier interrupted. He shook his fists in anger. "How dare you insult me? Guards, flog them!"

The soldiers knocked Levi and Lana to the ground and whipped them for several minutes.

Finally, the soldiers lifted the couple, who could barely stand, to their feet. The crowd was silent, and Xavier looked around the stadium, frustration setting in. He lifted his hands again. "Boo them!" he shouted.

The crowd, shaken out of their stupor, started to boo.

Xavier again waved them to silence and then stood glaring at Levi and Lana. "You will regret what you just said, Levi. I have a price on your children. I will stop at nothing to find them, and when I do, I will kill them."

Levi started to speak, coughing painfully as he did so. "You will never find them," he croaked.

"Oh, I will find them," Xavier promised, then raised his hands to the crowd. "I now have increased the price on their head. Instead of one hundred bars of gold, it will be a thousand gold bars, and they both don't have to be alive as long as one of them is."

A gasp came from the crowd.

"I will also give to whomever apprehends them my favor, and that person will become very wealthy indeed." He gave Levi a self-satisfied smile. "Now they will be found for sure."

Lana looked up to Xavier. "Please don't," she pleaded.

"It is too late, Lana. They are as good as dead," Xavier laughed before addressing the crowd again. "Levi admitted he killed your empress. What is the punishment?"

"Death!" the crowd yelled in unison.

"Levi and Lana Eclipse, I sentence you to death by fire."

The crowd cheered.

"I am sorry, Lana," Levi said to his wife.

"All is forgiven, my love. The children will be safe," Lana said as the soldiers began dragging them to the pyre.

As Levi and Lana were shackled to the poles, Xavier called, "Figs! Where are my figs?" Xavier always ate during executions.

Maximus looked at his father in disgust as a servant handed the emperor a plate of figs.

The soldiers poured the flammable liquid on the kindling, then over the condemned pair's heads. Levi and Lana screamed in pain as the liquid burned their wounds.

As the soldiers moved to set fire to the pyre, Levi looked at his bride one last time and said, "I love you."

Chapter Ten

The Evil Spirit of the Forest

It was a cool evening. The sun was starting to set as two people on horseback rode through the silent forest. There were no signs of life anywhere—the birds were not chirping, and there were no sounds of animals. The only sound was that of the horses' hooves crunching through the dead foliage.

Enoch and Elaine Eclipse said nothing as they rode through the dark and menacing forest. It was said that this forest was cursed, and an evil spirit inhabited it and killed any unwary traveler. The forest was known as the Twisted Forest because of all the gnarled dead trees.

A dank and dark river flowed beside the riders, smelling of sulfur. Enoch looked at the river from time to time, imagining an evil creature leaping out and ripping them apart, then eating them. Legend said that a millennia ago, this forest had been a lush, thriving, beautiful land. Enoch found that hard to believe.

"How much further, Enoch? I really hate this forest; it sends shivers down my spine," Elaine said. Elaine, who had just turned eighteen, had long black hair that she wore in a braid, along with brown eyes in a round face. Her mouth was of medium size beneath a small, pointed nose. She wore a plain brown riding dress and slippers, along with a necklace with a silver medallion that her mother and father had given her on her birthday and that she kissed from time to time when she thought of her parents. On her back, she carried a bow and quiver, and a small dagger attached to her thigh, and was concealed by her skirt.

"Hopefully soon," her brother replied. "There should be a clearing up ahead. We will sleep there for the night. Sometime tomorrow, I promise—most likely by afternoon—we should be at the border of Antillean."

Elaine nodded as she looked at her brother. Enoch was twenty years old and was tall and slender., He had a triangular jaw, brown eyes, and a small, pointy nose and thin mouth separated by a brown mustache. He also had small ears. He was traveling in plain white shirt and brown trousers and boots. He wore a holstered sidearm at his waist and a sword in a scabbard on his back.

Elaine could tell by the way he answered that he hated traveling through this forest as well. It was a necessity, however, to keep hidden. Very few, if any, traversed this forest because of the evil spirit associated with it. These woods were also away from the war and its ownership was not disputed, which also helped.

It had been three weeks since they had left their homes, and three days since they had entered this forest. Enoch wished he could find out for sure if their father had been successful and had escaped with their mother. He hoped they would learn more when they entered Antillean. *Just a little further and we will be safe*, he thought. He remembered what his father had said before they had left: "Son, most likely, I won't make it out alive. Take care of your sister and your mother. You are a young, strong man, and I am proud of you." Then their mother and father hugged and kissed them before they had left. *We may never see them again*; Enoch had thought as he and his sister had ridden away. He looked over to Elaine and felt a huge weight on his shoulders. He knew that Elaine could take care of herself—she was young and strong and knew how to survive, as did their mother—but he still needed to be there for them, as they would be there for him.

Seeing the worry in Elaine's face, he asked, "Are you alright?"

She frowned back at him. "I am just worried, I hope and pray for Mother and Father," she said, kissing her necklace.

"I am sure they will be all right and we will rendezvous with them at the palace," he tried to reassure her. "King Talon hopefully will accept us and Mother and Father, and we will be safe until we return to Apollyon."

A tear ran down Elaine's cheek. "I am sorry. I am worried that they didn't make it. Oh, Enoch, I don't know if I could handle that."

Enoch brought his horse closer to his sister's so he could clasp her hand. He squeezed it as he said, "I am sure they made it out of Adaliah safely and we will see them soon and all will be well."

"I hope so. I miss them so. Thanks for comforting me," Elaine managed to smile. Enoch smiled back at her, and suddenly, they heard a noise in the distance behind them.

Their smiles faded quickly. Fear filled Elaine's eyes as she looked at Enoch. "Is it the evil spirit?" she asked with a quiver in her voice.

Enoch shook his head. When Elaine opened her mouth to speak again, Enoch put his finger to his mouth to shush her. The sound grew a little louder and they could tell it was the sound of horses' hooves. Then they heard voices.

"Let's ride!" Enoch whispered.

They rode at a gallop until they reached the clearing. Enoch let out a curse, looking around in desperation. He had forgotten about the clearing. It was a large plain, and they would likely be seen before they reached the other side. Which way to go?

Then he noticed a large boulder big enough to hide them and the horses. "Let us go behind that boulder," he told his sister.

They rode to it at a full gallop, Enoch praying they would reach the boulder before they were discovered. Finally, after what seemed like an eternity, they made it. They got off their horses and led them behind the boulder, trying desperately to calm the animals.

Levi handed the reins of his horse to Elaine so he could peer around the boulder. Looking at the woods, he did not see anyone. *Maybe they changed directions*, he thought. Then suddenly, they appeared, emerging like ants coming out of the woodwork.

They looked like Apollyon soldiers, perhaps a century of them, the setting sun casting devilish shadows of them across the plain.

Enoch looked back at Elaine, who had terror in her eyes. "Apollyon soldiers," he whispered to her.

Elaine nodded. "Should we escape?" she asked.

"No. They would see us, and they would chase us. Let us wait here. Hopefully, they will just keep moving on and we will circle the boulder."

The soldiers were all on horseback and wore swords on their hips. They appeared to be a cavalry division. They wore black metal helmets and armor, and they carried black metal shields with the man consumed by fire. "Looks like we're in luck. Come, Elaine," Enoch said as the army approached the side of the boulder.

As the pair were about to move, a soldier called a halt and the army stopped. Enoch held in a curse; luck was not on their side, after all.

"We make camp here for the night," announced the commander.

A groan arose from the soldiers. "Are you sure that is a good idea, sir?" one soldier asked. "This place is cursed. It is very bad to stay the night here." The other soldiers nodded in agreement.

The commander laughed. "Come now, men! You are too old for fairy tales and bedtime stories—that is what it is." Enoch saw the silent soldiers looking at the commander with nervous and hesitant eyes. Then the commander frowned at them. "Look, this place makes me nervous as well, but this is the only place that hasn't been searched. You saw Emperor Pulsar's decree. If we catch Enoch and Elaine Eclipse, we all will be wealthy beyond imagination."

Enoch and Elaine looked at each other in concern as the commander continued, "To me, that outweighs any silly story or legend. Now let's make camp." When the soldiers made no move, the commander yelled, "Do it now or you will all be punished for insubordination!"

The soldiers sprang into action, dismounting from their horses and starting to make camp. "Let us get out of here," Elaine whispered to her brother.

"We can't, Elaine. It is not dark enough, and they are too close. We will have to wait until dark, then we will sneak off, hopefully undetected," Enoch said as a nervous sweat beaded his forehead.

Elaine slowly nodded, sweat trickling down her face as well, and she heard the commander yell, "Someone take my horse. It has been hours since I made water."

A soldier took the reins from the commander, and the officer walked toward the boulder. Enoch pulled out his pistol and Elaine held in a gasp as the commander walked to within mere feet of them. At this distance, they could see that he was a general.

Brother and sister watched as the general, a tall, muscular man with a thick neck and broad shoulders, took off his helmet, placed it on the ground, and started to urinate. Elaine looked away in disgust as he started to sing of winning a fair maiden and of love lost.

As the general finished, Elaine's horse started to shuffle. When the man looked startled by the sound and moved to investigate, Enoch cocked the hammer of his gun.

"Sir, we need help here, please," a voice called. The general stopped and turned to walk toward the soldier who had called for help. Enoch and Elaine sighed in relief.

"Are you all that useless?" the general yelled. "I am not your mother; now get it done."

Enoch holstered his gun. "That was a close one," Elaine said.

"Too close," Enoch agreed. "Hopefully soon, it will be dark."

An hour passed, and finally it was dark. The army had their tents pitched and cookfires started, and the air was filled with the smell of roasting meat and potatoes. Enoch touched his stomach as it started to rumble. It had been a long time since they had had a hot meal. Once they had entered the forest, all they had had was jerky and hardtack.

The army was starting to settle down, playing cards and telling dirty jokes. Elaine was taken aback. "Men and their barbaric jokes," she said with much disdain. "Enoch, should we go?"

"Yes, this is as good a time as any." Enoch moved to help Elaine onto her horse, but an outburst caught his attention.

"Hey, you're cheating!" One soldier pointed at another.

"I am not, you lunatic." Then they started to fight.

Taking advantage of the distraction, Enoch managed to help Elaine on her horse.

The General fired his gun into the air. The soldiers went silent, and Elaine's horse reared and whinnied in panic. All the soldiers looked toward the boulder, and Enoch jumped on his horse, yelling, "Go!"

Enoch and Elaine put their horses into a full gallop. "Hey, that might be them. Get them!" the General yelled. Enoch felt the wind blowing through his hair and saw the trees getting larger as they approached. Luckily, they could see well; it was a full moon, and the woods were not as thick on this side of the clearing.

Enoch heard the soldiers in the distance. He was surprised at how fast they had been able to get on their horses.

"They are gaining on us!" Elaine screamed.

"Just keep riding!" Enoch yelled at her.

A shot rang over their heads. They flew past the trees, trying not to run into any. "They're shooting at us!" Elaine cried.

"Keep riding, Elaine! Try to keep up," Enoch said, trying to keep the panic from his voice, but panic seized him fully as the river came into view. He had forgotten that the river wound back and forth through the forest. "Please let it be shallow," he prayed as they approached the river.

His prayers were answered. The water came only to the horses' knees as they dove in. It slowed them down, however. He heard the army splashing through the river, almost on top of them, even as another shot rang out over his head. Enoch cried out, "Please let us escape!" as their pursuers' horses were nearly upon them.

Out of nowhere, Enoch felt a chill run down his spine as the air grew very chilly. He could see his breath, as well as that of the horses. Then the ground shook as an ear-piercing roar rang across the forest. A large, dark shadow lumbered past him and his sister, and Enoch heard the soldiers scream in terror.

The soldier's horses screeched, and trees started to crack. Shots were fired, and blood-curdling screams of agony rang out. "Was that the evil spirit?" Elaine asked.

"I don't know, but I'm not sticking around to find out." They kept riding.

They rode and they rode, until they had to rest their horses. As they rested, Enoch looked at the night sky. He could see a dim light in the distance; the sun was going to rise soon. How long had they been riding? he wondered as he led their horses to a creek for a drink.

Elaine shook her head. "What did that General mean by a price on our heads?"

Enoch shook his head, too. "I don't know. It could mean Father and Mother were spotted escaping and were recognized but still escaped."

"That does not make sense. They would be after them and us, and he didn't mention Mother and Father."

"I am sorry, we can only speculate. We will find out what happened as soon as we reach Antillean."

"We must find out. We must rescue them," Elaine insisted.

"We must go on," Enoch said.

"We do not know what happened, but we will serve Mother and Father better if we continue to Antillean after the horses are rested," Enoch persisted. When Elaine nodded her head in resignation, Enoch put his hand on her shoulder. "You must rest as well," he told her gently.

"But what of the evil spirit? What if it comes after us?" Elaine protested.

"I will stand guard. If that spirit or creature or whatever it is comes back, I will awaken you."

Elaine nodded. As she yawned, Enoch grabbed a pillow from one of his saddlebags. He put it on some leaves and gave her his coat for a blanket. Elaine blew a kiss at him and lay on the ground. In less than a minute, she was asleep, completely exhausted from the chase and long horse ride.

Come to think of it, Enoch was exhausted too, but he must stay awake to protect his sister from this evil thing. Looking down at his sword and gun, he wondered how these weapons would protect them from such a creature. He leaned back against a rock, ready for the sun to peak above the forest, and wondered what it would be like to sleep.

Enoch gasped as cold water was dumped on his head. He wiped his eyes. When his vision cleared, he saw Elaine standing before him. He looked at her, confused. *Wait a minute . . .* his sluggish mind thought. It was daylight.

Elaine laughed at him. "So much for standing guard, my knight in shining armor."

Then he started to laugh. They continued to laugh, a wonderful release after such a stressful ordeal. "I was just resting my eyes," Enoch said with a devious grin.

"Oh, is that what you call it?" Elaine grinned back.

"Let us get something to eat," Enoch suggested. Elaine nodded in agreement. Enoch reached into his saddlebag, then stopped, looking at their surroundings. The trees were straight and tall and had leaves. Were those birds he heard chirping? He looked around and saw squirrels and rabbits. They were out of the twisted forest.

Elaine crossed her arms under her breasts. "I was wondering how long it was going to be before you noticed, muttonhead".

Enoch ran up to Elaine and embraced her, kissing her on the forehead. He twirled her around. "We are almost there!" he laughed. "Just a few more miles."

Suddenly, they heard a noise. Enoch let go of Elaine and reached for his gun, but it was not in its holster. He had left it next to the rock he had been leaning against.

His sword was there as well. How could he be so stupid?

"Looking for this?" a soldier asked, walking out of some brush with Enoch's gun and sword in his hands. Several more soldiers came out of the woods surrounding them.

"No! This cannot be, not after all we've been through! This cannot be happening!" Enoch yelled as the soldiers closed in.

Chapter Eleven

To Dance with Death

A loud clatter resounded across the training grounds as wooden swords clashed between teachers and students. The practice grounds were a beehive of activity. Archers practiced with their bows and arrows, either riding on horses or standing still as they shot at targets. Sounds of gunfire also filled the air as students practiced with the newer weapons, such as pistols and muzzleloaders. Still other students were training in hand-to-hand combat and battle staffs.

The practice area stood adjacent to the Talons' palace and was a large square arena with high rock walls. The grass, which stretched from one end of the field to the other, had been worn down by all the fighting. In the middle of the field was a stone walkway leading to a giant statue of Tiban Talon with his hands outstretched, holding the Eye of the Cyclops, representing the moment when he had put the eye in the cyclops statue.

Sweat beaded heavily on seventeen-year-old Aurora Talon's forehead as her wooden sword clashed with her teacher's. "Good job, Aurora, just like that. Do it again." Her teacher attacked in a fury, and Aurora blocked every attack. The teacher stepped back. "You can sheathe your sword, Aurora." When she did what she had been told, her teacher told her, "I give you thirty minutes to rest and think strategy, for when I return, it will be the true test."

Aurora bowed her head, as did her teacher, Amanda,

a tall and muscular woman who was thirty years old. Amanda had long black braided hair, and she had blue eyes and a thin- lipped mouth. She had been training Aurora for five years and, despite Aurora being royalty, had been extremely hard on her. Aurora was glad of this, for it made her strong both physically and mentally.

Aurora also cared for her teacher very much. As she watched Amanda walk away, she prayed, "Please let me graduate." It was vitally important for her to know she could fight to defend the city, and the nation even if she never saw battle.

When the war had started, her grandfather, Victor Talon, had decreed that everyone over the age of twelve who was physically able go through battle training. He wanted the city to be able to defend itself in case it was surrounded. She remembered that on the day he had made the decree, he had also said a prayer that it would never happen.

Two years ago, Aurora had graduated gunfire training and hand-to-hand training. Last summer, she had graduated bow-and-arrow training and battle-staff training, and now, after five years, she was on the verge of graduating sword training, which was the most difficult to learn. If she passed this, she would be considered fully trained, and if she opted to, she would qualify to join the army when she turned eighteen. She wanted desperately to join the army and fight for Antillean's freedom. She wanted to follow in her aunt Alana's footsteps, not wishing to be a wallflower. After her aunt's injury, convincing her father would not be an easy task, however. Aurora would turn eighteen in a few months, and she knew that if Aunt Alana had been able to convince Grandfather, she could convince her own father.

Abruptly, the fighting all around her stopped. Aurora smiled. for she knew what that meant Father and Grandfather were there to see her fight. Everyone had stopped what they were doing to bow as King Victor Talon arrived. The king smiled and waved at the crowd, and Aurora noted how her grandfather always looked uncomfortable when people bowed. He felt like he was equal with his people. But the people loved him and loved to honor him and being bowed to was part of being royalty.

Suddenly, Aurora started to feel nervous. Butterflies filled her stomach. She was happy and terrified at the same time. She was glad her family had come to support her, but what if she failed? She was not sure if she could handle that.

At this point, however, there was no turning back. Her family was approaching. Her grandfather was followed by Grandmother, Aunt Alana,

Father, her brother Hunter, and Mother. A cold chill ran down Aurora's back when she saw her mother, and she gasped. Aurora had remembered to wear her brown battle dress, but she had forgotten to change her shoes. She was wearing her best slippers! *Mother is going to kill me*, she thought, feeling like she was going to vomit.

~ ~ ~

Aldar smiled as he followed his father. Aurora had trained and fought long and hard for this day. He also was happy to be here with family, with his beloved sister's arm in his. On the other side of him was his mother, the queen of Antillean, Amber Talon, in a wheelchair being pushed by her nurse.

The queen had become ill with a bone and muscle disease soon after the war had started. It had ravaged her body, leaving her hands gnarled and leaving her very skinny and no longer able to walk. Her blue-gray hair reached her shoulders, and brown eyes were set in her round face, along with a small, stout mouth. In honor of the occasion, along with the crown on her head with the Antillean symbol, she wore a pearl necklace and a long blue velvet dress. She smiled and said to no one in particular, "I cannot wait to see my granddaughter do us proud."

Aldar smiled at her.

"Well, she'd better. If she doesn't, I'll have to pretend she is not my sister," Hunter said with laughter in his voice. He was Aurora's younger brother and was just a few weeks shy of his twelfth birthday. He could not wait to be old enough to train and to learn to fight like his sister. He had short brown hair and hazel eyes, and a long narrow nose, medium mouth, round jaw, and freckled face. He was wearing a white shirt, royal-blue trousers, and brown boots, along with a medallion bearing the Antillean symbol.

Everyone laughed as they approached the seats awaiting them. As they took their seats, a loud gasp from Zena interrupted the merriment. "She's wearing her silk slippers, not her boots. Oh, that child!" Zena scowled. Zena was Aurora's mother and wife to Aldar Talon. A short, stout woman, she had a round face, shoulder-length red hair, and green eyes. She had freckles on her cheeks, a large mouth, and a long, upturned nose.

Zena was wearing a gold tiara, a long green velvet dress, and green slippers. She was also wearing a gold medallion showing a rider, bow drawn on a horse, the symbol of Violida, her home country, of which she was a princess, and her mother and father were king and queen. She had a thick, distinct accent that was common in her homeland. Her voice was beautiful when she was happy but vile as a viper when she was mad. She had met and fallen in love with Aldar at a summit between their two nations, and a year later, they had been married. With the marriage came an agreement between the two nations that if one was under attack, the other would come to its aid. Sadly, when the war had broken out with Apollyon, Violida had backed out of the agreement. Zena was incredibly angry with her father.

Everyone looked at Zena, who had her hands on her hips and was tapping her foot. Then everyone looked over at Aurora. She turned her head away in embarrassment. Aldar moved to his wife, saying, "Now, Zena, they are just slippers."

Zena glared at him. "Just slippers. What do you mean, *just slippers*?"

Victor grinned. "Here we go again." Everyone tried not to laugh as Zena continued in a huff.

"I got them for her birthday last year. Now they're ruined!" she exclaimed.

When Aldar put his arm around her, she tried to pull away. "We will get her new slippers," he said calmly.

"But they were imported from Mirodia," she protested.

Aldar kissed her on the cheek. "Please, dear, don't be upset with her; this is her big day. We don't want her to have any distractions."

Zena rolled her eyes, then smiled. "You are right, my love." She waved to get Aurora's attention. When Aurora looked back at her, Zena blew her daughter a kiss. Aurora smiled and blew a kiss back at her. "Let's watch our daughter make us proud," Zena said to Aldar.

Aldar could not help but to smile and look out at his daughter. What had happened to his little child, the one who had run around in pigtails? Where once had stood a little girl now stood a young woman grown tall and strong, her red hair running in a ponytail down her back, though her freckled face was still childlike.

Finally, Aurora's teacher arrived. This was it. In order to pass, Aurora must defeat Amanda in an all-out sword fight—no easy task, considering Amanda was a master swordswoman and was the most decorated teacher in Antillean City. Everyone applauded as Aurora and Amanda turned to face them and bowed before facing each other and doing the same.

The combatants unsheathed their wooden swords and gave each other a salute. Then they stood staring at each other for a long time. Aldar could feel the tension between them.

Without warning, Amanda charged. Aurora, caught off guard, backpedaled at the onslaught. She barely managed to block the attack, then scrambled sideways to regroup.

Once again, Amanda attacked, but this time, Aurora was ready and blocked every attack. Then Aurora counterattacked, swinging her sword in an amazing flurry of movement.

Aldar looked on in awe. It was amazing to watch, like an incredible and terrifying dance with death. He was reminded of his sister; Aurora's fighting style was almost the same, and watching it sent chills down his spine.

Amanda swung her sword at Aurora's neck as if to decapitate her, but Aurora dodged the attack. Amanda went for her knees, but Aurora jumped over Amanda's swipe and landed on her feet. "Come on, Aurora, you can do better than that," Amanda chastised her as they continued to fight.

Aldar looked over to Zena, who had stood up. Anger filled her face, and she was trying to walk over to yell at Amanda. Aldar grabbed her arm. "Unhand me!" she demanded. "No one treats our daughter like that."

Aldar smiled. “Relax, this is part of the fighting. She is testing her; that is all, my love.”

Zena ripped her arm out of Aldar’s hand. “Fine, but I don’t like it,” she hissed as she sat down. Everyone in their seats sighed in relief, as did Aldar. He wiped sweat from his brow wondering what Zena had planned to do if he had let her interfere with the fight.

“Look at Aurora go!” Hunter yelled as Aurora started to attack. “I can’t wait to learn.”

“When you turn twelve, you whippersnapper,” Aldar reminded him. Aldar looked at his son, then looked at his daughter fighting. Although he was proud of his children, he wished things could be different. He hoped and prayed that neither of them would see battle, and it angered him that they might. He wanted his children to have a happy and normal life. “Curse Xavier Pulsar to the hottest part of the underworld,” he muttered under his breath.

Amanda interrupted Aldar’s thoughts as she yelled at Aurora. “What is wrong with you? Have I wasted my time? Come on!” They continued to fight, moving back and forth, seeming like they would never tire.

Amanda roared as she gave Aurora her most aggressive attack. Aurora stumbled backward. Zena let out a gasp, and Aldar stood up as Aurora fell to the ground. Amanda straddled Aurora and raised her sword to stab her student in the chest.

~ ~ ~

“I’ve got you now, Aurora!” Amanda shouted as she straddled Aurora, the tip of her sword aimed at the girl’s chest.

Aurora looked up at Amanda in shock. Everything seemed to be going in slow motion. *How did this happen? This cannot be! I fought and trained hard for this day,* she thought with tears in her eyes.

Amanda frowned as she raised her sword for the winning blow. She screamed, “Die!” as she thrust her sword down toward Aurora’s chest.

A fire suddenly started to burn in her soul, and a determined Aurora screamed, "No!" With all her strength, Aurora grabbed Amanda's legs and pulled Amanda off her feet. She rolled over and leapt to her own feet.

Amanda smiled as she scrambled back up to her feet. They heard a great applause reach a fever pitch. "That is it, Aurora, fight! Come fight me. Fight, fight, fight." Aurora let out an ear-piercing scream, and a surprised look came across Amanda's face as Aurora attacked. Aurora did as Amanda had told her: she attacked and attacked with all her might.

They continued to fight for several more minutes before Aurora screamed again and slapped Amanda's sword out of her hands. The sword clattered across the field, and Aurora jabbed her sword against Amanda's chest.

Amanda looked down at the tip of the sword against her chest for an exceptionally long time. If the sword had been made of steel, it would have pierced her heart. All was quiet.

Finally, Amanda looked up and smiled. "Well, Aurora, looks like you won."

Aurora pulled her sword back and sheathed it, and Amanda grabbed Aurora's wrist to raise her hand in victory, calling out, "Today I decree that Aurora Talon has graduated sword-fighting class and has reached full combatant status."

A great cheer roared across the practice grounds, causing Aurora to realize that everyone there had stopped to watch her fight. Amanda gave Aurora a hug and kissed her on the cheek. "I am so proud of you," she said. Aurora smiled. She had waited five long years to hear those words from Amanda.

Aldar ran up and picked up Aurora, twirling her around. Aurora laughed and hugged him when he let her down. Hunter had come up and patted her on the shoulder. "You are an amazing fighter even if you are a girl," he told her. Aurora punched him in the shoulder, and they both laughed as they hugged each other.

Aurora stiffened as her mother approached. Zena looked down at Aurora's slippers and then tried to straighten Aurora's hair. Then she smiled. "Very good, Aurora. You did us proud, child." Aurora sighed in relief as her mother hugged her.

"My turn," Amber said with a smile as she was wheeled up to Aurora." Aurora hugged her grandmother, who smiled as the girl kissed her cheek.

"Love you, Grandmother."

"As do I," Amber replied.

Then came Victor. As Aurora ran to him and wrapped her arms around him, he said, "I am so proud of you, my little honeybee." Aurora loved it when he used the nickname, he had given her when she had been little and always busy as a bee. "I am so proud of you. You did Antillean proud today. I love you so."

Aurora kissed him on the cheek. "I love you too, Grandfather. Thank you for being there for me."

"Everyone," said Amanda, getting everyone's attention as she approached Aurora with a scabbarded sword and a bracelet in her hands. "Give me your sword hand," she told Aurora. Aurora did as she was told, and Amanda put the bracelet on her wrist. The bracelet was blue and white, with the Antillean symbol on it. Aurora looked at in admiration. Next, Amanda placed the sword in Aurora's hands. The leather scabbard bore the same symbol.

Aurora pulled out the sword, which had a very sharp steel blade and a bronze guard. On the hilt was a blue gem. She raised it high for all to see, and another cheer came from the crowd.

After several minutes, everyone had fallen into silence. Amanda yelled at the students, "Well, you will not graduate just standing there!" In unison, all the students ran to their stations to continue their training. Amanda gave Aurora one more hug. "You have done me proud, Aurora. If you ever need me, come to my apartments. You can visit any time, for you are no longer my student but are now Your Highness." She kissed Aurora on the cheek. "I must go now, for I will have to find another scrappy youngling to train."

Aurora waved to Amanda as she disappeared in the crowd of students.

"Well, now you're a full-status combatant, eh? There will be no more living with you now." The familiar voice caught Aurora's attention.

"Bethany!" Aurora said, running up to Bethany Dawn and giving her a huge hug. "I thought you weren't able to come see me tonight because you had another commitment."

Bethany kissed her on the cheek. "I had to cancel. I had to come and watch the girl I watched grow up graduate."

Zena sniffed, and Aurora shook her head. Mother had always been jealous of Bethany, thinking Aurora spent too much time with Bethany and not enough with her.

Bethany and Zena exchanged looks. Zena was about to speak when Victor walked between them. "This is a cause for celebration! Are you hungry, my little honeybee?"

Aurora put her hand to her stomach. "Am I ever, Grandfather!"

Victor smiled. "I have had a special dinner prepared in your honor." Aurora smiled. "I have had your favorite meal prepared for you: roasted pig, buttered beans, mashed potatoes, and molasses pie."

"Grandfather, this meal would have taken hours to make. What if I had not graduated?"

Victor smiled. "Well, my little honeybee, I had every confidence you would graduate; however, if not, we still would eat well." Everyone laughed, and Victor put his arm around Aurora's shoulders. "Come, let us feast." He waved to Bethany. "Come join us. You played just as big a part as all of us raising Aurora."

"Thank you, Your Majesty." Bethany smiled as Zena rolled her eyes.

"Come let us celebrate!" Victor said as he led the way to a much-deserved celebration.

Chapter Twelve

To Dance with a Demon

After dinner, Aurora and Bethany laughed as they entered Aurora's rooms. Bethany started a fire in the fireplace. Aurora's bedroom was spacious and had many paintings, a vanity, and a large bed. They took their seats in ornate chairs in front of the fireplace, and Bethany smiled at Aurora. Bethany spent countless hours with Aurora even when her teaching duties were done, for the two were much more than teacher and pupil; they were also best friends.

Aurora began to rub her shoulders. Bethany stood up and walked behind Aurora, then began to massage her shoulders. Aurora closed her eyes. "Thank you, Bethany. I hurt everywhere."

Bethany smiled. "Well now, that was quite a battle you had with Amanda."

"Oh, Bethany, for a while I did not know if I was going to make it. I have never fought that hard before."

"Ah, but you did make it, and you earned that sword and bracelet. Do not forget that child. I couldn't have been prouder of you when you defeated Amanda."

Aurora smiled. "Thank you, Bethany. Perhaps I will not fight but now I'm ready, either way I pray this war will end soon."

Bethany frowned. "It is sad that Empress Shiva was killed. What a tragedy."

Aurora nodded. "It truly is sad. my prayer is that somehow, this tragedy will end this war, that at least with her death, somehow something positive will come out of this and Emperor Pulsar will have a change of heart."

"While it is not likely, it certainly would be a good thing," Bethany agreed.

Aurora sighed. "That poor woman. She had been through so much, and on top of everything, she lost her life. She was such a beautiful woman. I remember the first time I saw her, I thought she was an angel."

Bethany stopped massaging Aurora's shoulders and took a seat. "Tell me about that time," she said.

Aurora smiled. "Oh, Bethany, if you could have been there! It was a most amazing time.

"I was just a child, and it was the summit of the nations, a time when all the rulers of the nearby lands would meet. It was time for Antillean to host the meeting. I know there was a lot of tension, but I was too young to understand. I now know that Emperor Pulsar and Emperor Savage were under fire for the way they treated their people. All I cared about was the feast and the dance and the fact that Mother and Father let me come.

"I remember I had a silken white-and-blue dress and gold tiara. I felt so special that day! Everyone was dressed in their best. Mother and Father also wore silk. I remember it was the first time I was in the grand ballroom. I remember all the tables were set up with all the nations' flags, and on the table in the center was a grand cake. It was a massive cake and was adorned with the same flags.

"There was an orchestra with all manner of instruments next to the dance floor. I couldn't wait to dance. Then Mother called me to my seat. I could hardly contain myself as I ran over to take my seat. In front of us was a long table for all the rulers of all the nations to take their seats. The table stood in front of the grand staircase. Then the orchestra started to play as an announcer came down to his podium. I remember jumping to my feet when we were called to stand.

"I clapped as loud as I could when he introduced Grandfather and Grandmother Zanthor. Mother looked so proud to see them. Then Emperor and Empress Savage of Salonia were introduced. There was little applause for them. I looked around in confusion; I had no idea they were slave traders. Then King and Queen Unidad from Mirodia. I was fascinated with their animal-pattern royal garb. I did not know it was a jungle nation. Of course, my slippers I ruined were from there," Aurora laughed.

"Then Emperor and Empress Pulsar were introduced, and the applause died down to a trickle. I saw Emperor Pulsar for the first time, and he looked terrifying even before Father cut his eye out. I could tell then he was an evil man and did evil things to the weak and the innocent. Then I saw Shiva and my jaw dropped. She was wearing a red silken gown that had flame patterns on it. She was so beautiful.

"Then Shiva turned her back to the crowd; the dress opened to her bare back, and I saw it—that huge tattoo of that horrible image of the man consumed by fire. It looked dreadful. I remember Mother saying, not too quietly, 'Tattooed like an animal.' Shiva looked embarrassed at Mother's comment, but Xavier did not even notice.

"Then Grandfather and Grandmother Talon were introduced, and a great cheer came from the crowd. I remember Grandfather and Grandmother holding hands. It was before Grandmother got sick. She stood straight and tall. I was so incredibly happy.

"Grandfather stood up with a glass of wine and said a toast for peace and prosperity for all nations. Then we ate the food; it was amazing. During the meal, I could not help but stare at Shiva. Then my mother reminded me it was impolite to stare and to mind my manners.

"Finally, the time I waited for happened—the dance! The orchestra played the most joyous music. I remember dancing with Father, Grandfather Talon, and Grandfather Zanthor. Then came the most fun dance of them all: the king and queen dance.

"The orchestra played the song of the same name. The women stood on one side, the men on the other. Then when the music started, the men and woman bowed, then danced, and as the music played, they changed partners. I remember standing next to Grandmother Talon, then I started to dance with Father, and we continued to dance. I danced with men and boys alike. Some I knew, some I did not.

"Then I danced with Grandpa Zanthor. I laughed gleefully as he twirled me around. Then I turned to my next partner. I let out a small gasp as my hands clasped Emperor Pulsar's; I'd had no Idea he was part of the dance. He smiled at me; I tried hard to smile back. He had the darkest piercing eyes I had ever seen.

"I felt I was dancing with a demon from the underworld. I tried hard not to shiver or panic. Every part of me wanted to run and scream in terror. I could feel myself starting to sweat. I really hoped he did not notice. We danced for what seemed like an eternity, his creepy smile sending shivers down my spine. Finally, mercifully, the dance ended. I gave him a curtsy and he gave me a bow. 'You are a wonderful, beautiful dancer, young lady,' he said with the same creepy smile. I think I managed to say, 'Thank you.'

"Then he turned to Shiva, who was also part of the dance. 'Have you met my wife, Shiva?' he asked. 'No,' I managed to say. 'Shiva, this is Aurora Talon, the daughter of Aldar and Zena Talon.' We both curtsied. 'It is a pleasure to meet you,' she said. Her voice was like that of angels. 'It is a pleasure to meet you as well,' I said. I looked at her and him; *What a strange couple*, I thought, *an angel and a demon married. Strange indeed.*

"Then Emperor Pulsar let out a foul-smelling belch. He turned to Shiva. 'I am sorry, my love, I must find the privy. Make conversation with Aurora. I must go; I ate and drank too much, I am afraid.' Shiva and I watched as he hurried off to the privy. Then we looked at each other and laughed. 'I am sorry, little one. I am afraid my husband has little manners. He can be quite undignified at times,' she told me. We talked for what seemed like hours; she talked of their son, Maximus, and what a great ruler he was going to be.

"I remember she laughed and smiled a lot, but even at my young age, I could sense a sadness in her. I could see it in her eyes—a great sorrow lay deep inside her. She smiled, but her sad eyes betrayed her. Of course, I had no idea at the time what terrible things she had been through. Then

Xavier approached. He let out another belch as he put his arm around her and said, 'Looks like you two got along well.'

"I managed to say to him, 'Yes, we had a good conversation. Shiva is a wonderful woman.' 'Could not agree with you more,' he said as he held her tighter and belched yet again. This time Shiva scowled at him. He looked over at me. 'I am sorry, excuse me,' he managed to say. 'Well, Aurora, it is time for us to retire for the night,' he said as he winked at Shiva. Shiva looked at me. 'It was a pleasure to meet you, Aurora. I hope to meet you again,' she said. I told her, 'I am glad we met, too.' We then waved to each other, and she walked away. I will never forget that night; it was exciting and terrifying at the same time."

"What an amazing story," Bethany said.

"It was an amazing time. Of course, I have seen Shiva since then. She was always a pleasure to talk to. We would always have fun talking—at least until the war started."

"Ahem," a familiar voice interrupted.

"Mother." Aurora stood up.

"I see you two are having fun," Zena said with a scowl. "The hour is late, Aurora. You had a very exciting day, and you need to rest." She glared at Bethany.

Bethany stood up. "Well, I must be going."

Aurora gave Bethany a hug. "Good night," she said.

"Good night," Bethany said, then bowed to Zena. "Good night, Your Highness." Zena gave her a curt nod as Bethany walked out.

"Mother, why must you be so mean to Bethany? She is a very kind woman."

Zena was silent for a second. "Be that as it may, she is also your teacher, and she should spend more time teaching and less time having fun with you."

"But mother—" Zena's glare cut Aurora off, and Aurora realized there was no arguing with her.

"Tomorrow I want to contact that seamstress from Mirodia to get you new slippers."

"Yes, Mother," Aurora said stiffly.

Zena smiled. "Well, Aurora, I hope you sleep well."

Aurora hugged her mother "Good night, Mother."

"Good night, honey. Have a good sleep."

Aurora watched her mother leave, wishing her mother would treat Bethany better and would not be so jealous of her.

Aurora groaned as she took off her battle dress and grass-stained slippers. She washed her face in a basin of water. She groaned again as she slipped on her nightclothes; she could not believe how sore she was. She then gingerly walked over to her bookshelf, wanting to read before bed. What book to read? She saw an old, familiar book: *Eye of the Cyclops. I have not read this in a while.* She had forgotten what a fascinating story it was.

After reading several chapters, she put the book down, blew out her reading candle, and slipped under the covers, then fell into a deep sleep.

Chapter Thirteen

The Medallion

The commander looked at Enoch and Elaine suspiciously, pacing as their hands were being bound.

"Please, sir, there is no reason to tie us," Enoch pleaded. "We are here in peace."

The commander ignored him. "Sit," he commanded, and the soldiers helped Enoch and Elaine to the ground while the commander continued to pace. "My name is Mylon Clawbane. I am commander of the Sixty-Eighth Infantry of the Antillean army." Mylon was a tall and muscular middle-aged man with long black hair, brown eyes, and a square jaw. He wore white-and-blue armor with the Antillean symbol on the breastplate. "I would like to know who you are and what are you doing in this part of Antillean."

Enoch spoke up. "I am so glad you are from the Antillean army and not Apollyon! My name is Enoch, and this is my sister, Elaine. We have escaped Apollyon and we seek an audience with King Victor Talon."

Mylon pinched his chin in thought. "Okay, please tell me why you are on the run and why you seek an audience with King Talon."

Enoch told him about the assassination plan, about them sneaking out of Apollyon, about the evil spirit—everything. When he was done, Mylon stopped pacing and looked at him. "Quite a tall tale, son. You mean to tell me you two are the children of Levi and Lana Eclipse?"

"Yes, sir. We hope Mother and Father aren't far behind. However, we are confused."

"Confused? What do you mean?" Mylon asked.

"We don't know why there is a price on our heads. We don't know if Father was successful in killing Emperor Pulsar. We don't know if, heaven forbid, he got caught or was spotted and identified as he and Mother escaped."

"How do I know you tell the truth, son? For all I know, you two could be spies working for Pirena Solaris."

"I tell you, sir, what I say is true."

Mylon smirked. "You are telling me that you two snot-nosed kids have survived on your own in the woods? Then this evil spirit stopped an Apollyon century? I think we are a little old for fairy tales." Mylon started to laugh, and the other soldiers joined in.

"He's telling the truth, you buffoon!" Elaine yelled.

"Oh, we have a feisty one," Mylon said.

As the soldiers roared with laughter, Elaine's face grew dark with anger. "Men! It doesn't matter if they're from Apollyon or Antillean; they are all smelly, ignorant idiots."

The laughter stopped, and Mylon's face turned red in anger as he walked up to her. He kneeled in front of her. As she glared defiantly at him, he put his hand under her chin. "I am half-tempted to gag you, girl."

She gave him a pleading look. "Please, sir, we are telling the truth. We have proof of who we are."

Mylon gave her a considering look. "Okay, what proof do you have?"

"In one of the saddlebags is a letter. The letter is for King Talon to open; it is sealed with King Talon's seal to guarantee safe passage."

Mylon looked at one of the soldiers. "Go through the saddlebags and bring me the letter." The soldier complied. After several minutes, he handed Mylon the letter. Mylon examined the letter and the wax seal, which he touched with his finger. "This seal could be a fake."

Enoch and Elaine looked at each other in exasperation.

When she saw that Mylon was getting ready to open the letter, Elaine screamed, "No! If you open that letter, you will be disciplined for sure. That is for King Talon only."

"Are you threatening me?" Mylon shouted back. "I could just throw this letter in the fire."

Elaine tried to regain her composure. "I am not threatening you, sir. We tell the truth. Please."

Mylon sighed. "Do you have any other proof of who you are?"

Enoch and Elaine looked at each other. Finally, Elaine said, "I was hoping not to have to do this, but, yes, I have one more piece of truth I can give you."

Mylon looked at her curiously. "What do you mean?"

"You are going to have to trust me."

"Why in Tiban Talon's name should I trust you? I don't know who you are."

Elaine pleaded, "Please, sir, just trust me. There are a hundred of you and just me."

"I am losing my patience, but fine. What do you want me to do?"

"Untie me, sir," Elaine answered. Mylon rolled his eyes but motioned to a soldier to untie her.

Elaine rubbed her wrists once they were free. She reached behind her neck, and some of the soldiers unsheathed their swords.

"Put your swords away," Clawbane commanded, and the soldiers did as they had been told.

Elaine pulled her medallion off her neck. "I need a knife," she said.

Mylon groaned as he pulled out a dagger and handed it to her.

She cringed, saying, "I hate blood," then poked her finger with the dagger. The soldiers watched in amazement as she put a drop of her blood on the medallion. Holding the medallion in the palm of her hand, she shouted, "Long live King Talon!" Slowly, an image started to coalesce; it was Victor Talon. All the soldiers gasped at the sight.

Then the image spoke. "To whoever sees this image, listen to what I say. These two young people are Enoch and Elaine Eclipse; they are now my wards. You must treat them as you would treat me and my family.

Failure to do so is considered treason. Please bring them safely to me as soon as possible. Thank you."

The image disappeared, and there was a long silence. "Untie Enoch," Mylon finally commanded. "I am sorry, me lady. Give me a handkerchief, he commanded. A soldier brought him one, which he wrapped around Elaine's finger before turning to Enoch. "I am so sorry, sir. I am here to serve and protect."

Enoch and Elaine smiled at each other at this sudden turn of events. "It is all right, Commander," Enoch replied.

"Thank you, sir, and thank you, me lady. Is there anything you need? Food? Water? Anything?"

"Yes, Mylon," Enoch said, "We have been away from civilization for a few weeks. Do you have any news of our father and mother?"

Once again, silence filled the air. Mylon gave them a somber look. "I am not sure how to tell you this. . . . "

"Please tell us," Elaine pleaded. "We need to know what happened."

"I am sorry, but your father failed. He was spotted, and in the chaos, he accidentally killed Empress Shiva." Tears filled Elaine's eyes as he told them that their parents had been captured and, by now, probably dead. He also told them that there was a cease in battle in honor of Shiva.

Enoch wrapped his arms around Elaine as she started to sob uncontrollably.

"I truly am sorry," Mylon said with sadness in his voice. "I wish I could have given you better news."

"What do we do now, Enoch?" Elaine asked between sobs.

"We must carry on. We must go to see King Talon. We must do our part in defeating Xavier Pulsar. We must somehow bring honor back to our family name."

Elaine nodded. "You are right. We must fight to our last breath for Mother and Father and freedom."

Mylon put his arms around the siblings' shoulders. "I will prepare you an escort," he said. "Jonathan, come over here."

A young Apollyon man walked over. "Yes, sir." Enoch and Elaine stared at him. He looked strange. He had brownish olive skin, black hair, brown eyes, a curved nose, a round face, and a firm jaw—an Apollyon man wearing Antillean armor and fighting for Antillean, quite a sight to behold.

Mylon smiled at them. "This is Jonathan, my right-hand man. He and a dozen men will escort you to Antillean City and the king's palace."

Finally, Elaine spoke. "You are Apollyon," she said to Jonathan.

Jonathan smiled. "Yes, I am. I fled Apollyon just before the war started. I then joined the army to free Apollyon from that evil beast. There are many soldiers like me who have joined the fight to bring our land back to its former glory."

Mylon slapped Jonathan on the back. "We have to hold this perimeter, so make sure these two make it to Antillean City safely."

"Yes, sir." Jonathan saluted him, then collected twelve volunteers to come with them. "Bring them their horses and belongings," he told the volunteers. "We have already burned a lot of daylight and have a long way to go."

Before long, Enoch and Elaine were on their mounts, Mylon waving to them as they rode away to see the king.

Chapter Fourteen

The High Cost of Betrayal

Xavier Pulsar waited impatiently in the foyer for his supreme general to arrive. The funeral was to start soon. The foyer had a large marble floor and tall walls with a vaulted ceiling. Several paintings of Shiva hung on the walls, and a tall statue of her stood in the center of the foyer. Xavier had had the statue created for their tenth anniversary.

He heard the door to the outside open and exclaimed, "Finally, he's here!"

Virion walked quickly to Xavier and kneeled. "Forgive me, Xavier. We ran into a storm, and it delayed me. I am so sorry about Shiva; she was the most beloved woman in all the world." Virion had been a close friend since before Xavier had become emperor and had been his main supporter during the transition after Killian's death, and he, along with Shiva and Pirena, was the only person in all the land permitted to call Xavier by his given name.

Xavier smiled. "It is okay, old friend; I am just glad you made it in time. You may rise."

Virion, sixty-five years old, tall, and thin, rose. His short gray hair was balding, and his face, long and gaunt, was clean-shaven. His nose was long and narrow, his mouth stern, his jaw long and pointed, and his eyes blue. His olive-brown skin gave his gaunt features a leathery look. He was a seasoned warrior, indeed. He wore the black uniform of Apollyon, with the Apollyon symbol on his chest. All the medals and honors that an Apollyon officer could get were attached to his uniform.

Xavier put his arm around Virion's shoulders. "Tomorrow we will have a meeting. We will discuss our next move in the war."

Virion nodded somberly. "Are you sure, Xavier? Don't you need more time? This has been a very trying time for you."

"Thank you for your concern. Today we say good-bye to my rose; tomorrow I will be ready to start anew."

"Hello, Virion," Maximus said as he approached.

Virion gave him a curt nod. "Maximus," he said.

"Father, the director says everyone is seated and everything is ready when you are."

"Thank you, son. Well, let's go and say good-bye to your mother." The emperor put his arms around Maximus's and Virion's shoulders.

The director stood at the entryway leading to the auditorium. The auditorium was huge and contained several pews. One large walkway led across the marble floor. A podium stood on a stage, and in front of the stage was the glass coffin of Shiva.

Xavier looked out at the massive crowd; there were some high-ranking officials there. There were also several families present that met his favor, as well as representatives from other countries. Next, Xavier looked at the coffin. He could just see Shiva in it. She had been dressed in a gold silken dress. Her hair had been braided, and her fire-shaped tiara sat on her head.

He scanned the room until he spotted Shiva's mother, Quill Quasar, and younger sister, Shannon. Shannon had their father's features, but Shiva had looked exactly like her mother, only younger Quill, though older, was still beautiful.

Xavier nodded to the director.

"All rise for the emperor," the director announced. Everyone stood, and the director led the emperor and his party to their seats. Xavier stopped beside Quill and put his hand on her shoulder. "Thank you for raising such a lovely woman. I am sorry for everything."

Quill looked at him in stunned silence. It took a moment for her to regain her composure. "Thank you, Your Majesty" was all she could say.

Xavier nodded, then started down the aisle to take his seat. He looked at Shiva; she looked so beautiful that he wished he could hold her hand.

He wished he could love her one last time, and that conjured more memories of just before they had been married.

~ ~ ~

Virion rushed into Xavier's living quarters. "Xavier, I have some important news," he said, trying to catch his breath.

Xavier gave Virion a concerned look. "What is it, Virion? What is the matter?"

"I am sorry, Xavier, I really wish I could tell you better news." Virion hesitated, still trying to catch his breath.

"What in blazes is going on, Virion? Well, out with it, man! You're driving me mad here."

"It's Nova. Our spies have confirmed he is plotting with other high-ranking families to have you executed."

"What?" Xavier shouted incredulously. "How is this true? Are you sure? Is there any way this is not true?"

"I am sorry, but two of our spies have reached Nova's inner circle, and they our planning one last meeting after sunset."

Xavier grabbed a vase and smashed it to the floor, cursing. "How can this be? Nova betray me.? I gave him my favor. I gave him a mansion! I married him to Quill. I have given him servants, horses, livestock, and a lavish income, and this is how he repays me?" Xavier looked out his window; the sun was going to set in an hour. He tapped his fingers at the base of the window, in shock. Next to Virion, Nova was his most trusted friend.

He pondered for several minutes, his shock turning to hurt, then to anger, and then to fury.

"Xavier?" Virion finally asked. Xavier turned to face him, and Virion took a step back. He had never seen such a horrifying look of anger in Xavier before.

"Virion, get as many soldiers as you can. We are going to pay Nova a little visit."

Xavier's voice was so quiet and cold, it sent shivers down Virion's spine. "Right away," he said before turning and hurrying out the door.

Xavier walked to his sword, which was hanging on a spike. He pulled the sword down and attached the scabbard to his belt. "Death is the last gift I give you, Nova," he snarled.

~ ~ ~

Nova sat nervously at the conference table in his personal office building in the outskirts of the city. Xavier had had it built so Nova could conduct business on his behalf with those who met the emperor's favor. Nova knew what was at stake and what a great risk this was. Ten more people were to arrive—ten people who represented five of the twenty houses that met Xavier's favor. If they were able to pull this off, they would be rid of that tyrant and would get a new ruler. However, if this failed, they would be ruined—and they would be tortured and executed.

A knock came at the door. Nova walked up and cracked the door open. He saw nothing, but there was a long quiet pause. A voice in the darkness gave Nova the appropriate password, and Nova opened the door. Two people came through the door.

This happened four more times, and finally, everyone arrived. They were husbands and wives, their respective families' patriots, ready to do what was right.

Once all were seated, Nova stood. "Thank you for coming. This is it, the final meeting." He smiled. "Tomorrow night, Xavier Pulsar will be dead, and Apollyon will be free." He looked over to one of the family members. "Josiah, have you everything in place?

Josiah stood up. "Yes, Nova I—"

The window behind Josiah shattered. He had been shot. Everyone looked in shock as blood spurted from his mouth and his eyes rolled backward. He fell face first onto the table. For one eerie moment, all was silent.

Then chaos ensued. Apollyon soldiers broke into the conference room as Nova stood there in shock. He watched all but two of his fellow conspirators get slaughtered in front of him, and then suddenly, he was in pain as a chair was smashed across his back. Nova crumpled to the ground and looked up to see Virion Nebula shaking hands with the two family members who were still alive. Nova had been betrayed.

"Thank you. You will have double the wealth you have now," Virion told the two traitors, then looked down at Nova and scowled. "Bind him and pick him up," he said with great disdain.

Xavier was sitting on his mount when two soldiers threw Nova to the ground in front of him. Nova looked up at Xavier. Xavier snarled as he got off his horse and walked up to Nova, then looked down at his old friend and frowned. "Why, Nova, why?" Xavier screamed. "You were my friend. I can't believe it. I gave you everything you own. I gave you a home. I gave you a lavish salary. I gave you livestock. I gave you slaves and servants to fulfill your every whim. I even married you to your wife. I have had you eat at my table, and you betray me. What do you have to say for yourself?"

Nova looked up into Xavier's piercing eyes. "Xavier, I—"

Xavier slapped Nova across the face. "You no longer have the right to call me by my name. From now on, it's *Your Majesty.* Do you understand?"

Nova nodded. "I am sorry, Your Majesty. It will never happen again."

Xavier tapped his foot impatiently. "Well?"

"Yes, Your Majesty, I know all I have, all I possess, is because of you, and for that I was truly thankful. For years, I enjoyed our friendship, but as time marched on, I realized how the people were struggling. After a while, I became dissatisfied with all the wealth I had. How could I enjoy it when some people had no food? I also know that you were never going to do anything about it, so, yes, my former friend, I planned to kill you." A tear ran down Nova's cheek. "I am sorry, Your Majesty. I did not want to do it, but you left me no choice."

Xavier looked down at Nova for a moment. He felt as though he might cry, but he did not. Again, he slapped Nova across the face. "Scum! So, it seems you don't like wealth. Well, I will certainly take care of that. There is a high cost of betrayal, and you are going to pay dearly for your betrayal."

"Xavier," Virion said as he walked up to the emperor, "I have all the names of the houses that were part of this betrayal." He named the first three, then named the fourth: William and Karen Enigma.

Xavier's eyes opened in shock. The Enigmas were also a prominent family that had met his favor. Xavier sighed. This indeed was a terrible night. Not only his friend but four other families had betrayed him. Then an idea took form in his head: he could use this horrible night to his advantage—yes, indeed. He turned to Virion. "Take your soldiers and go to the four houses. Gather the servants, the children, and the livestock—they will make great slaves—then set fire to their houses. Let them burn to the ground. Let nothing be built in their place. Let the charred remains be an example to all who oppose me. Let them know I am the Apollyon."

Virion nodded and got on his horse, riding off with his soldiers.

Xavier looked at Nova and gave him a wicked smile that caused Nova to lean back, it was so unnerving. "Well, Nova, it looks like we have some talking to do. I will give you this chance to make things a little bit easier."

"I am listening, Your Majesty.

"I will give you as quick and painless a death as I can. Apollyon needs an empress. I will take Shiva's hand in marriage; she will be my wife. I will have mercy on Quill and Shannon; they will become my servants and will be able to see Shiva. What say you?"

Nova laughed. "I will die a thousand agonizing deaths before I give you my blessing, you tyrant." Xavier slapped Nova again, and Nova spit out blood.

"You dare insult me? Well, I guess we will do things the hard way. I will still marry her, and I will kill your servants. I will kill Quill and Shannon. I will tie them all up as I set fire to the house, and you can hear their screams in the inferno. I think that would be far worse than dying a thousand agonizing deaths."

Tears welled in Nova's eyes as he started to shake. "Please don't kill them, please. They are innocent; they don't deserve to die. Please do what you with me, but please don't harm them."

"I will marry Shiva with your blessing, and I will spare your younger daughter and wife; I will see to their comfort. I will take care of Shiva, and she will want for nothing; I will do anything to make her happy."

Nova sighed. "I guess I have no choice; however, there is a problem."

Xavier looked confused. "What do you mean, *problem*?"

"You see, Your Majesty, Shiva is already engaged. It was going to be announced after your death."

Nova braced himself for another slap, but instead of hitting him, Xavier scratched his head and started to pace. "Who is her suitor? Tell me now or I will renege on my promise."

Nova hesitated for a moment.

"Now!" Xavier yelled.

"Daniel Enigma, the son of William and Karen Enigma. Shiva and Daniel have been courting for a year. I gave him my blessing last week and they were to be married a year from now. Please, Your Majesty, do not harm him; he just lost his parents Shiva would be devastated as well; she loves him."

"Well, he must die. I am sure over time Shiva will forgive me and will love me just as much as Daniel." Xavier turned to one of his soldiers. "Find Daniel Enigma and bring him to me at the Quasar house."

As the soldier left to do the emperor's bidding, Nova said, "She would never forgive you, Your Majesty. She will never love you the way she loves Daniel. Please don't kill him."

Xavier yelled, "You should have thought about all this before you betrayed me! This is all your fault. Remember that high cost of betrayal I told you about? Well, this is part of it. Because of you, four houses are doomed, you are ruined, and Shiva will lose Daniel. Was it worth it?"

"Yes!" Nova screamed back. "I knew what risk I and the others were taking. We knew it meant our doom if we failed. We may have failed, but someday, Your Majesty, you will pay. Someone will kill you. Someone else will rise and be willing to sacrifice everything like I have, and you will be the one paying the price."

Xavier screamed and punched Nova in the face. Nova crumpled to the ground. Xavier picked Nova up by the shirt and shook him. "You slime. No one will be killing me. I will thwart any attempt on my life. I am going to live a long, prosperous life," he hissed, then threw Nova back to the ground.

"Gag him," he ordered a nearby soldier. "I don't want him to warn them. Throw that piece of garbage on a horse, for we ride to the Quasar house."

It took several minutes to reach Nova's home, for it was on the farthest outskirts of town. They rode up as quietly as they could.

The house was a huge, beautiful three-story mansion. Xavier remembered having it built for Nova as a wedding gift. It had taken three years to be ready enough for Nova to move in. Xavier shook his head. What a shame; even though it had been built by slave labor, it had come at a high cost.

"Go inside the mansion. Gather all the servants and slaves; kill any that resist except for Shiva, Quill, and Shannon," he ordered his men. "Failure to do so will result in death by fire. Do you understand?" His soldiers nodded. "Go," he commanded.

The soldiers sprang into action, kicking down the door and storming the house. Nova tensed as screams and shouts rang out.

After several minutes, people started to funnel out. Once most were out, along with some of the soldiers, Xavier commanded his soldiers to get Nova off his horse.

Xavier got off his own horse, waiting as patiently as he could to finally see Shiva. It had been quite a while since he had last seen her. Then his heart fluttered. Shiva was walking out with her mother and her sister. She was wearing her nightclothes and her hair was all askew; apparently, she had gone to bed. Despite all that, however, she was still the most beautiful woman he had ever laid eyes on, and he stood gawking.

"What in the name of Apollyon is the meaning of this, Xavier?" Quill demanded, interrupting Xavier's stupor. "We all get ready for bed, and then all this. Why? Xavier, why do you do this?" she asked in shock.

Xavier smiled grimly. "I'm afraid you have your husband to thank for this interruption. I will let him explain. Bring him forward," he commanded.

Quill, Shannon, and Shiva gasped as Nova came into sight. "What is going on here?" Quill asked incredulously. Why is he bound and gagged? He is your friend."

The soldiers roughly removed Nova's gag at Xavier's order, and he looked at his family and started to cry. "Go ahead, Nova," Xavier said. "tell them why you are bound. Tell them why I did this. Tell them everything."

Nova took a moment to regain his composure. "I am sorry, my love; I am sorry, children, but I failed and let you down. I am sorry I did not tell you I planned to assassinate His Majesty. I should have sent you away." His family's eyes grew big in surprise as Nova continued. "One family betrayed me; the others died. I'm sorry, but Daniel's parents are among the dead." Shiva covered her mouth as tears ran down her cheeks. "His Majesty has agreed to give me as painless a death as possible and you all as comfortable lives as possible."

"And why are you going to do this, Xavier?" Quill demanded.

Xavier gritted his teeth. "From now on, you will call me *Your Majesty.* You have lost the right to call me by name. Nova, please tell them the terms of my mercy." He folded his arms and gave Nova a smug smile.

Nova started to quiver as he looked at Shiva. "I am so sorry, Shiva. I only agreed to this for you to be safe."

Shiva looked confused. "What do you mean, Father? what do I have to do with this?"

"I have agreed to give your hand in marriage to Emperor Pulsar."

Shiva's eyes widened in shock. "But, Father, you gave Daniel your blessing. I love him; he is my soul mate. I don't understand. He just lost his parents, and now he is going to lose me as well. How can you agree to this?"

"He is going to marry you whether I agree or not, but if I refuse him, he will kill everyone, including your mother and Shannon."

"You monster!" Quill shouted, and she charged Xavier with her fists swinging. Xavier punched her in the face, and she hit the ground hard.

"Mother!" Shiva screamed. She and Shannon ran to Quill's side, and a new and strange feeling came over Xavier—a little bit of guilt.

Xavier did his best to ignore the feeling. "You are lucky I did not kill you, woman," he told Quill's prone form.

Shiva glared at Xavier defiantly as she and Shannon tried their best to revive their unconscious mother.

Nova growled, and the soldiers had to hold him back from charging as well. "I curse the day you were born!" he shouted at Xavier.

Xavier moved to punch Nova but stopped when he saw the tears streaming down Shiva's face. *What is wrong with me? I am an emperor; I am the Apollyon. I have no guilt*, he thought.

Quill came to, and Shiva and Shannon helped her to her feet. She wobbled a bit as they kept her steady.

Shiva looked at Xavier, hate filling her eyes, and Xavier thought they were beautiful.

Xavier turned his attention to Nova. "So do I have your blessing?"

Nova hung his head. "Yes, Your Majesty."

"I hate you!" Shiva screamed as she marched up to Xavier. When she tried to slap him, he grabbed her hand and twisted it behind her back. She howled in pain.

"Please, Shiva, I don't want to hurt you. Please don't do this again." He let her go gently, and she slowly walked back to her mother and sister, rubbing her elbow as she went. Xavier unsheathed his sword. "It is time to die, Nova. Say your final words to your family."

"No!" Shiva screamed. She approached Xavier, slowly and carefully this time, and fell to her knees. "Please, Your Majesty, I implore you, don't kill my father." She put her hands on his feet. "Please. I know the punishment for treason is death. I know he was your friend, and this must hurt badly. Please have mercy. Please do it for me." She looked up at him with pleading eyes.

Xavier started to quiver. *Stop it*, he said to himself and tried to keep his composure.

"Fine, I will let him live," he said.

A look of shock crossed Shiva's face, as well as the faces of everyone else there. Even Xavier was shocked. He had never listened to anyone before, especially a woman, but he had said it, and so it would be. He turned to face the equally shocked Nova. "Instead of death, I sentence you to the slave pits. After five years' time, you will return to work in my palace and will be able to see your family. However, you will never know freedom again; you will forever be my slave." He looked down at Shiva. "It is time to say good-bye to your father," he said with a thin smile.

Shiva kissed his feet. "Thank you, Your Majesty. Thank you for your mercy."

"Go to your father," Xavier told her uncomfortably.

Shiva rose to her feet, and she and Shannon helped their mother walk over to Nova, where they hugged and kissed each other. After several minutes, Xavier nodded to his soldiers. The soldiers pulled Nova from his family's embrace. Shiva screamed and cried as her father was tied to a horse.

Nova gave them one last smile as he walked slowly away with two soldiers in tow, and Shiva fell to the ground, sobbing uncontrollably. *She will be fine*," Xavier tried to convince himself.

"Your Majesty," said an approaching soldier, "we are here with Daniel Enigma like you requested."

Xavier let out a groan as Shiva jumped up and ran to Daniel, crying out his name as she embraced him. He had forgotten about Daniel.

Xavier looked at Daniel and had to admit he was a very handsome young man.

Xavier knew he was in a conundrum. He had to kill Daniel, lest the young man attempt to kill him. Xavier clenched his fists as Shiva kissed Daniel passionately. She really did love Daniel. What was he to do?

Xavier set his jaw. "Separate them," he commanded.

The soldiers who had brought Daniel quickly pulled them apart, and Shiva stared at the emperor. "Your Majesty, what do you plan to do to Daniel?" she asked.

Xavier tried to swallow, but his mouth had gone dry. "I am sorry, Shiva, but Daniel must die. I cannot tolerate competition," he managed to say.

"No, Your Majesty, please do not kill him. Please promise me as a wedding gift," she pleaded.

Xavier hesitated for a moment, then straightened himself. "I am sorry. I hope someday you will forgive me."

"I will never forgive you, Your Majesty, as long as I live. You can make me marry you, but you can never have my forgiveness."

Xavier felt like a knife had been thrust into his chest, but he was steadfast as he raised his sword and approached Daniel. "Hold her," he commanded two of his soldiers. He looked at Daniel. "Before I kill you, I will give you this chance to talk to Shiva."

Tears filled Daniel's eyes. "Shiva, I love you, but if I cannot have you, I would rather be dead." "Just remember I will forever love you and I will be waiting for you at heaven's gate, and we will spend eternity together."

"I will forever love you too," Shiva told Daniel between sobs. "I will look forward to meet you at heaven's gate."

Xavier looked into Daniel's eyes. "I am sorry, Daniel. This is nothing personal, so I will kill you quickly."

"Thank you for your mercy, Your Majesty." Daniel bowed his head. "I am ready."

"Sit," Xavier commanded.

Daniel did as he was told and once again bowed his head, bracing himself for the killing blow. Xavier tried not to look at Shiva, but he heard her crying in the background as he raised his sword to take off Daniels's head.

Xavier started to tremble.

Yelling at the top of his lungs, he threw his sword to the ground. "Fine! I promise I will not kill the welp."

Shiva ran up to Xavier and, to his surprise, hugged him. "Thank you for your mercy, Your Majesty." She let go of him and kneeled. "I am sorry, Your Majesty, I should have asked."

Xavier let out a booming laugh. "We are to be married, Shiva. It is all right that you hug me."

"Yes, Your Majesty," she replied with resignation in her voice as she placed her hand on Daniel's back.

Daniel looked at Shiva. "My love, you should not have made this bargain. I will be in torture all my life, seeing you with him." He spit on the ground. "I hate you. Your Majesty. As long as I live, I will hate you." Xavier punched him in the nose, and Daniel cried out in pain as blood spurted out of his nose.

Shiva looked up at Xavier. "Your Majesty, why do you hurt him? You promised."

“No, Shiva, I promised I would not kill him, and so I shall not; however, I never promised not to hurt him. He is now my personal slave. I do not trust him, so he shall never be free. If he gives me disrespect or does not follow my orders, he will be punished any way I see fit.”

Shiva glared at Xavier. “As you wish, Your Majesty,” she said with a hint of venom in her voice.

Xavier was taken aback by her glare and her tone. Was it not enough that he spared Daniel? What more did she want? “Take him away,” he commanded.

Shiva hugged Daniel one last time before two soldiers grabbed Daniel and disappeared into the darkness.

“Set fire to this house,” Xavier ordered. The remaining soldiers walked into the mansion with torches and flammable liquid.

“Please don’t burn the house down, Your Majesty, please!” Shiva pleaded.

“I am sorry, Shiva, but I must set an example for your father’s betrayal; thus, this has to be done.”

In a short while, the mansion was engulfed, the flames lighting up the night sky. Xavier watched the blaze consume the house and waited until the roof caved in with a loud crash,

then turned to his soldiers. “Take the servants to the slave quarters. Find horses for Quill and Shannon.” He turned and smiled at Shiva. “You will ride with me.”

Shiva nodded. “Yes, Your Majesty,” she said somberly.

“Shiva, please call me Xavier. You will be my wife; you do not need to be so formal.”

Shiva nodded again, still in shock from seeing her home burning to the ground. “Okay, Xavier,” she said coldly.

Xavier got onto his horse and reached his hand out to her. She clasped his hand, and he pulled her up in front of him. The city of Adaliah was aglow from mansions on fire as they rode to the palace.

~ ~ ~

Xavier came back to reality and looked over to Daniel, who sat by his side. He had thought about not letting Daniel attend, but he thought it would have pleased Shiva for Daniel to be there, so he had allowed it.

As he craned his neck to look over to Quill and Shannon, he took pity on them and decided to free them. They would no longer be slaves, and he would give them a home to live, though they would never be allowed to leave the city.

The funeral director spoke, drawing his attention. "His Highness Maximus Pulsar, please come." Xavier smiled with pride as he watched his son move to the podium to speak of his mother.

Chapter Fifteen

A Wedding and a Funeral

Xavier smiled at his son. Although he thought Maximus was weak in many ways, he had to admit Maximus was good at speaking. Watching him on this stage reminded Xavier that this was the same stage on which he and Shiva had been married, and his thoughts once again went back in time.

~ ~ ~

Shiva yelped in pain as her mother tapped her tattooing tool with a wooden hammer. Shannon held Shiva's hand to comfort her as Quill worked diligently on Shiva's back.

Quill was a master tattoo artist. She had done all of Xavier's tattoos, and now he had commanded her, to her chagrin, to tattoo the man consumed by fire on Shiva's back. He had threatened violence if she disobeyed.

None of them knew of the peephole that Xavier was looking through, or that Xavier cringed at every cry Shiva made. He did not want her to have any pain, but in his mind, this was necessary. He wanted his empire—and Daniel—to know that she was his and his alone and that no one else could have her.

"Mother, I don't know if I can do this. I don't know what to do. This was not supposed to happen. I was to marry Daniel," Shiva said, her voice straining in pain. "I keep asking why. It is not fair; this is wrong. This can't be happening." Shiva yelped in more pain as Quill continued to tap her tool against Shiva's back. "I should have let Daniel die. Now he must spend the rest of his life with me married to another man. What was I thinking? I was being selfish. My poor love! I wish both of us were dead.

"I hate that man for taking my Daniel away! I hate him for taking Father from us. I hate him for making me marry him. The thought of kissing him, Xavier touching me, making love to him makes my skin crawl."

Xavier clenched his fists. *She will love me not now but someday*, he tried to convince himself.

Shiva started to cry, and Quill tried desperately not to cry as she continued her work on the massive tattoo. Shannon, with tears in her own eyes, kissed the back of her sister's head.

Guilt took hold of Xavier like a vice and then tore at his soul like a wild animal ripping apart its prey. Emotion filled his heart. He felt like he was going to cry, but he did not, because a true emperor never cries. He paced back and forth, trying to figure out why he felt this guilt. He was giving Shiva a much better life than Daniel ever could. He was going to give her wealth beyond imagination, and an entire empire to rule with him.

After several minutes, he had gotten himself back together and again looked through the peephole. He faintly heard Shannon say, "I am so sorry, sister, that this has happened to you, but there must be a reason for this to happen."

Shiva let out a humorless laugh. "I love you, Shannon, but what reason do you think this is happening?"

"I don't know," Shannon admitted. "I know you hate him, but His Majesty loves you a lot. Maybe over time you can change his mind. Maybe you can make a difference and bring healing to Apollyon."

Xavier felt his blood boil. *How dare that brat say that Shiva can control me.*

Quill put her tools down. "Sit up for a while," she told her elder daughter. When Shiva sat up with tears streaming down her face, Quill put her hand on the girl's cheek. "Shannon is right; you will have immense power and influence. You can be a champion of the people. That might be the reason this has happened, child."

"But why me?" Shiva asked.

"I know you have been put in this position and it is certainly not fair. I am sorry, but there is a lot you must do that will not be fair. At times you will feel sorrow, but you must endure," her mother told her. "You must kiss him, do anything to please him, for your safety, ours, and perhaps even the empire's. You must not cry in front of him, only when you are with us or when you are alone. Try your best not to anger him or frustrate him. Smile when you can, even when you do not feel like it. I know you, Shiva. You are a strong-willed woman, and I know you will speak your mind. I am not asking you not to speak your mind; just be careful how you say it. Try to talk nicely to him to change his mind."

Xavier had had enough. He stormed out through his door and into the hallway. The soldiers guarding the door to Shiva's room did not even have time to bow as he slammed the door open. The three-woman jumped as Xavier stopped in front of them, Shiva frantically pulling up a towel to cover her bare chest. "What is going on here? Why have you stopped, Quill?" he demanded.

Quill trembled and quickly picked up her tools but then dropped them because she was shaking so much. "I am sorry, Your Majesty. I was just giving Shiva a little break. This is a large tattoo, and it hurts her."

"I know getting tattoos hurts. You did mine, stupid sow. My soldiers tell me all you have been doing is talking," he lied. "How much have you completed, Quill?" Quill looked as if she were trying to speak, but nothing came out. "Speak!" he demanded as he raised his hand to slap her.

"I'll show you, Xavier," Shiva said. As Shiva turned her back to him, Xavier put his hand down. The tattoo was almost complete. She gave him a big smile as she turned back to face him. "You see, your future mother-in-law does good work."

Xavier's jaw dropped. He was completely stupefied.

Then he found himself smiling back at that wonderful smile—that wonderful, beautiful, angelic smile. He loved her smile; it sent shivers down his spine.

When he realized what he was doing, his smile disappeared abruptly, and he turned to Quill. "I have to admit your work is impeccable; however, I need this to be done as soon as possible, We are to be married in three days."

"Yes, Your Majesty," Quill said with a bow, finally finding her voice.

Xavier walked up to Shiva and put his hand on her face. He felt his heart race when she placed her hand on his. "I am sorry, my love," he told her. "I know this is painful, but when your mother is finished, you can wear this tattoo with pride. You will be the most powerful woman in all the land; you will be empress of Apollyon." Shiva brought his hand to her mouth and kissed it, and Xavier felt more shivers go down his spine and the smile once again on his lips.

"Yes, Xavier, I will wear this tattoo with pride and honor, for soon I will be your bride."

When she let his hand go, he said, "Well, I must be on my way," with a very foreign cheer in his voice. "Go ahead, Quill, back to work."

Xavier watched as Shiva lay back down and Quill resumed her work. Then he blew Shiva a kiss, which she blew back to him. "I will see you in three days, my love," he told her, and she smiled at him before he turned to walk out. He walked away with a spring in his step, like he had no care in the world. He tried to remember why he had been so angry before but couldn't. Everything was going to be well. He was excited; in three days, he would have a bride, an empress, to spend the rest of his life with. Three days seemed so long; what was he going to do with all that time?

Three days later, Xavier was amazed at how fast the time had gone, and his excitement was replaced by an unfamiliar feeling. He was nervous.

He stood on the stage with the minister, sweat beading on his forehead as musicians played. Looking out at the crowd, he saw the families that still met his favor, as well as heads of state from other countries. He saw Quill and Shannon in back but had forbidden Daniel to attend. He had Daniel locked up in the dungeons until the wedding was over.

The priest nodded to the musicians, and they stopped for a moment, then started to play the wedding tune. Xavier felt like his heart was going to pound out of his chest as everyone rose and he saw her. Shiva walked down the aisle with Virion escorting her to give her away in her father's stead. She wore a white silken dress with reddish-orange flames jetting up from the bottom. She wore white slippers, as well as a red shawl around her neck. Her blonde hair was in a ponytail with red and orange flowers attached. Xavier swore he had died and gone to heaven, for she was the most beautiful angel he had ever seen.

Virion handed Shiva off to Xavier, and then she faced him, and they held each other's hands. Xavier smiled at her, and she smiled back at him. He barely heard what the priest had to say. Finally, Xavier placed the wedding ring on her finger and then she did the same to him, continuing to smile. Then they kissed. Xavier had kissed other women before, but those kisses paled in comparison to this.

Then Xavier placed the flame tiara on her head, for she was not only his bride but also now the empress. The crowd erupted in thunderous applause as Emperor and Empress Pulsar marched down the aisle.

Xavier looked over to his bride. She had a smile on her face, but he noticed that a tear had run down her cheek. Again, guilt reared his head. Xavier turned his head away for a moment, then smiled as he turned back to her. He would ignore this feeling. He just knew someday she would love him for real; she just needed time.

~ ~ ~

Xavier came back to reality as Maximus finished his eulogy honoring his mother. When his son had walked down and taken his seat next to his father, Xavier patted Maximus on the back and smiled at him. "Good job, son."

Maximus smiled back, always eager to meet his father's approval. "Thank you, Father."

Soon, Xavier found himself standing next to Shiva. She was just as beautiful as she had been on her wedding day. He touched her hair, then kissed her forehead. “I love you, my rose of Apollyon.” He walked back up the aisle, then at the door, turned back and blew a kiss. Then he walked out, leaving his love behind.

Chapter Sixteen

A Perilous Trip

Enoch blew into his hands to keep them warm as he, Elaine, Jonathan, and the other soldiers rode through the valley. They were surrounded by the Antillean Mountains, the snowcapped peaks rising hundreds of feet above them. They had been traveling through this valley for four days now. In another four days, they would be out of the valley, and a few more days after that, they would reach Antillean City.

The valley was very wide in places but in others was just barely wide to ride their horses through. Normally, the valley was a quick shortcut to Antillean City, especially during the spring and summer months. Unfortunately, despite it being late spring and sunny, it was unusually cold, and a fresh coating of snow covered the valley. Enoch was grateful that Jonathan and his soldiers had supplied him and Elaine with woolen coats and mittens; however, the mittens did not do as good a job keeping his hands warm as he would have liked.

He looked over to Elaine, who rode beside him. She was shivering in the cold and looked miserable. He rode closer to her. "Are you alright?" he asked.

She looked back at him with a frown. "I am cold," she said.

"I am sorry. We will be out of this misery in a few days, and then things will get better," Enoch said to her.

"I hope so," Elaine responded simply.

Enoch was worried about her. Before they had reached the mountains, she had smiled often. Since they had reached the mountains, her smiles had been few and far between.

Jonathan rode up to them, and Elaine smiled. *Except for when she talks to Jonathan,* Enoch thought. He had noticed that his sister had grown fond of the soldier.

Jonathan seemed to have grown fond of her, as well. He returned her smile. "I am sorry, Elaine. You look so cold," he said. "I am sorry it has been so unusually cold."

"I am fine," Elaine said, and Enoch chuckled to himself. Yes, she most definitely was fond of him.

"I am glad to hear that," Jonathan said, his smile getting bigger.

He seems to be very fond of her, Enoch thought with a smirk.

"Well, hang in there a little bit longer. In a little while, we will reach a cave. We have firewood and supplies stashed in there. It will be good to get in out of the cold and rest the horses—and maybe some talking and merriment?"

Elaine smiled again and blinked her eyes. *Hopelessly in love, I think.* Enoch chuckled, and Elaine looked at him and frowned.

"What is so funny?" she asked.

Enoch smiled, embarrassed. Before he could reply, a soldier galloped up. "Sir, a storm is coming our way!"

They all turned to look behind them. Enoch frowned all he could see was blue skies. Then he squinted. In the far distance was a fog.

"Get the rope," Jonathan commanded. Within a minute, he had ridden up to Enoch and Elaine and handed them a length of the rope. "Do not let go, or it could mean death." He looked directly at Elaine. "Please hang on, Elaine; I do not want you to get lost or worse." Elaine nodded.

Enoch looked behind them, and his eyes grew big in shock. He could no longer see the mountains. The fog had covered the mountains, and in the distance, he could hear the wind roar.

Jonathan got into position and said, "Hang on tight."

As they started to move, Elaine looked back at Enoch. "I am scared," she told him. She said something else, but her voice was drowned out by the storm's arrival. Enoch felt his breath being taken away as the cold wind cut through his coat like a knife. The flying snow stung his face, and he could see neither Elaine nor Jonathan. He looked behind him and saw nothing but white. His horse whinnied in protest as he coaxed it to move forward, trying his best not to panic. He shook violently, though he was not sure if it was because of the cold or fear—or maybe both.

After an hour, the snow and wind started to taper off and Enoch could just make out Elaine. He was relieved to see her. After several more minutes, the storm had subsided, and the sunshine returned as if nothing had happened. Elaine looked at him and smiled, clearly relieved they had made it through alive.

Jonathan Called them all to a halt, then rode up to Elaine. "I will take that," he said, smiling, as he took the rope from her. He then took the rope from the others and rolled it up and put it away before pointing to the distance. They could see the cave. "We are almost there," he announced, and everyone cheered loudly as they headed toward the cave.

When the ground started to shake, Elaine yelled, "What now?"

Jonathan looked back and let out a curse. "Avalanche! Ride for your lives!" he shouted.

Elaine put her horse into a full gallop, as did the others. She looked back in horror at the huge wall of snow headed for them. She saw that Jonathan, Enoch, and several others had fallen behind. "Don't look back!" Jonathan yelled at her.

Elaine could not believe what was happening. It seemed like the hand of Emperor Pulsar was there to stop them. The cave was getting closer, but the ground seemed to be shaking more violently beneath her. The avalanche made a deafening roar as she rode into the cave with six other riders.

As the avalanche slammed into the cave, a cloud of snow showered them inside. It took a minute for the cloud to clear. She looked at the six riders with her. Enoch and Jonathan were not among them. "Enoch! Jonathan!" she screamed.

"I am here," Enoch said from the partially plugged entrance. He was struggling to walk through the snow, which came to his stomach, as he led the horse by the reins.

Elaine struggled to reach him, but when she did, she hugged him. "Oh, Enoch, I could not bear the thought of losing you."

Then she panicked. "Jonathan!" she yelled as they breached the mouth of the cave.

"Everyone let us search for the others," Enoch said. They all went out searching, but after an hour of fruitless searching, it was starting to get dark—and it got dark quickly in the valley. The sun had fallen behind the mountains.

"I am afraid they are lost," one of the soldiers said.

Elaine hugged Enoch and sobbed, "I cannot believe it." Jonathan and the others were gone.

The search party all hung their heads as they made their way back to the cave.

"Wait," Elaine said.

Everyone stopped, not saying a word. Then they all heard a muffled groan. Enoch ran to the source of the sound. "Right here!" he shouted, and the soldiers helped him dig.

"Jonathan!" Elaine shouted as they pulled the man out of the snow. He moaned as they picked him up and got him into the cave. Within minutes, they had a fire started. Jonathan shook violently as the soldiers—one of them a healer—brushed snow off him. Elaine looked away as they took his clothes off and wrapped him in a blanket. An hour had passed after the healer put bandages on his head.

Elaine worried. In the time they had been together, she had grown attached to him. "Will he be all right?" she asked.

The healer looked at her grimly. "Well, it is hard to say. He took quite a blow to the head, but he has no broken bones that I can tell. If he awakes, he has a fighting chance and he will be back to his old self. We will see."

Another soldier spoke up, trying to lighten the mood. "I hope he comes through—although I am not sure if I can handle it if he gets back to his old self."

The other soldiers chuckled.

"Oh, shut up," a weak voice said.

"Jonathan!" Elaine exclaimed as she ran over to him.

He opened his eyes and smiled at her. When she then carefully kissed him on the cheek, he said, "Well now, I need to bump my head more often."

Everyone laughed. "Back to his old self. Well, we are all doomed," said the first soldier, slapping his hands on his knees. It felt good to laugh after a stressful day of riding and loss, and Jonathan surviving made for a good night.

After a restful night and a hearty breakfast, they broke camp. As the soldiers shoveled a pathway out of the cave, Elaine sat with Jonathan, who was still very weak but managed to smile at her.

"Well, it is time for us to ride out of here", Enoch said as he helped Jonathan to his feet.

They all stood at the mouth of the cave. It was a warm and sunny day, and the snow was starting to melt. They all bowed their heads as the healer said a prayer for those who had been lost, and then they all got on their horses.

Jonathan rode with Elaine, for his horse had not survived the avalanche. He put his hands on hers as they started out of the cave with the others, and Elaine felt her heart flutter. She looked back at him and smiled; he smiled back at her as they began their ride down through the valley. She felt something that had been missing from her life—hope—and prayed that hope would carry her through the rest of the trip.

Chapter Seventeen

An Accord

Pirena Solaris walked quickly down the hallway. Uncle Xavier had summoned her to his meeting room. She detested being late for anything, and this summons was surprising and unexpected. She was anxious and excited, for the meeting was about the next phase in the war. It was rare for her to be invited to such a meeting—one involving battle strategy. Although her role was equally important, it involved espionage, stealth, murder, thievery, and Uncle's special wishes, not war. It was hard for her to believe that Uncle Xavier had called for a meeting so soon after Aunt Shiva's death.

She finally made it to the entrance, and two soldiers bowed their heads as they opened the large ornate doors. She walked into a large room, where a large oaken chandelier hung from a high arched ceiling. Wall sconces lit the gray brick walls, and a large oak table stretched the length of the room through the middle. Seated at the table were Uncle Xavier, Maximus, Virion Nebula, and several high-ranking officials and scribes. Running around the table were the ever-nervous Daniel and a few other servants, serving hot coffee and scones.

"Pirena, glad you are here." Xavier smiled as he patted the chair next to him. "Come sit here next to me." Pirena smiled back and walked around the table. She removed the small swords from her back, then took her seat.

Xavier scowled at Daniel. "Make yourself useful and get Pirena some coffee and a scone."

"Yes, Your Majesty," Daniel said, quickly running over and pouring her a cup then giving her a scone. "I hope this is to your liking, General Solaris," he told her, bowing his head.

Pirena gave him a curt nod. She raised her cup of coffee to her lips, then paused for a moment and looked at Xavier. She had not noticed before how tired he looked as if he had not slept at all. His eye was bloodshot, and he was wearing the same clothes he had worn the day before; they were wrinkled, and he smelled of alcohol.

When he noticed Pirena staring at him, he gave her a very tired smile. "Are you all right, Uncle?" she asked with great concern. "Is there anything I can do for you?"

"He needs to get some rest," Maximus interjected. "I asked him to call off this meeting so he could rest, but he refused."

Xavier glowered at him. "I am fine. I will rest later. This meeting is far more important than rest."

"But Father, wouldn't the meeting go better if you were rested?" Maximus protested.

"Perhaps," Xavier admitted, "but everyone is here, and I will be fine. I will rest right after."

"But Father—"

"Enough," said Xavier, cutting him off, as he slammed his fist on the table, knocking his cup over and spilling coffee on the table.

Xavier let out a curse. "Daniel, get your lazy carcass over here and clean up this mess," he growled. Daniel scrambled over with a cloth and started to clean the mess. "Pour me another cup while you're at it."

"Yes, Your Majesty." Daniel set the cup back up and went to pour more coffee in it. In his rushed panic, he missed the cup and spilled more coffee on the table.

"You clumsy idiot!" Xavier yelled. "Clean this up and give me my coffee, or I'll knock your teeth in."

"Yes, Your Majesty." Daniel steadied himself, cleaned the mess, and poured the coffee in Xavier's cup.

"Now stand in your corner, dog," Xavier said, pointing to the corner in question. Daniel bowed his head and went back to his station. Xavier looked at Pirena and saw a look of concern on her face, then turned to look at everyone else in the room. All were staring at him, completely silent. Xavier hung his head. "I am sorry for this outburst. I am very tired;

I was up all night planning this meeting." He looked at Maximus and then Pirena. "I promise I shall retire after this meeting."

Pirena and Maximus nodded their heads.

Xavier looked at everyone and smiled. "I have called you all here for I have made an important decision that will greatly affect us all. I have decided to make an accord with Antillean that will finally end this war."

Pirena gasped, and everyone's faces wore looks of shock and surprise. Pirena could not contain herself and stood up. "What in the name of Apollyon are you talking about? You want peace? After five years of war, you just give up. You are not thinking rationally. It is too soon after Aunt Shiva's death to make such a decision. Please take time to think this over."

"I have made my decision, Pirena. There is no changing my mind about this; it is what is best," Xavier said.

Pirena's face grew dark "Then why in blazes did you invite me to this meeting? I know nothing of peace, only of death. You raised me to be a killer, not a peacemaker."

"Pirena, I do not wish for peace either," Xavier interrupted.

Pirena gaped at him. "But you just said you wanted peace with Antillean."

"I said nothing of the sort." When Pirena started to speak, Xavier held up his index finger to silence her. "I said I wish to make an accord with them. They will think I want peace, and for a while it will seem that way."

"You mean you are going to deceive them? How do you plan on doing that, Uncle? How is deceiving them going to stop the war? This makes no sense to me," she said, taking her seat again.

Xavier reached under the table and pulled something out of a satchel lying on the floor. He placed the object on the table in front of her. It was a book.

Pirena looked at it intently. Everyone else leaned forward, trying to get a better look at the book. Pirena picked the book up and looked at the cover. "*Eye of the Cyclops.* Is this about that orb in that statue in the Talon palace?" she asked.

Xavier smiled. "Yes, it is. I found it in the library. I could not put it down; I was up all night reading it."

"So, what does this eye have to do with anything, Uncle? How will this bring an end to the war? Please explain."

Xavier spent the next hour explaining the story of Ivan Albatross and Tiban Talon, and about the power of the eye and its control over nature. He told them about Ivan trying to resurrect his wife.

By the time he had finished, the room was silent, and everyone was looking at him like he was mad. Xavier scowled. "Does anyone have anything to say?" he asked with great discomfort in his voice.

Finally, Virion broke the silence. "It sounds like a great story. Forgive me, old friend, but I'm confused and concerned. You called this meeting based off an old legend about an all-powerful orb?"

Anger and irritation showed on Xavier's face. "Yes, I have, Virion. Do you question my sanity?"

"No, I do not, and I do not wish to anger you, but I question your judgement. You need more time for mourning."

Xavier stood up and shouted, "I do not need more time for mourning! I need to do something. I want to win this war. I want to conquer Antillean, and I want to conquer the world." He glared at everyone in the room. "Stop staring at me like I am mad!"

Everyone jumped in startled surprise and stopped staring at him.

"I am sorry, Xavier. I did not mean to offend. I love you, my friend, and I just want you to be all right," Virion said gently.

Xavier sat down and wiped the sweat off his forehead with the back of his hand. "I know. I am sorry." He looked around the table. "Please hear me out. I have a plan. It might work; it might not. I think this is a risk worth taking, but I will need your cooperation, so please hear me out." Everyone at the table slowly nodded their agreement, and Xavier smiled as anticipation filled the room.

"Before the end of the month and just before the cease in battle ends, I plan on contacting King Talon. Then I will inform him that I wish to send delegates to his palace to negotiate peace. The fool is so desperate for peace, he will take my offer without question or hesitation. As a peace offering, I will have five hundred slaves come, too, and will offer them freedom to live in Antillean. I can spare five hundred slaves; I will have them back soon enough." He pointed at Virion. "You will lead the delegation." Next, he pointed at Maximus. "And you will come along with them."

Virion and Maximus rolled their eyes but bowed their heads in agreement.

"Good. Virion, I know you and Maximus don't get along, but if my son is going to rule my nation someday, he will need experience." That brought a smile to Maximus's face; he wanted to make his father proud.

"It will be done," Virion replied, "but we will have to figure out terms for negotiations—and what part does the eye play?"

"We will figure out what to negotiate in the days to come. As far as the eye goes"—Xavier looked to Pirena— "this is the reason I called you to this meeting. I need your skills." Pirena straightened into her chair. "I need you to disguise yourself as one of the slaves and steal the eye."

Pirena's eyes lit up in surprise.

"You will wait a few days after Virion and Maximus leave; then you will jump into action. If all goes well, you will have no problem taking out the guards and stealing the eye out of the cyclops statue. Hopefully when you have it in your hands, you should know what to do with it and escape."

Pirena smiled, intrigued. This would be one of the biggest operations of her career.

"Do you think you can pull this off? Do you have any knowledge of the palace there?" Xavier asked.

Pirena pondered for a moment. "I don't have as much as I wish, but some of my contacts do. I will contact them as soon as I can." She scowled. "I have contacts throughout Antillean but was never able to get one privy to King Talon's inner circle."

Xavier smiled. "You are an amazing niece, Pirena. I know you will be successful."

Pirena smiled as she looked over to Maximus, who was frowning. He was always jealous of her.

"Does anyone else think this is madness, or is everyone in the room too afraid to say it?" Maximus said, his arms folded across his chest. All eyes gazed upon Maximus, and Xavier's eye widened in surprise. "I am sorry, Father, but someone has to be the voice of reason here. This sounds like a good children's story."

Xavier scowled at him. "You think I did not consider this? I think it was no accident I came across this book."

Maximus snorted. "So, you think this is some prophesied destiny or something, that you will have the eye and rule the world?"

"I don't like the tone of your voice or your attitude, you little welp!" Xavier shouted.

"I don't like the sound of your stupid insane plan!" Maximus shouted back, looking surprised himself. He hesitated for a moment, then continued. "What if this does not work, Father? Then what? If King Talon accused you of stealing the eye, I suppose you could deny it and say bandits stole it. But what if it turns out this story is false? would you honor the accord or continue the war?"

"I would continue the war, but this story is true; I feel it in my bones. This legend is true, and I will conquer the world. All of you will benefit from this; you will rule along with me, and I will make this new world a paradise."

"Will the fighting stop, Father? I am tired of this war. I am tired of all the death and destruction."

Xavier sighed. "Of course, son, the war will end. Of course, if anyone opposes me, there will be consequences."

"One more thing, Father—what of the Talon family? Would you spare them? I know Prince Aldar hurt you, but . . ." Maximus trailed off.

Xavier crossed his arms. "You expect me to spare Aldar after he did this to me?" Xavier said, touching the scar on his face.

"Perhaps not, Father," Maximus conceded, "but King Talon is a nice man, and so is his family—except maybe Zena. Please, Father, I beg you—no more death."

"Fine, I promise I will not kill them. I might let King Talon keep his throne as an honorary position. However, Aldar I will not kill, but I will make him my slave; he can assist Daniel."

Maximus smiled. "Thank you, Father. You will not regret this, for sure. I sure hope you are right."

"I am right, son, and unlike that fool Ivan Albatross, I will not let my guard down and no one will take the eye from me. Which brings me to this one last important detail. I plan on bringing your mother back from the dead."

Maximus's smile disappeared, replaced by a look of shock and disbelief. Then his face turned dark with anger.

All was silent as tension filled the room.

"What is the matter, son? Why are you angry? I would think this news would make you happy."

Maximus stood up, clenching his fists. "Bring Mother back from the dead? What do you mean?"

"I am going to do what Ivan Albatross attempted. Unlike him, I won't let some servant stop me. I truly believe that if Tiban Talon had not interfered, Ivan would have been successful. When I have this power, I will most certainly bring your mother, my love, back. I miss her. I miss her beauty, her smile, her touch. I want her back. She was taken away from me, and it was unfair."

"No, Father." Maximus protested. "I miss her so much—what I would do to see her smile again!—but she is dead and that is how it should be. Father, it would not be right. It goes against nature. You are not a god, and this is not a decision for a mortal man to make; it would be an abomination."

Xavier snarled at Maximus. "I don't care! I will be a god, and I will bring her back and she will rule by my side."

Maximus, screaming, grabbed his chair and smashed it against the wall. "You are a selfish cretin." Once again, Xavier looked at his son, surprised by his outburst, and Maximus pointed his finger at him. "The only reason she stood by your side was because she had no choice, and she was miserable. You took her happiness away from her. She was always sad, and now you want her back. You make me sick."

Maximus's eyes widened, for he knew he had said too much. He trembled as a shiver ran down his spine.

Xavier slowly stood, a most unnerving grin on his face. "You yellow, cowardly welp. I do not care how old you are—I am about to take you over my knee and swat you. I want an apology from you, and I'll forget you ever said those words." There was a long silence.

"Well, I am waiting," Xavier said. More silence greeted this proclamation.

As his son had done so recently, Xavier grabbed his chair and smashed it against the wall. "You apologize now!" he shouted.

"No!" Maximus shouted back, grabbing his coffee cup and smashing it against the wall.

"I should never have let your mother coddle you so much. Now you are a spoiled brat with no backbone."

Maximus drew his sword and charged Xavier, but soon dropped his sword and stopped. Before Maximus could think, Xavier's blade was against his throat. "Wow that was fast," Maximus managed to croak as the blade just barely broke the skin. He felt a small trickle of blood run down his neck. "You are still good with a blade, Father."

Xavier grinned. "Don't you forget that young man. Now, don't you have something to say, son, like an apology?"

"I am sorry, Father. I take back what I said. Please forgive me. Even though I do not understand all of this, I will stand by your side; you can trust me."

Xavier pulled his sword away and hugged Maximus. "I accept your apology. I know all this is hard on you. Soon, son, you will see that this was the best decision I have ever made; you will not regret it." He pulled away from Maximus and addressed the crowd. "I am sorry for all of this. I think for now it is best we adjourn. Soon I'll call for another meeting to iron out the details." Xavier patted Maximus on the back. "Have the healer patch you up."

Maximus nodded as he touched his cut and walked off.

The room slowly cleared out, finally leaving only Xavier and Pirena. She looked at him and chuckled.

Xavier smiled. "What is so funny?" he asked.

"You and Maximus have a strange way of working things out."

Xavier laughed. "I guess we do. I know I'm hard on him—perhaps too hard—but I must be." Xavier paused for a second before continuing. "I worry, Pirena. I'm not sure if he can rule. He is physically strong, yes, but . . ." He trailed off.

"I don't know what to tell you, Uncle. Maybe if this all works out, he will prove himself." Pirena kissed him on the cheek. "All I know is the way you two fight, I don't think I want children."

They both laughed, and Xavier kissed her on the forehead. "That is why I love you so; you know how to make me laugh."

"My pleasure, Uncle. Well, I had better get going and get in touch with my contacts."

Xavier smiled as she walked out the door; he knew this was going to work and everything would go as planned. Then he looked at the mess he and Maximus had made, and he frowned. "Daniel clean this mess up now!" he yelled.

Chapter Eighteen

Antillean City

"We finally made it!" Elaine smiled at Enoch. After several days of traveling, Antillean City had finally come into view. A mixture of relief and exhaustion filled them as they took in the sight of the city. Enoch and Elaine stopped their mounts and gaped. The view was breathtaking, to say the least. The city seemed to sprawl over several miles. The morning sun cast a glow on the massive spires of the palace. Behind the city was a massive blue-green ocean.

They both breathed in the salty sea air as they stared in amazement at the ocean. It was the biggest body of water they had ever seen.

As a tear ran down Elaine's cheek, Jonathan rode up beside them on the horse he had been fortunate enough to purchase from a farmer. He smiled. "Yup, I had the same stupefied look when I saw Antillean City for the first time."

"Hey!" Elaine said, laughter in her voice. Enoch, Jonathan, and the other soldiers laughed.

Jonathan turned to his soldiers. "You may go and see your families. I will send for you when you are needed." The soldiers grinned and bowed their heads as they rode ahead of them to the city. Jonathan winked at Elaine. "Come on, you two. We still have a long way to go, and daylight is burning."

Elaine was amazed at the massive city. They had ridden at least half an hour before they had reached the city gates. Jonathan turned his horse to face them. "Welcome to Antillean City."

As they rode in, brother and sister gaped again. "Elaine, look!" Enoch pointed at an Apollyon family walking down the street. As they looked down the streets, they saw people from all the five nations. They were amazed at how many Apollyon people were there and how they mingled with the Antillean people.

Although the city was busy, it moved at a steady pace. No one seemed to be in a rushed panic like in Adaliah.

Elaine felt her stomach growl as the smell of fresh bread from a nearby bakery permeated the air. The streets of Antillean were a bit dusty, but the city did not smell of sewers and sweat like Enoch and Elaine were used to. They smiled as they rode down the streets, and people smiled and waved at them.

At the end of this long ride, they finally reached the back gate of the palace. Enoch and Elaine looked up. It seemed that the spires of the palace almost touched the sky. "Amazing!" was all Elaine could say.

"Well, here we are," Jonathan said, interrupting the trance they were in.

"Identify yourself!" a voice called loudly. They looked up toward the voice and saw a soldier standing atop the wall next to the gate.

"It is I, Jonathan Morrison, second commander of the sixty-eight division of the Antillean army. Accompanying me are Enoch and Elaine Eclipse of Apollyon. They seek audience with King Talon."

"Do you have your identification tag and a letter from your commander?" the soldier asked.

"Yes, I do," Jonathan said as he took the necklace off from around his neck and pulled a letter from a pocket in his chest plate.

Enoch and Elaine were startled as two soldiers came from what seemed nowhere and pointed muzzleloaders at them. A nervous sweat ran down Elaine's neck as the soldiers approached. Another soldier appeared in front of Jonathan and reached out his hand, and Jonathan handed his identification and letter to him.

The soldier opened the letter and looked over Jonathan's identification. After several tense minutes, the soldier said, "Everything checks out." The soldiers put down their weapons. "Welcome, Jonathan, Enoch, and Elaine." He bowed to them, then yelled, "Open the gate."

Elaine let out a breath she hadn't realized she was holding, and she looked at her brother, who was sweating profusely. Jonathan gave them a sympathetic look. "I'm sorry, you two, but all precaution must be made for the king. I promise you will have a much better experience once you come in."

Elaine and Enoch were startled as the gate slowly rumbled open in front of them, revealing a large lawn and garden. A stone walkway led up to the back entrance, whose doors were huge and ornate with gold accents. On both sides of the walkway were roses, calla lilies, tulips, and all manner of other flowers. "Beautiful," Elaine managed to say.

"If you think this is beautiful, you should see the front entrance," Jonathan said.

"More beautiful than this?" Enoch asked in amazement.

"Indeed, it is," Jonathan said with a smile.

A soldier approached them. "Second Commander Morrison, please come with me," he said.

Seeing the concerned look on Elaine's face, Jonathan smiled. "It is going to be okay, Elaine. They probably have questions for me. They must wonder who you are and why you seek an audience. I should not be long."

Elaine smiled back as he got off his horse and walked away with the soldier who had come for him. More soldiers approached one stood with Jonathan's horse, and Elaine watched as two soldiers standing next to the doors opened the doors to let Jonathan in.

"Me lady," a voice said, startling her. A young boy was standing next to her. "May I help you off your horse?" He reached out to take her hand, and when she hesitantly allowed him to do so, he helped her off her horse. Elaine was surprised; no one had ever offered to help her off her horse, save Enoch and her father.

Enoch got off his horse as some stable hands arrived. "We will make sure your horses are stabled, watered, and fed," they were assured by the boy who had helped Elaine down. "They will be ready for you when you need them again. We will need your weapons, please, for the protection of His Majesty." Enoch and Elaine handed their weapons over without hesitation, then looked at each other as they and their horses were led away; they were not used to special treatment like this.

The soldier leading Jonathan's horse pointed to a bench by the garden. "You can rest if you wish; it could be some time before you see the king."

He was right; it seemed like an eternity before Jonathan came back, giving them a tired smile. "I am sorry this took longer than expected." He put his hand on Elaine's shoulder, who felt her heart flutter at his touch and gave him a big smile. He smiled back at her. "Well, I must take leave of you two for now. It has been fun getting to know you—especially you, Elaine—nothing against you, Enoch."

Enoch laughed as he stood up and shook Jonathan's hand. "Thank you for bringing us here. You truly are a good man," Enoch said.

"It was my pleasure," Jonathan said.

Elaine stood up and gave Jonathan a hug. "I would love to see you again," she whispered in his ear.

"As would I. When the moment is right, I will seek you out and we can spend more time together," he whispered back. Then Elaine kissed him on the cheek, and they broke their embrace.

Jonathan's mood changed, and he took on a somber tone. "Unfortunately, I have other visits to make today. I must tell five families that their loved ones will not be returning," he said with a frown.

Elaine looked at Jonathan. "Please give them my condolences; they died giving us passage. For that, I will forever be grateful, and if there's anything Enoch and I can do, they can let us know."

Jonathan nodded. "I will let them know, and please do not blame yourselves; it was beyond your control." Elaine was about to respond when a loud noise interrupted her. She turned to see that the doors to the palace were opening. "Ah, it looks like your escort has arrived," Jonathan said with a smile as he got on his horse. He waved. "Farewell. I will see you soon."

Enoch and Elaine waved back as Jonathan rode toward the gate, then they turned their attention toward the open palace doors. A woman with two guards on either side of her walked out of the palace. She looked a little older than them, maybe in her early thirties, and was wearing a blue dress with the Antillean symbol embroidered on the boddice. She was a tall woman with red-blonde hair, blue eyes, a round nose, and a thin mouth. She walked up to them and smiled. "Hello, I am Danielle Hawk." She gave them a curtsy. "I am the personal liaison to His Majesty King Talon. Welcome." Enoch and Elaine gave her a bow, then thanked her. "Come with me," she said, turning toward the palace doors.

They walked beside her, the guards framing her and them. "I am sorry, but King Talon is busy at the moment. I have been instructed to take you to a holding chamber, and you will wait for your audience there."

Enoch and Elaine gaped again as they walked through the palace doors and looked down the long hallway that seemed to stretch into infinity. The twenty-foot walls stretched into an arched ceiling from which hung long ornate chandeliers. On the walls were paintings and wall sconces. A long blue carpet ran the length of the hallway, and there was furniture throughout.

Danielle chuckled at their amazement. "You should see the main entrance; it is far grander than this one."

"Jonathan said the same thing," Elaine replied in utter disbelief.

"Perhaps sometime you will be able to see the main entrance," Danielle said.

Several minutes and hallways later, they finally stopped at a door. One of the soldiers accompanying them opened the door. The smell of food wafted through the doorway, and Enoch's and Elaine's stomachs growled at the smell; they had not had breakfast yet. Danielle smiled. "It may be a while before your audience with King Talon. Please come in."

They walked into a spacious room. The walls and the ceiling were similar in size to those of the hallways. In the middle of the room was a large oaken table and chairs. On the table was all manner of food, including a large pitcher of milk, ham, eggs, potatoes, bread, cheese, and an abundance of fruits and vegetables. Enoch and Elaine stood speechless at the sight. “Jonathan said you had not eaten today, so I had the cook make you breakfast,” Danielle told them. “I certainly hope this meets your approval.” All Enoch and Elaine could do was nod.

“I am not sure when His Majesty will be able to meet with you; heaven knows he is a busy man these days.” Danielle pointed at another door at the end of the room. “There’s the privy, and water and a washbasin for freshening up.

“You have an indoor privy?” Elaine asked incredulously.

Danielle laughed. “Yes, we do.”

Elaine looked away, embarrassed that she had said it out loud, and Enoch smiled at her embarrassment.

“Well, I am off,” Danielle told them. “I will go and see when His Majesty will be able to see you. Enjoy the meal. If you have any needs, these two guards will be at the door. I will return when the king is ready for you.” She gave them a courteous nod, then walked out the door with the guards following her.

Enoch and Elaine watched the guard close the door, then looked at each other and over at the food. There was a long moment of silence; then they laughed as they ran to the table and took their chairs. Enoch grabbed the pitcher of milk, which was nicely chilled. He poured Elaine a glass, then filled his cup. Although the food they had eaten on the journey with Jonathan was better than the jerky and hardtack they had had while traveling on their own, this was a feast. “Oh, my goodness, this is so good,” Enoch said with food still in his mouth.

“I have never seen this much food in my life,” Elaine replied, also with food in her mouth. They laughed again as they continued to eat. Elaine looked at her surroundings, feeling as if she had died and gone to heaven.

They ate and ate, until they could not eat anymore. “I think I ate too much,” Enoch said, holding his stomach.

Elaine smiled as she held her stomach. “Same here,” she said. “I wonder how long it will be,” she wondered aloud.

“Hopefully not too much longer,” Enoch said.

A couple of hours and a couple of trips to the privy later, they were still waiting. Enoch tapped the table nervously.

"I hope there's nothing wrong," Elaine said, subconsciously playing with her hair.

"I am sure there is nothing to worry about," Enoch said as he folded his arms across his chest. "King Talon has many duties to worry about; maybe he has taken his lunch." Elaine gave him a doubtful look.

Every time they heard a noise outside the door, they looked at the door expectantly, but every time, it was a false alarm. Enoch felt his eyelids get heavy, as he was ready to drift off.

He and Elaine both started as the door finally opened and Danielle Hawk walked through. "His Majesty will see you now."

Chapter Nineteen

An Audience

Enoch and Elaine were relieved to finally get moving after such a long wait. After more hallways, they made it to a foyer large enough to fit a small army. The fifty-foot walls reached up to a grand ceiling with a mural of Tiban Talon and his wife and child. A grand chandelier hung from the ceiling above a fountain in which water cascaded into a pool. In the pool were fish of all kinds swimming aimlessly in every direction. Across the fountain was the grand entrance to the audience chamber, where two guards stood beside the large oaken doors.

"Wait here," Danielle said as she walked up to one of the guards. She said something to him, and he nodded. The guard cracked the door open and walked in. Elaine felt a tinge of nervousness as the guard disappeared behind the door. She did not know why she was nervous; King Talon was known to be a fair man. Still, she felt like something was not quite right. She looked over to Enoch. He had the same concerned look, so she decided to watch the fish swim to keep her distracted.

"King Talon is ready to see you."

Elaine looked up to Danielle, who was smiling at them expectantly. She then looked at Enoch, who nodded. They both walked up to Danielle as the guards opened the grand doors, which led down a smaller hallway. At the end of the hallway was an archway. Elaine could make out two guards, one standing on either side of the opening. She and Enoch walked cautiously into the audience chamber behind Danielle.

Of all the amazing things they had seen, nothing had prepared them for the sight that awaited them. Elaine's jaw dropped. The audience chamber looked as though it could fit a large army.

The hundred-foot walls reached up to another arched ceiling, this one with a mural of the hawk with its talons outstretched. The hawk filled the ceiling. *It must have taken years to paint*, Elaine thought. The blue-streaked white marble floors shone brilliantly, and a large blue carpet ran the length of the room. Elaine started as she looked down to the end of the carpet. A white throne with gold accents held an old man—obviously King Talon.

Danielle motioned them forward, and as they approached the throne, Elaine noticed more people. Another man sat on the exact same type of throne—a younger man with sandy blonde hair whom she thought was perhaps Prince Aldar, though she was not sure.

A heavyset man standing behind the thrones had several insignias on his uniform—a general of some sort, Elaine thought. Several guards surrounded the thrones. All three of them had scowls on their faces.

When they finally reached the throne, Danielle gave a deep bow and Enoch and Elaine followed suit. "Your Majesty, I would like to introduce to you Enoch Eclipse and Elaine Eclipse of Apollyon," Danielle said as she rose. They all looked at Victor as he scowled at them, his eyes looking incredibly angry.

A long, awkward silence filled the room, the only sound King Talon tapping his finger on the arm of his throne. "Thank you, Danielle, you may take leave of us," he finally said.

Danielle bowed again and walked away. *I thought Jonathan said that we were going to be treated nice*, Elaine thought.

More silence followed as King Talon continued his tapping. The sound was unbearable.

Enoch broke the silence. "Your Majesty—"

"You will speak when spoken to," the king said, cutting him off.

"I am sorry, Your Majesty. I—"

King Talon pounded on his chair, cutting Enoch off again. "Silence!" he yelled. "Did you not hear what I said? Can you not hear, boy? You speak only when spoken to. Understand?" Enoch and Elaine nodded.

Elaine felt as though she were going to vomit. This was unexpected.

"You say you are Enoch and Elaine Eclipse, son and daughter of Levi and Lana Eclipse. Is this true?"

Enoch and Elaine stood quietly.

"Did I not ask you a question? Speak," Victor said with ice in his voice.

"Yes, we are, Your Majesty," Enoch finally managed.

Victor's eyes narrowed. "How do I know what you say is true? How do I know you're telling the truth? For all I know, you are spies working for Pirena Solaris."

"We are not spies, Your Majesty," Elaine managed to say.

The king rubbed his chin in thought. "I talked to Second Commander Jonathan. He seemed pretty convinced you are who you say you are. He was very adamant about it; however, I'm not convinced. Pirena is a crafty spy. Some of her recruits are trained diligently and can do a wonderful job of looking and acting their part."

"We are not spying, Your Majesty. Our father worked for you and most likely died for you. Mother as well!" Elaine shouted. Then Elaine's eyes widened as she realized in horror that she had overstepped her bounds.

The king's face reddened as he looked over to the man in the throne next to him. "What would you do with Aurora if she talked to you in that manner?"

The younger man scowled at them. "Well, it certainly would not be pleasant for her, that's for sure."

"Indeed," the king said. "Well, girl, what do you have to say for yourself? Perhaps an apology?"

Elaine started to shake, fear overtaking her. She bowed her head, a tear running down her cheek. "I am sorry; I meant no disrespect. Please forgive me, Your Majesty. I am sorry, so very sorry," she said, tears now streaming down her cheeks.

The king's angry glare was replaced by a more somber look as he looked at the two men with him. "What do you think?" he asked.

The man standing behind the thrones rubbed his chin. "She seems to be sincere. However, she could be a great actress." Aldar nodded in agreement.

"Look at me child. What proof do you have that what you say is true?" Victor asked in a softer voice.

Elaine looked up at him and said, "I have a letter and the medallion my father gave me. I have the letter in my pocket." She reached her hand into her pocket.

"Stop!" a voice behind her yelled. She froze as she heard some clicking noises and saw out of the corner of her eye a guard with a gun pointed at her. She could sense another guard on her other side—the guards who had been standing at the archway when they had come in. They had followed her and her brother in. Then Elaine looked forward and realized all the guards were pointing their guns at them. She looked over at Enoch; he was shaking like a leaf. Elaine felt her throat go dry, on the verge of panic.

Victor sighed. "Foolish girl. You should have not reached into your pocket like that. My guards are trained to protect me at all costs." Elaine nodded slowly. Victor nodded to one of the guards behind her. "Get the letter out of her pocket." The guard slowly walked over to her and pulled her hand out of her pocket, then reached into the pocket himself and pulled out a letter, which he carried to the king and handed to him.

The king turned the letter over and looked at the seal on the back. "Aldar, come over here," he said. Aldar walked over to him. "What do you think? Is it authentic?" the king asked, handing the letter to him.

Aldar looked at the seal with great scrutiny and carefully touched it. "It looks authentic; however, it could be replicated. Pirena is particularly good at replicating things."

Enoch and Elaine looked at each other, sweat beading on their foreheads.

Victor gestured to Aldar to hand him the letter. When Aldar had handed it to him, Victor pulled out a knife. He carefully broke the seal, opened the envelope, and pulled out the letter. Enoch and Elaine watched him eagerly. His face was stone-cold, with no expression whatsoever.

Elaine felt faint. She was not sure how much more she could take.

The king looked at Aldar and the general, then handed the letter to Aldar, who read it expressionlessly before handing it to the general. After reading it, the general handed the letter back to the king, who sat in silence, resuming his tapping on the arm of the throne.

The tapping irritated Elaine. It was like a blacksmith pounding on an anvil, ringing her ears.

"Guards, put down your weapons," King Talon commanded.

Elaine felt her heart skip a beat, startled by the break in silence.

The guards put down their guns, and the guards around the king and his son withdrew. The king looked at Elaine. "Can you show me the medallion you mentioned earlier?" he asked in a kind voice.

"Yes, Your Majesty," Elaine croaked as she tried to clear her dry throat.

"Can you take it off and show me?" he asked.

Elaine nodded, then looked at Victor hesitantly.

"It is all right, child, go ahead. No one will point a weapon at you."

Elaine carefully reached behind her neck and produced the medallion, which she held out on the palm of her hand. The king stood and, to her surprise, started to walk forward with a knife in his hand. She started to tremble. Was he going to kill her and Enoch?

"It is all right. I will not harm you." He stood in front of her and carefully turned the knife to present the handle to her.

Elaine was dumbfounded.

"Go ahead, child. You know what to do," King Talon said, and his eyes softened.

Was that sympathy she saw? she wondered, carefully taking the knife from his hand. She poked her finger with the blade and dropped a little of her blood on the medallion. It glowed, and an image of Victor appeared, with the same message as before appeared. Everyone there watched in awe.

"Hand me the knife, Elaine Eclipse, daughter of Levi and Lana Eclipse," King Victor said.

"What did you say, Your Majesty?" she asked incredulously.

"Please, Elaine, hand me the knife," he said.

She handed him the knife, and he poked his own finger and dropped some of his blood on the medallion. The medallion glowed a little more brightly. Elaine gasped as an image of her mother and father appeared. Her parents held each other's hands and smiled. "Hello, my dear children," Levi said. "We love you with all our hearts. If you are seeing this message . . . well, I failed, and we are dead."

Tears streamed down Elaine and Enoch's faces. "I know this is hard to take, but you must be steadfast. We are so proud of you two for making it to the palace and meeting King Victor Talon. I'm sorry you had to go through all this. I'm sure His Majesty was harsh, but he had to make sure you were not imposters. "When I met him to plan this assassination, he agreed to take you in if I were to fail. He is a good man and will take care of you. You will live here in this palace if you wish, and you will want for nothing; however, do not be lax. I want you two to do everything in your power to help the cause. Join in the fight for the freedom of Apollyon. Join the fight for Antillean's freedom. Fight for your freedom. Do it for your mother and me. I know you will do us proud as we look down at you from heaven."

Lana's smile broadened as she spoke. "My dear children! Oh my, have you two grown into wonderful adults. Enoch, take care of your sister; she is strong, but she will need your shoulder to lean on. Elaine, you must be there for Enoch as well; even though he is strong, he will need your shoulder as well." Tears welled up in Lana's eyes, as well as Levi's. "We love you two with all our hearts. We will be watching and waiting for that wonderful day we will be reunited again."

Levi and Lana unclasped their hands, and then each blew a kiss before holding each other's hands again, then turning and disappearing.

Overwhelmed by grief and sorrow, Elaine collapsed to the floor, the medallion clattering across the room. She sobbed and cried, shaking uncontrollably as the reality of her parents' death finally sank in.

~ ~ ~

Everyone else looked on in surprise as Victor got to his knees beside her and put his hands on her back. "That's all right, child, let it all out," he said, trying to comfort her. She looked over to him with pain in her eyes. To his surprise, she wrapped her arms around him. He patted her on the back. With tears in his eyes, he looked up to Enoch. "What about you, son?"

Enoch touched his chest. "Me?" he asked.

"Yes, you are in mourning; you need to let it out as well." When Enoch looked at him, dumbfounded, Victor gave him a fatherly smile and reached his right hand out to him.

Enoch lost his control at this. He kneeled next to the king and Elaine and sobbed, wrapping his arms around them.

After several minutes, the three broke the embrace and Enoch and Elaine helped Victor to his feet. Elaine, taking in her surroundings once more, saw that everyone—even the guards—had tears in their eyes. "Thank you, Your Majesty, for your kindness and compassion. We did not deserve this," Elaine said as she and her brother bowed.

"Nonsense. You most certainly deserved it. You two have been through a lot. By the way, you can call me Victor."

"But, Your Majesty, we cannot do that; it wouldn't be appropriate."

Victor smiled. "You now live with us in this palace. You are to be treated as family, and so you call me by my given name."

Elaine was going to protest again, but Victor held up his hand and smiled. "No protests, please. You are part of the family now." "

Yes, Your Majesty—er, I mean Victor," she said.

"That's a good girl." Victor nodded approvingly. Then he gestured to the guards. "Please bring them chairs."

~ ~ ~

After a few minutes, Enoch and Elaine were sitting opposite of Victor and the other two men, whom he introduced as Aldar and Isaiah to them as they all nodded their heads to each other. "Like your father said, I apologize for treating you so badly. We had no idea if you had been captured and tortured and, if you had, what information you would have told Pirena. I did not relish doing this to you, but we had to make sure you were the real Enoch and Elaine Eclipse."

"How did you figure out for sure we were who we said we were before I showed you the medallion?" Elaine asked. When Victor smiled and handed the letter to her, she looked at it and frowned. "It is blank," she said in surprise.

"So it seems," Victor replied as he stood up. He walked over to her and handed her his ring, but she looked at him in puzzlement. "Touch the letter with the ring," he said. When she did as he had told her, she was startled as writing appeared on the letter:

These are my children, Enoch and Elaine Eclipse. If they are handing you this letter, I have failed. Please take them in as you promised.

It was signed "Levi Eclipse."

"You were to have no idea about this secret message so if you had been captured you would not be able to tell them. If you would have been captured, your captors would have broken the seal and would have seen just blank paper," Victor explained. "My assistant, Violet Silverwood, invented this strange ink that only shows when my ring makes contact. Aldar and Isaiah have the same type of ring as well. She also created that medallion. You probably wondered why your father had you put a droplet of blood on it."

"Oh, it was dreadful, but father explained that it was important for the mission, so I did what I was told," Elaine said.

"Of course, I did the same, Elaine. The first message from me could only be activated by your blood. The second message had to be activated by your blood and mine as well. I know Jonathan and others saw the first message, but I was not sure if somehow, the Apollyon's had figured out how it worked. They might have figured out, somehow, how to replicate my message to convince Mylon, Jonathan, and the others.

"That is why I was so harsh and mean to you," the king continued. "I had to know if you and Enoch could be trusted. No amount of acting can show the real emotions you and Enoch showed. It really pained me to treat you in that manner. When I opened the letter, I was convinced the only person who knows how this works is Violet; I did not even ask her to explain. I never understand her explanations," Victor sighed. "Then when I dropped my blood on the medallion and saw your parents' message, well, that pretty much settled it.

"Your father knew you would arrive before he and your mother, so he had a checkpoint he was to check in at. He was going to contact me via a message cystallis—a message I unfortunately never received. I, however, talked to Emperor Pulsar. I tried hard to remain calm when I found out he had captured your parents. I'm sorry your father killed Shiva. I know in my heart it was an honest mistake.

"I hope you two don't feel shame for your father's accident. Unfortunately, he has been branded a murderer. It is good you've arrived. Emperor Pulsar put a large price on your heads and will stop at nothing to have you killed."

Enoch nodded. "I feel bad for Father's accident but feel no shame." Elaine nodded. "I know the Eclipse name is now tarnished and we will be hated for being his offspring. Elaine and I will do whatever we can to bring honor back to our name and help you in the fight for freedom."

"I am so glad to hear that. Your mother and father would be so proud of you two. I know you will do your best. Now, we have another matter to discuss. Jonathan told me of your encounter with a creature in the woods. I am interested. Could you explain more?"

"Yes, I can," Enoch said. Enoch told him of the Apollyon century, the pursuit, the shadowy beast, and the screams—everything. Victor, Aldar, and Isaiah's jaws dropped at the story.

"Did you get a good view of the beast?" Victor asked when Enoch had finished.

"Unfortunately, I did not," Enoch replied. "I just saw a large shadow pass by me in the dark and the trees falling to the ground as it passed."

Victor scratched his beard. "Interesting indeed. Unfortunately, we can't go hunting for the creature. Maybe someday we will be able to find out what that creature is. but for now, it will remain a mystery." He turned to Aldar. "These two are probably exhausted; they must be shown their rooms."

Aldar nodded his agreement. "I will send for Aurora and Zena; I'm sure they won't mind at all showing them their rooms." After getting their orders, two guards went off to get the women. Aldar smiled at Elaine. "You will like Aurora. She is a very friendly girl, and I'm sure you will make friends quickly."

Chapter Twenty

Introductions

Zena stormed down the hallway, infuriated. She hated to be interrupted when she was working on a project. What on earth was so important for Aldar to call her away? Did he not know she was busy? She had just a few more adjustments to make to Aurora's new ball gown and then it would be finished. She'd had to leave her daughter behind because Aurora had the gown on and could not sit until the fitting was done.

When Zena reached the foyer, the guards hurriedly opened the doors, and she ran past them. The guards at the archway had no time to bow as she stomped her way up to the throne. Zena stopped, put her hands on her hips, and glared at Aldar.

He looked back at her and smiled. "Where is Aurora?" he asked.

Zena tapped her toe on the floor. "Where do you think she is, dear?" she snarled at him.

"Um, am I supposed to know?" Aldar asked.

"Aurora's fitting," she reminded him.

"What fitting?" Aldar asked.

Zena groaned. "Honestly, Aldar, I swear there is no hope for you. Her ball gown—the gown I have been working on. She has outgrown her old ball gown and I have been working hard on it these last few weeks."

Aldar frowned. "We haven't had a ball since the last meeting of the nations."

"What is your point?" Zena asked,

"Why does Aurora need a ball gown when we haven't had a ball in years?"

Zena's face darkened. "Aldar Allen Talon, you are impossible; that is entirely beside the point!" she yelled.

"So, what is the point?" Aldar asked slowly as Isaiah laughed. Zena waved her hands in the air and cried out in frustration.

"Ahem," a voice said, interrupting Zena's gesturing.

She looked over to Victor, who wore a huge smile on his face. "Father," she said, her face turning red from embarrassment. Then she realized they had company and her embarrassment deepened as she saw the looks of surprise on Enoch and Elaine's faces.

Aldar stood up. "Enoch, Elaine, let me introduce you to my wife, Zena."

Enoch and Elaine stood up. "Pleasure to meet you, Zena," Elaine said as Enoch nodded.

Zena scowled at them. "Hello," she said slowly.

After a moment of silence, Aldar asked, "Is there a problem, dear?"

"Yes, there is," Zena said. "These two did not address me by my title. They are to address me as 'Your Highness,' not by my name." She gave them an accusatory look.

"That is fine, Zena," Victor said. "They are to be considered family."

Zena's eyes narrowed as she looked at Victor. "These two children have just arrived and are considered family? We don't even know them."

Victor's face reddened. "These two are the children of Levi and Lana Eclipse. I gave my word I would protect them and treat them as family."

"How do you know they are who they say?" Zena asked. "For all we know, they could be spies."

Victor rolled his eyes. "Do you really think we did not check that out already? They are who they say, there is no doubt about it," Victor said through gritted teeth.

"That is fine, Father, but they are still strangers and I prefer them to call me Highness, not Zena."

"That is enough!" Victor slammed his hand on the arm of his throne, making everyone jump. "I swear, woman, you make my blood boil." All eyes were on Zena, who squirmed under Victor's gaze as he tapped his finger. "I will tell you how it will be. They address me by my given name, so that means everyone will be addressed as such, especially you. You will treat them with respect and dignity, as I expect them to do the same."

Zena held her head high in the air and sniffed indignantly. "Yes, Father," she said with a tight voice.

Victor gave Enoch and Elaine a sympathetic look as he addressed them. "I apologize for my daughter-in-law's actions. She gets a bit testy at times—I blame that on the Zanthor side of the family—however, she can be kind and caring once you get to know her better and she is less suspicious of you." Zena stiffened as he continued, turning to her. "Now, my daughter, are you ready to take them to their quarters?"

Zena looked down. "Yes, Father, I will do as I am told. However, . . ." She paused.

"What is it?" Victor asked.

"I left Aurora behind in the living room; she is waiting for me there. I need to finish the ball gown first."

Victor sighed. "Of course. They will be able to meet Aurora; then you two will be able to show them their quarters." He stood up. "Well, Enoch, Elaine, I hope you find my palace comfortable. I will be looking forward to talking to you over dinner tonight."

Zena looked at Victor, shocked.

"Yes, Zena, they will be joining us for meals as well. After all—"

"I know, they're family," Zena said.

Instead of getting angry, Victor laughed. "Good, Zena. Now you must be going to Aurora; she is waiting for you. Aldar will be joining you soon. We have very secret and important things to discuss," he said with a smile.

She started, and his smile got even bigger, for he knew Zena always had to know what was happening. He watched as Zena then turned to Enoch and Elaine and put on a forced smile. "Come with me," she said as she led the way.

~ ~ ~

Zena stormed down the hallway to the living quarters. "They will address you by your given name," she muttered under her breath. "You will treat them with dignity and respect. We have secret and important things to discuss. Oh, that man infuriates me so."

"Zena," Enoch interrupted.

"What?" she screamed, turning around, and was startled to see them far behind her.

"I'm sorry, Zena; we are travel-weary and cannot keep up with you."

Zena sighed. "I apologize," she said. She stood and waited for them to catch up. "I guess I am in a hurry, for I know Aurora has been waiting a long time for me to return." Enoch and Elaine nodded as they caught up with Zena.

"It is just a little bit farther, I promise," she said in a friendlier voice.

When they finally entered the living quarters and saw Aurora, Enoch smiled. She smiled back as Zena approached her.

"I am sorry, dear, for making you wait. I was held up."

"No worries, Mother. I see you have brought company," she said jovially.

"Yes, the reason for my delay. Aurora, this is Enoch and Elaine Eclipse."

"Pleasure to meet you," Aurora said as Enoch and Elaine said the same. "I am so glad you made it here safely. I'm sure it had to be a perilous journey for you. I am glad my prayers for you were answered. Well, where are my manners? Please take a seat," Aurora said as she pointed to some chairs.

Enoch and Elaine exchanged looks of surprise; Aurora seemed much friendlier than her mother. She continued to talk as they took their seats and Zena fussed over her gown. "Where did you get that medallion? It is so beautiful."

Elaine put her hand on the medallion once more hanging around her neck. "My father and mother gave it to me. It helped bring us passage to see Victor," Elaine said after kissing it.

Aurora frowned. "I am so sorry for your loss. Your father was a brave man, and your mother a brave woman."

"Thank you, Aurora; it means a lot, hearing that from you. I'm afraid the people of Apollyon don't think so."

"Maybe someday they will change their minds. It was an honest accident. In this world, all things are possible." Aurora huffed. "Once again, where are my manners? Do you two want something to eat or drink?"

"No thank you. We just had a feast, so we're not hungry," Enoch replied with a big smile on his face, amazed at Aurora's friendliness. She certainly did not get that from her mother. *What a beautiful girl,* he thought, as he noticed her red silken dress sparkling in the candlelight. Her green eyes also sparkled.

"Ahem." A voice interrupted his gaze, and he looked over to a glaring Zena. Enoch quickly looked away. "Well, dear, you are all finished. Let us look and see."

Aurora walked to the middle of the room and twirled around.

Zena smiled in satisfaction. "You look wonderful child." She clasped her hands together. "The gown fits perfectly. Look in the mirror, Aurora."

Aurora walked to a full-sized mirror hanging on the wall and smiled. "You are right, Mother, it fits me perfectly. You did a wonderful job. Thank you so much!" She ran up and hugged her mother.

"Careful, dear, not too hard; we don't want your gown to get wrinkled."

"Yes, Mother," Aurora said as she left her mother's embrace. "What do you think, Elaine?"

Elaine was surprised. "You want my opinion?"

"Yes, please," Aurora responded.

"You look very beautiful in that gown; it makes your eyes glow in the candlelight," Elaine said with a smile.

"Thank you, Elaine. Well, Enoch, what do you think?" Aurora asked.

Enoch jumped a little at her question. He looked at Zena, who glared at him. "You look good," he said.

Aurora frowned, but her smile returned as she turned to her mother. "I suppose we should show them their quarters."

Zena smiled back. "I suppose so. Could you be a dear and show them? I need to go somewhere important."

"I sure can, Mother. I should have just enough time to show them before my next lesson with Bethany."

"Very good, child. Make sure you change your clothes before your lesson."

Aurora nodded. "Well, you two are you ready?" she asked.

Enoch and Elaine smiled and stood up. Enoch started to walk toward Aurora. As she and Elaine started to talk, he froze; Zena had put her hand on his arm. He looked into Zena's angry eyes. "I expect you to behave yourself, young man. Victor expects me to treat you with kindness and respect. I will do as I am told; however, if you even think about touching her . . ." Zena said, tightening her grip.

Enoch gritted his teeth. "I have no intention of doing that, Zena," he managed to say as pain shot down his arm.

Zena let go and smiled. "Thank you. I hope you and your sister enjoy your time here." When Aurora looked at her mother and smiled, Zena said, "I will see you later, dear."

"Yes, Mother," Aurora replied.

Enoch watched Zena walk out as he rubbed his arm.

"Are you all right? Elaine asked.

"What do you mean?" Enoch asked.

"You are rubbing your arm," Elaine said.

“Oh, I probably hurt in on the trip. Nothing to worry about,” he told her.

“It looks red,” Aurora said. “I could have a healer look at it if you want.”

Enoch smiled at her. “No thanks. I appreciate it, but I will be okay. Really, I am fine.”

“Okay then,” Aurora said, “follow me.” Aurora and Elaine continued to talk as Enoch followed, still rubbing his arm.

Chapter Twenty-One

New Friends

"This is your room, Elaine; I hope it meets your approval," Aurora announced.

Elaine's eyes widened at the sight of her room. Her bed was big enough to fit two people. It had ornate posts supporting a beautiful canopy. The room's plush white carpeting fascinated her, and the brass candelabra were breathtaking. The room also contained an oaken vanity and a stone hearth and fireplace, and the stained-glass windows overwhelmed her.

"Are you not satisfied? we can make changes if you wish, Elaine—anything to make you happy."

"No, Aurora! This room is perfect—just perfect. I've always slept on a floor mat. This bed will be like sleeping in the clouds of heaven."

Aurora smiled. "I am glad you like it. For a moment when you got quiet, I thought you did not like it. We will have your luggage brought up, plus we will need to get your measurements."

"My measurements?" Elaine asked.

"Yes, and yours also, Enoch." Enoch looked at Aurora, surprised. "We will have a tailor take your measurements and make you new clothes," she explained.

"But, Aurora, you don't have to do this," Elaine protested.

"I know I don't have to, but I want to. I imagine you two have been through a lot," Aurora said. "You probably have few clothes. You needed to pack light for your trip; you certainly will need a change of clothes. Well, Enoch," she continued, "let me show you your room."

At the sight of his room, Enoch smiled. It was as impressive as Elaine's. As the three headed down the hallway back toward the living room, they heard footsteps coming toward them. A young man appeared in the hallway.

"Oh good, Hunter," Aurora said.

"Hello, Aurora. Who are these two?" Hunter asked.

"Enoch, Elaine, this is my little brother, Hunter."

"Pleasure to meet you," Hunter said, smiling, and Enoch and Elaine both said hello.

"I see you are back from battle training," Aurora said.

"Well, whatever gave you that idea?" Hunter said, tugging at his battle training uniform.

Aurora laughed. "Somebody is grumpy today," she jested as he rubbed his shoulder.

"Hey, firearm training is hard. Ow!" he yelped as Aurora jabbed his shoulder. "What was that for?"

"Oh, I don't know, maybe because I'm older than you and I already know firearm training is hard."

Hunter snorted as he looked over to Enoch. "Does your sister give you this much grief?" he asked.

"You'd better believe it," Enoch said with a grin.

It was Elaine's turn to snort. "Oh, ha-ha," she said with a smile. They all laughed as they continued down the hallway to the living room.

"Please take a seat," Aurora told Elaine and Enoch. As they took their seats, Aurora said, "Now pardon me, but I must change my clothes. My teacher will be here any minute, and Mother doesn't want me to get my gown dirty. Hunter, please keep them company."

Hunter nodded. "Where is Mother?" he asked.

"Knowing Mother, she is probably spying on Father and Grandfather," she replied. They both chuckled, and Enoch rubbed his arm, thinking about how Zena had squeezed it.

A knock came at the door, and Bethany opened the door and walked in. She looked at Aurora, her eyes widening. "What in the name of

Apollyon is this?" she asked as she walked up to Aurora. "Who is this lass?" Aurora grinned as Bethany walked around her. "This can't be Aurora Talon, princess of Antillean! Why, this tough-as-nails sword-fighting, terror-inducing warrior in a frilly gown? This cannot be." She laughed as she gave Aurora a hug. "You look like an angel," she told Aurora. "Your mother does great work. What a wonderful, beautiful gown. It suits you perfectly."

Aurora smiled. "Thank you, Bethany."

Bethany next smiled at Hunter. "How are you doing, young man?" she asked.

"I am well, except for maybe a few bruises from firing that musket. That thing about knocks me on the ground," he complained.

"I remember your sister complaining about the same thing," she said as Hunter chuckled, and Aurora sighed with her hands on her hips.

"I didn't complain that bad," Aurora protested.

"Oh please, Aurora! You complained for days about your shoulder."

Hunter roared with laughter. "Aurora has been teasing me about my shoulder," he said.

"Well now, that's what big sisters are for," Bethany said, winking at him. Then she turned her attention to Enoch and Elaine. "I see we have some guests from Apollyon."

Aurora walked up beside their guests. "Bethany, this is Enoch and Elaine Eclipse; they are going to live with us."

"I see," Bethany said. "I have heard a little bit about your plight. I am sorry for your loss, but I'm glad you arrived safely."

Elaine and Enoch nodded their heads. "Thank you; we are glad we are here," Enoch said.

"Well, welcome to the Talon home. I will be glad to know you better, and I'm sure Aurora and Hunter will make you great friends."

Elaine smiled broadly. She could hardly believe how fortunate she and Enoch were. Here they were, common people, in a palace with the royal family, who were acting just like any other family. She could tell that she and Aurora were going to be good friends—Hunter and Enoch, too. Bethany seemed like a nice and trustworthy woman—perhaps a mother figure—as well, and because she was from Apollyon, Elaine hoped they could relate to each other. She really hoped to get to know the older woman well.

"Well, Bethany, give me a few minutes to get changed for my lesson today," Aurora said, interrupting Elaine's thoughts.

"Never mind, dear," Bethany said. "We have time to do it another day. I would like to talk more with these two." Enoch and Elaine smiled as she continued. "Let us all go to the kitchens for a snack instead."

"We could," Aurora said, "but they just ate, and—"

"That would be delightful," Elaine interjected.

"Are you sure?" Aurora asked.

Elaine looked at Enoch, and he nodded. "Well, that settles it," Bethany said. "I walked by the kitchens on the way here, and they were making this great-smelling apple-cinnamon cake. I am friends with the head chef, and I am sure they will have extra for us to share." Everyone nodded their approval.

Several minutes later, they were all sitting around a makeshift table in the kitchen that the kitchen staff had provided. The kitchen staff scurried about, handing them cake and milk.

Bethany eyed Enoch, then looked over to Aurora. "My, he sure is a handsome young man."

Enoch's eyes widened. "Oh, stop," Aurora said. "Look, you're embarrassing him."

Bethany winked at him. "Nonsense," she said. "It is too bad I am so much older than him, or I would have to take him with me." Enoch turned his head away.

"Bethany, stop. You really are embarrassing him," Aurora chuckled.

"I am sorry, young lad. Don't mind me; I can be quite a jokester. What's an old lady to do?"

"Yes, you will have to excuse her," Aurora said. "Bethany is quite humorous and is quite the storyteller." When Bethany gave her a devious grin, Aurora asked, "What is that smile for?"

"I just remembered a funny story."

Aurora rolled her eyes. "Looks like I am in trouble."

"Yes, you are, young lady. Remember the time they installed the new privy?"

Milk shot out of Hunter's nose as he started to laugh, and Aurora's face turned red in embarrassment. "Not that story! Please not that one," she protested.

"About two years ago," Bethany said, ignoring the younger woman's plea, "a privy was installed across from Aurora's room. She was so excited. Before then, she had to walk a long way to use the privy, so she could hardly wait to be able to use it. She was so excited that she went into the privy and did not notice that the seat had not been installed. She let out the loudest scream I have ever heard! She screamed so loud, I thought someone was killing her. I ran in and saw her with her legs and arms flailing in the air!" Everyone started to laugh.

"Her mother, Hunter, and I tried to pull her out, but to no avail. Finally, Hunter ran for help.

"You should have seen the look on her face when her father and two soldiers arrived and pulled her out. She walked funny for days." Everyone else roared with laughter, and Aurora found herself laughing as well.

"Any more stories you have to tell?" Aurora asked, grinning and shaking her head.

"No, young lady, I think I will have mercy on your poor soul."

"Thank you. Now let's talk about someone or something else." Aurora looked over to Enoch and Elaine. "Do you have anything you would like to share?"

Looking around the table at Aurora, Hunter, and Bethany, Elaine could tell they were trustworthy even though she had just met them. "Let me tell you about our trip here," she said, and told them of all the trials they had gone through: the trip through the woods, the mysterious creature, the avalanche, and everything else. When Elaine had finished the tale, Aurora stood up, walked over to her, and hugged her.

"My, oh my," Bethany said, "it is truly a miracle you two made it here."

Enoch and Elaine both nodded. "How about you, Bethany? What is your story?" Elaine asked.

Bethany's eyes widened. She had a very somber look on her face. "I am sorry, child, it is very hard for me to share. I can tell you this much, though: I got myself into trouble—so much, in fact, it landed me in the slave pits. After a year, I managed to escape and ran to Antillean for my freedom. Apollyon was in the worst part of the drought, and it was before the war. I had no food or water. I finally reached the border, but I was too weak to go any farther, and I lay on the ground to die. I fell asleep.

"I was awakened by an Antillean soldier who lifted my head and gave me a drink of water. That soldier happened to be General Isaiah Phoenix, and he nursed me back to health.

"He and a century of soldiers brought me here to the palace and I befriended the king, and, well, here I am."

Everyone was silent for a while. "Wow, Bethany, that is the most I have ever heard you talk about that," Aurora said.

A tear ran down Bethany's cheek. "It was hard for me to share even that. Maybe someday I will tell more, but that is it for now," Bethany said as more tears ran down her cheeks.

Aurora stood up to hug Bethany and yelped as she accidentally bumped her glass of milk. Milk spilled on her gown, and she moaned, "Why didn't I change my clothes before we came?"

Bethany shook her head. “I must say, Aurora, for a master swordswoman, you sure are clumsy.” Bethany walked over to her and *tsk*ed. “Well, if we hurry, I think I can clean that up before it stains.”

Aurora threw her hands up in the air. “You think you can clean this up? Mother, is going to kill me.”

Chapter Twenty-Two

Heir to the Throne

Xavier Pulsar looked out from a balcony, watching his son sparring with Virion. Their swords clashed with a loud clang. Xavier was happy to see Virion helping Maximus. Normally, with the war raging on, Virion would have had no time for such a thing. Now with this cease in battle and the final details of his plan worked out, they had time to spar. Xavier hoped that spending more time together will help them get along, though he understood why his old friend was not fond of his son. Maximus was strong physically, but his will, determination, and brutality were certainly weak. He hoped that Virion could work on those weaknesses. Maximus and Virion were going to spend at least two and a half months together just getting to Antillean City, with such a large caravan of soldiers, horses, carriages, and slaves.

Everything was going as planned; Xavier just had to wait for Victor to respond to his request. The cease in battle was to end in three days, and today, he was to set the trap. He had to be patient, for it took a long time to set up these meetings, and at great expense. To pass the time, he waited here.

It looked like Virion and Maximus were taking a break. Maximus smiled as Virion handed him a canteen. That was good; they seemed to be getting along. Apparently, Virion told a joke, for Maximus started to laugh. *Oh, that laugh is just like Shiva's,* Xavier thought, looking at his son fondly. Sometimes Maximus reminded him of Shiva, and he missed her so much. That laugh brought back memories of times gone by.

~ ~ ~

Xavier was sitting on their bed, reading a book. The bed sat on a dark oaken pedestal and was covered in red silken sheets and warm pillows. Hanging on the wall above was his father's sword and the decree his father had signed, to remind him of that triumphant day when he had become emperor.

Shiva sat in a chair across from him, in front of a vanity with a large mirror, so he could see her reflection. She had just got into her nightgown and was brushing her hair. He did enjoy watching her. Something was a little different about her tonight—something strange. She had a different air about her. Then she started humming to herself, and—that was strange—she seemed to be sitting up straighter than usual. Even the way she brushed her hair seemed different tonight. She seemed—well . . . happy. "Are you all right, my love?" he asked her.

Shiva turned toward him and gave him a big smile. He gave her a confused smile in return. She had smiled many times before, but never like this. She was grinning from ear to ear. "Yes, Xavier, I am well. Why do you ask?"

Xavier hesitated. "Just making sure," he finally said. *What is wrong? Has she gone mad?* he wondered.

When she stood up, Xavier was startled at the sight of her. Her silken nightgown shimmered in the candlelight, giving her face a brilliant glow. She gestured with her index finger for him to come to her, and he wondered, *what in the name of Apollyon is wrong with her?*

He got out of bed and stood up, but then, without warning, she ran and jumped at him. He barely had time to catch her. "Shiva, what is going—"

Before he could finish his sentence, she was kissing him passionately. She had kissed him many times, but never with this much passion. He almost dropped her in shock. It took him a minute to get his bearings. Once he had done so, he pulled away from her kiss and set her back on the floor. "What is the matter?" he asked. "Something is wrong. Why are you acting this way?" he demanded.

Shiva laughed. "There is nothing wrong; everything is right," she said gleefully.

"Oh, for crying out loud, woman, what is going on? You are acting so strangely. Out with it," he said with great frustration.

"I am with child!" she exclaimed.

Xavier started. "What did you say?"

"We are going to have a baby," she replied.

Xavier stood there in stunned silence. Then without warning, he swooped her up in his arms and kissed her. They kissed like they had never kissed before. He twirled her around, he was so excited. "I am going to be a father!" he shouted.

Shiva smiled and kissed his forehead. "I will bear you a child, and he or she will be wonderful."

Xavier smiled as Shiva looked into his eyes. Was that love he saw in them? Had she finally forgiven him for all he had done to her father, mother, sister, and lover? The moment had finally come—the moment he had waited for what seemed like an eternity. She loved him.

They kissed again, and this time, he carried her over and laid her down on the bed. He could see the passion in her eyes. He crawled onto the bed beside her and reached over to embrace her.

Suddenly, there was a loud knock on the door. Xavier looked toward the door, rage filling his eyes. He could hear a commotion—a muffled argument—outside. Xavier grunted in anger as he stormed to the door. He threw the door open so that it crashed loudly. Two guards and Daniel jumped and stood at attention. "What in blazes is going on here?" Xavier screamed at them.

"Sorry, Your Majesty. We tried to stop him," one of the soldiers said.

Xavier, his face contorted in anger, looked to Daniel. "Daniel, what are you doing here?"

Daniel shook in fear and tried to speak, but nothing came out.

"Out with it!"

Daniel jumped. "Your Majesty, I have an urgent message for Empress Shiva."

"Can it wait? I am trying to enjoy some alone time with my wife," he hissed.

"What is it, Daniel?" Shiva asked as she raced to the door. Daniel and the guards blushed.

"My love, you are not decent; you must cover up," Xavier said.

Shiva ignored him. "What is the message, Daniel?" she urged. Daniel looked down at the floor, hesitating.

"Well, say something!" Xavier shouted. He was taken aback when Shiva gave him a scornful look.

"Take your time, Daniel It is all right; you can tell me."

Daniel looked her in the eyes, tears running down his cheeks. "Oh, Your Majesty, I have grave news. There was an accident at the slave pits. I . . ." Daniel trailed off.

"Accident? What do you mean, accident?" Shiva asked. "Is Father all right?" she asked with a tremble in her voice.

"I am sorry, Your Majesty. A large boulder fell on him and ten others. He is dead."

Shiva let out a loud shriek, then fell to her knees and started to sob. As they looked on, she stood again and wrapped her arms around Daniel.

Daniel was shocked. He stood stiff as a board, not knowing what to do. Finally, he wrapped his arms around her.

Jealousy overtook Xavier, and he pulled Daniel away from Shiva and screamed, "Get your grubby hands off my wife!" as he punched the slave in the face. Daniel crumpled to the ground.

"Daniel!" Shiva cried, and Xavier grabbed her arm to prevent her from falling to her knees next to him. She pulled her arm from Xavier's grasp and sank to Daniel's side. "Are you alright?" she asked him.

A bruise had formed on Daniel's cheek. "I am fine, Your Majesty. I deserved what I got; I should not have touched you," he said as she helped him to his feet. Daniel steadied himself against the wall and did his best not to fall when he bowed. "I am sorry, Your Majesty. It will never happen again."

"You'd better believe it won't happen again! Next time, I'll rip your arm off. Now, out of my sight," Xavier growled.

Daniel bowed his head again and wobbled down the hallway. Shiva watched him as he walked away, then she turned to face Xavier. Gone were the love and passion in her eyes; they had been replaced by anger and hate. Xavier took a step backward as she glared at him.

"My father is dead, and you didn't console me. Daniel consoled me, and you punished him. I have been hoping that maybe somewhere in your cold heart there was some form of compassion, but there is none."

Xavier felt as though he had been stabbed in the heart. Her rebuke cut him to the core. "I don't know what to say, my love, I really don't," Xavier said with a frown.

"I know you don't." Shiva sighed in resignation. "I am tired. So very tired."

"Come to bed, my love, and you can rest," Xavier offered.

"I cannot sleep with you . . . at least not tonight. I must go see my mother and my sister, for, like me, they will be in mourning. I will sleep with them tonight."

Xavier wanted to say something appropriate, but he could not find the words. "I will post a guard outside their door," he managed.

Shiva walked into their bedchamber and grabbed her pillow and a blanket. She did not look at him as she walked down the hallway with a soldier in tow.

Xavier walked into the bedchamber and shut the door. He looked at Shiva's mirror and scowled at his reflection, then let out a curse. "You are an idiot!" he shouted. "A stupid idiot!" He lay in bed but did not sleep that night; it was one of the longest nights of his life.

A loud clang brought Xavier back to reality. He was glad for the distraction and wished he had not conjured up that bad memory, but as he watched Virion and Maximus fight, another memory filled his mind.

~ ~ ~

Xavier winced as Shiva screamed in pain. He paced the hallway. The day had arrived—the day he was going to be a father. He was excited and terrified at the same time. It seemed like an eternity since Shiva had gone into labor "How long does it take?" he asked himself impatiently.

Xavier heard Shiva scream again as a nurse told her to push. He had had no idea that childbirth could be so painful. He shook his head. It *cannot be that painful, can it?* he pondered. He wished she would not scream like that; he did not want his love to be in such pain.

"Push, push, push!" a nurse shouted, then there was silence. Xavier put his ear to the door, then jumped as the loud, high-pitched cry of a baby filled the air. He heard all the nurses cheering and celebrating.

He walked up to the door and knocked in excited anticipation. "Give as a few minutes, Your Majesty," one of the nurses called.

After what seemed like hours, the door opened. Xavier walked in and smiled. Shiva lay in her bed, holding a tiny baby in a blanket. She gave Xavier a tired smile. A tear ran down her cheek. "We have a son—a wonderful, beautiful son."

Xavier beamed with pride. He walked to stand beside Shiva and the new life they had made together. "A son," he said in disbelief. "Our son will be a great ruler someday. He will be even a greater emperor than myself. For that reason, his name shall be Maximus; he will be the greatest of all the rulers of the world."

Shiva nodded her approval. "A wonderful name, Xavier. I believe he will be a great ruler someday. Do you want to hold him?" Shiva asked.

Terror filled Xavier's heart. "Hold him?" he asked, very slowly.

"Yes, hold him."

"I guess I can," he said nervously.

Shiva lifted the baby toward him and explained how to hold the baby. Sweat beaded on Xavier's brow. The baby was so tiny, so fragile. How could he possibly hold it? Then he took his son in his arms and saw that

Maximus had the same dark eyes as him. Maximus looked at his father while sucking his fingers, and for a moment, Xavier thought he might cry from joy, but he did not. He was overjoyed but was not going to be weak, and he promised himself that his son would also not be weak.

After several minutes, he handed Maximus back to Shiva. He kissed her on the forehead, then let out a yawn. "This childbearing is exhausting. I need a nap," he complained.

Shiva rolled her eyes and scowled at him.

"What?" he asked.

"Never mind," she said, shaking her head. "Enjoy your nap."

To this day, Xavier couldn't figure out why she had been upset with him for wanting to take a nap. That reminded him of when Maximus had turned sixteen—a special birthday, indeed, for that was when he became a young man. They had had a special birthday for him. All the families who met Xavier's favor had attended a grand feast, with music, dancing, and games. When all the other presents had finally been opened, Xavier had approached Maximus.

"Here, son," Xavier said with a smile as he handed Maximus a long present wrapped in cloth. Maximus looked at the long gift, puzzled. "Unwrap it," Xavier urged.

Maximus eagerly unwrapped the cloth, and his eyes widened as the cloth fell to the floor. "A sword!" he exclaimed in excitement, looking at the ornate bronze hilt with its red gem.

"Pull out the sword, son," Xavier urged him.

Maximus unsheathed the sword and was amazed at the ornate blade. "It's beautiful, Father! Thank you so much."

Xavier smiled as Maximus hugged him. "Careful, son; it is a very sharp sword."

"Yes, Father, I will be," Maximus reassured him. He pulled away and moved to put the sword back in its scabbard. As he did, he let out a gasp, seeing writing engraved on the sword. He read it aloud: "Emperor Killian

Pulsar, ruler of Avarlon." He dropped the sword. It clanged loudly as it hit the floor.

Maximus looked over to Shiva in surprise, but Shiva only shook her head with a shrug and gave him a sympathetic look.

"You're a clumsy oaf. I just had that sword sharpened!" Xavier yelled as Maximus backed away from the sword.

"You gave me Grandfather's sword—the very sword you killed him with?" Maximus asked, clearly shaking.

Xavier scowled at him. "Yes, it is. I grew tired of seeing it mounted on my wall. I figured it might as well be useful. It is a perfectly good sword; I thought you would be pleased."

Maximus frowned, looking down at the sword like it was a poisonous snake ready to strike.

"That sword is perfectly fine, and even though your grandfather was a tyrannical battle-axe, this sword is a part of our heritage." When Maximus only stood staring at the sword, Xavier demanded, "Pick the sword up." Maximus looked at the sword, then at Xavier as if he did not know what to do. "Did you not hear me, boy? I said pick it up."

Maximus glared at Xavier. "No," he replied. "I will not carry a weapon that you used to kill Grandfather. I just can't. I refuse to." Xavier glared at him, and Maximus squirmed internally; he could not stand the soul-piercing stare his father would give him.

"This is what you're going to do, son. You are going to put that sword back in its scabbard, and you are going to put it on your belt and like it."

"No, Father, I will not," Maximus proclaimed, but when Xavier snarled as he marched toward him, Maximus scrambled, quickly putting the sword back into its scabbard.

Xavier stood over him. He raised his hand to slap Maximus, but from behind, someone slapped his hand away. Raged filled Xavier. *Who dared slap his hand away?* He turned, raising his fist to hit the person who had dared defy him.

Shiva raised her hands defensively and turned her head away as Xavier turned, and her tiara clattered across the floor.

Xavier's eyes grew big in shock as he barely stopped his punch from hitting her. He put his fist down to his side. He looked at Maximus, then Shiva, then hung his head.

Shiva straightened herself out and calmly walked over to her tiara, which her mother and sister had run over to pick up. All was silent as Shiva waved them away and then reached down to pick the tiara up and place it on her head. Next, she walked over to Maximus and helped him to his feet, then helped him put the sword on his belt. "Is that to your satisfaction, Xavier?" Shiva asked.

Xavier quietly nodded his head, and she smiled, but Xavier knew the anger behind that smile.

"Good," Shiva said, then looked at her mother and sister. "Help Maximus with the cake; cut it up and pass it around. Go ahead, dear, enjoy your cake," she said to her son. "Your father and I will return to you shortly." She then smiled to the people who were there. "Everyone, please enjoy the cake and refreshments; let's celebrate our son's special day."

The music started back up, and everyone returned to what they had been doing as Shiva gave Xavier a stern look and nodded toward a hallway. When they reached the end of the hallway, Shiva turned on Xavier. "You bullheaded, lumbering lummox of a man." She pointed her finger in his face. "Why can't you treat our son with some dignity and respect?" Xavier's eyes widened at her outburst. She had been angry with him many times before, but never like this.

Shiva kept shaking her finger in his face. "He is our one and only child. You are way too hard on him; he is just a young man."

Xavier's face grew dark. "Well, you are too soft. You treat our son like he is a child. He is not a baby, but you coddle him like one. He is a man, and he should be treated as such. He has become too soft. He is supposed to be strong, merciless and have no weaknesses. He is to be emperor someday, and I want him to be a man, not a laughingstock, but right now, he is an embarrassment."

Shiva frowned at Xavier. "You want our son to be a monster, not a man. You want him to be heartless. Well, a good man can have compassion and kindness and still be a strong leader. Our son is strong, but you insist on intimidating him and making him feel worthless. He is worthy to be an emperor, and he is a man—and unlike you, he does not have to be ugly to do it. He is our son. He is strong and compassionate—something you have no concept of. In my opinion, Maximus is more of a man than you will ever be." Her eyes widened, and she backed away, starting to tremble. She realized she had gone too far. She had overstepped.

Xavier snarled at her as anger welled up in his eyes. All he could think of was backhanding her. He watched as she closed her eyes and braced herself for the slap that was sure to come. He wanted to hit her so badly. He raised his hand, but then it dawned on him that he had never hit her before. He looked at her trembling frame, then put his hand down. He could not slap her; she was his love. How could he hurt his rose?

He put his hand down, then smiled a little. Then he smiled broadly, trying with all his might not to laugh. He burst out laughing.

Shiva opened her eyes, startled by this unexpected outburst. She looked at him wonderingly, dumbfounded. Why was he laughing? "What is so funny?" she finally asked.

Xavier started to laugh hysterically. He tried to speak, but he could not, so he embraced her.

She stood stiff as a board as wonderment turned to annoyance. "Why are you laughing?" As Xavier pulled away, she put her hands on her hips and started tapping her foot, glaring at him.

"Never in our marriage have you ever spoken to me in such a manner. Only you, my love, would dare say those things to me. You are right he is our son, and I must treat him better. My father never treated me like a human being. I have to break that habit; I am sorry, my love. Forgive me."

Shiva stood in stunned surprise. Rarely did Xavier apologize for anything. She managed to smile. "Accepted," she said. "There is one thing that is bothering me, though—what was so funny?" she asked.

He smirked. "That insult you hurled at me. What did you say, again? It was so funny."

Shiva thought for a moment. "A bullheaded, lumbering lummox," she repeated, then a smirk filled her face. They both looked at each other and then burst out laughing.

"It has been many years since I was insulted, but a bullheaded, lumbering lummox—well, now, that is funny." Shiva embraced Xavier and kissed his cheek. "Come, my love, let us put this all behind us and celebrate the rest of our son's birthday." They turned, and Xavier put his arm around her as they returned to the celebration.

Maximus looked at them with concern in his eyes but then saw them smiling as they approached. Xavier smiled at him. "How about some of that cake, son?"

Maximus smiled broadly as he handed Xavier and Shiva cake.

~ ~ ~

Xavier returned to reality, frowning at himself for his failings as he continued to watch his son fight. It bothered him so to still treat his son the way he did. He tried so hard to keep that promise to Shiva, but Maximus made it incredibly difficult.

"Your Majesty," said a voice behind him.

Xavier turned to a servant who was bowing. "What is it?" he asked.

The servant stood up. "We have contacted King Talon," she said. "He is at his cystallis, awaiting you to connect to him."

"Very good." Xavier smiled. He followed the servant to the cystallis room. It was finally time to set everything in motion. As he took his seat and waited patiently for the servant to set up the cystallis, he tried not to smile. Then he started to sweat, knowing he had to be careful not to make a mistake, for he knew if he did not come across as genuine, this would not work.

Suddenly, the cystallis started to glow and an image of Victor Talon started to coalesce on it. Victor nodded, and so did Xavier. They looked at each other in silence.

Finally, Xavier spoke. "Victor, I have decided to reach out to you because I have changed my mind. I want peace."

Chapter Twenty-Three

The Approaching Storm

Aldar Talon was happy as Aurora, Enoch, Elaine, and Jonathan approached him in the battle practice area. It was evening, and all the teachers and apprentices were done for the day, but this group all were dressed for some battle training of their own—not because they were planning on going to war but because it was always good and relaxing to keep their skills honed even though there was to be peace.

It had been two months since Xavier Pulsar had contacted Aldar's father and sent a delegation to work out a peace accord. It was good to end this war, but somehow, he did not feel at ease about the whole thing; he did not trust Xavier Pulsar. His father did not feel ill at ease at all, so Aldar wondered why he could not get rid of this feeling. He sighed in frustration but smiled in spite of this; the others were laughing and smiling as they came closer. He had grown to love Enoch and Elaine. Over the past two months, they had become like an adopted son and daughter.

Aldar also smiled about the budding romance between Elaine and Jonathan. He remembered being young and in love. It was so special to see that in such a lovely couple. Luckily for Elaine, Jonathan had been promoted to one of the general positions of security at the palace, and they were able to spend time with each other on his days off. Jonathan was a perfect match for Elaine, for she was more reserved while he was footloose and fancy-free. When they fell behind the rest and kissed, Enoch teased, "Come on, you two love birds, quit smooching!"

Everyone laughed as they finally reached Aldar.

They had decided to have an archery contest. Aldar already had the targets set up and bows and arrows for all of them.

Enoch smiled at Aldar. "Well, Aldar, what do you want to bet on now? Your crown this time?" Enoch teased.

"Oh, Father, please don't. Last time you bet Enoch, it cost you one of your vests," Aurora said, laughing.

Aldar looked up toward his crown, then smiled at Enoch. "And everyone will be calling you Majesty," he said.

Everyone laughed at that, and Jonathan bowed his head and shouted, "All hail Prince Enoch, ruler of all that is in his mind!"

Enoch punched Jonathan in the shoulder as he laughed. "Careful," Elaine said.

"It is fine, my love, it didn't hurt," Jonathan assured her as he rubbed his shoulder mockingly. He looked at Aldar. "Are not Zena and Hunter going to compete in this contest?" he asked.

"I'm afraid not. Hunter, of course, is resting up after a day of hard training, and Zena—well . . ." Aldar hesitated.

Aurora walked up to Aldar and put her arm around his waist. "What Father is trying to say is Mother is far from graceful in this sort of thing."

Aldar nodded. "I'm afraid so, and she did not want to be embarrassed about it, so she stayed back to read." Everyone nodded in understanding. Zena was a proud woman and did not want to appear weak.

Aldar smiled, eager to change the subject. "Well, you jesters, are you ready to be put in your place by this old man?"

"Well how about this, you jesters—how would you like to be put in your place by a *very* old man?" said a voice behind Aldar.

Aldar and Aurora turned to see Victor Talon wearing a huge grin on his face.

"Grandfather!" Aurora exclaimed as she ran to him and gave him a hug.

"Hello, my little honeybee," he said.

Everyone else looked at Victor; no one wanted to say it, but they all knew what the others were thinking: Victor was too old. Victor noticed their looks as he left Aurora's embrace. "You think I'm too old, eh?"

When no one spoke, he said, "Well, I'm here to tell you that this old coot is as good as when he was young and spry."

"That's all right, Grandfather, you can join the competition," Aurora said.

"Of course, I can! I am king, after all," he said with a big grin on his face. The others all looked at each other again.

"Well, we can't argue that point," Jonathan said.

"Very good, Jonathan, you are wise beyond your years. Elaine, you'd better hang on to this man," Victor said.

"You'd better believe I will!" she said as she put her arm around his waist as she smiled up at him.

"All right, already. Enough of this sissy mushy stuff. Let's compete," Enoch said with a smile.

"Agreed." Aldar nodded, and they started the competition.

Everyone but the king took a turn, with varying results but no bull's-eyes. Victor had insisted on being last. When it was his turn, he nocked his arrow and groaned slightly as he drew the bowstring. He grimaced and looked pained as he aimed. Aurora moved to say something, but the king loosed the arrow, which flew swiftly and hit the target. "Bull's-eye!" Victor shouted as everyone looked, dumbfounded, at the arrow stuck straight and true in the bull's-eye. "Not bad for a man with one foot in the grave," he said with a wink.

The stunned silence that followed was finally broken by cheering and laughing.

The contest continued for another hour, after which Victor was declared the winner. They celebrated with punch, then talked for a while until Aldar suggested that they all go to the lookout. Everyone nodded their agreement.

After several steps, they reached the top of the lookout wall. Aldar had always liked the view from here, and this evening it was particularly lovely, as the sun, close to setting, was giving the ocean a golden glow.

Victor patted Aldar on the back. "Beautiful, isn't it?" When Aldar nodded in agreement, Victor said. "Unfortunately, it looks like there's a storm a brewing."

Aldar squinted. Indeed, dark clouds were forming in the distance.

They heard a soldier come up behind them, and Victor turned to him the soldier kneeled ."You may rise," Victor told him.

The soldier did so, then announced, "Your Majesty, I have news from one of our scouts. The entourage from Apollyon is about two days' ride out. They have made great progress and are at least two days ahead of schedule."

"Very good, soldier. You may leave us." The soldier bowed his head and scurried off.

"That's wonderful news," Aurora said as everyone smiled and cheered. "Soon this war will be over and there will be peace." Victor smiled broadly, until his eyes fell upon Aldar.

Aldar was not cheering. He was not celebrating or smiling. Victor frowned at him. "What is wrong, son?" he asked.

Before Aldar could respond, a thunder rolled in the distance as the sun disappeared behind the clouds. "I am sorry, Father, I feel that something is not right. Something doesn't feel right."

Everyone looked at Aldar in silence. "I'm not sure what you mean," Victor said, confused. "I don't feel we are missing anything. We have everything prepared for the occasion."

"I know, Father. I cannot explain it, but something doesn't feel right. There is something wrong about this meeting." More thunder rumbled in the distance.

"I don't understand you, son. What do you mean, there's something wrong? We have soldiers following the entourage; we will have some of our best soldiers escorting them when they arrive. Isaiah will have his most elite soldiers with us when we negotiate peace with Virion and Maximus. Enoch and Elaine will be in hiding so no harm will come to them. It will be impossible for them to harm us; we have everything covered."

"I know," Aldar said, a lot more harshly than he intended.

"So what is the matter?" Victor asked with a hint of frustration.

"I don't know, Father, I don't know. Something is not right." Aldar shook his head. The sky was starting to darken slightly, and the wind picked up a little. "I don't think we should do this," Aldar said.

"What do you mean, we should not do this? Why do you wait until now, when they are practically at our gates, to tell me this?" The wind picked up, and a bright flash of lightning followed by a louder boom of thunder rumbled across the sea. "What do you want me to do when they arrive, tell them to go back to the hell from whence they came?"

A large bolt of lightning streaked across the sky, and thunder shook the wall.

"We'd best get inside," Jonathan suggested.

Victor stormed ahead of everyone into an enclosed lookout tower. Everyone huddled together and looked out the window as the storm slammed into the tower. Rain fell in sheets, and another thunderclap shook the tower. everyone looked in awe at the tempest. Standing next to his father, Aldar turned to look at him, saying, "I am sorry, Father. I did not mean to make you upset. I really have no idea why I feel this way."

Victor hugged him. "I am sorry as well. I guess the stress of all this is getting to us all." He patted Aldar's shoulder. "Everything will be all right, I assure you. Everything will be fine, you will see."

Aldar smiled. "You are right, Father. I am sure everything will be all right, I guess I was acting childish."

"You were not acting childish; you were concerned. That's a good quality, to be cautious. Everything will be all right." Without any warning, the storm abruptly stopped, the clouds began to clear, and the sun shone again. The sun was setting, turning the clouds red and purple. "What an odd storm," Victor noted. "Well, it certainly gave us a wonderful sunset." Aldar nodded in agreement.

"Well, everyone, the show is over, and I must retire for the night," Victor announced.

Everyone nodded their agreement, and they talked and laughed as they headed down the stairs before saying their good-byes and good-nights. Aldar stayed behind to put all the equipment away and was surprised to see Aurora standing near him.

"Let me help, Father," she said. He smiled and handed her one of the bows. As they collected the rest of the equipment, Aurora spoke. "Father, you really seemed worried back there. You told Grandfather you were sure everything was going to be all right, but you don't really believe that; I can tell."

He patted her on the head. "Nothing gets past my eldest child," he said, kissing her forehead. "I will try my best to support your grandfather. He is confident things will be all right; I guess I should feel the same. I want all of us to keep steadfast and keep our eyes open during this time."

"We all will, Father, I promise; I'm sure things will be fine. Do you have any idea why you feel this way?"

Aldar looked at the sky beginning to turn to night, then looked at Aurora and said, "I have no idea, child."

"Everything is in place. Like Grandfather said, we all should be safe. Enoch and Elaine will remain in our quarters during this time. There is certainly no need for Xavier Pulsar to know we have them, at least for now. Then there was that odd storm that came up when Grandfather and I were arguing. Was it a warning?" he mused. "It is as though the Apollyon entourage is like a storm approaching us."

Aurora nodded. "And the way the storm abruptly stopped—very strange indeed," she said.

"I am not sure, Aurora; I want you to keep the way I feel about this away from your grandfather. He has worked hard to make this happen, and I certainly don't want to disappoint him."

"I will," Aurora said. "I have to admit, now that I think about it, I feel a bit ill at ease about this too. I pray this feeling goes away."

Aldar nodded his agreement. "All I can say, I will not draw an easy breath until this treaty is signed and the entourage returns to Apollyon."

Then he smiled. “Come on, let us get this job done and maybe we can sneak some milk from the kitchens.”

They both laughed as they gathered the remaining equipment.

Chapter Twenty-Four

Arrival

As they approached, Maximus Pulsar looked out of the carriage, in awe of the spectacle of Antillean City. In all his life, he had never seen such a beautiful city. His eyes widened as they passed through the gates. He was amazed at all the people from all the other nations who were there; he could not believe how many Apollyon people were also there. He could not help but think that if his father had had more mercy, not so many would have fled to Antillean. He could not fault them for living there; Antillean was a wonderful nation.

Maximus stifled a yawn. It had been a long, hard journey. The slaves behind them had slowed things significantly. The trip home would be much quicker without the slaves slowing them down, he knew, but for the sake of the negotiations it was worth it. He hoped these slaves would enjoy their freedom—albeit a short-lived freedom ending when Pirena would get his father the eye. He still thought this was a crazy idea, but even if the legend of the eye were a fairy tale, what would the harm be? Pirena would just get a worthless orb and an extremely long walk back home. He smiled at the thought of Pirena sputtering to herself as she made her way back to Adaliah.

His smile faded as he looked at the mass of humanity that had crowded the city sidewalks. They were silent. They all gave his entourage looks of disdain and anger. It was most unnerving, to say the least.

Virion interrupted his thoughts. "Relax, Maximus, we will be fine. King Talon assured our safety. No harm will come to us; Victor is a man of his word. If you look around, you will see we're flanked by Antillean soldiers." Maximus did just that and saw that the Antillean soldiers had indeed flanked them. He was not sure if that was comforting or terrifying; he could feel himself sweat.

Maximus nearly jumped out of his seat as a loud cheer broke the silence. He let out a curse. "What was that?" he asked as cheers and applause echoed down the streets.

Virion started to laugh. "They're cheering for the slaves; they are certainly not cheering for us. The look on your face!" Virion continued to laugh, and Maximus frowned and crossed his arms at the outburst. Once Virion had stopped laughing, his face became more somber. "You know, your father would be displeased with you. He would have scolded you something fierce. Be glad he was not here. I have to admit, I'm worried, Maximus. I worked hard with you so you can have proper etiquette, so please do not mess this up. This is extremely important, and your father will have both our hides if this does not work out."

"I know, Virion. I will try to do my best," Maximus said.

"No, you *will* do your best," Virion corrected.

"I know," Maximus said, "I will only speak when spoken to, and I will let you lead. I will do my best."

Virion's smile returned. "That is all your father and I ask for—you to do your best—and he will be proud of you."

Maximus smiled at that, and Virion returned the smile as they continued down the street. They rode in silence until finally, they came to a stop and a loud voice rang out. "Open the gate! The entourage from Apollyon has arrived."

Once again, Maximus jumped. Virion sighed but said nothing and shook his head. The gates groaned loudly as the gate was slowly raised. The gate made a loud thud as it reached the top. Virion looked at Maximus, looking surprised that Maximus had not jump at the sound. The carriage driver opened the door and bowed as Virion and Maximus climbed out.

Maximus looked at the palace, and his jaw dropped. Virion put his hand on the younger man's shoulder and smiled. "I had the same reaction when I saw this palace for the first time." They stood looking around as they awaited the welcoming committee to take them to King Talon.

Looking toward a massive wide staircase that led to the palace entrance, they watched as a group of soldiers walked down the stairs in single file then split apart and turned to face each other. This left a wide gap for what Virion assumed was the welcoming committee.

A woman with reddish-blonde hair and wearing a long, flowing gown appeared at the top of the steps. She curtsied. "Greetings. I am Danielle Hawk, His Majesty's personal liaison. Supreme General Nebula, Prince Pulsar, soldiers, and slaves, welcome to Antillean."

All stood in silence as Virion and Maximus nodded their heads in acknowledgement. There was a long pause in which Virion could not figure out why she was not coming down to them. Did she expect them to walk up to her? He felt anger building inside him. *An insult before they had even met the king. How reprehensible!* he thought.

He was about to storm up the stairs and yell at her, but then she curtsied again and said, "Here he is, His Majesty King Victor Talon."

Virion's eyes widened in shock. Sure enough, a gray-haired old man wearing a crown and silken robes appeared at the top of the stairs. What in the name of Apollyon was this? Royalty giving a personal greeting like this was a rare honor. He realized he was frowning, and he quickly put on a forced smile. This greeting had him thrown off.

The king started down the steps, and his soldiers saluted him. Virion panicked, completely stupefied. This was so unexpected that it had left him feeling off-balance. Sweat beaded on his forehead, and he was not sure what he was going to say. *Blast it all! I do this all the time*, he thought.

When the king made it to the bottom of the stairs and smiled at them, Virion's eyes widened. Then Victor held out his hand. Virion paused for a second and, realizing he was being rude, held his hand out to shake. He was startled as Victor shook his hand vigorously, but he still managed to smile. "Welcome, Virion, I am glad to see you again. I pray your journey was not too taxing."

Virion tried to say something, but the words seemed stuck in his throat. "The trip was fine," he finally managed. *Fool!* he cursed at himself.

Here he was, messing up after he had been so worried about Maximus messing up. Why was he so off?

The king turned his attention to Maximus and gave him a handshake as well. "You must be Maximus. Welcome to our great city."

Maximus smiled. "Thank you, Your Majesty. Thank you for welcoming us to your lovely home."

Virion looked over at Maximus in disbelief. The younger man was calm and collected. *What in the name of Apollyon is wrong with me? Why am I so blasted nervous?*

"I am so sorry for your loss," the king told Maximus. "Your mother was a wonderful woman, and I was always pleased to talk to her."

Maximus nodded. "Thank you, Your Majesty. She was a wonderful mother, and I miss her so."

The king put his hand on Maximus's shoulder. "As does the rest of the world," he said. Then he smiled. "Please, you do not have to call me Majesty; Victor will suffice." He returned his attention to Virion. "If I may, I would like to address your soldiers and then the slaves."

Virion could not believe what he had just heard. Here they were, the enemy, on Antillean land, yet the king had just asked permission to speak. Who was this man? If the roles had been reversed, he certainly would not have asked for permission.

Virion nodded. "Of course. You are more than welcome to address them, and certainly the slaves." Virion looked at Maximus. "Stay here until we are finished." Maximus nodded his understanding, and Virion made his way with the king to the top of the steps, where they turned to face the soldiers and the slaves. Virion raised his hands in the air to get their attention. "King Talon wishes to address you; you will respect him as you do me."

The king looked out at the soldiers, then at Virion. "Thank you, Supreme Commander Nebula." Turning back to the soldiers, he continued. "First of all, welcome to my palace. Thank you for surrendering your weapons. They will be returned to you when you head back home. We will take your horses to the stables, where they will be watered and fed and well taken care of. We have special dormitories in the wing of the palace to your left. There, you will have access to baths. You will have comfortable beds, your uniforms will be washed, and you will be fed three meals a day. We also will restock all your supplies for the journey home. My supreme commander, Isaiah Phoenix, will lead you to your dormitories."

Isaiah rode up to the head of the Apollyon soldiers with two of his men. "Everyone, please follow me," he shouted. When the soldiers looked at Virion nervously, he nodded at them with a smile, so they followed Isaiah.

Next, the king looked at the slaves and waved to them. "Please come closer. Don't be afraid."

The slaves nervously walked to the steps but were careful not to get too close to Maximus, who looked at them disdainfully.

"Maximus, you can join us," Virion called, and Maximus graciously and quickly ran up the stairs so the slaves could get closer.

The king frowned as he looked at the slaves' dirty faces, muddy bare feet, and ragged clothes. There were men, women, and young teenagers. He was surprised to see no children—probably too long a walk. It angered him that people could be treated as animals, but he forced a smile upon his face. "Welcome, everyone. I pray that you are all well and this long journey was not too hard on you.

"Emperor Pulsar has graciously granted your freedom in an act of peace—a peace I pray will be everlasting. I pray that with time and negotiations, we can abolish slavery altogether. It may take some time, but I will do my best to rid the world of this great atrocity."

Virion frowned and folded his arms. He was not sure he liked the king's tone, but he said nothing.

Victor could see the fear in the slaves' eyes. He could tell they wanted to applaud but were too afraid. "I have opened up temporary housing in the wing of my palace that is to your right," he told them. "You will be treated to the same amenities as the soldiers, and there will be healers on hand if one is needed. You will also have access to new clothes and proper sanitation. A thousand of my best builders have been working day and night on a housing complex for you. It should be done in a few more weeks, and at that time, it will be your home and you will have all the rights and privileges as all our citizens. We have many of our businesses interested in hiring you for a multitude of jobs, including jobs at my palace."

Virion could not believe what he was hearing. Was Talon really going to do that for common slaves? As the king continued to speak, Virion noticed that some of the slaves had tears in their eyes.

"As King of Antillean, I officially decree that you are no longer slaves and are now citizens of Antillean. Welcome to Antillean, my countrymen and -women! Welcome home, welcome home."

The former slaves erupted in loud cheers and cries of celebration, shouting, "Long live King Talon!"

Victor could not help but smile a little at Virion and Maximus's angry, disdainful looks. He looked over to a few of his soldiers. "Please lead these wonderful citizens to their rooms."

The people continued to chant, "Long live King Talon!" as they were led off to their housing.

"Well, that was impressive," Virion managed to say in total dismay. "Xavier would have been infuriated; I am glad he didn't see this," he said aloud.

Victor turned to address him. "I am sorry; I don't mean to create friction between us."

Virion managed a smile. "No worries, Victor, all is forgiven; they are, after all, free."

The king smiled and nodded. "I have special rooms set up in the palace for you. Let me show you. There will be servants at your beck and call. The dinner hour will be soon; you will need to freshen up."

An hour later, Virion and Maximus had freshened up and changed into clean clothes for dinner. Virion was impressed. He and Maximus had adjoining rooms and a wonderful living space, and the beds were quite comfortable—far more comfortable than he was accustomed to. He and Maximus stood up as a knock came at the door. Virion walked over and opened the door, and once again to his surprise, Victor Talon stood before him with his liaison. This time, Virion held his composure as the king smiled.

"Hello, Virion, Maximus."

"Good evening," Virion said with a forced smile."

Victor nodded. "I am sure you are famished."

"We sure are, Victor," Maximus said eagerly.

Virion shot him a look, and Maximus frowned. Virion turned to Victor. "Thank you, Victor, we look forward to dining with you," he said with a smile.

"Very good," Victor said enthusiastically. "My personal chef has a special meal for this occasion. I hope it is to your liking."

As they walked down the hallways to the dining room, Maximus gawked at the beauty of the palace. Virion had been there before, so he could not blame the boy, and he decided not to scold him; he had to give some allowances. Instead, he thought furiously. He could not understand Victor Talon. He had met the man before, briefly, but had had no idea he was this gracious. What a strange man! He was nothing like all the other rulers of the five nations. None of them would have done a fraction of the things Victor had done this evening. *For certain, he is the only one who would walk you to the dinner table*, Virion thought.

Finally, they made it to the grand dining room. As they walked in, everyone already at the table stood and bowed. Virion held in a curse at yet another surprise. Victor's family was there to eat with them, yet another honor. The first meal with another ruler was just that—a meal with the ruler. If the whole family was there, it was a sign of trust.

The king smiled again. "Virion, I know you know most of my family, but Maximus does not, so if you can indulge me, I wish to introduce them."

"Of course," Virion said. *Asking permission again?* he thought.

"This is my youngest grandchild, Hunter," the king said.

Hunter bowed his head. "Welcome to our home," he said with a smile.

"This is my eldest grandchild, Aurora."

She smiled, and Maximus smile broadly in return. Virion scowled at him; he certainly was not going to allow that.

"This is my youngest child, Alana."

She bowed her head, and Virion remembered she was the blind one.

"This is my eldest, my son Aldar."

"Virion, Maximus," Aldar said nervously. After all, he was the one who had wounded Maximus's father.

"This is his wife and my daughter-in-law, Zena."

She scowled at them as she nodded. *She is a feisty one*, Virion remembered.

"Excuse me," Victor said as he walked to the end of the table, where the queen sat in her wheelchair. He grabbed the handles and backed the chair up, then wheeled his wife over to Virion and Maximus. "This is my queen, my lovely wife, Amber."

"Nice to meet you again, Virion. And who is this fine young lad? You must be Xavier and Shiva's boy. Well, it certainly is a pleasure to meet you."

To Virion's surprise, Maximus took her hand and kissed it, saying, "It is a pleasure to meet you."

"Aw, and a sweet young lad, too." The queen looked at him sympathetically. "I am sorry about your mother, God rest her soul."

Maximus stood in silence. *Don't you dare cry*, Virion thought at the boy.

"Thank you, Amber, she truly was a great mother," Maximus said with a smile.

Good job, Maximus, Virion thought. *He actually kept his emotions in check.*

Victor took Amber back to her place at the table, then escorted Virion and Maximus to the head of the table. This was yet another honor. Visitors from rival countries usually sat at the middle of the table.

I guess I should no longer be surprised at this, Virion thought in resignation as he took his place next to Maximus at the table.

Victor also took his place, and then they stood in awkward silence for a moment. Virion almost let out a sigh but then remembered the whole family was waiting for him and Maximus to take their seats. He indicated to the younger man that they should sit, and everyone else followed. Virion felt a little bit ill. Why were they all so friendly?

They ate their appetizers over general conversation about the weather and other neutral topics. When the main course came, Maximus's eyes widened at the lavish spread. The wine was poured, and the food served, and Maximus blurted, "What is this meat? It is so rich and delicious! Even Father, with his great riches, has never had food such as this." When Virion hit him in the side and glared at him, Maximus gritted his teeth.

"I am sorry about Maximus's outburst. He is still very young and new to such things," Virion said to the family.

Victor smiled. "No need for Apologies. The boy is just curious, and I am happy to answer. It is called leg of lamb. We don't have it often, only for occasions such as this."

"What is lamb?" Maximus asked.

Virion was smiling, but deep inside, he was fuming, Maximus was going to get a talking-to later. He sat in silence while Victor explained to Maximus what a lamb was.

"Really?" Maximus said, "We have no such animals in Apollyon, just wild boar, chicken, and the occasional cow. We probably would have more fish, too, but most of our rivers are contaminated."

That boy is talking too much, thought Virion, who was trying with all his might not to yell at the lad. He watched Victor smile and talk kindly to Maximus. Why was the king being so friendly to them? *It was us who invaded their land. We ravaged their towns and enslaved their people at the beginning. It was us who killed so many of their countrymen and -women in this long-drawn-out war.* Yet they were so friendly. Why? They had no reason to, yet here Virion was with Maximus, being treated with the utmost respect. Virion was starting to get extremely angry; he could feel the anger roiling just beneath the surface.

He treats us like special guests, he treats my soldiers with kindness, he treats the slaves with compassion. He has his family greet us so nicely, then he feeds us this special dinner. I hate that smile on his face; I hate his cheery disposition. I hate his kindness and compassion. And even worse, I am beginning to like this man.

"Is something the matter, Virion?" Victor asked, interrupting his thoughts.

It was then that Virion realized he was holding a cloth napkin and had twisted it into knots, his knuckles white from the strain of twisting the napkin. He quickly put the napkin back on his lap and looked at Victor, embarrassed. "I am sorry, everyone. I have a bad habit of doing that when I am deep in thought."

"I see," Aldar said, his eyes widening, then he changed the subject. "Let us have dessert. It is molasses pie, Aurora's favorite."

After dinner was over, Victor led Virion and Maximus back to their rooms. "I look forward to our meeting tomorrow," he told them. "I pray that we can all come up with a mutual agreement."

Virion nodded. "As do I, Victor. Xavier has grown tired of all the fighting and is eager to move forward from this war."

"Very good, Virion. Well, I am off. You gentlemen have a good night. I will see you tomorrow."

Virion waited for a few moments to make sure Victor was out of earshot before he shouted at Maximus. "Stupid idiotic fool!"

Maximus hung his head. "I am sorry, Virion, I overstepped my bounds. Please forgive me."

"I wasn't talking to you, idiot! I was yelling at myself. I mean, yes, you could have done better, but overall, you did fairly well. I, on the other hand, was a miserable failure. Oh, Xavier would be most disappointed in me. Victor Talon is so infuriatingly nice; it borders on being sickening. Why is he so blasted nice?"

"He is a very nice man, and his family is also so nice. Amber is so nice, and Aurora is so beautiful," Maximus said.

"Don't get any ideas," Virion told him. "Even though she will be a servant, you have no chance with her, so forget it."

Maximus frowned but nodded his head. "I understand," he said.

"You'd better!" Virion sighed. "I am sorry, Maximus. I am in such a foul mood right now; all this kindness is too much for me, and I'm letting it out on you. It makes what we must do harder than I anticipated. I cannot let their kindness cloud my judgement. I must keep myself together and do my part so Pirena can do her part—the sooner the better—and your father can rule the world, your mother will return, and order can be restored." Virion let out a yawn. "Let us go to bed; we have a big day tomorrow."

Chapter Twenty-Five

Negotiations

After a nice breakfast, it was time for negotiations to begin. Victor led Virion and Maximus into the meeting room, where Aldar, Alana, Isaiah, Danielle, and other dignitaries sat. All stood up as Victor, Virion, and Maximus came to their seats. Everyone sat down again in unison, and Aldar felt a chill go down his spine. He put on his best smile, but the feeling returned. Something was not right; he could sense it. Some sort of wrongness was there, but he could not put his finger on what it was.

The meeting started like most, with small talk and chatter about how things were going on in their lands. "I have a question for you, Victor," Virion said.

Victor nodded. "Please ask away, anything."

"As you know, after the tragic death of Her Majesty Empress Shiva, Levi and Lana Eclipse were caught, sentenced, and executed. Their children, Enoch and Elaine, escaped and have not been seen for months. I want to know, have you seen them? I know we are here to talk peace, but the emperor needs to know. If you have them, Emperor Pulsar demands you release them to me, and I will take custody of them. They will return to Apollyon and will face their judgement in this matter. There is no negotiation." The air grew thick with tension as Virion folded his arms.

I knew things were going to go wrong, I just knew it, Aldar thought.

Victor smiled. "Virion, I assure you, we have not seen the children. I admit we have been looking for them, but so far, no luck," he said calmly, then, "Now I have a question for you, Virion. Why should the children be punished for what their father has done? How is that justice, punishing their children? It does not seem right."

Maximus slammed his fist on the table and stood up. "Father and I do not care about justice; we want revenge. Their father killed my mother.

My heart and soul have been ripped apart. So have Father's. There is a price that must be paid, and that price must be their lives. I want them dead."

"I am sorry for your loss," Victor said, "but killing them will not bring your mother back."

Maximus glared at Victor. "You have no clue what pain Father and I have felt. Mother did not deserve what came to her."

Virion put his hand on Maximus's arm to make him stop, but Maximus ripped his arm away. Virion groaned and rubbed his temples.

"I think you are a liar," Maximus went on. "I think they are here, and you are hiding them from us. They could not have just disappeared; they must be somewhere, and I am willing to bet they are somewhere in Antillean City. It is kind of funny, we also had a century of soldiers disappear; they must have run into the abyss with them."

"Enough!" Virion yelled, standing up and grabbing Maximus by the shoulders. He shook the prince. "I told you to shut up and let me lead. What in the name of Apollyon is wrong with you? King Talon is a man of his word; he would not lie about such a thing. You are too emotional, and I should have left you home, you stupid little whelp." Virion turned to face the quiet and stunned crowd. "I am sorry for this unprofessional conduct displayed by Prince Maximus."

After a long silence, Maximus faced Victor and hung his head. "I am sorry, Victor, I truly am. I have been overwhelmed by this great loss in my life, and sometimes it clouds my judgement. I know you are a man of your word, and you would not lie about such a thing. I pray I have not ruined our negotiations. Please, will you find it in your heart to forgive me?"

Victor scowled and started tapping his finger on the table. Aldar hated it when his father did that; usually, nothing good came after he did that. *I just knew something was wrong and bad things were going to happen*, he thought.

After what seemed an eternity, Victor stopped tapping and stood up, opening his mouth to speak.

~ ~ ~

Bethany paced nervously in the Talon family living quarters. Aurora, Enoch, Elaine, and Hunter were sitting around, talking with each other.

Aurora could not help but notice Bethany's pacing. She even saw sweat on Bethany's face. "What is the matter, Bethany? You are not your cheery self," Aurora asked.

Bethany stopped, now realizing she had been pacing. "I am fine, Aurora."

Aurora smiled at her. "Remember when I was little, and you could always tell when I was not being truthful?"

Bethany nodded.

"Well, I have known you almost my entire life, and I can tell when you are not being truthful."

Bethany smiled and took a seat next to Aurora, everyone looking at her in concern. "I guess I cannot hide anything from you, now, can I?" Bethany said as she put her arm around Aurora. "I have to admit, having Virion Nebula here makes me nervous. Thank heavens he has not seen me yet."

"Why do you care if he sees you?" Elaine asked. A tear ran down Bethany's cheek, surprising everyone. Bethany was always cheery and lighthearted.

Then Bethany burst into tears. Aurora wrapped her arms around her. "It's all right, Bethany. I am here for you. It's all right."

After a few moments, Bethany pulled away. "I am so sorry for this, everyone," she apologized, but they all assured her there was nothing to be sorry for."

"I guess I should give you all an explanation."

"You don't have to," Hunter and Enoch said in unison.

"But I need to. The time has come to tell you all about my experience as a slave," Bethany said.

Everyone looked at her, surprised that she was willing to talk about her days in slavery.

"My family was in Killian Pulsar's favor when Xavier Pulsar took over. We were fortunate, and Xavier Pulsar also took favor upon us. That is until he found out that my mother and father were plotting to kill him. That was about fifteen years ago." She looked over to Enoch and Elaine. "In a way, we have similar stories," she told them.

"My father was friends with Virion before this happened, so Virion was stunned and angered when he found out. I have a younger brother and sister, Nathaniel and Bella. Occasionally, Virion would come down to humiliate father. He would take turns beating us in front of Father. Oh, it tormented him so!

"Father and Mother are now dead; they grew too old and weak. The work was too much for their hearts," she explained. "They then separated my brother, sister, and I because they found out we had planned to escape. Virion beat us again before we were separated. He said if we ever escaped and we were found, he would execute us personally. I do not know if Nathaniel and Bella are still alive or not, or if they escaped. That is also why I did not attend last night's dinner when your father invited me. I told him I would explain later, and considering I was an escaped slave, he understood and told me to lay low as well.

"I pray that someday, somehow, I will see my brother and sister again. I know Nathaniel and Bella would be happy for me. They would want me to live the best possible life I could have, and I have found it here. You are my family, and I am proud and happy to be a part of your family."

Everyone left their seats and gathered around Bethany. They took turns hugging her and kissing her forehead.

"Ahem," a voice sounded. Everyone turned to see Zena, who had just walked into the room.

Zena frowned at Bethany, then gave her a confused look as she saw tears running down Bethany's cheeks. Then her look changed to one of concern. "Are you all right?" she asked with genuine concern, surprising everyone; most of the time, she gave Bethany scorn.

Bethany smiled. "Everything is fine, just fine."

Zena looked as though she were going to ask what was going on, but she dropped the subject. Then it was her turn to pace.

"Are you all right, Mother?" Aurora asked.

Zena stopped. "No, I am not all right. I have to admit I am a little bit nervous. I know your father has been nervous about all this as well." Zena resumed her pacing, then continued speaking. "It has been hours since the negotiations started. I do not understand why I was not invited; your grandfather said I was too ill-tempered. Well, I beg to differ. I am not ill-tempered; I am just deeply passionate, is all."

Bethany looked at Aurora, smiled, and rolled her eyes. Aurora covered her mouth, trying not to laugh.

"I am worried it can't be good. It is taking so long, I pray everything is all right."

"I am sure everything will be all right, Mother," Aurora said.

"This could take days," Bethany said.

Zena stopped pacing and crossed her arms. "I suppose you think you're an expert on this, Bethany?"

Well, her sympathy didn't last long, Bethany thought.

"I am sorry. You all were here, spending quality time with each other, and I came in and spouted off," Zena said. "Well, I am going to leave you all, and I am going down to the meeting room and find out what is going on." She turned to leave.

"Grandfather will not be happy," Aurora said.

Zena turned to look at her. "I really don't care, child," she said, then turned and left.

~ ~ ~

Zena walked as fast as she could without looking hurried or improper. She was going to get to the bottom of all this.

After several minutes, she made it to the hallway leading to the meeting rooms. Two guards were standing at the entrance to the hallway. She approached them and smiled. They both bowed and said, "Your Highness," in unison. "Is there anything we can do for you?" one of them asked.

"Yes, I was wondering if you know if any progress has been made in the negotiations."

The guard on her right spoke. "I am sorry, Your Highness, we do not have access to that information; we are here for protection."

"Well, has anyone left the room at all?"

"Yes, Danielle Hawk left for a while and returned with servants bearing food and drink."

Zena was getting frustrated. "You mean no one has left even for a privy break?"

The soldier, now visibly trying not to laugh, said, "You forget there is a privy attached to the meeting room."

Zena let out a curse. "That certainly does not help me at all. Well, I need to find out what is going on in there," Zena said as she walked toward the guards.

"I am sorry, Your Highness, we are under strict orders by King Talon himself not to let anyone enter without his consent."

"Well, I am your princess and I say you must let me pass this very instant," she demanded.

"I am sorry, Your Majesty, but your authority does not supersede his; he has the final say here."

"I don't care what His Majesty says, I am going to find out what is going on if it's the last thing I do." She moved to walk past the guards, but they stepped in front of the doorway, blocking her way.

She groaned in exasperation. "Get out of my way, you cretins!" she shouted, then kicked one of the guards in the shin. He grunted in pain as the other soldier grabbed her arm. "Unhand me, you barbarian!"

Suddenly, the door to the meeting room opened with a loud creak. The soldiers turned to face the door. Victor Talon poked his head out. The soldiers bowed their heads, and Zena turned away in embarrassment.

"Hello, Zena, how are you? I thought that was you making all that commotion; everyone could hear what was going on out here. I figured sooner or later you would come over to see what was happening here; however, I am quite surprised it took you this long to come pay us all a visit." Zena began to walk away. "Where are you going? I thought you wanted to visit us on such an important day."

Zena stopped in her tracks and turned around. She opened her mouth to speak, but Victor spoke before she could say anything. "Guards, Princess Zena may enter."

The guards bowed their heads and stepped out of Zena's way. Zena continued to stand at the end of the hallway, looking at Victor sheepishly. "Come. It is all right, Zena. Come in."

Zena walked to Victor slowly as he opened the door. She walked into the room with her head low, bracing herself for the scolding that Victor inevitably gave her in these situations. She looked over to Aldar and the rest, expecting looks of scorn, but instead saw several smiles; Danielle Hawk and the scribes seemed to be writing an accord.

Zena jumped as Victor put his arm around her. "I was going to send for you, but you came here just in time," he told her.

Aldar looked up at Zena again, then walked over and gave her a hug. "We did it! The war is finally over."

Zena wrapped her arms around him as a tear ran down her cheek. "I thought I'd never hear those words."

"All is ready, Your Majesty," Danielle said. Victor and Virion read their copies, then nodded. "Very good, indeed," Danielle said with a smile as Victor and Virion shook hands. "Everything will be ready for the signing ceremony tomorrow," she told them. "We will have messengers hang up flyers and make announcements throughout the city."

"Very good, Danielle; very good, indeed," Victor said with a smile. In fact, Zena saw that everyone in the room was smiling. The smile on Victor's face made him look younger. All the stress that had been on his face for the past five years had vanished and he was genuinely happy. Everyone shook hands, an amazing sight to behold.

Virion bowed his head. "Well, it is time for us to retire for the night. I look forward to tomorrow." When Victor walked over to escort them to their rooms, Virion said, "No need. I think we can make it back to our rooms." Victor nodded, and Virion and Maximus, bowing their heads one last time, left the room.

Once the Apollyon men were gone, Victor ran up to Zena and hugged her. Zena gasped. It had been years since her father-in-law had hugged her. When he kissed her cheek, she blushed a little and touched her cheek; he never did that.

Victor laughed gleefully. "What a wonderful day this turned out to be," he said as he pulled away from her.

Isaiah put his arm around Aldar. "Well, I guess this means we will have to get along too."

"I don't know about that. I'm not sure if I could handle that," Aldar said with a smirk as he gleefully punched Isaiah's arm. They all laughed.

It was refreshing to see all the stress leave the room, Zena thought.

Aldar hugged Victor. "I am sorry, Father, for worrying so much. I wasn't sure if this was going to work for a long time, especially after Maximus blew up at you. For a moment there, I thought you were going to throw him out."

"Well, I certainly felt like throwing him out—especially when he accused me of lying," Victor said, winking at Aldar.

"He accused you of lying?" Zena said with a slight smile. Everyone softly chuckled as they gave each other a knowing look.

That must have been the bad feeling Aldar had been having, because with the treaty signed, it was over nothing bad was going to happen, nothing to worry about. *We will have to keep Enoch and Elaine out of sight until Virion and Maximus are far away,* Aldar thought.

"Well now, I think this calls for a celebration. Let's drink!" Isaiah said with a bottle in his hand.

Chapter Twenty-Six

To Sign an Accord

Victor smiled as a large crowd gathered at the palace gates. A large platform had been made quickly for this event, with a table and four chairs set in place for Virion, Maximus, Aldar, and himself to sign the accord. He could hear riders in the distance proclaiming that a peace accord had been struck and calling for people to come to the signing. Then he heard another sound—the sound of complaining.

He turned to face the sound. Sure enough, there were Zena with Aldar, Alana, Aurora, and Hunter. She continued speaking as Aldar let out a yawn. "Well, it serves you right to have a headache. You and your new best friend was up half the night drinking." Victor chuckled to himself as Zena continued to scold Aldar, and he watched as Isaiah walked up behind Zena and put his arm around her, causing her to jump and scowled at him.

"Would you rather we would still not get along?" Isaiah asked.

Zena pulled away, then looked at Aldar and back at Isaiah, and sighed. "I guess you are right." She kissed Aldar's cheek. "I guess I cannot fault you all on such a momentous occasion."

Next came Virion and Maximus with smiles on their faces. Victor was happy that they were happy as well. The negotiations for peace had not been easy, but the fact that everyone was happy with the accord was amazing.

Virion walked up to Victor and shook his hand, saying, "Well, the time has come."

Victor patted Virion on the back as they shook hands, and he smiled at Maximus, who also smiled. "I pray this peace will be an everlasting one, Virion. As soon as it can happen, I wish to speak with Xavier again."

"I was able to speak to Xavier briefly. He is quite satisfied with this agreement and will contact you as soon as he can. Right now, there has been trouble with the cystallis; his engineers are working on the problem."

Victor smiled. "I understand, and I am excited to speak with him again soon."

"I hope and pray you will be able to meet with him in person someday, maybe sooner rather than later," Virion said with a huge grin.

Before Victor could respond, a voice called out to him. "Everything is ready," Danielle Hawk announced.

Victor smiled. "Lead the way, Danielle."

She smiled and curtsied. A great applause rang through the streets and across Antillean City as she stood in front of the table. She introduced the royal family as they came to the stage and took their seats. When she introduced Virion and Maximus, the crowd gave them soft but courteous applause. Then the crowd cheered in thunderous applause as Victor and Aldar took their seats.

"Scribes," Danielle called. Two scribes walked up to the stage and set the documents on the table. After giving a long explanation of what the documents contained, Danielle asked, "Your Majesties, are you in agreement?" Victor and Maximus stood up and nodded their agreement. The scribes then handed all four men their own quills and ink bottles. The four took turns signing the documents, and a great cheer arose as they all shook hands.

Victor smiled as the Antillean people cried, clapped, and cheered. *Finally, peace has come*, he thought.

Chapter Twenty-Seven

Celebration of Freedom

"Aurora, are you ready, dear?" Zena asked.

"Almost, mother," Aurora replied. Aurora was excited. It was going to be a big day. The peace treaty had been signed almost a month before, and today, the former slaves were getting their new homes. A lot of planning had been put into place. There was to be a ceremony at the palace's grand plaza, and Grandfather was to give a speech. Then the new Antillean citizens would march over with Grandfather to their new home. She was happy to see these freed slaves live as citizens of Antillean. There were to be food and drink when they arrived. Danielle had done a stellar job arranging the whole thing, and Aurora was going to thank her when she saw her.

Aurora looked in the mirror. Mother had also done a stellar job, on Aurora's new dress, of blue and white silk. Aunt Alana had the same. Aurora had been surprised that her mother had also made the same dress for Elaine. Zena had also made matching jackets for Father, Hunter, and Enoch. This made Aurora incredibly happy. Finally, after all these months, Mother seemed to accept Enoch and Elaine.

"I am ready," Aurora announced as she walked into the living quarters, smiling as she looked at her mother.

Zena scowled at her. "Why your father agreed for you, Alana, and Elaine to wear your swords is beyond me." Zena tapped her foot disapprovingly. "I think it is not ladylike and is undignified." Then she smiled and gave Aurora a kiss on the cheek. "However, my daughter, you are beautiful."

Aurora smiled. "Thank you, Mother."

Zena's smile widened as Aldar walked in, and she then turned her attention to him, straightening his jacket. "I, on the other hand, will not be carrying a sword. I still think it is unladylike."

Aldar kissed Zena's cheek. "That is all right, dear, you already look ravishing without a sword."

She laughed. "Well of course I look ravishing. I wouldn't have it any other way." They both laughed and kissed. "Is Hunter ready?" Zena asked her husband, her face becoming more serious.

"I am here," Hunter said, entering the room.

Zena looked at him and smiled yet again. "You look perfect, child. If only your father could do a better job; I am always fixing his clothes for him." Everyone laughed. "Well, we must get Aunt Alana, Enoch, and Elaine," Zena said.

"It is too bad Bethany couldn't make it," Aurora said. "She has a really bad headache."

Zena gave Aurora an indifferent look. "Well, let us go," she said and led the way out of their living quarters and into the hallway.

After they had met with the others, the group walked to the grand plaza, an enormous meeting place. Today, a raised platform with a podium was set up, with chairs for the royal family. The plaza was surrounded by large walls and balconies throughout. Several hundred excited people were there to join in the celebration.

"Grandfather, Grandmother!" Aurora called out as Victor arrived with a servant pushing Amber in her wheelchair. She gave them both hugs.

"Hello, my little honeybee," Victor said with a smile. He turned his attention to the rest of the family. "My, you all look wonderful today! Zena, you did a wonderful job."

Zena blushed a little. "It was my pleasure, Father; thank you so very much," she said.

"Hunter, my, oh my, you have grown so much this last year! I am so proud of you, young man. Alana, you are so radiant today; you look so beautiful."

"Thank you, Father," Alana said, smiling.

"Ah, Enoch and Elaine! I imagine you two are glad to finally be out of hiding."

They both smiled, and Enoch said, "Yes, indeed. What do you think, Elaine?"

Elaine's smile widened as she replied, "For sure, indeed."

"Where is your beau?" Amber asked, giving Elaine a wink.

Elaine laughed. "He is on duty today, making sure the guards under him are doing their job. He is in charge of the interior of the palace today; otherwise, he would be out here on duty. He hopes to be here for the feast."

Victor nodded. "Well, I certainly hope he will be able to make it to the feast."

Elaine also nodded. "I hope so. He has been busy of late, and I do wish I can spend more time with him when this celebration is over."

Victor smiled. "I will see to that personally, young lady," he said with a wink. "Now that you are all here, I have something to say."

All eyes turned to him as the family wondered what he was going to say. "After this celebration is over, Grandmother and I are going on a much-needed retreat." After everyone applauded, he added, "I plan on being gone a month. Aldar and Alana will rule in my stead." Victor slapped Aldar on the back. "It will be good practice for your future king of Antillean. Just don't get too used to it. I still plan on being here a long time, son"

Aldar smiled. "I certainly don't plan to get used to it, Father," he said.

"Your Majesty," called Danielle, approaching the family. With her were what appeared to be four Apollyon teenagers: two boys and two girls. Danielle bowed her head. "Here are the four teenagers you have selected to speak."

"Thank you, Danielle," Victor said, and his liaison curtsied and walked off. "Very good, indeed," Victor said, then introduced the speakers to his gathered family. "This is Ivan, Allan, Julia, and Olivia." All four bowed their heads to the family. "They will be sharing the stories of their experiences as slaves, and I am looking forward to it."

The Apollyon teenagers nodded, and one of them said, "It is our pleasure, Your Majesty."

"Thank you," Victor replied. "This is a momentous occasion. I pray this will be a stepping-stone for future freedom." The Apollyon teenagers nodded again and smiled, as did everyone else.

"Your Majesty, it is time," said Danielle, approaching again.

"Good, let us get this started," he replied and led the group to the platform.

~ ~ ~

Elaine smiled, happy to see Victor so happy. To her, though, this was bittersweet; she wished Jonathan were with her. She so looked forward to spending more time with him. There was no doubt in her mind that he was the one, and she prayed he felt the same. She wanted to be married to him and to bear him children. She could not wait to see him at the feast.

~ ~ ~

Jonathan walked down the hallway, bemoaning the fact that he was not with his love on such an occasion. He was happy for his countrymen to be free, and he prayed someday Apollyon would no longer have slaves. For now, he had to do his job. He had checked all but one of the guards, the one who guarded the Eye. He himself had done that job before; it was boring. He thought it was also a silly waste of time. At least he rotated the soldiers who guarded the door with other positions.

He had just one soldier guarding the statue, with the chamber door open so people could just walk in and see. Maybe a handful of people would come and see the eye each week, so he supposed it was a good idea for one soldier to be there, but he did not think the Eye was worth all that much, so why would anybody want to steal it? If he had his way, they would just lock up the attraction and open it upon request.

He approached the door. "Sir," a soldier said, saluting him.

"Hello, James. How are you today?" he asked.

James frowned. "I am doing fine," he replied.

"How are your wife and newborn doing today?"

James smiled. "Darla is fine, and our little Charline is well. She just turned a month old."

"I suppose they are at the celebration," Jonathan said.

"Yes, sir, they are. As you know, my wife has helped with the new citizens and wanted to be there."

"You know what? Why don't you go to the celebration?" Jonathan smiled.

James's eyes widened. "Are you sure?"

"Yes, I am sure. Spend time with your wife and child. I will lock this door up and I will take responsibility for this. You will not get in trouble. I plan on talking to His Majesty about this personally. This truly is a waste of time and resources. Enjoy your time with your wife and child."

"Yes, sir!" James saluted him and hurriedly marched off.

Jonathan smiled; this made him feel good. He hoped that would be him someday. He really loved Elaine, and he wanted her to be his wife and, hopefully, bear his children. He hoped she felt the same way; after all, he planned to propose to her after the celebration. He felt for the ring in his pocket. He felt bad for not spending as much time with her as he would have liked. He had worked extra hours so he could get this ring, and he hoped and prayed she would say yes.

Well, it is time to lock up, he thought, moving to extinguish the candles in the sconces. As he did so, he looked up at the statue. "What a grotesque and ugly cyclops," he said aloud.

He heard a noise in the hallway. "James, did you forget something?" he asked, but there was no answer. "Must have been my imagination," he told himself. Then he heard footsteps and turned toward the entryway to see a shadowy figure. The figure appeared to be a woman in dark clothing and hood.

Jonathan stared at the figure for a moment. "May I help you?" he asked.

"Yes, I have a question," the dark figure replied and began approaching.

Why did that voice sound familiar? He couldn't quite place it. "If you are looking for the celebration, it is in the plaza," he said nervously.

"I am sorry about this, Jonathan," the dark figure said.

His eyes widened as he recognized the person, and he laughed. "Why are you dressed in that getup, and why are you sorry?" Without warning, the dark figure stabbed him in the chest. His eyes bulged in shock, and an unbelievable pain shot through his body.

As he fell to the floor, the dark figure let out a curse. "I am so sorry, Jonathan. Why did you come here?" the dark figure said, tears running down her cheeks. "Hurry!" she called out.

Two other figures in dark clothing raced in, and one of them climbed the statue and pulled the eye out of its socket. He yelped as it started to glow, and he quickly handed it to the other figure who had come in with him. This one wrapped the eye in a blanket and handed it to the woman who had stabbed Jonathan, who put the eye in a satchel on her back.

Jonathan did not know if he was hallucinating. "Did the eye glow?" He felt weak as he looked up at the woman who had stabbed him.

She took down her hood, tears streaking her face. "I am so sorry, lad; I am sorry I ruined your future with your love."

Jonathan could feel the life leaving his body as he struggled to keep his eyes open. "Why?" he asked. "How could you do this?" Just before his eyes closed, he asked, "Why, Bethany? Why?"

Chapter Twenty-Eight

To Celebrate

Victor smiled as he followed Danielle with everyone else in tow. He had waited a long time for this moment—one of many more, he hoped. A tear ran down his cheek as he looked at his bride being wheeled beside him. It was going to be wonderful to go on a vacation with her. With her disease's slow progression, it was only a matter of time before it killed her. A vacation was going to be complicated with her disability, but it would be worth it.

"My love," he said to Amber, his smile growing broader, "I am almost as happy as I was on our wedding day."

Amber smiled. "Well, if you are almost as happy. Not sure I would handle it if you were happier." They laughed together as Victor kissed her forehead and held her hand.

Finally, they reached the platform, and Victor looked at his family. "What a beautiful sight. I am so happy to share this moment with you all."

"We would not miss this for the world, Grandfather," Aurora said.

Everyone nodded in agreement, and then Danielle, who also was smiling, said, "Well, it is time." She walked onto the platform, and everyone in the plaza cheered. She addressed the crowd, then introduced the king's children and grandchildren, along with Enoch and Elaine, who took their seats as the gathered people cheered and shouted. Danielle then introduced the teenagers.

When Amber was introduced, the crowd roared, "Long live Queen Talon! Long live Queen Talon!" Then Victor was introduced, and the people roared again. "Long live King Talon! Long live King Talon!"

Victor stood at the front of the platform for several minutes, waiting for the people to quiet. He had not seen such an expansive crowd since his coronation. *I will never forget this day as long as I live*, he thought, and then he addressed the crowd. "Welcome to this homecoming ceremony. This is an incredibly happy day, indeed. Today we celebrate five hundred new citizens of Antillean and their new place to live. These former slaves have suffered atrocities and hardships most of us could not imagine." He gestured to the four teenagers waiting to speak. "These young men and ladies have a story to tell you—their amazing story of hardship and survival.

"But first, let me introduce our new fellow citizens." On both ends of the plaza were large doors. They opened, and the five hundred former slaves walked out, smiling. The former slaves all wore robes made especially for this ceremony, with the Antillean symbol on them.

After a few moments, the crowd had settled down, and Victor beamed at the new citizens with pride. "Welcome, citizens of Antillean! Welcome to your new home, and welcome to freedom. You are free from the savagery of torture. You are free from the tyranny of oppression. You are free to pursue happiness in any way you can. You are free to be creative and express yourselves. You are free to go to bed and wake up in a warm bed. You are free to enjoy a sunny day such as this. You are free to love. You are free; you are free. You are free Antillean citizens. You are free."

The new Antillean citizens shouted, "We are free! We are free! Long live King Talon! Long live King Talon!"

After several minutes, the cheering subsided, and Victor resumed his speech. "Now it is time for these young people to tell—" A sharp pain hit him in the chest, and he heard a loud gasp in the crowd. He looked out at the crowd and saw that their smiles were gone. It was like time stood still. He groaned as the pain grew worse, and he looked down to see a poison dart in the right side of his chest. He stumbled.

Aldar ran up to catch his father.

Isaiah, who was monitoring the crowd, shouted, "Assassin on that balcony!"

Suddenly, the freed slaves pulled swords from beneath their robes. "Death to King Talon! Death to Antillean!" they shouted, attacking the crowd. Chaos ensued as Antillean soldiers clashed with the Apollyon attackers. The four teenagers on the platform pulled out swords of their own, and Aurora looked at them in shock. The girl named Olivia charged at Aurora as the others charged at other family members.

Aurora unsheathed her sword. She wanted to protect her family, but Olivia was blocking her way, so she fought. This girl from Apollyon was good; no way was she a slave, Aurora thought as she backpedaled from the onslaught of Olivia's attack. The girl took a swipe at Aurora's head, but Aurora ducked, dodging the attack, and thrust her sword into Olivia's chest. The Apollyon girl crumpled to the ground, dead.

Aurora looked down at Olivia in shock. She had never killed before; it was surreal. How could this be happening? As she pulled her sword from the girl's chest, Aurora looked out at the battle in the plaza. Dead bodies were everywhere. Antillean soldiers were trying to protect the Antillean people gathered in the plaza, and more soldiers were entering the fray.

"Aurora!" Zena's frantic voice broke her out of her stupor, and she turned around to see the other teens dead on the platform.

Aunt Alana was pulling her sword out of one of them. "Aunt Alana!" Aurora yelled. *How in the world was she able to fight while being blind?* she wondered. Then she saw Zena behind Alana. "Mother!" Aurora ran to her.

Zena was shaking violently and had soiled her dress. "Alana, saved me," she said as she broke down in tears.

"Where are Enoch and Elaine?" Aurora asked.

"We're here," Enoch replied.

She looked over to them and saw Enoch wiping blood off his sword. She ran to them and gave them hugs. "Thank the name of Tiban Talon you are all right!" she cried as she squeezed them tightly. Then dread hit her. "Grandfather, Grandmother!" she yelled, leaving her friends' embrace and running toward the podium.

Aldar was there. He had a cut on his arm but was otherwise all right. "No, Aurora," he said, trying to stop her as she ran past.

Aurora looked at her grandmother crumpled dead on her chair. Her throat had been slit. Her nurse lay next to her on the floor, dead, with a knife by her hand; it looked like the nurse might have killed Grandmother. Danielle Hawk lay dead near them. "I never got to thank her for being such a great friend." Aurora hung her head. She started to feel sick, then turned away from the gore and death and vomited violently.

"My little honeybee," a weak voice said.

"Grandfather!" Aurora yelled as she saw him lying on the floor. A healer sat by his side.

The healer looked at Aurora and said, "I am sorry, Your Highness. He is at death's door." Aurora sat next to her grandfather and held his hand.

"Oh, my little honeybee, I am so sorry. I put too much trust in Xavier Pulsar. The war has restarted. Instead of peace, I have allowed death to come."

"This is not your fault, Grandfather. You wanted what was best for our country; you didn't know."

"Thank you, my little honeybee." Victor managed to smile. "Where is your father? I grow weak; I must see him."

"I am here, Father."

Victor started to cough violently, but after a few moments, it subsided. "My son, I am so proud of you. I soon will be with your mother in paradise, so I need you to listen. I am not sure why this happened. I pray that it will be revealed soon. The road ahead will be a rough one. You will have to make hard decisions. You must have a clear head; don't let hate and anger cloud your judgement."

Aldar was visibly shaking. "I promise, Father, I will not let hate cloud my judgement."

Victor managed to smile. "I guess I am going on a much better vacation with your mother for now. She will be standing with me in paradise."

Aldar stood still in shock, quietly talking to himself. Aurora heard him say, "Why did I not stop this? Why, oh why, did I not stop this?" he muttered.

Suddenly, Victor started to cough up blood, and his breathing became ragged. He turned to Aurora and smiled. His eyes started to flutter violently, and his body started to shake. Then, suddenly, he stopped shaking, his eyes opened wide, and he said, "I love you, my little honeybee." Then he died.

Tears streaked down Aurora's face as she kissed her grandfather's forehead. "I love you, Grandfather," she said.

A soldier approached. "Your Majesty, we must leave the area; you are still in grave danger." Aldar said nothing. "Your Majesty," the soldier repeated.

Aldar snapped out of his shock. "Yes, soldier, let us leave."

As those left alive on the platform gathered to leave the area, Enoch yelled, "Aurora, look out!" as he ran toward her. Aurora turned around to see one of the Apollyon teens aiming a pistol at her. Before she could react, Enoch had knocked her out of the way. The teen fired the pistol, and Enoch grunted in pain.

"Enoch!" Elaine screamed as she ran to her brother's side.

As soldiers quickly subdued the Apollyon teen, Aurora moved to Enoch's side and saw that the bullet had grazed his right arm. "I am all right, just a scratch," Enoch told his sister. "Let's go."

"You saved my life," Aurora said.

"Well, of course I did. That's what close friends do for each other. Now, let us go," he repeated.

They all left the scene as fast as their feet could carry them, leaving the carnage behind.

Chapter Twenty-Nine

Avenged

"Aunt Shiva is avenged!" Pirena said to herself as she ran from her balcony. She was wearing a dress from a servant she killed, she wished she had her battle dress. She was glad that finally, after weeks of being undercover as a former slave, the day had come for her to gain her revenge. She tossed the poison dart gun on the floor; it had done its job. It was fitting that she had used the same gun to kill Victor Talon that Levi Eclipse had used to kill her aunt Shiva. What a wonderful feeling. She was amazed at how lax security was. "The fools really thought we wanted peace," Pirena laughed. It was funny they checked all the soldiers for weapons but never checked the slaves.

She hoped the young people she had hired were able to kill Enoch and Elaine Eclipse. "Cursed little whelps," she muttered. At least she knew that the king was dead and there was no way the healers could hope to save him. The plan that she and Uncle had devised had been wonderful, and she was amazed that it had gone perfectly. Five hundred loyal soldiers had posed as slaves, even willing to have slave marks branded on their necks. They had all known that they were likely to die but had known it would be for the betterment of Apollyon. Before she left the room, she pulled out all her weapons she had hidden under the bed.

Bethany had better have got the eye, or she will face my wrath, Pirena thought as she neared the end of the hallway.

"Stop right there!" a voice shouted behind her, and she heard the click of a hammer being pushed down on a pistol. "Turn around!" the voice demanded.

She did as she was told and saw a soldier. He seemed surprised that she was a woman. "Hands in the air!" he commanded. Pirena did just that as he approached.

The soldier started as he saw the arsenal of weapons on her person. Looking at her closely, he said, "Who in the name of Tiban Talon are you?"

Pirena smiled. "Unfortunately for you, my name is death." Before the soldier could reply, a dagger appeared in Pirena's hand, which she threw into the soldier's throat. The soldier let out a gasp. As he staggered, his gun fired harmlessly into the floor, and then he fell dead to the floor.

Better make haste, Pirena thought. The gunshot would attract others' attention. She made her way to a large hallway that led to a foyer with a large window. That would be her escape. From there, she would sneak to the rendezvous point she and Bethany had agreed upon.

Other hallways led to the same foyer, and as she neared the window, she heard approaching footsteps. She let out a curse; no time to escape through the window. As six soldiers charged into the foyer, she withdrew her swords and assumed a battle stance. The soldiers surrounded her, and one of them asked, "Who are you?"

Before she could reply, a voice behind the soldiers spoke. "She is Pirena Solaris."

Pirena noticed the soldiers' faces turn pale. *I really do have a reputation*, she thought. But who had spoken those words? The voice had sounded so familiar.

The speaker came into sight, and she recognized him. "Isaiah?" she said in surprise.

"She is also known as the Lady of Death, but she certainly is no lady," Isaiah added. He scowled at her. "Well, Pirena, it has been a long time. I see the cut on your cheek I gave you a while back has healed." Pirena touched the scar on her cheek from a wound that he had inflicted on her during the war. "It is unfortunate you escaped before I was able to kill you. This time you will not be so fortunate." Pirena cursed at herself remembering the day Isaiah caught her spying, she was still green.

Pirena gave him a sardonic smile. "I wouldn't be too sure about that."

Isaiah unsheathed his sword. "Oh no, I plan on killing you and putting your head on a spike for killing His Majesty."

Pirena sniffed. "Well, now. That is not very friendly—certainly no way to talk to a lady."

"Like I told my men, you are not a lady. You are a treacherous, filthy, disgusting, insufferable monster."

Pirena laughed. "My, oh, those words really hurt. Please, Isaiah, tell me how you really feel about me. Such talk from such a distinguished gentleman to a woman—no wonder you have never been with one."

Isaiah's face turned red. "That is enough, you wretched harlot. I want you dead." He turned to his soldiers. "Stand down. I wish to fight her by myself."

"But sir—" a soldier protested.

"That is an order!" he yelled.

The soldiers stepped back as Pirena chuckled. "What is the matter, Isaiah? Did I strike a nerve?"

Enraged, Isaiah shouted and charged at her, his knuckles white as he thrust his sword at her. Pirena dodged the attack and cut his left cheek. He groaned in pain as he ran past her.

Isaiah touched his cheek as blood trickled down his face. Pirena smiled. "Tit for tat, my friend."

Isaiah frowned. "You are not my friend," he growled. This time, his attack was not so reckless. His sword clashed with her two swords. Pirena tried to cut him again, but this time he dodged her attack.

"Not bad for a fat old man. I thought by now you would have lost your touch," Pirena said as their swords clashed again. They went back and forth for several minutes.

Pirena dodged another of his attacks, this time cutting his right hip. Isaiah groaned and held his hip, and Pirena charged for the killing blow. Isaiah dodged her attack, however, and punched her in the face. Her swords clattered across the floor, and Pirena fell hard.

She lay on the floor, her eyes shut, and Isaiah carefully hobbled to her. When he kicked her leg to see if she was unconscious, she did not make a sound. He straddled her, planning to stab her in the chest. He lifted his sword, and she hit him in the groin with her hand. She scrambled to her feet and tried to kick him in the face, but the dress was too long. She punched his face instead, and to her surprise, he fell to the ground, unconscious.

The soldiers only stood in place, stunned, so Pirena quickly ripped her dress, revealing her shorter underskirt, and grabbed her swords. At this point, decency did not matter. The soldiers had collected themselves and were charging her. In one fluid motion, Pirena kicked one of the soldiers across the face and stabbed another in the chest. As she pulled her sword out of that soldier's chest, two other soldiers came at her from both sides. She twirled her razor-sharp swords and decapitated them.

The two remaining soldiers stopped in their tracks. They looked at each other, hesitating, leaving themselves exposed. Pirena stabbed them in their chests simultaneously, and they crumpled to the floor, dead.

She pulled her swords from their chests, then turned to the soldier she had kicked, stabbing him as well. She turned to Isaiah. "Your turn," she announced, but then she heard more footsteps in the distance. She sighed. She had to leave now. She sheathed her bloody swords and opened the window. "Until next time, love," she said as she jumped out the window.

Pirena landed in a tree and chuckled as she listened to the commotion through the window. Although she had not had the chance to kill Isaiah, she took comfort in knowing he would have a scar on his cheek. Not to mention the humiliation of being defeated by her and not avenging the king.

She made her way to the bottom of the tree and hid in the shadows of the palace walls, darting from one spot to the next, carefully planning her moves so as not to be seen. After several minutes, she reached the rendezvous point, under a low bridge that connected two sections of the palace. She looked around but did not see Bethany there. *Where in blazes is that old hag?* she wondered.

At the sound of footsteps, she drew her swords. Three darkly cloaked figures appeared. "Could you be any louder?" Pirena hissed as she sheathed her swords. "You walk like drunken cows." She looked at Bethany, who had tears in her eyes "Why are you crying? Crying is for weaklings."

"I'm sorry, Pirena."

Pirena slapped her face. "That's General Solaris, thank you very much. You have been gone too long."

"I am sorry, General Solaris."

"That is better," Pirena said. "So why the tears?"

"I killed someone," Bethany said.

"So what? I kill all the time," Pirena said.

"I killed Elaine's love." Bethany's tears flowed.

"Quiet, you sow," Pirena scolded. "Why did you get so close to them? You should have never got so close. It certainly has clouded your judgement." Bethany nodded in agreement, and Pirena added, "It does not matter anyway. Hopefully, Elaine is dead with her brother, along with the rest of them."

"What?" Bethany said in dismay.

"You're a stupid idiot. Why do you think I had you steal the eye? Did you think I just waited for you, just twiddling my thumbs? I killed Victor Talon."

"You did what?" Bethany said, her eyes wide. She shook in shock, then anger. "I thought we were just going to get the eye." Bethany clenched her fist and walked toward Pirena, and Pirena reached for her sword.

"Not a good idea, Bethany, especially if you want to see your brother and sister."

Bethany stopped her advance. She bowed her head. "You are right, General Solaris. I am sorry for my actions."

Pirena nodded. "We need to make haste. There are some bushes in front of that wall. I want to see the eye; then all of us can escape."

When they reached the bushes, Pirena said, "Let me see the eye. Did it glow?"

"It did, General Solaris."

"Let me see," Pirena repeated.

Bethany took off her satchel and opened it, then pulled out the eye. A dim glow shone through the cloth.

Pirena pulled the cloth off the eye. The glow was almost blinding. It was mesmerizing. She put her hands on the eye and gasped as a strange euphoria took over. She could feel the power. It coursed through her veins. She felt invincible. She felt immortal. She smiled.

"General Solaris, you probably should figure out how to use the eye. It is really glowing brightly," Bethany said.

Was someone speaking to her? Pirena wondered. Well, it did not matter. She enjoyed this power. It was intoxicating. She was experiencing every emotion at once. She was happy; she was angry. She felt wonderful; she felt sick. She felt nothing; she felt everything. What a strange and wonderful thing.

A scream broke her trance, and she looked at Bethany, who had an arrow stuck in her right shoulder. The two cloaked soldiers who had stolen the eye with Bethany panicked and ran. Pirena heard them scream as gunshots were fired. She could feel something headed her way, and she dodged with supernatural speed as an arrow landed where she had been only a moment before.

Pirena cursed herself. How could she be so careless?

"General Solaris, please come here, and we can escape," Bethany cried.

Pirena smiled. "I think not."

Bethany looked at her in shock. "But my brother and sister—you promised".

Pirena dodged another arrow as she said, "Your brother and sister died a year ago in a cave-in."

"Why, you wench!" Bethany charged her.

Pirena kicked her in the side of the head. "Well, that is too bad for you, Bethany. You were only a tool—a tool I used and don't need anymore."

Bethany groaned in pain. As several soldiers charged in, Pirena took off running. "How to go home?" Pirena asked herself. She could not believe how fast she was running. She felt she could outrun a horse.

Then another feeling hit her, and a chant she did not understand came to her mind. "This had better work, or I am dead," she muttered. She reached a wall just as soldiers approached her from all sides. A soldier pointed a crossbow at her.

Pirena held the eye up high. Time seemed to slow tremendously. She could see the soldier pull the crossbow's trigger, and she saw the bolt approach, slowing almost to a halt. Pirena chanted, then a blinding light flashed, and everything went black.

The soldier who had fired the crossbow yelled, "Where did she go?" He ran to the wall and touched the bolt that was stuck where she had once stood.

Chapter Thirty

Aftermath

Aurora put her hand on her forehead her Head was pounding, and she felt faint. She groaned in pain. She barely managed to keep steady on her feet. She was still in shock, unable to accept what had just happened. One minute, the world had been filled with joy and happiness, and the next, the world had come crashing down around her.

She and her family, along with Enoch and Elaine, were on the largest uppermost balcony, out of firing range of most weapons. They were not to move until things had completely settled down.

Aurora looked out at the horror in the plaza. The smell of blood hung thick in the air like a heavy cloud of misery and dread. The carnage was unbelievable. Bodies of Antillean soldiers, Apollyon traitors, and innocent bystanders littered the plaza. The cries of the wounded and dying were unbearable. Several soldiers and non-soldiers walked around dazed and confused. Thank goodness the Apollyon attackers had been stopped, Most of them lay dead. Only a handful had been captured.

Aurora hoped they would get to the bottom of what had happened. The whole thing made her sick, literally. She felt as though she were going to vomit again, but instead, she began to cry. Elaine walked over and wrapped her arms around Aurora, and they sobbed together.

"I received word that the young man who tried to kill Princess Aurora has passed away," a healer announced, and Aurora heard her father curse.

"One less person to interview," he said, pacing. He had not stopped pacing since they had moved to the balcony, and he kept muttering to himself. He was pale. Sweat beaded on his brow, and he was shaking like it was a frigid winter day. Mother sat on a chair with Hunter and Aunt Alana on either side of her. She, too, looked shocked. Next to them were Grandmother, Grandfather, and Danielle, respectfully covered in blankets.

Enoch was sitting on a chair, a healer bandaging his arm. "I would not call that a scratch, young man," the healer said. "That bullet cut through you good."

Aurora and Elaine left their embrace and walked over to Enoch. Aurora kissed him on the forehead. "Thank you for saving my life," she said.

"No worries. I know you would have done the same for me," Enoch replied.

Aurora hugged him, careful not to hurt his arm, and kissed his cheek. Then she heard another commotion, this one at the far end of their balcony. "What now?" she said. In the distance, she saw Isaiah. Behind him was a woman bound in chains, with two soldiers at her side.

As the group drew closer, Aurora could see that Isaiah was hobbling and was holding a bloody towel against his cheek. Then she yelled, "Bethany!" and ran as fast as she could, stopped in front of them and blocking their way. "Isaiah, what is the meaning of this?" she demanded. She noticed the bloodstain on Bethany's shoulder. "She is hurt. Free her from these bonds immediately," Aurora said, her hands on her hips.

Isaiah looked at her sympathetically. "I am sorry, but I am afraid that is not possible."

"What do you mean, it is not possible?" Aurora screamed. "I need answers," she demanded.

Aldar approached, wide-eyed. "Isaiah, what is going on? Why is Bethany shackled?"

Isaiah bowed his head. "Your Majesty, I'm afraid I have more painful news. Bethany had a part in the plot to kill your father and mother."

Aurora laughed. "You must be mistaken. Bethany would not do such a thing."

Isaiah shook his head. "I have been told she was spotted with Pirena Solaris and two other people."

Aldar cursed. "Pirena Solaris. We were fools. We let our guard down, and that viper struck. How could we be so blind? That is the reason

Xavier Pulsar was not responding to Father's requests to talk; he was pretending his cystallis was not working."

"How do you know that was Bethany with Pirena?" Aurora asked. "It could have been mistaken identity."

Once again, Isaiah shook his head. "She was spotted and identified by several of my soldiers. One of them shot her in the shoulder as she was attempting to escape."

Aurora stood in stunned silence as Aldar spoke again. "What happened to Pirena? Where is she?"

"I am not sure, Your Majesty. Several of my soldiers said she had some sort of glowing object. They had her surrounded as she said something no one understood, and then there was a flash of light. The soldiers were temporarily blinded by the flash. When they could see, she had disappeared. It is a very strange story, Your Majesty. I have my soldiers checking every nook and cranny of the palace. Hopefully, we can find her."

Aldar nodded his approval. "I am afraid I do not have much hope you will find her. She is a master escape artist."

Isaiah took the towel off his cheek. "Believe me, Your Majesty, I know."

"This cannot be true," Aurora interrupted. She looked at Bethany. "Please tell them this is not true." Bethany looked away, refusing to look Aurora in the eye. "Please, Bethany, you are our friend."

Elaine walked up and spoke. "This cannot be true, Bethany. You would not betray us; you are a wonderful person."

Bethany looked back at them, and her eyes widened. Then she burst into tears. She tried to say something but was unable to.

"This cannot be true. Please, Bethany, please say it is not true and you had nothing to do with this," Aurora pleaded.

Bethany looked at Aurora with pained eyes. "It is true, child. I betrayed you and your family," she finally managed to say. "I am sorry. I had no idea that Pirena was going to kill your grandparents. Please believe me." Bethany groaned when she looked at Elaine again. "Elaine, I am so sorry. So very sorry."

Elaine looked at Bethany, confused. "What are you talking about?" she asked.

"Jonathan—it just happened," Bethany said, and Elaine gasped.

"What do you mean, Jonathan? Is he all right? What did you do?"

Bethany hesitated before answering. "I killed him."

"You killed him?" Elaine cried. "Why? Where is he, you murderous wench?"

Aurora stepped forward and glared at Bethany, her face turning red and contorting with anger. "Why, Bethany? We trusted you. You were like a mother to me. How could you do such a thing?" she screamed.

Bethany took a step backward, and then Aurora charged, tackling Bethany. The two soldiers tried to stop Aurora, but she punched Bethany in the face several times.

"Murderer!" Aurora screamed as the soldiers pulled her away. Bethany got to her knees, her nose bleeding freely.

Aurora broke free from the soldiers' grip and kicked Bethany in the face. Bethany crumpled to the ground, and before the soldiers could grab Aurora again, she stomped Bethany's face.

They pulled her away, and she screamed, "I want that traitor dead!" as she continued to fight against their grip.

"Enough, Aurora!" Aldar commanded, but his daughter ignored him as she continued to struggle.

"No, Aurora," said a voice in front of her. She had been so busy fighting the guards that she had not noticed that Enoch had walked between her and Bethany.

Tears streamed down Aurora's cheeks. "I want her dead. She was involved in Grandmother and Grandfather's deaths. She killed Jonathan; I want her to die for all she has done. I want justice!" she screamed.

"I know you do," Enoch said. "She will be tried, and I assure you justice will be served, but not this way, Aurora."

Aurora screamed, "She killed Jonathan, and I want her to hurt."

"I know you do, but this is not who you are, Aurora. I know you want justice, but what you want at this moment is revenge." This caused Aurora to pause. "Aurora, you are not the only one in pain here," Enoch said, nodding to the side.

Aurora looked at Elaine, who was lying on the floor, sobbing, "My Jonathan!" Aurora stopped struggling.

"Let her go," Enoch told the soldiers. They did so, and Aurora wrapped her arms around Enoch.

"Thank you, Enoch, you are a true friend."

Enoch grunted in pain and wrapped his left arm around her. Aurora turned and extended her hand out to Elaine, who got up and embraced them both. The three of them sobbed together.

Without any warning, Aurora started to collapse. Enoch managed to keep her from falling to the ground. "Aurora!" Elaine shouted.

"Get a healer," Aldar commanded.

A healer approached as Enoch lay Aurora on the floor. The healer touched her head, then put his ear to her chest, and then looked to Aldar. "She will be all right. She just passed out, probably from stress and exhaustion. She will be fine; she just needs rest."

Everyone sighed in relief. "What is the condition of Bethany?" Aldar asked.

Another healer who was examining Bethany said. "Well, Your Majesty, she took quite a few blows to the head. She is unconscious. I think her jaw may be broken. We will have to get her to an examination table. I have seen this kind of blow before. Time will tell if she recovers or not."

Aldar gritted his teeth. He could not fault Aurora for being so angry, but because of her anger, they might not be able to find out why Bethany had done this.

Several soldiers approached with gurneys, on which they placed Victor, Amber, and Danielle. Everyone stood and bowed their heads in respect as the three were carried away.

Aurora was placed on a gurney after this, and Aldar commanded that she be taken her to her own quarters. Elaine, Enoch, Zena, and Hunter followed the soldiers who carried Aurora, but Aldar stopped Elaine. "I promise you we will find Jonathan. I will order soldiers to try to find his body." Elaine nodded as Aldar hugged her. "We will get to the bottom of this, I promise. Jonathan was a good man; I am truly sorry."

Elaine nodded, wiping tears from her eyes. "Thank you," she managed to say as Aldar kissed her on the cheek.

After Elaine had walked away, Aldar turned his attention to the healer monitoring Bethany, now on a gurney. "We will update you on her condition and we will let you know when or if she awakens," the healer said.

"Very good, thank you," Aldar said. The healer nodded and left with Bethany, leaving Aldar and Isaiah by themselves.

Isaiah looked at Aldar sympathetically. "No one is here. Soon, you will be king. This might be your last chance for a while," he said, opening his arms.

Aldar looked at Isaiah, surprised, and then the wall he had put up came crashing down and he shook violently. He wrapped his arms around Isaiah and cried. "I should have done better. I should had stopped this. I knew something was wrong, but I could not figure out what, so I just ignored it. This whole thing was just a farce; they wanted to kill us all so Xavier could finish his conquest." He pulled away. "Thank you, Isaiah; I needed that."

"No problem, Your Majesty. I know we have had our differences, but I am here for you. I will fight by your side; you have my full and utter loyalty. I will fight for you; I will fight for our people. I will help you figure out for sure why this happened. We will defeat Xavier Pulsar, no matter what."

Aldar put his hand on Isaiah's shoulder. "Thank you. Together we will make my father and mother proud. We will avenge them and all who died and bring peace and prosperity back to our land. This I pledge my life to."

"Sir!" shouted a soldier, who bowed his head as he approached. "Your Majesty, we have searched everywhere; no sign of Pirena Solaris."

Isaiah snorted. "Well, she must be somewhere. I know what everyone saw—that flash. It must have been some sort of trick; she could not have disappeared. I have new orders; spread the news: I need whoever can look for General Jonathan Morrison. He apparently is dead."

"Yes, sir, we will start looking," the soldier said. "I will let others know." The soldier saluted, then took off quickly.

"Well, Your Majesty, I must be off to find out how many men we lost."

Aldar nodded. "As soon as we can, we need to call a meeting," he said, then added. "Please, Isaiah, you can call me Aldar. I don't want that to change."

Isaiah smiled and then walked off, leaving Aldar by himself, and he watched as soldiers moved bodies out of the mass of dead humanity in the plaza. He wanted to scream. He wanted to cry. He wanted to lie on the ground and pound his fist. But no, he was going to have to be strong, so he stood up tall and straightened his crown. He needed to tend to his family, so he walked straight and tall with all the weight of Antillean on his shoulders.

Chapter Thirty-One

The Legend

A*m I dead?* Pirena asked herself, her eyes still closed. She still held the eye, cradled in her arms. She felt no pain, no arrow embedded in her chest, and heard no cries of the soldiers. There was only silence. She slowly opened her eyes and looked around. All she could see were blue skies and clouds. *Am I in heaven?* she wondered. *There's no way I am in heaven. I have too much blood on my hands. I have caused too much pain and suffering.* It was so peaceful and quiet. Where was she?

She looked down at her feet, but all she saw was white. It looked like she was standing on a cloud. She noticed that the cloud was moving beneath her feet, and she watched in wonderment as it slipped past her. She let out a gasp, then screamed as the cloud moved on. She was hundreds of feet in the air. She panicked, trying to wrap her body around the eye, scrambling, afraid she was going to fall. After what seemed like several minutes, however, she gained her composure, finally realizing she was not going to fall.

She saw the Talons' palace below, and thousands of soldiers scattered throughout Antillean City. They looked like scrambling ants. "Looking for me, no doubt," she said aloud, then laughed. "Stupid fools!" she shouted.

She could not believe it—Uncle was right; the legend was true. The euphoria she felt was amazing. Uncle had given her the book about the eye to read, and she had laughingly said, "How could Uncle believe this nonsense?" But whether the legend was true had not been as important as her true mission.

She had found out from Bethany, who had been a useful informant, that the Talons had Enoch and Elaine Eclipse. *Stupid old fool. All I had to do was to give her false hope that she would see her brother and sister again.* Then when Bethany had found out that King Talon had personally hired

Levi Eclipse to assassinate Uncle . . . priceless. Now the icing on the cake was that the legend of the Eye of the Cyclops was true. *I could fly down there and kill that old cow and put her out of her misery.* That was one thing she could do for Bethany; she could give her that mercy, she supposed.

She could also go down there and kill anyone in the Talon family who had survived; she could kill everyone there. Now that she thought about it, she realized she could take over the world by herself; she could rule. She did not need Uncle; she could try to revive Aunt Shiva and let Uncle rule Apollyon, and she could have the rest.

"What am I thinking?" Pirena said to herself in shock. "The eye is affecting my mind. She loved him and could not betray him. "I must make haste and bring the eye to Uncle."

She looked at the eye in puzzlement. "How exactly does this thing work?" She remembered thinking about escaping earlier, and how those strange words had formed, and she had spoken them. Now she was high in the air and was safe, so it must have to do with what she was thinking or what she was wishing for, she decided. She raised the eye over her head. *I want to see Uncle,* she thought, and chanted more strange words. Nothing happened. Then she started to streak across the sky. Once again, panic filled her heart, but soon, panic was replaced by happiness. "This must be what is like to be a bird," she laughed. She flew through the sky faster and faster. She flew past the majestic mountains, and she did not feel cold. She flew past the plain where the first battle had commenced, where Uncle had lost his eye. She flew at lightning speed, and she could see her uncle's palace in the distance getting closer. Once again, she smiled gleefully. "Uncle, I am coming!" she yelled when the palace was in full view.

~ ~ ~

Xavier Pulsar paced back and forth in front of Shiva's dead body. He had had her, in her glass coffin, brought to one of his spare rooms, where her coffin sat on a large platform. He walked up and looked at his love, still beautiful as ever. Her body had been preserved by healers who used a special chemical that kept it in a frozen state. After the seal of the coffin was broken, however, he would have only an hour to revive her before her body would start to decompose. He would not need an hour, he thought with confidence.

He had had a craftsman build a holder out of the marble material that neutralized the eye so he could place the eye in it when not using it. He had learned that the name of the material was tsundium, though it really did not matter to him what the name was if it worked. He sweated profusely as he continued his endless pacing. It had been at least two hours since he had spoken to Pirena via cystallis, and the waiting was excruciating. He had no idea if Pirena had been successful, but he hoped he would know soon. Either she was going to walk through his door or she was going to contact him and let him know of the failure. Worse, he might not hear from her at all, which would mean she was dead or captured. He would have a lot of explaining to Victor Talon if that were the case, but no matter, he could handle the old fool. He also knew Maximus and Virion had just made it into Apollyon, so at least he did not have to worry about them.

He looked down at Shiva and smiled. "Soon, my love, you will return to me, and we can live in happiness." Then he frowned. "I am a fool. I sent our son and my dear friend on a fool's errand that could have endangered them both. I sent Pirena to kill the Talon family and those Eclipse brats. Even if she were successful in killing them, if the eye did not work, it would be for naught. This war will go on indefinitely and the wrath of the Antillean army will be upon me. What was I thinking, believing in such rubbish? What a fool I am for endangering everyone for such a folly." He hung his head. "I know you were never happy, my love. I am sorry. I did want you to be happy."

Suddenly, he could sense something wrong. Something was off. He did not know how he knew, but he knew something was about to happen. He gasped and felt a chill go down his spine as a great light appeared in front of him. He fell to his knees, knowing it was the wrath of God coming to judge him for all his sins. "I know I am a horrible person.

Please have mercy on my pitiful soul!" he cried out. Then the light started to take the shape of a woman holding an object in the air.

The light faded and the figure stepped forward. "Hello, Uncle," Pirena said with a smile.

Chapter Thirty-Two

Never Hold on to Anger

"I am not sure I can trust them," Zena said. "If Bethany was a spy, how do we know Enoch and Elaine are not? They might just pretend to be them, and the real Enoch and Elaine might be dead." Zena paced in their living quarters. She had been on edge since the attack.

"Zena, you know that is impossible," Aldar said calmly. The medallion proved they were the real Enoch and Elaine Eclipse. You are not thinking logically. If they were a part of this, they would have drawn their swords and attacked us. Enoch took a shot in the arm saving Aurora. They are wonderful children, and I love them like they are our own."

"Well, I still don't trust them. They are from Apollyon, and all Apollyon people are evil."

"Now, Zena, you know that is not true. The Apollyon people have been oppressed under Xavier Pulsar's rule. Yes, these soldiers that attacked were evil, and of course Pirena is as well. They were working for Xavier. They are good and bad Antillean people. The point is you should never place an entire race of people in the same category.

"Right now," he continued, "Enoch and Elaine do not need this, especially Elaine. We have not found Jonathan, and it has been a day now."

Zena scowled at Aldar. "I am sorry, but I will never trust anyone from Apollyon again, including Enoch and Elaine." Aldar stormed over to Zena, who gasped as he grabbed her by the arms and shook her.

"What is the matter with you? Why do you have to be so stubborn and bullheaded? I know you are hurting, and your trust has been broken, and I understand that. Bethany's betrayal hurt us all—especially Aurora—and it hurts bad, and I understand your mistrust. But I will not sit idly by and have you accuse Enoch and Elaine of treason. They love us and are there for us."

He stopped shaking his wife as she started to cry. "I am sorry; I did not mean to hurt you," he said gently. He had been angry at her before, but not like this.

"You don't need to apologize, Aldar." Zena wrapped her arms around him. "You are right, I am stubborn and bullheaded, and it has clouded my judgement. I am sorry for doubting them. I really do love them; I just hurt so bad."

Aldar kissed her cheek. "I know, my love. I know this is hard right now, but I swear we will overcome."

After several minutes, they left their embrace. "Thank you, my dear, I really needed that," Zena said.

Aldar looked at her, surprised. "You are thanking me for shaking you?"

Zena smiled at him. "Yes, I am. I needed to have some sense shaken into me and for me to realize how much I really do love Enoch and Elaine."

Hunter came into the room just then and saw the tears in his mother's eyes. "Are you all right, Mother?" he asked.

"Yes, I am, Hunter. All things considered; I am all right. Is your sister up?" she asked, wanting to change the subject.

"No, Mother, not yet. I have not heard so much as a peep since she went to bed last night; she was pretty tired."

Zena moved to leave the room to check on Aurora, but Aldar said, "I will check in on her. Sometimes a girl needs her father." Zena nodded as he left the room. Down the hallway, Aldar softly rapped on Aurora's door.

"Come in," Aurora said, so softly that he barely heard.

He walked in gingerly and looked at her. Aurora was lying on her back on her bed, dressed in black, as everyone in the kingdom was. He forced a smile as he looked at her. "How is my lovely daughter today?" He groaned as Aurora rolled her eyes and turned onto her side to face away from him. "I am sorry, that was a stupid thing to say."

She turned back to him with tears streaking her face. "It is all right, Father; you were just trying to cheer me up." She crawled out of bed and hugged him. "Oh, Father, I am sorry."

"What do you mean?" he asked, confused.

"I am sorry for the way I acted yesterday and for attacking Bethany. I was so angry at her; I could not control myself. I hurt her badly, and it is not in my nature to do that to anyone." She pulled away from him.

"Bethany was part of this assassination, and she hurt us all," Aldar told his daughter. "I understand your shock and anger, and I do not fault you in attacking her. I might have done the same."

Aurora trembled as she looked into his eyes. "I am scared, Father. I am so scared. I killed someone. I had never done that before, and it has shaken me to the core. I have never hurt someone. I was so angry, I wanted to rip Bethany's eyes out of their sockets. I am afraid I will never be the same; I am afraid I have become a monster. I am afraid that I will always be angry, and I will never be happy again."

Aldar touched her cheek. "I am afraid that you will never be the same again, Aurora. What happened to us is life changing. You will have times of anger, and there will be times that will be appropriate. We need to be angry for what Xavier Pulsar and Pirena Solaris have done, and they need to be brought to justice. However, we must change that anger into determination and not let it take over our lives. If you are angry all the time, it will fester in your heart, mind, and soul and it will eat you alive. I want your grandfather to be proud of us, and I will do everything in my power to win this war—not for revenge, not for anger, but for justice for your grandparents, for us, and for Antillean."

Aurora hugged him again. "Thank you, Father. I love you so much."

"I love you too," Aldar told her.

A knock on the door interrupted their embrace. "Come in," Aurora said.

The door opened, and Enoch and Elaine came in. Aurora rushed to Elaine and wrapped her arms around her friend. They hugged for a long time. Then Aurora hugged Enoch and kissed him on the cheek. "Thank you for stopping me," she told him.

Enoch smiled. "That is what friends are for. I know you would have done the same for me."

Aurora smiled back at him. *Would I have stopped him?* she wondered. She was not sure she would have.

"We came to check on you; we wanted to make sure you were all right," Elaine said.

Aurora looked at them fondly. "You truly are good friends. You both have suffered tremendously and then take the time to check on me.

"Well, you all," Aldar said, speaking up from Aurora's bed, "I must be going. I have a busy day; Zena and I have funerals to plan and a coronation to prepare. Of course, there is a war to prepare for as well."

The three young people nodded somberly at him, for they knew the coming weeks were going to be long and painful.

"Aldar, there are soldiers here!" Zena called out from down the hall, and Aldar hurried to the door of the family's living quarters.

"Your Majesty, Bethany Dawn has awoken. The healer says her jaw is bruised and she can talk, although not very coherently. He is also not sure she is going to live much longer. Bethany requested that Elaine Eclipse and Princess Aurora Talon see her."

"I'll be ready in just a minute," Aldar heard Aurora say behind him. He looked back at Aurora and Elaine with concern in his eyes. Seeing his concern, Aurora looked at Elaine, and they both nodded. "We are coming with you, Father," Aurora said.

~ ~ ~

The medical ward was filled with injured Antillean and Apollyon soldiers and Antillean civilians. Aldar, Aurora, and Elaine approached Bethany, who had a healer sitting by her side. They all took places next to the bed.

Bethany's eyes were shut. "Bethany?" Aurora said, and Bethany opened her eyes. Aurora struggled; she felt terrible that Bethany was going to die because of her, but nothing could stop that now.

Bethany's eyes widened when she saw that both Elaine and Aurora were there, as though she had not expected them to come. Then tears started to stream from her eyes. "I am so sorry for what I have done," she said in a slurred voice. "I will not ask for forgiveness, for I do not deserve your forgiveness."

Bethany mumbled as her eyes moved from side to side, and then she seemed to regain her clarity. "Aldar, I am sorry for your mother and father. I had no idea Pirena was going to have them killed. I really am sorry." She started to cough. After she had finished coughing, her voice was a lot weaker, and they could barely hear her. "I am sorry, Aurora; I know you thought of me as a mother, and I know you don't believe me, but I thought of you as a daughter." Bethany began coughing again, this time coughing up blood. The healer put a cloth to Bethany's mouth as the patient gasped for air.

Once the coughing fit had ended, Aldar spoke. "If you had no idea that Pirena was going to do this, what part did you have in it?"

Bethany looked at him with crossed eyes. "I had a different job," she said, trying hard to concentrate.

"Yes, but what job did you have? What responsibility did Pirena give you?" Aldar asked.

Bethany looked at Elaine, and her eyes grew wide. "I am sorry about your love. I did not mean to kill him."

"Why did you kill him? Where is he?" Aldar asked with increasing frustration.

Bethany coughed again, struggling to breathe. "She is fading fast," the healer announced.

Bethany reached her hand to Elaine, and to Elaine's surprise, she took it. "I am sorry," Bethany repeated. Her eyes closed, but they could see she was still breathing. "I am sorry, so very sorry." Bethany's voice was haggard as she continued, "Elaine, he is at . . . he is at . . . " she mumbled, her breath growing shallow, "the cyclops." Then she stopped breathing.

The healer announced that Bethany was dead, and Aldar asked, "What did she say? I did not hear her."

"I am not sure," Elaine said. "Something like 'a clops.' What is a clops?" she asked.

A soldier lying in the bed next to Bethany's spoke up. "I am sorry to interrupt, Your Majesty. I just woke up a little while ago. My name is James. I am sorry to listen in, but you are looking for General Jonathan Morrison?"

"Elaine ran over to the soldier's bed. "You know where he might be?" she asked. "Please tell me."

"I am not sure where he is now, but I was guarding the *Eye of the Cyclops* and he decided to let me go to the celebration. I met my wife and daughter there, and you know the rest. I protected them. Me, I got stabbed, but I will survive."

Aurora gasped, and Elaine looked at her. "What is this eye of the cyclops?"

Aurora gave her a stunned look before she was able to speak again. "I know where Jonathan is."

Aurora looked at Aldar meaningfully, and he nodded. He called for a soldier and ordered, "Get a dozen soldiers and have them come with me." He looked at Elaine. "You might not want to come."

Elaine looked at Aldar sternly. "I don't understand where you are going, but I want to be there. I want to see him."

Aldar nodded.

Several minutes later, with the soldiers in tow, they made their way toward the *Eye of the Cyclops*. Aurora and Elaine ran as fast as their feet could carry them, leaving Aldar and the soldiers far behind. Aldar called out behind them, "Slow down! There might be danger ahead," but they ignored him. When they finally reached the chamber that housed the *Eye of the Cyclops*, they found the doors shut. Aurora pulled on the handles, but they did not budge. Elaine joined her, and they both pulled. "They are locked," Aurora said in frustration, and they turned to see Aldar and the soldiers approaching.

Aldar scowled and looked like he was going to scold them, but because of the circumstances, he did not. "The door is locked," Elaine told him, trying to hold back her tears of sorrow and frustration.

Aldar pondered for a moment. Obviously, Bethany had locked the door. "Let us break the door down," he said.

"I have a battle-axe, sir," one soldier announced, pulling the weapon from his belt.

After several minutes of effort with the axe, Aldar broke the doors open. The room was pitch-dark. "Get some candles from the candelabra!" he commanded. The soldiers did as they were told, and once the group had been furnished with candles, everyone walked into the chamber slowly. The faint light glinting against the face of the cyclops made it look even more menacing than usual. The soldiers found the candelabra in the chamber and lit them.

Elaine screamed as she saw Jonathan lying on his back with a knife wound in his chest. She ran to him, fell to her knees, put her arm around him, and cried. Aurora went to her friend and wrapped an arm around her, trying to give her comfort.

Aldar looked at the scene before him, unable to believe that Jonathan was dead. This whole situation made no sense. Jonathan had been a good man and had loved Elaine with all his heart, and he had told Aldar that he had bought a ring for her. Jonathan's death angered him so that he did not have the heart to tell Elaine about Jonathan's plans. Why would Bethany kill Jonathan, and here of all places? It made no sense no sense at all.

His thoughts were interrupted when Aurora pointed at the cyclops and announced, "The eye of the cyclops is gone." Everyone looked at the cyclops, and sure enough, the eye was gone.

"What in the world?" Aldar said in disbelief. "Bethany killed Jonathan for a rock?"

"That's it," Aurora said. "Not only did they kill Grandfather and Grandmother and tried to kill us, but they also came to steal the eye. I remember when I was a child when Bethany took me to see the eye, I was terrified. She told me the story of Ivan Albatross, the eye and its power, and how our ancestor Tiban Talon defeated him. She even gave me a book about the legend, *The Eye of the Cyclops*. It was quite intriguing."

Aldar shook his head. "That is just it, Aurora—it is a legend, nothing more. It is an exaggerated story."

"Maybe, Father, but what of the witnesses reporting Pirena holding a glowing object and running at inhuman speeds, dodging all of those arrows? The fact she was surrounded, and she held that object up high and spoke strange words? Then the bright flash of light and she just disappeared as the arrow that the soldier fired hit the wall?"

Aldar scratched his head. "Unfortunately, I have not paid much attention to this legend; you know a lot more than me. But now that you mention it, it is very odd indeed that Pirena had that glowing object and did all those things."

Aurora walked closer to the statue and pointed at the empty eye socket. "That is what Pirena had in her hands, the eye of the cyclops. It makes sense. She sent Bethany to steal the eye while she went over to kill us and had those soldiers posing as slaves to create a distraction."

Elaine stood up. "And it cost us all. You lost your loved ones and cost my love his life."

Aurora ran over and hugged Elaine. "I am sorry. I did not mean to ignore you or be insensitive."

Elaine kissed Aurora's forehead. "You were not being insensitive; you were just trying to figure things out. We need to figure out what is going on, why this happened, and what to do next."

Aurora nodded and turned to Aldar. "This is very serious, Father. The kingdom is in grave danger. I will have to go to my library and get that book. It explained what powers the orb gave Ivan Albatross. I have not read it in a long time, but I do remember it gave him power over nature. He could disappear and reappear in thin air; he created those cyclopes. They wreaked havoc across the land and thousands of people died." She paused, then her eyes widened, and she stood in stunned silence. She looked like she had seen a ghost.

"What is it, Aurora? What is wrong?" Elaine asked.

"Oh my. Pirena Solaris stole the eye so Emperor Pulsar can bring Shiva back to life."

"Did you just say what I thought you just said?" Aldar asked in disbelief. "Xavier Pulsar wants to bring Shiva back?"

"Yes, Father, I did. In the book, Ivan had Tiban dig up his wife and attempted to revive her. Tiban stopped him and killed him with the eye before he could do it, so it is unknown if such a thing could be done. That is why the eye sat in that statue all this time—the statue is made of a type of marble named tsundium. It neutralized the power of the eye. How it did that was never determined, but now that power has been released."

Aldar pondered for a moment before speaking. "Well, that all makes sense. Unfortunately, there's not a lot that can be done now. We have funerals to prepare for and my coronation; then I'll meet with my cabinet. Then we will have to plan our next move in the war and hope that we can overcome this."

Several soldiers, who had left to find a gurney, came back in with one, on which they placed Jonathan. When they picked up his body, something fell out of his pocket. A small box hit the floor and opened, and a ring rolled out of it. Elaine picked the ring up and looked at it curiously. Aldar walked up to her and kissed her on the cheek. "I am sorry, Elaine. Jonathan was going to propose to you. He loved you so much."

Elaine looked at Aldar, shocked, and then her tears flowed again as she hugged him.

Aldar stood and held Elaine as she cried. Much needed to be done at that moment. Aldar was now the most important man in Antillean. He had decrees to make and a war to fight, but at that moment, Elaine needed a father.

Chapter Thirty-Three

A Parting of Ways

Maximus Pulsar sat in the carriage alone, his arms folded in frustration. He felt like breaking something. What he really wanted to do was break Virion Nebula's neck; he hated that old man. His thoughts went back to the night before. They had just set up camp for the night, Maximus relieved at having entered Apollyon. At least if Pirena failed in her mission to get the eye, he and Virion would not be caught.

He had thought about the Talon family. They were a very lovely and nice family, and he was jealous. He had no siblings, only he and his father, and he wished his father could be at least a little like King Talon. It saddened him that if the legend were true, Father would enslave the Talons, but at least they would stay a family. He also wondered about the fate of Enoch and Elaine Eclipse, as Victor had had no idea where they were. Maybe if the eye worked, Father could seek them out, capture them, and execute them.

In many ways, he hoped the eye would not work, for what Father planned—to revive Mother—made his stomach turn. It was not natural. Mother had died. That was the nature of things, and reviving her would be an abomination.

Maximus had sat in front of the campfire with Virion by his side reading some book about battle strategy, when a soldier had approached. "Sir, I have a handwritten message from one of General Solaris's spies. I apologize, sir, for not calling you to the portable cystallis; the spy had fled the palace and was in a rush as not to get caught."

Virion had scowled. "Not ideal, but under the circumstances, I guess I have no choice but to accept the message." The soldier had saluted and handed Virion the note. Maximus had looked at Virion, curious about what the note said. Virion had read the note, stone-faced, then, when he finished, had worn a thin smile. "What did the note say, Virion?" Maximus had asked.

Virion had ignored the question and stood up. "I have an announcement!" he had shouted. All the soldiers had gathered around, quiet. "I have good news and some bad. Pirena was successful in her mission. King and Queen Talon are dead." Maximus had looked at Virion, shocked. "It has not been confirmed if any other members have perished, or their wards. It has not been confirmed but looks as though Pirena's servant was able to steal the eye. Pirena was seen running with some sort of object and was being chased by Antillean soldiers. She apparently has disappeared without a trace and there is a massive search for her. "In short, the assassination of King Talon was successful, and the fate of General Solaris and the eye is unknown. Let us pray if the eye works, Emperor Pulsar will kill any surviving members. That is all."

Maximus had sat in silence as all the soldiers dispersed and Virion walked over and sat next to him. They had sat in awkward silence, Maximus was angry—incredibly angry—feeling like he was going to explode. He had stood up and yelled, "What in the name of Apollyon is this, Virion? Did you know that this execution was going to happen?"

Virion had nodded calmly. "Yes, I did. I am sorry, boy, but it was your father's command."

"I can't believe Father lied to me. Why did he lie to me? Why did he lie to me?" He had pointed an accusatory finger at Virion. "You lied to me." Virion had only nodded. "Why did he do this? He promised me he would not have any of them killed. Why? I don't understand. Father said Pirena was going to steal the eye and was not to have them killed. They are good people. When I get home, I am going to give him a piece of my mind, I am so mad. He had no right to do what he did without telling me! If he were here right now, I would hit him, I hate him so."

Virion had stood up and slapped Maximus. "Never talk that way about your father. Have respect."

Maximus's face had grown dark. "I've had it with you, old man." He had tried to punch Virion in the face. Virion had dodged and punched Maximus in the face and then in the stomach. Then he had punched Maximus in the face again. When Maximus had groaned and fallen to the ground, Virion had kicked him in the side.

Soldiers had run up, but Virion had waved them away, telling them, "I can handle this. You are a spoiled, ungrateful little child, Maximus Pulsar," Virion had said as he had sat down beside the groaning Maximus. "Your father did what he had to do, what is best for his rule, and unlike you, he knows how to rule. He will not admit it, but he knows you are weak. He has no faith in your ability to be a good ruler. He lied to you because he wanted to pacify you. He hoped this was going to be a good experience for you. I am afraid he would be extremely disappointed in you; you are a failure. I admit King Talon was a nice man; he was a wise and compassionate man, and believe me, it made this difficult even for me."

Maximus had made his way to a seated position and wiped blood from his mouth with the back of his hand. When Virion stood, Maximus had spit blood on Virion's shoe. "You little whelp!" Virion had roared and kicked Maximus in the face. Maximus had howled in pain as Virion had turned him onto his back. Virion had stood above Maximus and scowled. "This is exactly why your father has no faith in you; you have no insight. Victor Talon was a nice man, but he was not perfect, and he was not as truthful as he seemed. You apparently did not catch what I said earlier that it was not confirmed that the rest of the Talon family or their wards survived. He lied to you and me. He had Enoch and Elaine at the palace all along. They were hiding in the Talon quarters."

Maximus had looked at Virion in disbelief. "Surprised?" Virion had asked. "Prepare yourself for another surprise. Victor Talon hired Levi Eclipse to kill your father; that is why your father ordered Pirena to execute him. Your father knew this all along, yet he still had no faith in you to hand you that knowledge."

A tear had run down Maximus's cheek, and he had said, "I am sorry."

Virion had laughed. "You are right, you really are sorry. You are a sorry excuse for a man. You are not a man; you are an overgrown child. Your father would be so angry at you. There you go, crying." Virion had shaken his head. "If I were him, I would rescind your claim to his throne and give it to Pirena."

Maximus had screamed in rage and tried to sit up, but Virion had stomped on his chest and held him down so Maximus had to gasp for air. "I have had enough of your company. Tomorrow, I will leave with half the men. You can follow another path back home. You can even take the carriage; I could use some fresh air. When I arrive, I will tell him of our success and of your failure, and you will have to answer for it."

Virion had lifted his foot from Maximus's chest, leaving Maximus coughing violently as Virion said, "Well, good-night," and then walked away.

Maximus frowned as he folded his arms. Every bump in the road hurt him, thanks to the abuse he had taken from Virion. It was late evening, and Maximus stuck his head out the window to ask, "Driver, how much longer until the sun sets?"

"Another hour or so. We are trying to make as much ground as we can, Your Highness. This trail goes around several forests; it will take longer to get to the palace."

Wonderful, Maximus thought. *I must wait longer to face Father's wrath.* He really hoped the eye did not work. He sat sulking as he looked out the window, then let out a yawn and drifted off to sleep.

When he awoke, the daylight was starting to fade. He looked out his window and started; the scenery had changed dramatically. He looked out the other window. The trail was surrounded by trees. There was no foliage, and the trees were crooked and gnarled. He put his head out the window. "Driver, where are we?"

"I am not sure, Your Highness. We seemed to have taken a wrong turn," the driver said nervously. The soldiers ahead of us are trying to find a clearing. Unfortunately, it is getting dark, and we will have to camp here for tonight."

Maximus sighed. "Could anything get any worse?" he said to himself.

A strange sense of foreboding overtook him, and a chill ran down his spine. Maximus heard a scream echo through the woods and then heard the driver gasp. He could hear crashing trees. "What is going on?" he asked.

More screams and the sounds of gunshots echoed through the woods, and the horses whinnied in panic. The driver screamed with an ear-piercing shriek as a roar shook the carriage and it rolled backward. Maximus panicked. As he reached for the door, the carriage exploded around him, and he flew through the air. He hit the ground hard and screamed in agony, then looked around to see what was going on.

His vision was swimming, but he could make out movement. When his vision cleared, he saw a large dark shadow against the twilit sky. The shadow appeared to have a man in both hands raised over its head. Was that the carriage driver?

The shadow roared and the man screamed as his body was ripped apart by the shadow's hands, then everything went dark.

Chapter Thirty-Four

Prayer for a Cursed Soul

Xavier looked at Pirena with his mouth wide open. He was shocked at the scene that had transformed in front of him. The orange glow from the eye shone around her, giving her a menacing look.

"Are you all right, Uncle? I apologize if I have startled you."

To Xavier's horror, he realized he was in a prone position. Embarrassed, he stood up quickly. "I am fine, Pirena, I dropped something. Oh well, I guess I will find it later." He looked at the eye and immediately forgot his embarrassment. The eye was mesmerizing.

Pirena reached her hands out, offering him the eye. "Here you go, Uncle, please take it. I feel the power taking me over." When he carefully took the eye from her, Pirena felt like she was going to faint, she felt so drained.

Xavier smiled as he felt the power coursing through his body. He could not believe it; the legend was true! His gamble had paid off, and he now had the power to do what he wanted. He could rule the world and he could not be stopped. He chanted a few words and laughed as he floated into the air.

He flew around the room. "I am Xavier Pulsar, and I am ruler of the world, for the world will cower in my presence!"

He returned to the ground and placed the eye on the pedestal that had been crafted for it. The eye stopped glowing.

Pirena looked surprised. "No worries," Xavier reassured her as he took the eye off the pedestal. "It still works. I had the pedestal specially made for the eye. I plan on always having this near me. I cannot always hold it. This will ensure that I will be able to sleep at night—can't exactly sleep with an object as bright as the sun." He laughed. "Come here," he said, opening his arms.

When Pirena ran into his arms, he kissed her cheek. "Now tell me, my lovely niece, what all happened?"

Pirena smiled. "It will be my pleasure." She talked to him for nearly an hour, telling him all that had transpired.

When she had finished her tale, Xavier smiled, then laughed. "I knew that old buzzard would fall for it, and now he is dead. So, you tell me you saw the spy who took care of Amber killed her as well."

Pirena nodded. "I had to escape, so I have no idea if the others I hired killed anyone else."

"No matter," Xavier said. "Once I am done returning my love to me, I shall go over there and kill the rest of them." He looked at Pirena, confused. "Were you supposed to have three others with you, including that slave spy?"

"I know the two soldiers are dead—they were shot—and I am sure the slave got caught. Most likely, she would have been executed by now."

"Well, I guess she is out of luck." They laughed. "Servant!" Xavier called. When a servant appeared, he commanded, "Bring wine." Several minutes later, he and Pirena were sitting at a table, drinking the wine. "I am so proud of you," he told her. "You have done well. You have never disappointed me. Your hard and diligent work will not go unrewarded; therefore, when this is all over, I will appoint you ruler of Antillean. You can rule in any way you wish," he went on. "The land is yours, from the Antillean Mountains to the ocean, it will be yours."

Pirena smiled and stood to kiss him on the cheek. "Thank you, Uncle. I love you so much."

"You are welcome. However, there is one condition to your rule," he said as Pirena resumed her seat.

Pirena's smile faded. "And that is?"

"You cannot wage war against me.' He laughed, and Pirena let out a snort.

"Uncle, you are so funny. Well, the hour is late," Pirena said. "I shall retire. I am going to take a long bath then go to bed. When do you plan on reviving Aunt Shiva?"

Xavier pondered for a moment. "On the morrow. It will take a while to unlock the coffin. I suppose I could do that myself, but I don't want to risk it." Pirena nodded as she got up. "Which reminds me . . . Daniel, get your good-for-nothing carcass in here!" Xavier yelled.

Daniel rushed into the room just as Pirena was leaving. He stopped and stared at her, shocked, then watched in disbelief as she left.

"What is your problem? You've seen General Solaris many times," Xavier scolded him.

Daniel bowed. "I am sorry, Your Majesty, but I thought she was part of the entourage that left for Antillean."

Xavier shook his head. "She was you idiot."

Daniel looked back at the door, then to Xavier. "I thought it was going to be a few more weeks before they arrived back. They are here already?" When Xavier stood up from his chair and walked over to stand in front of him, Daniel cowered. He flinched as Xavier reached out and put his hand on his shoulder. He looked at his shoulder and then at Xavier. When Xavier tilted his head toward where Shiva lay, Daniel gasped. "Is that the eye?" he asked, wide-eyed.

Xavier smiled. "You are in no position to ask me anything; however, today I am going to make an exception. Pirena arrived here with the eye. She flew all the way from Antillean City. It only took minutes. With this power, I intend to take over the world, and there will be peace and prosperity. I know you love Shiva, and she loves you, and there is nothing I can do about it. I love her too. That is why you are alive. I rarely keep my promises—no doubt my son has learned that by now—but I have with her. I plan on bringing her back tomorrow. She is mine and mine alone, but you will be able to see her again. I can only give you that comfort."

When Daniel backed away and looked at the floor, Xavier was confused. "What is wrong? I thought this would make you happy."

Daniel hung his head. "I am sorry, Your Majesty. Hurt me if you will—punch me, kick me, spit in my face, beat me to a pulp. Insult me, humiliate me, or make me a laughingstock. Starve me or take drink away from me. I would rather you do all of this to me than bring her back. I would rather be dead than see her sad eyes and pretend smile." Xavier's face grew dark. "Go ahead, Your Majesty. I don't care anymore what you do to me. There is nothing you can do to me that you have not already done. But please do not do this to her. She is dead, and that is what should be; it is unnatural to bring her back."

Xavier shook his fist and screamed, "You sound just like my ungrateful son, the little snot-nosed brat." He walked over to the eye and picked it up. The orb glowed brightly as he lifted it over his head. "I should blow you into oblivion."

Daniel smiled, spreading his legs and raising his arms into the air. Xavier gaped at him, then growled and put the eye back on the pedestal. "Well, Daniel, I have news for you: I am going to revive Shiva, and she will be happy. I will make her happy. I don't need my son's approval, and I certainly don't need yours. I promised Shiva, I would not kill you, but I never promised her you could ever see her again. Therefore, I am relieving you of your duties as my personal slave. I will give you another assignment. You are not to see her again. I will decide your fate after I am done reviving her. Now get out."

Daniel bowed, then moved toward the door. "You will be cursed in doing this, and I will pray for your cursed soul," he said as he walked out the door.

Chapter Thirty-Five

My Rose of Apollyon

The horizon glowed in pink and purple hues, getting ready for the grand entrance of the morning sun. Looking out from the balcony of his chambers, Xavier smiled. "This is the last sunrise I shall see without my rose of Apollyon." He began to pace the length of the balcony. Soon, the funeral director and his helpers were to arrive, and he was excited. He could not wait to see the life back in Shiva's eyes. He could not wait for her to walk by his side again. He had refused breakfast; how could he eat? He had butterflies in his stomach, for he knew today was going to be grand.

He scowled as he thought of Daniel and the night before. "That good-for-nothing, worthless dog." He had called Daniel in, planning to have him inform the funeral director to meet him this morning. "No thanks to him, I had to do it myself." He snorted in anger.

"What am I doing?" he asked himself. "Today is a happy day." Pushing the negative feelings away, he squinted as the sun finally rose.

When he heard a knock at his door, he walked into his chambers and called, "Enter."

The funeral director and two others came in. "Hello, Your Majesty. Benjamin, the funeral director bowed.

Xavier nodded. "Glad you are here." He led them into the room where Shiva lay, and Benjamin and the others gawked at the eye. Xavier walked to stand behind the eye and smiled, grabbing their attention. "Well?" he asked.

They all bowed. "I am sorry, Your Majesty," Benjamin said. "We will begin our work. We will get this seal broken in earnest." As the servants started working on the glass casket, Benjamin bowed his head. "If I may explain a few things." When Xavier gave him a curt nod, he went on. "Once this seal is broken, you will have one hour, Your Majesty. After that, and because of the process used, Her Majesty's body will begin the decomposition process. Her body will decompose extremely fast. She will need to be buried quickly."

Xavier nodded in understanding. "No need to worry about that." He laughed. "I will revive her on the first try."

After several minutes, the servant stopped and nodded their heads to Benjamin, who smiled and helped them remove the cover from the coffin. A hissing sound filled the air as they pulled the lid off and put it on the floor. "We shall now leave you, Your Majesty," Benjamin told Xavier. "I will return in an hour just in case, Your Majesty."

Xavier laughed. "You may come back in an hour, although that will not be necessary."

Benjamin and his assistants bowed and took their leave, shut the door behind them. Alone with his bride, Xavier walked up to her body and put his hand on her cheek. It was cold as ice. He touched her hair, which felt brittle.

"No matter, my love. You shall return to me, and you will be warm, and you shall love me."

He walked over to the eye and, looking at it, pondered for a moment. The words of his son and Daniel ran through his mind. *It is unnatural* and *I will pray for your cursed soul* kept repeating in his head. Was what he was doing right? Was he being selfish? Would his soul be cursed? He laughed. What foolish thoughts. He loved Shiva with all his heart, and that was all that mattered.

He smiled and picked up the eye and felt its power rage through him. This was it, the time he had waited for. He held the eye over his head. "For you, my love," he said, then thought, *Rise.*

He chanted the words that came into his mind, but nothing happened.

He looked up at the eye, then at Shiva, dumbfounded. Maybe he had chanted the words incorrectly, he thought. "Rise, Shiva, rise," he chanted.

Once again, nothing happened.

He tried several chants. "Rise, my love, rise. I command you to rise, my love." Still nothing.

"Eye, I command you to raise Shiva. I command you to raise Shiva now." Still, nothing happened.

"Please rise, Shiva. Rise I beg you, Shiva. Rise. I love you, Shiva. Rise." Nothing.

In desperation, he shifted the eye so he was holding with only his fingertips and chanted with all his might, "Rise, Shiva, rise!" He heard his voice echo around the room.

He gasped Shiva's body began to shake violently.

He kept chanting and chanting and chanting, and her body shook more and more violently. *It's working!* he thought and smiled. The shaking stopped, and her body lay still.

Xavier continued to chant as his arms grew tired. Shiva's body lay there, limp. Her face wore no expression, and her eyes remained shut. Xavier groaned as he lay the eye on the ground. He jumped as a knock came at the door. He sighed. "Come in," he said.

Benjamin walked in and bowed. "Your Majesty, an hour has passed." He looked at Xavier, then at Shiva. "I am so sorry, Your Majesty. I truly am sorry, but we must bury her immediately."

"No," Xavier said.

"Your Majesty?" Benjamin asked.

"I said no."

Benjamin stood in silence for a while before speaking again. "Your Majesty, she will decompose."

Xavier reached down and grabbed the eye, stood up again, and floated in the air. "I said no, you whelp!" Xavier shouted. "Now get out."

Benjamin scrambled out of the room, and Xavier floated back to the ground and screamed as he threw the eye across the floor. "Worthless rock!" he shouted, then cursed and stormed from one end of the room to the other. "All this planning, all of this waiting, and for what? What was the point of all of this? I have the power to do whatever I want, to go wherever I want to go." He looked at Shiva. "Yet I cannot bring you back to life. What was the point?" He wanted to die. "Life is not worth living without you, my love. I need you back," he pleaded.

He moved a chair beside her and said in it, holding her hand and laying his head on her chest. "My love, my rose, what am I to do without you?"

He drifted off to sleep and dreamed. He dreamed of her being alive. He dreamed of kissing her passionately. He dreamed of early-morning walks together. He dreamed of her angelic smile and her heavenly, amber-colored eyes. Then he dreamed of her dying in front of him, of her weak voice, her rasping breath, then of her taking her last breath.

Xavier jumped as he awoke. He had heard something. What was it that he had heard? he wondered. It was coming from Shiva's chest. Wondering if he was hearing a snake, he sat up and looked at her chest but saw nothing there. He stared at her, wondering how long he had been asleep and surprised because she did not seem to have decomposed yet.

The hand that Xavier was holding moved, and he jumped out of his chair, letting go of her hand as he did so. He looked at the hand, shocked. Was he imagining things?

He jumped again as he heard another noise. He looked at her chest again. Was it rising and falling? In disbelief, Xavier looked over to where the eye lay slowly pulsing, then returned his attention to Shiva.

Her eyes popped open.

Xavier shouted, jumping backward and knocking the chair over. he trembled in fear as Shiva lifted her head. Her eyes were wide as saucers and her face was expressionless as she stared blankly. She turned her head from side to side, and then a horrified look on her face.

Xavier backed away even more as Shiva sat up and looked directly at him. She stared at him for the longest time. Then her eyes returned to normal, and her expression of horror was replaced with confusion.

"Xavier?" she asked, and Xavier jumped again. "What happened? Why am I here?"

Xavier stared at her, not knowing what to say, but her voice—that beautiful, angelic voice—touched him. Xavier trembled, and for the first time since he was a child, Xavier cried.

Chapter Thirty-Six

A Funeral and a Coronation

"Father, I don't know if I can do this," Aldar said with tear-filled eyes as he kissed Victor's forehead. Victor Talon lay in his coffin, dressed in white and wearing his cape, with his crown on his head. He looked majestic in his royal best, and peaceful, as if he were napping. "Thank you, Father. If I become half the king you were, I would consider myself a good king. Thank you for being hard on me when I needed it. Thank you for giving me a shoulder to cry on. Thank you for being such a special grandfather to our children. Thank you, Father, for loving Mother so much." He kissed Victor one last time, on the forehead, and walked to where his mother lay.

Amber was wearing a white dress with a blue shawl. She lay straight in the casket, looking the best she had in years. "Thank you, Mother, for being there for me. Thank you for putting up with all my shenanigans. Thank you for skinning me alive when I did my shenanigans; I certainly deserved it. Thank you for being such a loving grandmother. I know these last few years were hard for you. Despite that, you were always there, giving us all moral support. I will never forget you," Aldar said, then kissed her cheek.

Everyone else in the family had already done their farewells, so Aldar nodded, and the funeral director bowed his head. The funeral director and another man shut the coffins, which were made of maple branded with the Antillean symbol. The caskets were loaded onto two carriages as Aldar and the rest of the family climbed into separate carriages.

Aldar was exhausted. This was his third funeral of the day. Early in the day, they had laid to rest Danielle Hawk. She had served the family for many years and, sadly, had no family of her own. Of course, to them, she was family, so the Talons had all gone to her funeral to support her.

Then Jonathan's funeral had followed. It had been hard. Jonathan had been an orphan and had been raised by his uncle, who had died a few years before. Elaine had sat across from Aldar and Zena, wearing the ring Jonathan had planned to give her, which she had turned into a necklace. She had unconsciously rubbed it, along with the necklace her father had given her. It tore Aldar apart to see her suffer, and he wished he could comfort her, but no amount would be enough.

Bethany had been unceremoniously laid to rest in a common cemetery. Aldar shook his head as he thought of Bethany. It would always be a mystery to him how she could have betrayed them when they had given her so much love.

The carriages finally made it to the royal cemetery, where generations of Talons were buried. Headstones abounded here. He knew Tiban Talon was buried there and told himself that somewhere, someday, he would have to find out where Tiban's grave was within the cemetery.

The carriages came to a halt, and everyone unloaded from them. At the gravesite, Isaiah stood in front of everyone and gave a wonderful eulogy honoring a king and queen who had served their country well. After the eulogy, the caskets were lowered into the ground, and everyone gathered around. They all tossed flowers onto the caskets "Good-bye, Father; good-bye, Mother, until we meet again," Aldar said, tossing flowers into their graves.

Before he knew it, Aldar was at his coronation. Everything was happening so fast; he could hardly believe it. Aldar felt like he was going to topple over as he kneeled on one knee and the priest put a new crown upon his head. "Introducing your new king!" the priest announced. Somber applause echoed across the plaza.

Aldar stood up and looked at Zena, who had just been crowned queen of Antillean. Then he looked over to Aurora, who nodded and mouthed, "You can do this, Father." *I love that child*, he thought as he walked up to the very spot where his father had died. The podium was a different one, but somehow, that different podium did not give him any comfort as he scanned the balconies and the people who were there for the ceremony. It did give him some comfort to see soldiers at every balcony, around the crowd, and at every exit, however. He paused for a minute and took a deep breath before speaking. "Citizens of Antillean, thank you for coming in this difficult time of mourning. Many people died here. I applaud your resolve and bravery for coming to this place of death and sorrow. Unfortunately, during this heinous attack, the eye of the cyclops was stolen—grave news, indeed."

He saw the looks of confusion that he had expected, and he explained to the crowd the legend of the eye, then continued, "We have evidence that the legend is true, and we are all in grave danger." The crowd shuffled nervously.

"As my father before me, I stand here in front of you and speak the truth; I shall never lie. We are facing dark times and even more darkness before this is over, but we must be steadfast. I have attempted to contact Emperor Pulsar myself, and he has not responded to me yet. Unfortunately, Emperor Pulsar has the power to destroy us all. He has the power to enslave us all and take away our freedoms. But he cannot take away our resolve. He cannot take away our will to live. He cannot take away our compassion and kindness. And most of all, he cannot take away our love."

The crowd started to come alive and started clapping. "No matter what Xavier Pulsar does, he will never take that away. I love my family; I love all of you; and I love this land we call Antillean. So, I promise you, as your king, I will fight Xavier Pulsar and his evil horde to my dying breath.

"Together, we will find the eye of the cyclops and we will figure out how to destroy it. We will defeat this evil." Aldar unsheathed his sword and raised it high in the air. "We must prepare, for soon, we go to battle. God bless you all; God bless this land; God bless freedom; and God bless Antillean."

The crowd erupted, cheering, "Long live King Talon! Long live Queen Talon! Long live the Talons! Long live Antillean!"

Aldar beamed with pride as he looked at Zena, who was also smiling. He looked at Aurora. She blew him a kiss and mouthed, “I knew you could do it, Father. I am so proud.”

“Long live the Talons! Long live Antillean! Long live freedom!”

Chapter Thirty-Seven

Shiva

Xavier just stood there in shock as Shiva climbed out of the casket. "What is wrong?" she asked. "I have never seen you cry before." Xavier looked at her with tear streaks on his cheeks. Her eyes were full of concern. "Please tell me what is going on. I am so confused." When Xavier continued to sob, she said, "Xavier, you are scaring me."

Xavier wiped the tears out of his eyes and did his best to regain his composure. "My love, your beautiful voice . . ."

Shiva shook her head. "It is the same voice I have always had. Today is no different."

Xavier looked at her, confused. "Do you not remember, my love? The audience? The assassin? The poison dart?"

"I have no idea what you are talking about. Why did I awake in this casket? I am not dead; please explain." So, Xavier explained all that had transpired: her death, the Eclipses' execution, the fake treaty, the assassination of Victor Talon, and the retrieval of the eye.

Shiva looked at Xavier in stunned disbelief. "Where is Maximus now?"

Xavier smiled. "He should be here in the next ten days or so. He will be so happy to see you."

Shiva smiled. "I knew you loved me, but I never thought you would go to such lengths to bring me back. I never dreamed that the legend was true; it was all just ghost stories to haunt children's dreams." Shiva chuckled.

Xavier looked at his wife in stunned disbelief. They were talking with each other. It felt like a dream. He looked at her and smiled. She looked beautiful; he wanted to touch her, kiss her.

Shiva smiled at him mischievously. "I know that look. You cannot hide that from me." Her smile widened as she approached him. "Kiss me, Xavier."

Xavier's heart fluttered as if it were about to beat out of his chest. Her beauty . . . those amber eyes . . . her long blonde hair. He drew close to her. He paused for a moment, and she smiled. "What are you waiting for? I am all yours," she said.

He grabbed her, wrapped his arms around her, and kissed her. Xavier felt a shiver go down his spine, and he backed away. Her lips were cold. It had been like kissing a corpse.

"What is wrong, Xavier? I thought you wanted to love me." Shiva looked at him, confused.

Xavier looked at her frantically. She did not look dead; her heart was beating, and she was breathing. He touched her hand. It was cold as ice. He quickly pulled his hand away.

"What is wrong, Xavier? Why are you afraid of me? Why do you refuse my love? Why do you not love me anymore?" Xavier said nothing and took a step back. "Why will you not love with me?" Xavier took another step back.

"Why won't you love me?" Shiva yelled in an inhuman shriek.

Xavier saw a flash out of the corner of his eye, and something hit him, knocking him across the room. Gasping for air, he looked in the direction where he had seen the flash of light. He saw only the eye. *Did I just get hit by a bolt from the eye?* he wondered, then noticed the eye was pulsating.

He struggled back to his feet. As he got his breath back, he looked over to Shiva and felt his soul fill with terror. Shiva wore a wicked snarl on her face, and her eyes had turned a reddish-orange and begun to pulsate in sync with the eye. Xavier screamed and ran.

Shiva ran after him at an unnatural speed, and Xavier grunted as she slammed into him. She had him pinned against the wall, with her hands wrapped around his neck. He felt a chill go down his spine as she tightened her grip. He could barely breathe.

"You selfish, self-centered beast! How dare you bring me back to this miserable existence? I curse the day you were born."

"Shiva, I am sorry. I—"

"Silence! I don't need your pathetic insincere apology. You took away from me the man I really loved. You took away my family's freedom and my father's life."

Xavier struggled against her grip, but she was too strong. He stomped on her foot, but she did not flinch.

She shrieked again and tossed him across the floor like he was a toy.

Xavier grunted as he landed. As he scrambled to his feet, another bolt shot out of the eye, knocking him onto his back. He looked at the ceiling; it was spinning. He closed his eyes, trying to get his bearings straight. He tried to get up again, but Shiva placed her foot on his chest.

"Please, my love, have mercy," he pleaded.

Shiva laughed. "Give you mercy? Really? The man who knows no mercy is begging for it. Was not that what you always preached to our poor crying son, that compassion and mercy were for the weak? Look at you now. You are no emperor; you are a pathetic weak little mouse. You make me sick.

"I am going to make you pay for all your sins and transgressions against all of humanity. You must pay for taking my Daniel away from me and the way you treated him. You must pay for what you did to Mother, my sister, and my father. You must pay for making me marry you and forcing your disgusting love upon me. You must pay for the way you have treated Maximus; he just wanted your love, but you just gave him grief. You must pay for all the death, pain, and suffering you have given to the people of Apollyon."

Tears streamed down Xavier's face. "I am so sorry. I am deeply sorry. Please forgive me. Please do not kill me."

Shiva laughed again. "I remember that story long ago about your father begging you not to kill him. You called him weak and pathetic. Is it not amazing when you are in the same position how the tide turns. No,

Xavier, I cannot let you live. You must pay for all you have done, and your punishment is death."

Xavier hit her on the shin, knocking her foot off of his chest enough to allow him to scramble back to his feet.

Shiva smiled. "Go ahead and run."

Xavier ran, but once again, she pinned him against the wall and put her hands around his throat. "You cannot escape me, for I am the lioness, and you are the hare," she said, slowly tightening her grip as she spoke. "I am going to be the sole ruler of Apollyon. Under my rule, there will be tears of joy, not oppression. Anyone who opposes me or tries to oppose me will most certainly die. I will rid the world of vermin like you who taint the world. Everyone will obey me and the eye or die."

A bloodred tear ran down her cheek. "The all-powerful eye and I will bring peace back to this land. I cannot wait." She gave him a wicked, toothy smile. "It is now time to pay. Now you shall die."

Xavier braced himself, expecting her to crush his neck with her icy grip. To his surprise, however, her grip lessened a little. Then he felt a strange sensation—Shiva's hands started to feel warm. They grew warmer and warmer.

To his horror, Shiva's hands continued to warm, until they were hot. Sweat beaded on his forehead as if he were too close to a fireplace. He started to squirm. He had to break loose. He had to get the eye so he could fight back. He screamed in agony as his boots caught fire. In desperation, he clapped his hands around Shiva's head.

Shiva let go, clearly stunned, and he punched her face. She crumpled to the floor.

Xavier quickly pulled his burning boots off his feet and looked at the eye sitting on the other side of the room. He hobbled toward it as fast as he could, yelling in pain from walking on his burned feet. He was getting closer to the eye. Just a few more feet, and he would be safe.

Just a few more feet.

Chapter Thirty-Eight

Chaos

Pirena Solaris walked toward her uncle's living quarters, excited to see Aunt Shiva again. It was midmorning, and she figured she had waited long enough for Uncle Xavier to spend quality time with Aunt Shiva before her visit. As she approached the hallway that led to her uncle's chambers, she saw Daniel. "What are you doing in the hallway?" she asked. "Shouldn't you be serving Uncle Xavier?" Daniel hesitated, so she turned him around and shoved him in front of her.

"General Solaris, I no longer am—"

"Shut up and move," she told him.

He did as he was told.

When they arrived at the door, Pirena scowled. Where were the guards, and why was the door cracked open? Something was off. Uncle always had guards at his door. Pirena drew one of her swords.

Daniel gasped. "I am sorry, General Solaris. I know you are mad at me."

Pirena rolled her eyes. "Shut up," she hissed. "I am not going to kill you, you buffoon. Something is wrong. I think Uncle and Aunt might be in danger." Pirena slowly pushed the door open and walked in, Daniel following.

When she saw two guards lying on the floor, she told Daniel, "Get out of here. You are too noisy. Leave now, or I will kill you myself." Daniel turned around and stumbled out of the door.

Stupid idiot. I should have just killed him, Pirena thought as she checked the guards. They were dead and had strange burn marks on their chests. What had happened here? She looked around the living room. All the furniture was broken. She walked down the hallway that led to the room where Aunt Shiva had laid. The door to the room was shut, so she opened it carefully, her eyes widening as she slipped into the room.

She skirted the room with her back against the wall, noticing that Shiva's casket had been shattered and the furniture smashed. As she continued scanning the room, Pirena drew her second sword. She saw two people lying in the corner, the eye glowing faintly next to them. When she realized the people on the floor were Uncle Xavier and Aunt Shiva, she took a step toward them. She heard a noise in the hallway and turned around, running quickly but silently toward it.

Seeing a figure slowly coming through the door, she was ready to pounce and deal a killing thrust, but she stopped in her tracks. "Daniel, I told you to get out of here, stupid idiot." She glared at him. Before he could react, she sliced off his right earlobe. He screamed in pain as he grabbed at his ear. "That will teach you to listen," she scolded. "It truly amazes me Uncle has kept you all these years."

~ ~ ~

Despite his pain, Daniel noticed the eye in the far corner as it glowed brighter and brighter while Pirena continued to scold him. Then the eye disappeared, and he blinked.

"Are you even listening to me?" Pirena slapped him. A strange feeling filled the room, and it suddenly turned cold.

~ ~ ~

Pirena stopped talking as she realized she could see her breath. Daniel gasped as a figure holding the eye up in the air materialized behind Pirena. He shook in fear and wet his pants. He tried to speak, but the words would not come out. Pirena looked at him quizzically. "Shiva," he finally said.

"Aunt Shiva?" Pirena asked, turning. There was a flash of light.

Part Two

Curse of the Eye

Chapter Thirty-Nine

An Unexpected Reunion

It was a beautiful day in the kingdom of Violida. The rays of the morning sun crept across a mighty sea. Seagulls flew over and landed in the sea, getting their morning breakfast, while fishermen brought in the morning catch. King Barnabas Zanthor looked out at nature's splendor with his wife, Abigail as they sat on their private balcony, enjoying their breakfast of pastries, fruit, and coffee. Morning was the best time of the day; it was when he could spend the most quality time with his wife.

Barnabas was bald and sixty-seven years old. He was strong, short, and stocky, with a barrel chest and brawny arms and feet. He wore a white silken shirt, purple trousers, silk slippers, and a gold crown with purple gems, along with a cape embroidered with the symbol of Violida, a man riding a horse and drawing a bow. Abigail, sixty-five, was a short, thin, wiry woman with long, flowing brown hair streaked with gray. She wore a purple dress, its boddice bearing the symbol of Violida, and a gold tiara and purple-gemmed necklace.

Barnabas sighed. The rest of the day was to be the same as always: talking to village leaders, hearing complaints, and such. He would have his daily audience with the townsfolk, settling disputes and hearing more complaints. To say the least, he had a busy yet mundane life. He raised his hands in the air and yawned.

Abigail smiled. "My dear, the day has just begun, and you are tired already. Do you need more coffee?"

Barnabas smiled back at her. "I am sorry, my queen, but I am growing weary. I need to go on a holiday. We have not gone on holiday since the war broke out between Antillean and Apollyon."

"Well, dear, now that we have heard the war is over, maybe we can see our lovely daughter. We have not seen her in a long time," Abigail said.

Barnabas sighed again. "That is, if she will ever talk to us again. She was very angry at me." Barnabas regretted his decision to not support King Talon in the war against Apollyon. The war probably would have ended much sooner with his army supporting the Antillean army, but he did not want to be at war. Violida had not been at war since its civil war when he was a child. He had seen the horrors of war and did not want his nation to be involved in any war whatsoever.

He missed his grandchildren, however. The last time he had seen Hunter, the boy had been little. Now he probably was a scrapping young lad. Aurora had been just a young girl, and she probably was now a lovely young woman. Then there was his lovely Zena, his young, high-spirited daughter. She was as beautiful as her mother. How he missed her. His last memory of her was of her scowling at him as she and Aldar entered their carriage after he had turned Aldar down.

That decision had cost him dearly—his relationship with the Talon family and his daughter. He had let Antillean down; he had let his friend Victor Talon down; he had let his grandchildren down; and, worst, he had let Zena down.

"What is the matter dear?" Abagail asked. "You were talking, then you stopped and started to stare out at the sea."

"I am sorry. I was just thinking of Zena. I miss her so. I would love to go to Antillean to see her."

A soldier stepped onto the balcony and bowed. "Your Majesty, I have an urgent message from Zena Talon. She is waiting for you via cystallis."

Barnabas looked at Abigail, stunned. "We speak of our daughter, and now she wants to speak. Amazing."

They both stood up, and Abigail hugged him. "This is wonderful, my love!" she exclaimed. They hurried as fast as they could to the cystallis room, where they took their seats.

After several minutes, the operator announced, "It is ready, Your Majesty."

The crystal panels started to light up, and an image started to spin before coalescing. Barnabas started as he saw Zena for the first time in more than five years. She looked like she had aged ten. Her eyes were bloodshot, and tears were running down her cheeks. They sat in silence for a moment as Zena wiped the tears from her cheeks.

Zena broke the silence. "Hello, Father. Hello, Mother."

"Hello, Zena," they both said. "What is wrong, child, why are you crying?" Abagail asked with great concern.

Zena grabbed a tissue and blew her nose. "I am sorry; this is so unladylike. I never intended to cry."

"Please, Zena, let us know what is wrong. Why are you crying? I thought all was well," Barnabas said.

Zena scowled at him. "Things are far from well, Father. I am sorry; I planned on contacting you sooner. I guess you could say I have been busy of late. Things have been chaotic over here. I have some very grave news to tell you. The war is far from over. In fact, it has become much worse. Victor and Amber Talon are dead."

Abagail covered her mouth, and Barnabas stared at Zena in disbelief. It was then Barnabas noticed that Zena was not wearing a tiara but a crown—a queen's crown. Zena explained to them all the horror and dread that had transpired, and tears returned to her eyes. "The legend of that eye is true, and we are all in grave danger, Father. Xavier Pulsar could attack anytime. We are not giving up. We are going to gather up all our armies and we are going to attack Apollyon. That is one of the reasons I contacted you, Father. I know you turned Aldar down all those years ago, so as your daughter, I am asking for your help. We need all the help we can get. With your armies, we might have a fighting chance. This is much bigger than just Antillean; we are talking about everyone. We are in danger. So are Salonia, Mirodia, and Violida, not to mention the innocent people of Apollyon. Father, I want to put this divide between us behind us. I am begging you, please."

Barnabas looked down, hesitating, then looked up into Zena's eyes and shook his head. "I am sorry, Zena, I cannot. How do you know for sure the eye has all that power? Has Xavier shown up at your doorstep yet?"

Zena's eyes widened, and then she frowned. "Not yet, Father, but that means nothing. He could be here any moment. Why, Father? Why do you continue to refuse to do anything with the obvious? You signed an alliance with us saying you would help defend us, and we agreed the same for you. "Can you not see the danger we are all in? Wake up, Father. This is real, and we need you. Please, Father, please."

Once again, Barnabas shook his head. "I am sorry, my daughter, but I cannot help you."

A tear ran down Zena's cheek. "Why do you deny us? I do not understand why you won't help us."

Full of shame, Barnabas looked at his daughter. "I just cannot. I am sorry, Zena, but I just cannot."

Zena's face darkened. "Victor and I had our arguments, and we had our disagreements. There were times I was so angry with him, I could just scream. I resented him quite a bit. Victor Talon was a good man. He loved his family, he loved his country, and he took care of both family and country. He even cared for me, even when I was a witch, a thorn in his side, and he probably wished Aldar had married someone else. I will say this: He was more of a father to me than you have ever been, for he stood up for what is right. I am going to say good-bye now. Mother. I am sorry. I love you, but I must go." Zena glared at Barnabas with hate-filled eyes "Father, I hope I never see you again, you coward." Zena's image faded away and the screen went dark.

Barnabas sat in stunned silence.

Abagail stood up. "Barnabas, you are an impossible man. What has happened to you? What has happened to the man I love?" She stormed from the room, crying.

Soon after, the operator left, clearly uncomfortable. Barnabas sat alone in silence for a moment before leaving the room, walking down the hallway with his head down. He passed a mirror, then stopped and walked back to look at his reflection looking back at him. He did not like what he saw, and the words Zena had said were burning him to the core. He fell to his knees. "I am a coward. A hopeless, good-for-nothing coward!" he yelled.

He stood up and stormed down the hallway. He knew what he had to do but was not sure he could.

Chapter Forty

Returning Home

Virion Nebula smiled as he approached the gates of Adaliah. It had been a long ride. He was quite tired, and he hated to admit it, but he wished he had taken the carriage and made Maximus ride the horse. He was getting too old for riding horseback long distances. He was saddle-sore, and he winced in pain as he rode. He wanted nothing more than to have a nice meal, a glass of chilled wine, and a long bath.

He slowed once he was through the city gates. Something was just a little off. The streets were empty, and all was silent. He and his soldiers looked up and down the streets for anyone, but they saw no one.

Virion got off his horse and walked up to one of the shops to look in the window. It was dark, and the door was locked. It was noon, usually the busiest time of day, when people were everywhere. Virion scratched his head nervously and looked at his men, who all wore looks of concern.

Virion returned to his horse and mounted, saying, "Let us ride to the palace." The soldiers followed him down the streets. The only living things they saw were some mice, a few horses, and some stray cats. "Halt!" Virion commanded. As his men stopped, he lifted a finger to his mouth for silence. In the distance, he heard a voice. He motioned for his men to ride forward, and they did so as slowly as possible.

When they turned the corner to the main road to the palace, Virion was surprised. That street and all its side streets were filled with the townspeople. Every man, woman, and child were there. As he got closer to the palace, he saw a person standing on the main balcony—a woman dressed in red—and heard the voice more clearly. Was that Shiva's voice? He could not tell for sure.

Once he had reached the rear of the crowd, there was no doubt that was Shiva's voice. Virion smiled. "Well, I'll be. Xavier's mad plan worked. The power of the eye is true, and Shiva is back." Virion had his men clear a path as they rode toward the palace. As they drew nearer, he saw Shiva better. He could see that she had the eye in her hands and was standing precariously on the ledge of the balcony. A tall, thin man wearing a red silk shirt and trousers was standing next to her, but Virion could tell it was not Xavier.

Finally, Virion's approach drew Shiva's attention. She smiled. "Virion, you finally arrived. Welcome home."

Virion got off his horse and bowed. "Shiva, I am filled with overwhelming joy to see you alive. It is unbelievable; the legend of the eye of the cyclops is true. I am incredibly happy to see you."

Everyone in attendance trembled in fear as Shiva lifted the eye over her head and it glowed brilliantly. Then she floated into the air, her brilliant blonde hair floating as she descended to the ground.

The horses started to panic as she touched the ground, and the soldiers had to hold the reins tightly. The people moved as far back as they could. As Shiva approached Virion, he noticed something was different about her. She was not wearing the crown of flames but a crown with a round reddish-orange gem. A reddish-orange orb was embroidered on the boddice of her red dress.

Virion started. Her eyes were no longer amber but were also reddish orange, with a faint glow. Curiosity took him over. "What is going on here? Why are you wearing a different crown? Why are you wearing this strange dress? Who is that strange man on the balcony, and where, in the name of Apollyon, is Xavier?"

Shiva frowned as she stopped right in front of him. Virion took a step backward. Shiva's mouth contorted into a scowl, and Virion yelped as she grabbed his shirt and wrapped her right fist in it. She lifted him up, and a great cold traveled up his spine and turned his breath to mist. "How dare you disrespect me, you mouse! You do not call me by my name. You call me *Your Majesty*. How dare you ask me questions like I am on trial. I am your empress, and don't you ever forget it."

The eye, in her left hand, continued to glow, and the two of them floated into the air. Virion kicked his feet in panic. They floated higher and higher, until they were as high as the tallest tower of the palace.

"You are an evil man, Virion Nebula. You must pay. You must die for your transgressions."

"Your Majesty, please don't kill me. I am your humble servant. I—" Before he could finish his sentence, she dropped him. "I am sorry!" he yelled as he twisted around. Plummeting face first toward the ground, he watched in horror as the ground got closer. He closed his eyes. Suddenly, he stopped falling.

He opened his eyes and was shocked. his face just inches from the ground. He looked up and saw that Shiva had him by his ankle. She smiled at him. Then she dropped him.

His face hit the ground hard, along with the rest of his body, and he rolled onto his back and looked up at the sky. Sitting up, he felt dizzy.

Shiva landed beside him, then looked at the crowd. "You are all dismissed back to your lives. And don't forget what I taught you." She looked around expectantly. "Well?" she shouted.

The crowd spoke in unison. "You are our empress, ruler of Apollyon. We will obey you without question or complaint. We will obey the eye of the cyclops, for it determines what is good and what is evil. All hail the eye; all hail our empress."

Shiva smiled. "I pray to the eye you all have a nice day." The people dispersed as quickly as they could, and Shiva looked at Virion, who pulled out a handkerchief and put it to his bloody nose. She smiled at him. "Virion, you are forgiven. The eye forgives you, and so do I."

Virion got to his knees and bowed his head. "Thank you for your kindness and mercy. I am not worthy."

Shiva nodded and reached her hand out. Virion reluctantly took it, and Shiva pulled him to his feet as easily as if he were a child. She turned to his soldiers. "You may enter the palace gates. There will be food and drink provided for you." All the soldiers bowed their heads and trotted through the palace gates. Shiva smiled at Virion. Her smile was unnerving—devious and demonic—and her glowing eyes looked as though they could see into his soul.

"So, where is Maximus?" she asked him. "I heard he was with you when you left for Antillean."

Virion felt his blood run cold. "He should be home in the next few days," he replied. "We split up. We felt that it was important for one of us to get here sooner rather than later to see if the eye had indeed been brought here."

"Oh, okay. I guess that makes sense. Well, I'll be looking forward to my son's return."

Virion let out an uneasy breath. He would have to think of an explanation when Maximus returned, for if he did not, he would be a dead man. Shiva offered him her hand again, and so he gave her his hand. He held in a scream as they floated into the air. This time, they landed safely on the balcony. It was then that he recognized the man who had been standing with Shiva. "Daniel?" Virion asked. He nearly asked the man what he was doing there but thought better of it.

Daniel nodded slowly, a look of horror on his face. "Virion, glad to see you," he managed to say.

Wait a minute, he did not call me sir! Virion managed to keep his anger in check, for in a way, Daniel was in the same boat as he.

"Where are my manners?" Shiva said. "You must be tired and famished, Virion. I will have my servants bring food and drink to your chambers and will have a bath drawn for you. Now that we are on better terms, I shall answer your questions. I was addressing the Apollyon people. I told them that now that I have returned, all evil has been vanquished and if they listen to me and the eye, no harm will come. However, if they defy me and the eye of the cyclops, they will be punished and die.

"The new crown with the orange gem and the orange eye on my dress," she continued, "is the new symbol of Apollyon. I am ridding

Apollyon of that dreadful symbol of the man consumed by fire. I have used the power of the eye to remove that abomination of a tattoo off my back. All flags, banners, and uniforms bearing that evil symbol will be burned and replaced by the almighty eye.

"Obviously, you see that the man you were wondering about is Daniel, my one and only true love." Shiva kissed Daniel on the cheek, and Virion saw the man shiver. "Well, Virion, you can go to your quarters now. You should have food and drink shortly.

Virion bowed. "Thank you, Your Majesty." He started to walk toward the doorway into the palace.

"Wait a minute, Virion, I forgot to tell you—" When Virion stopped and turned to look at her, she continued, "Daniel and I are to be married soon." When Virion looked confused, she said, "Daniel, can you tell Virion what happened to Xavier?"

Daniel's face wore a pained expression as he pointed upward. Virion looked up and saw something he had not noticed before—something hanging above the entryway.

Virion held in a gasp as he looked up in horror at the burned, hollow-eyed corpse of Xavier Pulsar.

Chapter Forty-One

Memories

The cyclops stood, menacing, as it stared down at her. Without the eye, however, it did not seem as scary as it once had been. Aurora stood in silence at the base of the cyclops as she remembered the first time she had seen the statue. She had been just a child, but she still remembered the story Bethany had told her and the book she had given her. She had not read the book in several years; however, since the assassination of her grandparents, she had read it from cover to cover several times. She looked at the bench that she and Bethany had sat on, and a tear ran down her face. Bethany's betrayal had changed her much. For one thing, she was far less trusting.

In some ways, she felt stronger. She felt like her heart was a little bit harder, like her heart had been scarred, like it had weathered a terrible storm, yet she felt like under that scar was a tender wound threatening to reopen.

As she sat on the bench, Aurora had to admit she missed Bethany's company. She missed her teacher's jokes and her laugh. She remembered nights when Bethany had made her warm milk to help her sleep, joking that she had slipped some mead into the milk. In spite herself, Aurora chuckled.

But that was the past, and that had not been the real Bethany. The real Bethany had been a traitor.

Aurora looked over to where Jonathan had been murdered. She stood up from the bench and walked over to where he had died, and she said a prayer. "Jonathan, I am sorry you never got the joy of marrying Elaine. She mourns you every day, and she will never forget you. I know you can hear me, and I pledge to you, you will be avenged."

A cough by the doorway interrupted her, and she looked over to the two guards standing there. "Babysitters," she sputtered quietly. Ever since the attack, Father had ordered that they all were to have escorts wherever they went, even inside the palace. She understood why Father had made this decision, but the lack of privacy was frustrating.

Aurora yawned; the midnight hour was approaching. She had been unable to sleep, so she had decided to go for a walk, to the dismay of her guards. She had walked all the way to the statue barefoot and in her nightclothes. *If Mother were to see me this way, she would be mad.* For some reason, the thought brought her a little bit of satisfaction. She started to walk around the statue, and she could see the guards watch her walk. She rolled her eyes. "I am surprised they don't follow me into the privy," she said to herself.

She started to laugh, and her guards looked at her like she had lost her mind. She was fine with that. She started pacing aimlessly, deep in thought. Father was going to assemble his armies to join the other armies at the border with Apollyon, then attack. With the full force of the Antillean army, he hoped he could somehow defeat Emperor Pulsar. She wanted so badly to be a part of that, but every time she tried to talk to her father about it, he would just smile. Last night, he had gently put his hand to her chin and said, "You are my little girl. I would never forgive myself if you were to die."

She knew her father wouldn't let her go because he loved her, but it was also very frustrating to her. She did not want to just sit and do nothing. She wanted to fight for the people, the land that she loved, and her family. She knew how to fight, she could shoot a gun, she could shoot an arrow, and she knew how to fight with a quarterstaff. She was deadly with a sword. She had trained years for this day, and her father would not let her join the fight.

She sighed. "You are wrong, Father, I am not a little girl. I am a woman, a princess, and a warrior. I love our land, I love our people, and I will defend it to my own death. Why won't he listen?" It was so frustrating that she felt like screaming.

Aurora's thoughts were interrupted by the sound of footsteps approaching. Her guards drew their swords and turned to look down the hallway. It was Enoch. He had two guards walking with him as well. Her guards nodded and sheathed their swords.

Enoch looked angry as he approached her. "What are you doing here and who are you talking to?" he asked.

Aurora blushed; she had not realized she was talking out loud. "I guess I was talking to myself," she admitted, embarrassed.

"Well, whatever it is you are doing, if your mother saw you here, she would have your hide. I got up to use the privy and saw your door was open and you were gone. I was not going to alarm your parents, so I decided to go looking for you myself."

Aurora frowned. "As you can see, Enoch, I have my guards with me. I was in no danger at all."

"That means nothing," Enoch said sharply. "With Xavier having the eye and all that has happened, anything can happen."

Aurora was surprised by this outburst, and she felt her face warm as she felt a touch of anger creeping in.

Enoch hung his head. "I am sorry. I overstepped my bounds. When I saw you were gone, it scared me. I care about you and was afraid something happened to you, is all, and I am sorry for my outburst."

Aurora felt the anger leave her. He was afraid for her; he had said he cared about her. She found herself smiling. "I forgive you. You were just afraid, and you wanted to make sure I was safe. Considering all we have been through and considering what Elaine has been going through, I cannot blame you."

Enoch replied, "So as a concerned friend, I still want to know why you are still up."

Aurora frowned. "I am frustrated, Enoch. I want to join in the battle, and Father will not let me. He has allowed you and Elaine to join, but not me; it is infuriating."

Enoch gave her a sympathetic look. "He is your father. In a lot of ways, he reminds me of my father. He taught Elaine and I well; he taught us how to survive in the wilderness and how to fight with weapons. He knew all of this, and yet he treated Elaine like she was a fragile flower and he wanted to do everything he could to protect her. Your father is no different. I think he does not want you to get hurt like Aunt Alana did. No matter how old you get, no matter what you do, he will always see you as his little girl."

Aurora sighed. "I know, Enoch, I know, but it does not change the fact I am a woman. It does not change that I want to fight for freedom. I think I will go mad if I stay behind."

"Maybe I could talk to your father," Enoch offered. "Maybe he would listen to me. It certainly wouldn't hurt."

Aurora looked at him, surprised. "That is a wonderful idea! That might work," she said.

"Tomorrow after breakfast, I will talk to him. Worst case, he will say no; best case, he might say yes," Enoch said.

Aurora let out another yawn. "Thank you so much, but I guess we should go back to bed, or we won't be awake for breakfast." They smiled at each other, and without warning, Aurora kissed Enoch on the cheek. "Good-night, Enoch." Aurora looked to her guards. "I am ready to go back to my room."

Enoch touched his cheek, stupefied, as he watched Aurora walk down the hallway.

Chapter Forty-Two

Carnage

The world was dark, but there was peace, serenity, a cool calm. There was no pain and no suffering. There was no reality, no up, no down, no left or right, no forward, no backward, just darkness.

Then, in the distance, there was a small pinpoint of light. It was just a minor annoyance, nothing to worry about. But the light slowly started to expand, threatening to destroy the peace and tranquility.

"No,"

The light began to expand quickly, peace and serenity being replaced by fear and chaos.

"No."

The darkness was swallowed by the light. The light got brighter and brighter until it was as bright as the sun.

"No!" Maximus Pulsar screamed as he awoke, the midday sunlight beating down unmercifully on his sunburned face. He groaned in pain as he was overtaken by the reality of the situation, he was in. "What in the name of Apollyon happened?" he asked himself. Then he started to take inventory of himself. He was bruised and battered, but nothing seemed broken.

He winced as he started pulling wood splinters from his face and body. He felt dizzy as he slowly and carefully made his way to his feet. He stumbled, trying to keep his balance, and remembered he had taken a huge blow to the head.

He squinted in the sunlight. His head hurt, feeling like it might burst like a melon. He gritted his teeth. His vision was a little blurry at first, but after about a minute, his vision cleared, and he vomited. He wished his vision were still blurry, for the sight before him was sickening. There was carnage everywhere. Pieces of the carriage were scattered across the pathway, and there was blood and gore as far as he could see. Several bodies were broken and lying-in unnatural positions. He saw the driver's body that had indeed been ripped in half. Dead horses lay twisted. It looked as if a spoiled child in a tantrum had run through, destroying its toys.

A putrid smell hit his nostrils, and he felt another wave of dizziness hit him hard. He fell to his hands and knees and vomited again. The smell was unbearable. Some of the bodies were already decomposing in the hot sun. "How did I wind up in this hell?" he shouted as he got back to his feet.

He heard a weak voice call, "Help me, please," and he walked through the rubble and bodies until he found the caller. He saw it was a woman soldier. "Please help me, Your Highness, please," she called again. "Please take my helmet off."

Maximus walked up to her. Her legs and her right arm were crushed, and she was breathing heavily. He pulled off her helmet and looked at her in shock; she looked a lot like his mother. Her hair was much shorter, and she was more muscular, but otherwise, she looked just like Shiva.

The soldier looked at him sheepishly. "I need water, please, Your Highness."

Maximus felt a twinge of anger. He was a prince, and she was a soldier; she had no right whatsoever to ask him to serve her.

His anger went away quickly, however. She was a citizen of Apollyon, and she was thirsty. Come to think of it, he was thirsty himself. Looking through the rubble, he found several broken canteens and smashed food barrels. He finally found an unbroken canteen, but it was empty. "Just my luck," he muttered. He had to find a source of water.

He reached for his sword but realized it was not with him. He had forgotten that he had taken it off in the carriage. He looked everywhere but could not find it. He was not about to go into the forest without a weapon to defend himself, so he picked up one of the many swords scattered on the ground.

He walked up to the edge of the forest and took a deep breath, then walked in. The dead trees and dead foliage offered little shade, but the air did seem cooler. Hearing a sound in the distance, he stopped and looked around but saw nothing. Wondering what that sound could have been, he continued to walk deeper into the woods. Then he realized the sound was running water. He hurried his pace. Sure enough, the sound was being made by a shallow river.

Maximus smiled as he reached the river. He put his hands in the water and splashed his face, The water felt cold on his sunburned skin. The river smelled of sulfur, but he did not care. He filled his canteen and took a drink. It tasted awful, but it was wet and soothed his dry throat. He drank as much as he could, then refilled the canteen. He walked back to the road cautiously, canteen in one hand and sword in the other. So far, no sign of that awful creature, whatever it was. He hoped never to see it again. He looked at his sword and wondered what good this weapon would be against such a creature.

He finally made it to the road and back to the carnage that had once been his entourage, and to the soldier. Her head was slumped over, and her skin looked pale and clammy. She looked like she was on death's door.

He touched her face, and she gasped. She had fallen asleep. He offered the canteen, putting it to her lips, and she drank greedily. "It does not taste good, but it is wet," he told her. The soldier did not care; she emptied the canteen.

"Thank you for your mercy, Your Highness," she said with a smile.

He gave her a smile, unable to get past how much she looked like Mother. "You are welcome," he found himself saying.

The soldier coughed up a little blood and was shivering despite the hot day. Maximus pulled his cape off his back and placed it on her. She managed a smile. "Well, I am certainly a mess," she chuckled, then coughed up more blood, this time more than the last. She gasped for air, starting to choke, and she tried to talk but she could not. She coughed again, then croaked, "I saw that creature. It looked like—" She coughed up more blood. Her eyes closed as she settled down a little, and her breath became shallow. Then she stopped breathing.

Maximus looked at the woman, frustrated. He wanted to know what she had been trying to tell him. Unfortunately, she would never talk again. He moved his cape up from where it lay on her body, to cover her face.

He looked around. Everyone but him was dead. He wondered why he was the only one who had survived. He had no time to ponder such things, so he rummaged through the debris, finding a pack and filling it with whatever rations he could find, and found a scabbard for his sword.

He decided to go back to the creek to refill his canteen because he had a long walk ahead of him. When he made it to the river, he splashed water on his face again and filled the canteen. He turned to leave but heard another noise. He froze in his tracks and slowly turned around, afraid of what might be behind him. He saw nothing, but the sound continued. Despite his fear, curiosity took over. A much wiser man would have walked away.

Was that snoring he heard? He crossed the shallow river to the other side. *Someone must be camping here*, he thought, *but who in their right mind would camp here?* He walked further in toward the sound but stopped, feeling a chill run down his spine. It was the creature.

It had its back to Maximus, and though its arms were folded in front of it, Maximus could tell they were muscular, like its back, which shook as the creature snored. It was wearing a loincloth, and its massive legs were crossed.

Maximus felt his heart beat out of his chest, then jumped as the creature stretched its arms and let out what seemed to be a yawn. The creature started to roll over, and Maximus ran.

He ran through the river. He ran to the path, and he ran down the path as fast as his feet could carry him. He ran and ran, leaving the entourage, the carnage and the creature far behind him.

Chapter Forty-Three

For Antillean

Twenty thousand soldiers stood facing the palace, all of them in full battle armor, standing ready for the new king. King Aldar Talon walked up to the podium with Queen Zena, Alana, General Phoenix, Enoch, Elaine, and other ranking officers behind him. Aurora sat in the shadows beside the platform on which her father was giving his army last instructions before they left for battle the next morning. She was nervous, feeling sweat bead on her back. She was also in full armor.

When Enoch had tried to convince Aldar to let her join, Aldar had simply told Enoch that Aurora was too young. She had cried on Aunt Alana's shoulder that night, and now, therefore, Aurora stood in hiding. Aunt Alana had had Aurora try her old battle uniform, and it had fit perfectly. Now the hard part was to begin—she had to confront her father. What she was going to do had never been done, for a king was never confronted—at least not in public, whether you were family or not. What she was about to do could be considered insubordination, but what else could she do? This was her last shot. She doubt her father would punish her too severely.

It was time to move. Aurora walked out from the shadow of the platform.

Enoch was the first to notice her. Somehow, he recognized her even though she had a helmet on. He shook his head and mouthed, "Don't do it." She ignored him and continued to walk.

Then she caught her father's attention as she stood in front of the army. Aldar frowned. "Who are you, and what is the meaning of this?" he demanded. Several guards pointed their guns at Aurora.

"Don't shoot!" Enoch yelled.

Aldar looked at him, confused. Then he looked at the mysterious soldier. "Stand down," he commanded.

Aurora kneeled. Then everyone was shocked as she took off her helmet and placed it on the ground.

Aldar's jaw dropped. "Aurora?" he asked, and she nodded. "I thought you were sick. And where are your guards?"

Aurora stood up. "I snuck out my window, Father" Aldar looked at her, concerned.

From the platform, the queen screamed, "Aurora Talon, what am I going to do with you? I don't care how old you are, I am going to take a stick to you when we get back."

Aurora stood still with no expression, then bowed to her mother. "I am sorry, Mother. I love and respect you, but this conversation is between Father and me."

Zena looked at Aurora, surprised, and paused for a moment, looking hurt but not slighted. "As you wish," she said, then looked at Aldar. "Dear, your daughter wishes to speak."

Aldar's face turned red in anger. "I want you to go back to your room, young lady, this instant, and I will forget this stunt."

"But, Father," Aurora protested, "we need to discuss this. Please listen to me."

"This is neither the time nor the place to talk of such things. I have made my decision, and it is final. Guards, please take my confused and distraught daughter back to her living quarters. Guard her door, and someone stand outside her window."

"Father!" Aurora cried as the guards approached.

"Oh, for crying out loud, stop being so stubborn!" Alana shouted at her brother.

Aldar looked over to Alana, whose face was beet red in anger. "Give your daughter the chance to talk. She deserves to be listened to. Please give her a chance to plead her case. She loves you and respects you." Aldar stared at Alana for a moment, then looked at Aurora. "Stand down," he commanded, and the soldiers backed away.

Everyone stood in silence, and then Aldar spoke. "All right, Aurora, I am willing to listen."

"Father, I love you. I love our family. I love the Antillean people, and I love this land. I am willing to lay down my life for our freedom. I want to fight for this land. We are all in danger, and we all might die. Well, if I am to die anyway, I would rather die fighting.

"I know I am your little girl," she continued, "and I realize that you will always think of me as that little girl with freckles and a ponytail. Well, Father, your child has grown up. I am not a girl anymore. I am not just a princess; I am a fighter. So please, Father, let me do this. Let me be a part of this battle. Let me fight for Antillean."

Aldar sighed. "I am sorry, Aurora, I cannot stand the thought of losing you. I could not live with that."

"Father, with the eye of the cyclops in the hands of Emperor Pulsar, I am probably going to die anyway."

Aldar looked away from her, trying to find another excuse. "I am sorry, Aurora, you are not old enough. You must be eighteen to join the army. You are seventeen. It was a decree your grandfather signed into law; I cannot change that."

Aurora smiled. "You are wrong, Father."

Aldar looked at her in confusion. "What do you mean?" he asked.

"Father, I know you have been unbearably busy of late and you don't realize . . . "

Aldar shook his head. "What am I not realizing?"

Aurora's smile broadened. "As of today, I am eighteen."

Aldar hung his head. "I am sorry, Aurora. I had no idea it was your birthday. With everything going on, I have been so busy." He looked at his daughter and then smiled. "Well, young lady, I guess I have run out of excuses." Aldar motioned to her. "Please come up here," he said.

Aurora walked up onto the stage and reluctantly walked to her father, who looked at her, then at Alana and back to Aurora. "Your aunt is the one who talked you into this and you are wearing her armor aren't you?"

Aurora grinned sheepishly. "Maybe," she replied.

They looked at each other, straight-faced, for a long time. Then they burst out laughing and Aldar hugged his daughter and kissed her on the forehead. "I love you," he told her.

"I love you, Father," Aurora replied as they continued to hug.

When they broke their embrace, Aldar turned to the rest of his army. "This is my eighteen-year-old daughter, of whom I am proud. So as your king, I decree that Princess Aurora Talon, my lovely daughter, is a member of the Antillean army!"

The army erupted in thunderous applause. Aurora teared up at all the excitement. The soldiers yelled, "Long live Princess Aurora!" as Aldar proudly raised his daughter's hand. Aurora smiled, knowing she would never forget this moment for the rest of her life.

~ ~ ~

The next day came sooner than Aurora had expected. The morning sun was rising as the army prepared to embark. Aurora had mixed feelings. On one hand, she was elated that she was going to make a difference by fighting for Antillean. On the other, she was saddened that the war was not over, and that Jonathan and her grandparents were dead.

Aldar walked up to Aurora and hugged her then he kissed her cheek. Aurora worried about her father, who always seemed on the brink of exhaustion. "I promise you, Father, you will not regret this. And thank you."

Aldar managed a smile. "I know, honey. I have no regrets. You will do me and Antillean proud."

Zena walked up to them, wearing her own battle armor. "When do we leave?" she asked.

Aldar shook his head. He did not want Zena to come, but she had insisted, arguing that if her father were not man enough to come, she would fight in his stead. That was a nice gesture, but Antillean needed King Zanthor's army as well. "Are you sure about this, Zena? You have no formal battle training," Aldar protested.

Zena rolled her eyes. "We have been over this. Alana is to run the kingdom in your stead. She can run the kingdom simply fine. She certainly can still defend herself; she, after all, saved my life. Hunter will be able to help guide her along; besides, I can be with you for moral support."

Aldar shook his head. "I just worry about your safety, dear, I am sorry. Last time you wielded a sword, you about took my head off. I don't want you to die."

Zena laughed and put her arm around Aurora. "Have you forgot what our lovely daughter said? Well, I am with her; if I am going to die, I want to do it defending our country."

Aldar hesitated. "You can also make a difference staying here. I just don't think you can—"

"Oh, for crying out loud!" Zena said. She stormed over to Isaiah, who happened to be standing nearby with a pistol in his hand and swiped the gun from him.

"Hey! That is my new pistol, and it's loaded!" he yelled at her.

Zena lifted the gun to shoot, and everyone—including Aldar—ducked. She took aim and fired at a pot of flowers several feet away. The pot shattered into pieces.

Aldar—and everyone else there—looked at Zena, dumbfounded as she blew the smoke from the barrel. "I hate daisies. Never thought they were all that pretty anyways."

Aldar laughed. "Well, I guess the Talon women know how to defend themselves. All right, I will stop. I am glad to have you, my love." They kissed as everyone else went back about their business.

“I’ll be back, dear,” Zena told him. “I have to make sure my luggage is ready.” She walked away with Isaiah’s pistol, putting it in the pocket of her dress.

“Don’t take too long, dear. We will leave when you get back,” Aldar called after her. Zena smiled.

“Hey, that’s my pistol!” Isaiah protested.

“Relax, Isaiah,” Aldar told him, “I will get you a new pistol.”

“Well, it probably won’t be as good as that—”

“Come on, Isaiah, it is just a pistol, you will be fine. I will have one for you before Zena returns.”

“All right, Aldar, but I have just one question: how long you think it will take for Her Majesty to pack?”

Aldar’s eyes widened as the horror of what Isaiah had asked sunk in.

Two hours later, they were on the road.

Chapter Forty-Four

Prisoner

Virion sat at his table, wearing a bathrobe. The bath he'd had had done little for his aching muscles. All he could think about was his emperor, his confidant, his best friend, Xavier Pulsar dead. His plate of food sat on his table, cold. He had lost his appetite. His only comfort came from the chilled wine he drank.

He was not sure what to do. The woman he had talked to was not the Shiva he admired and knew. She was cold, callous, and vile, yet he had seen some of her personality when she had been nice. Her behavior was so erratic, it seemed the evil in that eye had taken possession of her. It seemed her body, her being, her soul had been cursed by the eye of the cyclops. The power the eye possessed was terrifying.

Then it hit him—where was Pirena? She was the one who had brought the eye here. Was she still alive? Maybe she could give him some insight to what had happened here. He certainly was not going to ask Shiva; she might do to him what she had done to Xavier. He had to find a subtle way to figure out what had happened to Pirena.

Then he had an idea. He had just emptied his glass, so he lifted it to the young servant. He smiled at her as she nervously refilled the glass. "Do you know where General Solaris is?" he asked. "Is she staying here in the palace or is she on a new mission?" The servant dropped the wine bottle, and it smashed on the floor. "You clumsy girl," Virion scolded.

"I am sorry, sir," the girl said as she got on the floor and frantically started to clean the mess she had made. He could see the fear in her eyes; she looked on the verge of panic.

Virion got down on the floor next to her and started to help, speaking softly. "Please, I need your help. Do you know where General Solaris is? It is imperative that I speak to her. Please, any information at all."

The servant shook. "I don't know what to do, sir. I am so afraid Empress Shiva will kill me and my family."

Virion smiled. "I know you are afraid, but something needs to be done to stop Empress Shiva."

The servant nodded. "General Solaris is in the dungeons because she hurt Daniel. She is to remain there until she declares her loyalty to Empress Shiva and apologizes to Daniel."

Virion sighed in relief; Pirena was still alive. He would have to find her, and maybe then a solution would present itself to stop this evil. He put his hand on the servant's head. "Thank you for your bravery. This will not go unrewarded. I will do everything in my power to protect you and your family."

"Thank you, sir."

Virion stood up. "You are welcome. Return to your normal duties." As the servant bowed and returned to work, Virion thought, *oh, Xavier, instead of bringing life to your love, you have brought a curse on our land.*

Virion got dressed and left his apartments. He walked casually down the hallways of the palace, careful not to look hurried or panicked, although he wanted to get to the dungeons as fast as he could. He noticed that everyone in the palace wore looks of fear. Fear had been common in the palace under Xavier's rule, but the looks on the faces he saw now was unlike any he had ever seen before.

Virion regretted going on his mission to Antillean. He wished he had talked Xavier out of this mad plan, but there was no sense wasting time worrying about that now; the damage had been done. He finally reached the stairway to the dungeon and gagged. The vulgar smell of the dungeon was overpowering. He approached the guard and announced, "I am here to see General Solaris."

The guard bowed. "She is on the far side of the dungeon, in cell nineteen sixty-eight."

Virion nodded. That cell was where the most severe prisoners were held, usually by themselves. As he walked, he looked at the filthy prisoners. They all looked famished, and the chamber pots on the floor were overflowing. It had been a long time since he had been down here. He had forgotten what a miserable and forlorn place it was.

Virion walked as quickly as he could down the hallway and past the cells of the unfortunate prisoners, then made it to the hallway that led to Pirena's cell. It was dark; he grabbed a torch from the wall. The smell was only slightly better as he headed down this hallway. There seemed to be no one else here. When he finally came to Pirena's cell, he found her chained to the wall, her head was slumped. Virion investigated her cell, hoping she was not dead.

Thankfully, she was breathing, just asleep.

He was taken aback; he had never seen Pirena in this condition. It looked like her cheek was bruised and maybe she had a black eye. "Pirena," Virion said quietly, hoping not to startle her. Pirena's eyes opened. She struggled against her bonds, and her eyes widened. She started to thrash around. "Pirena, it is me, Virion. I am here to help."

Pirena stopped thrashing and looked into his eyes, then relaxed. Virion unlocked the cell with his master key and was able to get a closer look at her. Her dress was tattered and torn, and her face looked like someone had punched it or smashed it several times into a wall.

"What are you doing here, Virion? You must leave here immediately. You are in grave danger if Shiva sees you with me."

"No, Pirena, I must get you out of here. We must figure out a plan to get the eye away from Shiva."

Pirena hung her head. "I do not think there is a way to defeat her. She has unimaginable powers. She can appear out of thin air. Every morning, she appears in front of me to torment me."

Virion looked around, paranoid. "Has she been here already?" he asked nervously. When Pirena nodded her head, Virion smiled. "Well, then things should be all right. My key should unlock your bonds."

Virion kneeled and inserted his key into the keyhole of the lock of her shackles. "These bonds are old; this might take a while," he told her.

"What can you tell me of what happened?" he asked as he struggled to unlock her bonds.

"It was awful. I had walked into Aunt and Uncle's living chambers, and it looked like a great battle had taken place. I saw Aunt and Uncle lying on the floor. Daniel came in, and I was angry with him and sliced off his ear. Then Aunt Shiva appeared behind me and hit me with a lightning bolt. I hit the wall hard. I remember her picking me up and screaming at me never to harm Daniel again. She then threw me on the floor, and I passed out for a moment. When I awoke, she had Uncle up in the air. She then chanted and yelled, 'Death by fire!' and Uncle burst into flames and screamed. I will never forget the sound of his scream. A great rage came over me as I got up. I charged Aunt Shiva. I tried to take off her head, but she dodged my attack, and she hit me with another bolt.

"The next thing I knew, I was here. She has asked for my loyalty, and I will not give it to her. She says she could use my services, but I will not give them to her either. She gives me just enough food and water to survive. I think she will kill me soon, and maybe that would be best, just put me out of my misery."

"Nonsense, Pirena. I am going to get you out of here and we will think of something, you will see."

Pirena frowned. "I hope you are right. I should have not listened to Uncle; now he is dead. Speaking of death, bringing the eye here will do just that—bring death to this land, bring death to this world."

"Almost got it." Virion smiled as he struggled with the key, and he heard a click. "There we go. Now you are free," he said, looking at Pirena, and her eyes widened. He felt a strange feeling move up his spine. The room grew cold, and he could see Pirena's breath. He shook in fear.

"Hello, Pirena; hello, Virion," he heard a voice say, then saw a flash of light.

Virion groaned in pain. The lightning bolt had slammed him to the ground hard.

He shivered, the cell was as cold as a winter morning, and looked to Pirena. She was shivering as well. Virion made it to his feet and turned to face Shiva, who slapped him across the face. "So, when were you going to tell me the truth?" she asked him.

Virion looked at Shiva, confused. "The truth about what, Your Majesty?"

Shiva snarled at him. "I talked to one of your soldiers. He told me that you had a fight with Maximus and then left him behind."

Virion felt sick. "I am sorry, Your Majesty. He was most disagreeable about being lied to. Yes, I did leave him, but he was in capable hands; he had over a hundred of our best soldiers protecting him. We were far away from any Antillean regiments. He should be home any day now, you will see."

Shiva mused for a minute, and then her eyes started to glow. "I am not angry at you for arguing with my son. I know he can be argumentative sometimes. I am angry you did not tell me about this; it makes me wonder where your loyalties lie."

Virion got to one knee. "My loyalties lie with you, Your Majesty."

"Really? You say your loyalties lie with me? If that is true, why are you here talking to Pirena, a traitor? Are you plotting against me? This seems quite suspicious."

Despite the cold of the room, sweat beaded on Virion's forehead. He could feel his heart beating out of his chest. He had to think of a lie, and quick. "I am sorry, Your Majesty, but Pirena is an old friend, and I knew she had to be here somewhere. After all, she brought the eye here. I looked everywhere and, well, I came to the dungeon, and she was here. I meant no disrespect, Your Majesty; I was simply curious about what happened, is all."

"I guess I cannot blame you for your curiosity about what happened to my ex-husband; after all, he was your friend. All right, I believe you; however, I hold you responsible for my son's well-being. He had better be here soon. I need one more thing, Virion: I need you to pledge to me your loyalty."

Virion took Shiva's hand and kissed it. Her skin was cold and clammy, and it repulsed him, but he managed to hide it. "You have my loyalty, Your Majesty. I will fight for you, defend you unto my death."

Shiva smiled at Pirena. "You see, Pirena, it is that easy; all you have to do is pledge your loyalty to me and things will get better."

Pirena spit on the ground. "My loyalties lie with Uncle Xavier, not you."

Shiva's eyes pulsed, along with the eye, and another bolt shot out of the eye and hit Pirena in the chest. Pirena screamed and gasped for breath. After several seconds, she regained her breath and hung her head. "Why don't you just kill me and be done with it instead of torturing me so?"

Virion shook his head. *Stubborn fool. Why does she not give her loyalty? I need her to help me overthrow Shiva.*

"I have not killed you because I need you. I cannot be everywhere all the time. You are the best spy and assassin in Apollyon history. I need you to do my bidding for me. If you pledge your loyalty, I will reward you handsomely, plus you can leave this dungeon and have a nice meal and a hot bath."

Tears streamed down Pirena's face. "I loved Uncle so much, and you killed him. I am afraid I cannot give you, my loyalty."

Shiva shook her head. "Well, Pirena, I had hoped it would not come down to this. But I must do what I must do. Guards!" she called. Two guards rushed to her; their faces fearful. "Bring me a prisoner; anyone will do," Shiva commanded.

A few minutes later, the guards brought an old, grizzled man who looked as though he had spent a lifetime in the dungeon. His clothes were on the brink of disintegration. The prisoner's eyes widened as Shiva put her hand on his throat.

Pirena's eyes narrowed. "Do you think killing that man will change my mind? Go ahead, kill him; he means nothing to me." The man shook his head in fear.

"Oh, I know you don't care if I kill him; I just want to give you a reminder." When Pirena looked at her quizzically, Shiva said, "Remember how your uncle died? Well, I am going to kill this man the same way I killed Xavier—only this time, slower—and then I will do the same to you, slower still."

"No!" Pirena pleaded. "I cannot be reminded of how Uncle died. Please don't do it. I cannot bear it."

Shiva frowned. "Pirena, the most ruthless and fierce assassin, is afraid? I never thought I'd see the day." She squeezed her hands around the prisoner's throat and sweat started to beat on the prisoner's brow.

"All right, Aunt Shiva, I will pledge my loyalty to you."

Shiva smiled as the prisoner erupted in a flash of flames and instantly turned to ash. He had no time to scream. "Well, that is one less prisoner to feed. Guards, free her from her bonds."

Virion pulled out his keys, which he hadn't realized he had put away. "Allow me," he said as he kneeled next to Pirena. He certainly did not wish for Shiva to know he had already freed Pirena, or they both would certainly die. He winked at Pirena as they stood, hoping they would find a way to meet privately.

Pirena wobbled a bit as she stood up with Virion's help. Then she kneeled. "I pledge my loyalty unto my death."

Virion helped Pirena to her feet, and then Shiva hugged her and kissed her on the cheek. "That is my girl." Shiva then turned to the guards. "Send word to General Solaris's servants to prepare her food and wine and draw her a bath." The guards bowed and ran off to do their tasks as Shiva fussed over Pirena.

As they walked out of the dungeon, Virion knew what had to be done: Shiva had to be stopped. How, he did not know.

Chapter Forty-Five

A Long Walk Home

Maximus walked slowly down the dirt path—the path he hoped would lead him home. Sweat ran down his back. He was not sure how long he had been walking—seven days? Ten? He had lost track. He was constantly looking over his shoulder, anticipating the creature's appearance. So far, he had not seen it, nor had he seen another person. He looked at his sword and chuckled despite himself. If that creature attacked him, it would rip him into pieces, whether he had a sword or not. *What* was *that creature?* he wondered yet again.

He staggered down the road, feeling dizzy and nauseated, probably from drinking the nasty water, which was all he had found to drink. He supposed it could have been the food he had eaten. He knew nothing of harvesting food. He would find the occasional apple tree and had managed to find some delicious mushrooms, which he kept in his pockets.

The afternoon sun started to grow hot, and he managed to find a tree with lots of leaves. He walked to the trunk and collapsed to the ground, the cool shade giving him respite from the heat of the day. When he put his back to the trunk and looked up, the branches above him began to spin. He closed his eyes and groaned. When was he going to stop feeling dizzy? He kept his eyes firmly shut and finally fell asleep.

When his eyes opened again, it was early evening. Maximus panicked and grabbed his sword, hearing a noise in the distance. Then he saw the soldier he had given water to appear a few feet in front of him. Her body was broken, and she lay on her back. She looked over at him with a blank stare. "How are you here?" he asked her. "Are you not dead?"

The woman said nothing, but suddenly, Shiva appeared behind her. "Mother, you are alive? Pirena must have brought the eye back and it works! I cannot believe it, Mother, I missed you so."

Shiva smiled. She glowed like an angel, her crown of flames glittering in the sunlight and her gold dress shimmering. Maximus tried to stand but found that he could not. "My son, I am so proud of you and all you have done." She looked down at the soldier. "This soldier asked for a drink, and despite being royalty, you gave it to her. You could have just scoffed at her and spit in her face. You truly are a man. You must not follow in your father's footsteps, for he is ruthless, and you are more a man than he."

Suddenly, Shiva and the soldier disappeared, replaced by Xavier, who ran up to Maximus and screamed at him. Maximus yelped in fear.

"You call him a man?" Xavier screamed. "This little worm is a pathetic excuse for a man. You are a spineless coward. When are you going to wake up? When are you going to become a ruthless tyrant? What, in the name of Apollyon, is it going to take? What a disappointment you turned out to be. You are a disgrace. How many times must I tell you, kindness and compassion are for the weak. You must be ruthless."

Maximus started to cry. "Father, please forgive me. I am sorry. I can be a man. Please forgive me."

Xavier spat. "You cry? Only the weak cry! I should kill you; you're a worthless piece of trash."

Xavier pulled out his sword, and Maximus pleaded, "Don't kill me, Father! Don't kill me, please." He screamed as Xavier thrust his sword. Then Xavier disappeared.

Maximus breathed heavily, sweating profusely.

"Come, Maximus. You look famished. Come eat dinner with me."

Maximus was shocked. A table of food appeared in front of him, and Victor Talon sat at the table with a broad smile on his face. "Come. You are a growing young man. I have leg of lamb, roasted chicken, buttered peas, and molasses pie, Aurora's favorite." Victor grabbed a chicken leg and started to eat, and Maximus watched in horror as blood ran down Victor's nose and stained his white shirt. Victor put down the chicken leg and coughed up blood. His shirt was now crimson. "What is the matter, Maximus? Are you not well? Why do you not eat?"

"I am sorry, Victor. I had no idea Pirena was going to kill you. I really, truly, did not know."

Victor looked at Maximus, confused. "What are you talking about? I am fine."

Suddenly, Victor started coughing blood up violently and put his hands to his throat, gasping for air. Maximus screamed in panic.

Virion and Pirena appeared beside Victor and started to laugh. Victor continued to gasp, and they continued to laugh. "What a dumb fool," Virion said.

"Blind fool. He wanted peace, and because of his gullible, desperate need for peace, he is now dead," Pirena said laughingly.

"Stop that! Stop that now!" Maximus shouted. "Victor was a good man and did not deserve this."

Virion slapped his knee, laughing, tears running down his cheeks. "The old goat got exactly what he deserved."

Pirena snorted. "It is true, Victor did love his people to death." They both fell to the ground, rolling around in the grass while laughing hysterically.

"Stop it right now!" Maximus demanded.

Victor, Pirena, and Virion disappeared, and all was silent. Maximus looked around. "What just happened?" he asked. Was he dreaming, or were these hallucinations?

Then, suddenly, all the people who had spoken in the past few minutes appeared in front of him, wearing blank expressions. All at once, they broke their silence, Shiva telling him what a great man he was, Xavier telling him what a disappointment he was, Victor coughing up blood, Pirena and Virion rolling on the ground in laughter. Their voices grew louder, all the sounds combining until they became excruciating. Maximus covered his ears as the sound grew to a deafening pitch. "Stop!" Maximus screamed.

They all disappeared at once. “Thank you!” he shouted.

After several minutes, determining that they were not coming back, Maximus closed his eyes and fell into a nightmare-filled sleep.

Chapter Forty-Six

The Campfire

Aurora groaned as she rubbed her lower back. It was sore from the long day's ride—one of many more to come. When the sun rose, they broke camp and rode until sunset. She still managed a grin. She had nothing to complain about; she was grateful to be a part of something bigger than herself.

She walked up to some familiar faces. Enoch and Elaine were sitting on some straw bales, the glow of the campfire showing two tired faces. It truly had been a long, tiring day. "May I join you?" Aurora asked.

Enoch's tired expression turned into a smile, and he stood up. "Sit here," he said, offering a spot between himself and Elaine. He gave her an overly dramatic bow. "I am sorry, Your Highness, I can only offer you a meager throne of straw." Aurora and Enoch laughed, and even Elaine snickered a little as Aurora took her seat. It had been a long time since they had laughed and did that feel good!

Elaine looked at her, smiled, and put her arm around Aurora's shoulder. Aurora leaned into Elaine. "I am glad to see you smile," she told her friend.

"Aurora, I am tired of crying. I am tired of being in despair. I need to . . . I want to be happy again."

"I am sure that day will come someday," Aurora said, trying to give her comfort, and kissed Elaine's cheek.

"It feels strange, going back to the land we fled," Enoch said. "I pray we can defeat Xavier Pulsar and return peace to our lands." Aurora offered her arm to him, and he reluctantly let her put her arm around his shoulder. He looked around, nervous, not wishing to upset Zena. The words she had told him when they had first met burned in his mind.

"Going on such a long journey is much better with friends like you," Aurora told them.

"Couldn't agree with you more," Enoch said, and Elaine nodded in agreement.

"It has been quite a while since I have been on a trip such as this. I think the last time was when I and Hunter went to visit my grandparents in Violida. I was little, and before the war, we had gone to spend time with them. That was the last time we visited, and the last time I saw them was the meeting of the nations before the war. I often wonder how they are doing. I know there is bad blood between them and Mother. Mother and Father went to visit them because Grandfather Zanthor said he was not going to help. I was still young, but I remember Mother coming home crying.

"I hold nothing against my grandparents, but they broke Mother's heart and devastated Father and Grandfather Talon. She just recently contacted Grandfather via cystallis, and he still turned her down. I am not sure why he refuses to fight with us; he has a grand army, and it would have made a difference. I am sure that is why Mother is so stern sometimes; she is quite bitter, and it shows sometimes. She also has a lot of love in her heart—you don't always see it, but it is there."

"Hello, how are you doing tonight?" a familiar voice called from the shadows. Into the light of the campfire came Zena. Enoch quickly pulled away from Aurora, and Aurora stiffened, hoping her mother had not heard her.

"Hello, Mother," Aurora managed to say.

"So what have you three been up to? Hopefully not trouble," Zena said, grinning. All three laughed with just a hint of nervousness. "Mind if I join you?" she asked. When Enoch jumped up and offered her his seat, Zena said, "No need, Enoch, you can sit next to Aurora. I will sit on the bale beside of you." She sat next to Enoch and put her arm around his shoulder. He swallowed as his throat went dry. She smiled at him. "Are you all right, Enoch? You look a little ill."

Enoch swallowed again. Then he spoke in a nervous chatter. "I am fine, no problems here. I feel great! Fit as a fiddle, really. No problems."

Zena laughed. "Relax, Enoch, I am not going to hurt you, really. I don't bite."

Enoch thought for a second that her biting him had never entered his mind—until now. He started to sweat.

Then he was stunned. Zena reached over and kissed him on the cheek. He looked at her, and she smiled. He relaxed. "I know the road ahead will be rough on all of us, and, well, I want us all to get along with each other," Zena said. "Enoch, Elaine, I want to apologize to you. I know I haven't been the easiest person to get along with. I am not as open as Aurora is; I am much slower in accepting new people in my life. Then after Bethany's betrayal, I became suspicious of you until Aldar challenged me. It has taken me a while, and I have come to realize that I love you two and you will always be a part of our family."

Elaine got up and hugged Zena, sobbing, "Thank you, Zena."

Zena also began to cry. "I love you both, and don't you two forget it!" she said between sobs. Aurora beamed with pride at her mother. It had been a long time since her mother had opened herself like that.

"Hey, did I miss something?" Aldar asked as he walked up. Zena and Elaine broke their embrace, and Zena wiped tears from her eyes.

As Aldar sat next to Zena, she smiled at him. "Just having a family moment."

Aldar managed a smile. "Well, that is a good thing to have, and many more to come." Aurora smiled, until she looked at her father. He looked like he had aged ten years since he had taken over as king. He had a smile on his face, but the bags under his eyes betrayed that smile. The weight of the world was on his shoulders, and it was taking its toll. His forehead had wrinkles of worry, and he had some new gray in his hair.

"Well, I am glad you are all here. I am glad to spend time with family," Aldar said. He gave his biggest smile, and Aurora saw a spark in his eyes, something she had not seen in quite a while. "So, Zena, what have these three whippersnappers been up to? Mischief and mayhem, I suppose." They all laughed. Oh, did it feel good to laugh with everyone again! Aurora wished it would not end.

Elaine winked at Aldar. "You don't know the half of what we have been up to."

For some reason, hearing that from Elaine was so funny, they roared with laughter. All their stress was released in that one much-needed round of laughter. Unfortunately, that wonderful feeling was short-lived.

As a soldier approached, saying, "Your Majesty, I have a report from one of our scouts." The soldier handed Aldar a piece of paper, which he opened.

"Well, it looks like we should meet up with the other army tomorrow." Aldar stood up, the twinkle in his eyes gone and his frown returned. "Well, I am sorry to leave you all, but Isaiah and I have some planning to do."

"Don't stay up too late," Zena said.

"I will try not to, love," Aldar said, walking away.

Everyone sat in silence after his departure, saddened that he had to carry this terrible burden. Zena sighed, breaking the silence. "I worry about him. He wakes me when he crawls into bed just a little before sunrise. Then he is back up just as the sun rises. I don't think he has had a full night's rest since . . . well, since it happened." Everyone nodded in understanding.

"Well, I think I shall retire for the night," Enoch said.

"I think I shall too," Elaine said, and they went to their tents, leaving Aurora alone with her mother.

Aurora moved closer to her mother, who put her arm around Aurora's shoulder and kissed her forehead. "Pray for your father. He worries me. He does not sleep. He has not been eating well. I know it kills him not to have time to spend with you, Enoch, and Elaine, and he also misses Hunter and Alana as well. Pray that he will have the strength to face this new threat and we will overcome."

“I will, Mother, I will pray for Father.” Aurora kissed her mother, then said, “I am headed to bed Good night.”

“Good-night,” Zena said with a smile as she watched her little girl who was not little anymore walk off to her tent. She sat gazing up at the stars and their wonder for a while. Then she yawned, got up, put out the fire, and crawled into her cot to await a sleep that probably would not come.

Chapter Forty-Seven

Fury

Shiva paced on the balcony to her living chambers. She looked out at the horizon. She was hoping any moment, Maximus would approach the palace gates with his entourage. Behind the table in her living quarters stood three nervous figures: Daniel, Pirena, and Virion.

Virion shook in fear, sensing Shiva's anger starting to rise. *Where is that boy?* he thought. *He should have been here days ago. Did he go sight-seeing?*

Shiva stopped pacing and turned to stare at Virion, her reddish-orange eyes glowing brighter and looking like they would shoot darts at him. She lifted the eye above her head, and it gave off a blinding glow. Virion braced himself for the death blow.

Instead of striking him, Shiva shot up into the air, rising higher and higher and then floating in place. She slowly spun around, taking in a panoramic view of the horizon. She grew excited as she saw a cloud of dust rising on the main road to Adaliah, then frowned when she realized it was a bunch of farmers bringing their produce into the city. Anger and despair filled her heart. Her eyes began to pulsate with the eye as she screamed, "Maximus, my son, where are you?"

Her voice echoed across the land, and birds and animals scattered at the sound. Bloodred tears ran down her cheeks as a bolt of lightning shot up into the sky from the eye. Dark storm clouds swirled overhead in a vortex. Lightning flashed across the sky, and thunder shook the land. Rain came down in sheets. The townspeople below ran in a panic at this sudden storm.

Shiva screamed and howled, crying, "Maximus, where are you? Please come to your mother. I need you."

Virion jumped as Shiva landed on her feet on the balcony with a thud, looking at him furiously. The lightning and the eye shimmered on her wet crimson dress and blonde hair, emphasizing her fierceness. *This is it; I am a dead man,* Virion thought as Shiva walked into the room and again raised the eye over her head. He braced himself for the agonizing death blow, but Shiva chanted, and the storm slowly dissipated. She lowered the eye to hold it in one arm, then looked into a mirror and started to smile. She started to laugh as she touched her wet face, her hair, and her dress. She laughed louder and louder until she sounded manic.

Virion, Daniel, and Pirena looked at her in surprised shock. When Shiva walked up to Daniel and put her hand on his shoulder, he visibly shook, as if he had been touched by an icicle. She faced them all and said, "Just look at me; I am just a mess. I am sorry for my outburst. I guess I was not acting very civil and certainly not like an empress."

All three bowed their heads. "No apologies needed, Your Majesty, all is well."

She smiled back at them. "Thank you."

This woman's crazy mood changes like the wind, Virion thought. *It blows in all directions.* "Your Majesty, might I suggest we assemble some search parties? I think I could have them ready within the hour."

Shiva frowned and pointed a finger at him. "I suggest we don't. After all, it is your fault, Virion. Therefore, I am going to do what I should have done in the first place."

Virion cringed as Shiva raised the eye. She chanted, and all three of them floated along with her, flying out onto the balcony and shooting up into the sky. They all had panic in their eyes as Shiva spoke. "We shall find my son and you will apologize to him. Maximus will decide your fate, and I shall dish out whatever punishment he wishes."

Virion gritted his teeth. "Yes, Your Majesty," he said with closed eyes.

People down below looked up in amazement as the four streaked across the sky. After an hour of flying around, Shiva screamed, "No!" as she looked in horror.

They landed, and Virion opened his eyes, which widened in shock. Dead horses and dead bodies were scattered across a trail. They were badly decomposed, and the stench was overwhelming. He recognized the armor on one of the dead bodies as belonging to their entourage. Virion felt sick as they searched the carnage. "What happened here?" he asked himself.

"Maximus, where are you? Mother is here," Shiva shouted frantically. In that moment, she sounded like her old self searching for her lost child, Virion thought.

"What in the name of Apollyon happened here?" Pirena asked. "Everyone here has been ripped apart."

Shiva floated in the air, trying in vain to see Maximus in the woods. "Keep looking," she commanded them.

"Maximus's sword!" Pirena shouted as she pulled the sword out from under a broken wagon wheel.

Shiva landed near Pirena and took the sword from her and looked at it, deciding her son must be dead. She walked over to Virion. "I do not know who or what killed this entourage. All I know is my son is dead." She put down the sword and raised the eye. She chanted, and the corpses rattled.

Virion looked at her in disbelief. Was she really going to bring back these poor people in hopes of reviving Maximus? The thought repulsed him.

Shiva lowered the eye and once again wrapped her arm around it, hanging her head. "I cannot revive him; he is too decomposed. They are all torn apart. Even the eye does not have that kind of power." She picked up her son's sword and approached Virion, who backed away. "You must die. My son was to be heir to the throne, and I was to guide him in his reign as emperor. Now that dream is gone."

Once again, Virion braced himself. As Shiva pulled back the sword to thrust it into Virion's chest, Daniel cried, "I found his cape!"

Shiva lowered the sword and ran over to Daniel.

Virion sighed. He was not sure how much more he could take. The stress alone was going to kill him.

"Look, Shiva! His cape is wrapped around that soldier."

Shiva looked at the cape and smiled. "He might still be alive. It looks like he or someone put this cape on this soldier. It makes sense; this soldier is broken; there is no way she was able to wrap herself." She ran over to Virion and kissed him on the forehead. "You are one lucky man. The search continues. Let us go back to the palace and plan for some search parties. The sun is setting; let us make haste." She handed the sword to Pirena, then lifted the eye and chanted. They took off to the palace, Virion wondering how in blazes he had gotten so lucky.

Chapter Forty-Eight

Unexpected Visitors

A tired Aldar Talon yawned as he and Isaiah sat at the table in the tent of the general of the southern Antillean army. General Williams, an old, balding, gray-haired man with a stern nose and pointy chin, nodded his head. With Aldar's army of twenty thousand soldiers and General Williams's thirty thousand, Aldar hoped and prayed they would have enough to overwhelm Xavier Pulsar and his armies.

"It is strange, Your Majesty; for whatever reason, all of the Apollyon armies have backed away," General Williams said. "I am not sure why, other than they plan on defending the city. I would think it would have made better sense for them to defend themselves before we reached the city. This is not the way Virion would run the army unless he is doing Xavier's bidding."

Aldar put his hand on his chin. "You are right, General Williams, it does not make any sense, but be it as it may, we must march on."

Isaiah and General Williams nodded in agreement. "Aldar, we probably should show the general here our special weapon," Isaiah said.

Aldar nodded and lifted a heavy object covered in cloth, setting it on the table and pulling off the cloth to reveal a strange-looking battle-axe. General Williams looked confused. "What is this axe made from? It certainly is not made of metal. What is this strange material?"

Aldar smiled. "It is made of a material named tsundium. It is the same material that the cyclops is made of. my personal liaison, Violet Silverwood, is also an inventor. She was the woman who invented the cystallis; she is an amazing woman. She is confident that this weapon will destroy the eye of the cyclops. The trick will be to somehow retrieve the eye from Emperor Pulsar and smash it with this battle-axe."

"Let us pray this works," Isaiah said. "We have made fifty such weapons that we will split amongst our divisions."

General Williams nodded his approval. "And what if this weapon does not work?"

Aldar sighed. "Then heaven help us all."

A loud noise interrupted their conversation, and a frantic voice called out, "Your Majesty!"

A soldier walked into the tent and bowed. "I am sorry for this interruption. There is a massive army in the distance headed our way."

The king and generals jumped to their feet, knocking over their chairs. "That is impossible," General Williams said. "I have had my men scouting everywhere; they would have seen them coming. In what direction is this army coming, soldier?"

"The army is coming up from behind us, sir."

General Williams looked at the soldier, stupefied. "Is this some magic conjured up by Xavier and the eye?"

The four men ran out of their tent, the two generals running to their positions and calling out orders. The Antillean armies scattered, trying to get in position for an attack. "My horse!" Aldar commanded. Soon, he was on his mount and Isaiah joined him in riding in the direction of the army. "Do you have your army in position?" Aldar asked.

"My commanders are getting them ready," Isaiah said.

Aldar gaped, in awe of the massive army that was approaching; it looked like hundreds of thousands of soldiers. "How in Tiban Talon's name did Emperor Pulsar come up with such a massive army?" Then he cursed. He knew that Xavier's army was at least sixty thousand strong. He pulled his scope from his saddlebag to look at the approaching army, and his jaw dropped. "This is not the Apollyon army," he said.

Isaiah pulled out his own scope to see. "Well, I'll be. You are right, Your Majesty! It looks like three armies." Sure enough, the approaching forces wore three distinct colors and they had not taken any battle positions. "Where did these armies come from and why are they here?" Isaiah asked.

"I am not sure, Isaiah, but it might be a good idea to call off our army." Isaiah turned to see General Williams getting his troops into battle formation, and he rode toward them, frantically calling them off, as Aldar kept watch on the approaching troops. He could see the banners of each army, but they were too far away for him to make them out. He watched a moment longer, then turned his mount to join his generals. "Isaiah," he said, "there is an entourage headed our way; we must meet them. General Williams, join us. Let us bring a century of soldiers with us; we cannot assume they are friendly."

A few minutes later, they were on their way toward the advancing entourage. As they grew closer, Aldar could see them more clearly. Four soldiers were holding up flags. The soldier in front had a solid green flag which represented peace. He could not believe what he saw next—a purple flag with a rider with a drawn bow, the flag of Violida. "Barnabas?" he asked. Next, he saw a red-and-gold flag bearing a crouching tiger, the symbol of Mirodia. "King Unidad?" Aldar was stunned. The fourth flag was black, with a white image of a man striking an anvil with a hammer, the flag of Salonia. "Emperor Savage?" That was really shocking, considering Salonia was an ally of Apollyon.

Aldar and his men slowed their horses to a trot as they drew near the entourage. It was then that he saw Barnabas behind the first flagman. Everyone came to a halt and looked at each other in silence as Aldar looked at the other monarchs in disbelief. Then Aldar nodded. "King Unidad," he said, and Unidad nodded. "Emperor Savage." Savage also returned the nod. Then Aldar gave King Zanthor a long glance. "Barnabas," he said as King Zanthor nodded to him.

All the men sat in silence; Aldar not sure if he was dreaming.

Barnabas smiled. "Son, we need to talk."

Chapter Forty-Nine

Daniel's Lament

Daniel paced in his chambers. He was exhausted. He felt helpless. He had been through all kinds of hell, but even after having Shiva taken away from him and years of verbal and physical abuse, nothing had prepared him for this. He wished that Xavier had never made his promise to Shiva and had killed him with his parents. This woman was not the woman he loved. Sure, she looked like Shiva, beautiful as ever, but that cursed, forsaken eye had taken possession of her. Whether the real Shiva was buried deep inside, he did not know.

He tried to smile and do whatever it took to keep Shiva, or whatever she was, calm; she was so unstable. He hated it when she touched him. It sent shivers down his spine, and when they kissed, her lips were cold and waxy.

Now he was waiting for her to come. She had told him that she had something important to say. He cringed to think of what she might say.

A knock came at the door, and Shiva walked, in the glow of the eye making her look demonic. She walked up and kissed him, then said, "My love, I am sorry for keeping you waiting. I just had a meeting with Virion and Pirena. As you know, Maximus has not been found and there is a possibility we may never find him. I have forgiven Virion for his ignorant stupidity. I know he had no idea this was going to happen. I wish I knew what happened. I feel a presence in that forest and have tried to seek it out, but whenever I come close, I am repulsed and cannot get closer. I have told the army to steer clear of the forest."

She tried to hold back her tears. "I fear my son is dead," she said, hugging him and then putting her head against his chest.

Despite being repulsed, Daniel embraced her; her bloodred tears stained his shirt. For a moment, he felt like she was the real Shiva, but then she pulled away and ran around, excited. She twirled around, then ran over to him and kissed him again. "Do you know what this means, my love?"

Daniel shrugged. "I have no idea."

Shiva laughed. "You are a silly man, but that is what I love about you. I have decided to move our wedding to tomorrow. You must become emperor and I must bear us a son."

Daniel felt like he was about to vomit. "But we don't know if Maximus is dead or not. Should we take time for mourning?"

Shiva frowned. "I have already mourned. The time for mourning is over. If he is alive, he shall be emperor. We planned on getting married anyway, and I still want to have a child with you." She looked at him. "Are you not excited, my love?"

Daniel hesitated for a moment, then smiled. "Yes, my love, I cannot wait. I'm sorry, I guess I wasn't ready for such a wonderful surprise."

Shiva laughed gleefully. "Well, my love, the hour is late; we must get our rest. See you tomorrow."

The next morning came too soon for Daniel. He had not slept at all. With bloodshot eyes, he looked at himself in the mirror. A tear ran down his face. "This is not how this was supposed to be," he muttered quietly. "I was supposed to marry the woman I love years ago. We were going to spend the rest of our lives together. We were going to have children and live a long and happy, prosperous life. I am glad Emperor Pulsar is dead. He took my Shiva away, then turned her into this monster. He got what he deserved."

He picked up a vial of poison that he had made a long time ago—when Shiva had married Xavier. He had managed to keep the poison hidden all these years and never used it because, he had thought that somehow, someday, he would get back with her. But now he was in this hopeless situation. His eyes welled with tears, and he looked upward. "I am sorry, Mother and Father. I died the day Shiva got married, and I have been dead all these years. There is no reason for me to live. The woman I loved is no more, just an abomination." He started to shake as he pulled the cork from the vial and put the vial to his lips but then threw it to the floor. The vial smashed into pieces, leaving a stain on the floor. "What in the name of Apollyon am I doing?" he asked himself.

"Shiva—the real Shiva—would not have wanted me to give up. I must not give up. I must continue to live. I will not give up, and as disgusting as it is, I must marry her. I must gain her trust. I must figure out how to destroy the eye—not for myself but for the entire world." He looked in the mirror again and, instead of sorrow, he saw determination. "I am going to do this."

A knock came at the door and a soldier came in, announcing, "It is time."

Daniel set his jaw. "I am ready."

Everything moved quickly, and before Daniel knew it, he and Shiva had said their vows and were having their reception. Looking at the room they were in, he was amazed at how fast Shiva had removed the old symbol of Apollyon. All the tapestries and flags now were red, with the reddish-orange orb. He picked at his meal while Shiva ate beside him. Watching her eat, he thought, *She eats like anyone else would. She breathes and her heart beats, yet when I touch her and kiss her, it is like she is dead.* He still wondered if Shiva—the real Shiva—was trapped somewhere inside, fighting to get out. There was so much he did not know.

"What is wrong, my love? You seem distant. Are you all right?" Shiva asked, interrupting his thoughts.

"I am fine, my love. I guess I am overwhelmed by the excitement of the day. I never thought we would ever get together. I never dreamed we would ever get married."

Shiva smiled. "Well, we are, my husband, and I have never been happier in my life." She put her arm around him, and her smile turned into a devious grin. "We can cut this celebration short, and we could have an early honeymoon."

It took all of Daniel's strength to hold back a shiver. He forced a smile. "That sounds great, but what about our guests?"

Shiva laughed. "We have entertainment; Virion can tell stories about us, or something." She stood up and looked at the people who had shown up for their happy day. "Ladies and gentlemen, I appreciate your love and support on this happiest of occasions—"

Virion burst through the door. Shiva had apparently not noticed that he had already left the celebration. "Your Majesty, I have some news." Virion stopped as Shiva's angry face grew dark, and her eyes glowed brightly, as did the eye. He cursed. *Here we go again*, he thought as she raised the eye over her head and everyone in the room dropped to their knees. When he found himself floating in the air, he somehow found it amusing that he was getting used to this.

"This had better be good, Virion Nebula, or I will kill you this time for real, you worm."

Virion did not panic. "I have a report that the northern and southern Antillean armies have joined together to make one army. It looks as though they plan on invading our land."

Shiva let Virion gently back to the ground, her anger replaced by surprise. "Are you sure, Virion?"

Virion nodded. "They were spotted by one of Pirena's hidden scouts."

Shiva muttered, "I am a fool. Of course, Aldar would plan retaliation. I will have to meet with Aldar and apologize for my dead husband's stupidity. I really do feel bad about Victor and Amber's deaths; however, I also need to inform him that I and Daniel now rule the world. I will have to meet with every nation about this change. They can still rule their lands but will have to answer to us. They must respect the almighty eye of the cyclops or face our wrath and the dire consequences of disobedience."

Addressing the crowd, she said, "I am sorry for this outburst. Please enjoy the rest of your meal." When the crowd stood up and looked at her in silence, she screamed, "I said enjoy yourself!" in an inhuman voice. The crowd jumped into action and acted as though there had been no interruption.

"Virion, stay there. I will be with you in a minute. I need to discuss things with you." Virion nodded.

Shiva kissed Daniel passionately. "I am sorry, my love, but I must cancel our romantic evening, for I must plan."

Daniel held in a sigh of relief.

"I must make plans. Even with the power of the eye, it will take some time to meet with all of the rulers. You will be in charge in my stead. I expect you to make no decisions without me." When Daniel nodded, Shiva smiled, then turned to Virion. "Come with me, Virion, I need your help in planning."

Daniel watched her leave, feeling relieved that at least for now, they were not to celebrate their honeymoon. He also felt sorry, for the world was to face the reality of the evil that had been wrought upon it.

Chapter Fifty

Alliance

"I need more proof," said Emperor Raphael Savage of Salonia. "I am here with my army to see for ourselves. I am sorry, Aldar, for what Xavier has done to your family, and I do not blame you for attacking Apollyon; however, Xavier is an old ally of mine, and I am not convinced that this eye of the cyclops is what you claim it is. If I find out that he really is a threat to the world, you certainly will have my support; however, if I find out the eye's power is not real and out of grief, Xavier foolishly risked his empire, I will pull out.

"I know I am despised for what I have done," he continued, "and I do not want our disagreements to stand in the way. I am many things, but I am also a man of my word, and I will not interfere with the fight you have with Apollyon. Eye or not, what Xavier did to you was heinous and unforgivable, and I wish you luck in avenging your parents."

Aldar nodded in understanding. "Fair enough," he said as Emperor Savage took his seat.

King Theodore Unidad of Mirodia stood up to speak. He was a dark-skinned man with a thick accent. "As you know, Mirodia has been a neutral country for many years. That is why our jungles have remained unspoiled. My people have lived in happiness and prosperity. We only go to war if our way of life has been threatened. Even though we have not been involved with your conflict, I have always considered you a friend. I know of this legend of the eye, and I am a firm believer that mortal man should never delve into evil powers.

"Your father and mother were good people and did not deserve what was handed to them. I am so sorry for your loss and for the unbelievable trials you have been through. I also do not wish this to happen to me or the people of Mirodia, and you have my support and devotion, for the eye is a danger to us all. Xavier needs to be stopped and the eye needs to be destroyed." King Unidad took his seat, and Barnabas Zanthor stood up and smiled at Aldar, hoping his son-in-law would smile back.

Aldar looked at him indifferently. "Do you wish to say something, father-in-law?" Aldar asked.

"Yes, I do, son. As you know, my lovely daughter contacted me and told me of the situation you were in. Regretfully, I refused to help, further damaging my relationship with her, you, and your land. I have changed my mind. I contacted Emperor Savage and King Unidad and, with much effort, convinced them to join me. Between our three armies, we have two hundred thousand soldiers—one hundred and sixty if Emperor Savage pulls out. Combined with your army, we will be a formidable opponent." He looked at Aldar somberly. "I am sorry, son. I did you wrong; I did your father wrong. I let my grandchildren down; I let my daughter, whom I love so much, down; and I let Antillean down."

Barnabas walked forward to stand directly in front of Aldar and started to cry. He got down on his knees. "What I did was cowardly. I was afraid. I did not wish for Xavier Pulsar to invade our land as well. I committed a grievous error, and I am ashamed of myself. I know I have no right to ask, but I beg your forgiveness. I am willing to lay my life down and fight by your side and defeat this threat that can destroy us all."

Aldar stood up. "You have said enough, Father." He looked sternly at Barnabas. "You are right; what you did was cowardly, and it hurt Zena badly, especially this last time you refused to help. We could have used you. A lot of men and woman died in this senseless war, and heaven only knows how many would have lived if you had shown up. There is nothing that can be done about that; what is done is done. However, you are here now, and you brought us one, maybe two, more incredible armies." He put his hand on Barnabas's shoulder. "We still have a lot to work out between us. You certainly have your work cut out for you with Zena; she is not happy you are here. Despite all of this, I forgive you. We need you. We need your help. And thank you for coming with allies."

Barnabas stood up, and the two men shook hands. Aldar was about to say more when Zena walked in. When she saw Aldar shaking hands with Barnabas, her face turned red in anger. "So now you come crawling to us."

Barnabas looked at his daughter. "Zena, I am—"

"Save your pathetic apology," Zena said. "I don't know why Aldar has allowed you back. If it were up to me, I would have thrown you out. Because of your cowardice, Mother and Father Talon are dead. I hold you responsible for their deaths. My husband may have accepted your apology, but I will not give you my forgiveness, you coward. I love my mother, for I know she had no control of the situation, but as far as I am concerned, Father, you are dead to me."

Zena stormed out of the tent. Her words had cutting Barnabas to the core, and he stood visibly shaking from the verbal lashing he had received. Aldar spoke softly. "I am sorry, Father. Like I said, you have a lot of work ahead of you."

"Abigail is here with me. Zena loves her. Maybe she could talk to Zena; at least there is that."

There was another commotion as a soldier ran into the tent. "Your Majesty—"

Aldar threw his hands up. "What now?" he shouted.

The soldier bowed. "There's a woman outside; she is flying in the air."

Aldar looked at the soldier, dumbfounded. "What did you say?" he asked.

"A woman is flying around the camp. She has what might be the eye of the cyclops in her hands."

Aldar and the other monarchs ran out of the tent to find that the sun was nearly set, making the sky look red. The woman with the eye streaked across the sky like a shooting star. She stopped and slowly descended to the ground in front of them. Dark clouds started to swirl high in the air, and thunder rumbled as she landed. "Shiva?" Aldar asked, his voice trembling in surprise.

Shiva snarled, and her reddish-orange eyes and the eye pulsed. "What in the name of the eye is this?" she hissed. She glared at Aldar and the other monarchs, who all stared back in stunned surprise. "I come here expecting to see the Antillean army. Instead, I see armies from Violida, Mirodia, and Salonia? Why? How?" she said scornfully.

Aldar approached her and bowed. After she, in turn, respectfully bowed to him, Aldar spoke again. "Empress Pulsar, it is good to see you alive."

"Thank you, Aldar. It feels great to be alive. It has been a long time since we last saw each other. Please, you can call me Empress Enigma. Xavier Pulsar is dead. I am now married to Emperor Daniel Enigma."

A shocked silence permeated the air. "Xavier Pulsar is dead?" Aldar asked, not believing what he had just heard. "What happened to him? How did he die?"

Shiva laughed slightly, then smiled. "I killed that monster. I burned him alive with the purifying fire of the almighty eye of the cyclops. He used the power of the eye to bring me back to life, and I used the power of the eye to end his. He deserved to die. He took away my love; he killed my father; he enslaved my family. He is also responsible for my mother and sister turning against me, for they have begged me to give my responsibility away."

She looked at Aldar. "You already know what he did to you, what he did to your land and your parents. You should have seen the look on his face before I killed him. He cried like a child; he screamed like a girl. It was glorious. He suffered for all the evil things he had done." She laughed maniacally.

Aldar was taken aback. This was not the Shiva he knew. It looked like the eye had possessed her.

"I have purged this world of the evil my first husband unleashed upon this world," Shiva said. "I have purged Apollyon of that evil symbol of the man consumed by fire. Apollyon has a new symbol, of the eye of the cyclops, the symbol of hope and prosperity." Bloodred tears flowed down her cheeks, "My son, Maximus, is dead as well," she announced.

Aldar's eyes widened. *She killed him as well*, he thought in disbelief.

"He and Virion split away from each other, and he was killed by some strange force while he rode off the beaten path. At least we think he is dead."

Aldar looked to his side and saw Enoch and Elaine. They both shook in fear as they gave him a knowing look.

"His entourage was decimated. Soldiers and horses were torn apart, and I cannot get close to this force. It is evil, whatever it is.

"I am sorry, Aldar. You are a good man, and you and your family did not deserve this to happen to you. While what happened to you was reprehensible, it was also necessary."

Aldar scowled at her. "What do you mean? You are telling me their deaths were necessary?"

Shiva nodded solemnly. "My first husband's actions, while regrettable, where necessary, for if the eye had not been stolen, evil in this world would still reign. The almighty eye is here to judge the corrupt and bring justice to the weak. I am the ambassador of the eye. I do not blame you for attacking Apollyon, for I would have done the same if I were in the same situation. But Xavier is dead. There is no need for war and more bloodshed, no more suffering. I was going to travel to all your kingdoms and tell all of you this, but I guess I do not have to. So, I am here to announce that I, Empress Shiva Enigma, am supreme ruler of the world."

"What do you mean, Shiva?" Aldar asked.

Shiva glared at him but then smiled. "Please show me respect and call me *Your Majesty*."

"I am sorry, Your Majesty, I am confused at what you mean."

Shiva sighed. "It means I answer to the eye, and you answer to me. The almighty eye has told me these things. You still will rule your kingdoms. You will still have power. The difference is you answer to me.

However, if you refuse to obey the eye and you refuse to obey me, you will receive the eye's wrath."

Shiva raised the eye over her head. She rose into the air and chanted, and a bolt of lightning shot up into the sky. A dark cloud appeared in the sky, and thunder shook the ground. She chanted again, and the cloud slowly disappeared. Her smile returned. "I give you one month to return to your lands. I will meet with each of you. That is when I will expect your fealty to the eye and to me. If you do not swear your fealty, you will be destroyed by the eye. What I showed you today was just a snippet of my power. If you all do this, you will be rewarded with peace and prosperity and will be protected from evil."

She looked at Barnabas. "I expected your son-in-law, not you. I suppose the deaths of your in-laws changed your mind." She then regarded Theodore Unidad. "I am surprised to see you here. I thought you were a neutral country."

King Unidad started to sweat nervously. "I was approached by King Zanthor. He told me word of the eye being stolen and the unfortunate deaths of the king and queen of Antillean. We did not know what Xavier Pulsar's intent was, so we decided to join in the fight."

Shiva smiled. "A noble gesture for an old friend. That was a very brave thing to do, but you now have nothing to worry about." She next looked at Raphael Savage and frowned. "Now, seeing you here surprises me. I know you have worked with my first husband for decades. You have been friends for just as long. This concerns me. You plan on betraying your friend? How can I trust you will not do the same for me?"

Emperor Savage shook in fear. "I was just here to find out if all of this was true. I was going to pull out if the rumors turned out to be false and the eye was just a worthless rock."

Shiva snarled at him. "Well, as you can see, the rumor is true, and the eye is not a worthless rock. The eye will forgive you this time for your ignorant comment, but never disrespect it again."

Emperor Savage fell to his knees. "I will not disrespect the eye again, and I will not betray you," he pleaded.

"You had better not betray me or you will suffer a worse fate than my first husband's."

Shiva flew high into the air. "You have thirty days to return to your homes and prepare your people. You must decide to obey the almighty eye and me and live or to not and be destroyed." She smiled. "That will be a glorious day. We will be united in peace. Happiness will reign, and pain and sorrow will be no more." She turned to Emperor Savage and grimaced. "You will be the first one I will visit." Then she turned toward Apollyon and flew away, shouting, "May the eye bless you all."

Everyone watched in silence as she disappeared into the distance, and then Emperor Savage looked at Aldar. "Well, I guess you were right about that eye."

Chapter Fifty-One

To Conspire

Someone knocked on her door. Quill Quasar walked to her door, wondering who it could be. No one came to see her. People in general avoided her and her youngest daughter, Shannon. Especially now that her oldest daughter, Shiva, was the ruler of Apollyon. She opened her door cautiously, and her eyes fell upon an old, familiar face. "Daniel!" She wrapped her arms around him. "I am so happy to see you." She kissed him on the cheek. "I am sorry for what has happened to you and my daughter." Then she pulled back. "I am sorry, Daniel. You are royalty now; I should have asked."

Daniel smiled and kissed her on the cheek. "No worries. You can hug me anytime. Besides, being formal is the least of my concerns."

It was then that Quill noticed another person standing behind Daniel: Virion Nebula. She stiffened.

Daniel put his hand on her shoulder. "Do not fear. He is on our side."

Quill managed a thin smile. "General Nebula, welcome to my home."

"Mother, who is here?" Shannon asked, then stiffened when her eyes met Virion's.

When Shannon noticed Daniel, he smiled at her. "It is all right he is with me."

Shannon smiled but entered the living room reluctantly.

"Please take a seat," Quill offered. Daniel and Virion took their seats, and she said, "Let me make tea."

"Thank you, no," Daniel said. "It is vitally important that we talk about your daughter."

Quill sighed as she and Shannon took their seats, and Quill started to tear up. "I lost my lovely daughter when she married Xavier Pulsar. Then I lost her again when she was accidentally killed, and I lost her again when she was brought back. This time is worse because she has turned into a tyrant far worse than Xavier Pulsar. I hate that man for what he has done to my poor Shiva! Has she not suffered enough? She needs rest, eternal rest."

Tears welled in Daniel's eyes. "I know. I have felt the same; she did not deserve the hand that was dealt to her."

"That is why we are here, Quill," Virion said. "We need your and Shannon's help. She has become more and more erratic. It is only a matter of time before she starts killing innocent people. I am sorry for what Xavier has done to your family and Shiva, especially now. Xavier was blinded by his grief, and I was caught up in that. I had no idea this was going to happen to Shiva.

"I am sorry I was a part of this," he continued. "Because of my involvement, the whole world is in danger. I will not ask for forgiveness, for I do not deserve it. I do want to help in whatever capacity I can. I know it will not make up for what I was involved with."

Quill nodded. "Okay, Daniel, what is it you need from us? There is not much I can do. All I want is my daughter to get the peace she deserves."

Daniel smiled. "We are going to have you over for dinner." When he saw Quill and Shannon share confused looks, he explained, "We are hoping maybe you could talk sense to her. Maybe she might give up the eye."

Quill rolled her eyes. "You were not present when I talked to Shiva."

Daniel frowned. "I did not know that you had talked to her."

Quill teared up again. "I talked to her about when she was a child. I talked to her and the eye. When I mentioned my concerns, she grew angry with me. She told me not to mention it again. I still tried talking to her about it. Then she threatened me. She said that the almighty eye was angry. She told me if she saw me again, she would kill me."

A knock came at the door, and they all looked at each other. "Best you stay here," Quill said as she stood up. Quill opened the door.

"Hello, mother," Shiva said.

Quill's jaw dropped, and then lightning shot from the eye, hitting her in the chest. She flew backward into the living room, hitting the floor hard.

Everyone jumped off their chairs, Shannon running to Shiva, yelling, "No!" Another bolt hit her in the chest, throwing her backward and she landed next to her mother.

Daniel ran to Quill and Shannon and looked at their faces. He had seen that look before: the blank stare of death. He screamed at Shiva, and she hit him with a bolt as well. He screamed in agony as he slammed into the chair.

Shiva scowled at Virion. "Do you have anything to say?" When Virion shook his head and slowly backed away, Shiva walked over to Daniel. As he tried to catch his breath, she said, "My love, why are you here? Have you decided to betray me? Why were you talking with my mother? She is a betrayer of the eye." She turned her attention back to Virion. "You had better start explaining, or you will join my mother and sister."

Virion was not shaken and said calmly, "Daniel wanted to see Quill. After all, she was his mother-in-law and Shannon was his sister-in-law. He had no idea they were considered traitors."

Daniel gasped as he struggled to his feet. "We were just visiting. I was inviting them to dinner."

Shiva looked at the bodies of her mother and sister, hesitating. "This still does not explain why you are here, Virion."

Virion shook his head. "Did you forget, Your Majesty? Daniel and I go out sometimes for a walk."

Shiva blinked. "Oh, that is right. I forgot about that," she said quietly and then lowered her head.

"We decided to visit on a whim. We were not conspiring. It was an innocent mistake, nothing more."

Emboldened, Daniel asked, "Why are you here, Shiva? I thought you were going to be gone for a week."

Shiva found herself on the defensive. "All the armies from Antillean, Salonia, and Violida were there. They all were poised to attack because of my dead husband's actions. They were coming for him and the eye. I sent them away to swear fealty to me in thirty days. That is why I am here early. When I got home, I saw you were gone, so I went looking for you. One of Pirena's spies told me where you were."

She looked down at her mother and sister and started to cry. "I am sorry, Mother; I am sorry, Shannon." The Shiva of old returned as she sobbed, "I killed the rest of my family. I am a monster. I am so sorry." Daniel put his hand on her shoulder, and she pulled away, screaming, "This is your fault, Daniel!" Daniel looked at her, dumbfounded. "It is your fault. And yours as well, Virion. If you had not come here, they would still be alive. I should kill you both." She let loose an unholy scream, then fell to the floor.

"Shiva, I am sorry," Daniel told her.

Shiva trembled as she sobbed. "Just get out, both of you. Please just get out."

Virion and Daniel stood in silence for a moment, and then the eye flashed, knocking them to the ground. "I said get out!" Shiva screeched.

Daniel and Virion scrambled to their feet and left the house. Once in the street, Virion scratched his head. "I need to speak to Pirena on this matter. I need to figure out whose side she is on." He and Daniel wiped the dirt off their clothes, then turned and walked away, leaving a mourning Shiva behind.

Chapter Fifty-Two

Dealing with Guilt

The sun was setting on a long day as the rulers of Antillean, Salonia, Violida, and Mirodia were still in intense meetings. Word had gotten out throughout all the armies that they were not backing down. Zena scowled as she saw her father sitting in the tent and nodding his head as Aldar spoke.

"There's my child," an old familiar voice said behind her.

Zena turned and smiled. "Mother!" she yelled. Zena ran to her mother and gave her a big hug.

Abigail touched Zena's cheek and smiled. "My lovely child, now queen of Antillean. My, oh, am I proud of you! That crown looks glorious—although not as glorious as you. I am so proud of you and the woman you have become. You know your father is proud of you as well."

Zena's smile disappeared, and she lowered her head. Abigail put her arm around her shoulder. "I know you are angry with him. You know, I was not happy with him myself."

A tear ran down Zena's cheek. "Why, Mother? Why did Father refuse to help?"

Abigail pulled a handkerchief from her skirts and dabbed at Zena's cheek. "I am not exactly sure why. I asked him several times, and he would never give me an honest answer. It took all my strength not to scream.

"It pained me so to see you and Aldar leave," she continued, "and it pained me worse when you talked to us last. The only thing I could think of was we were in a civil war when he was a child and he saw people get slaughtered. I know that shook him to the core, and I think he was afraid. He did not wish to see that happen again. I understand, Zena. I understand the anger and frustration you are going through. I have been angry with him off and on all these years, but one thing has not changed—I love him. I have loved him despite his shortcomings, despite me thinking he was a coward."

Zena shook her head. "Well, I don't love him. He turned his back on us, and for that I cannot forgive him."

Abigail nodded. "I understand, dear, I really do. I cannot say I would not feel the same in your situation. All I know is he realizes that he made a grave mistake, and he is sorry for not being there. He is here now. I know he is terrified, but despite that, he came, and he brought two other kingdoms with him. I am not asking you to forgive him, for that is something you must decide in your own timing.

"I am, however, asking you to at least talk to him. Listen to what he has to say in a civil manner. He wants so desperately to talk to you. When the time is right, could you please talk to him? If not for him, do it for me, please. It pains me so to see you two at odds with each other."

Shiva looked pained. "I will try, Mother. I promise I will try. I cannot promise we will make amends, but I will try."

Abigail smiled. "That is all I ask of you. Hear him out, and I am sure he will hear you out as well." She hugged Zena again. "Thank you, Zena. I hope someway, somehow, you two will work this out." She smiled. "I wish Hunter were here, but I understand he is too young. But I am glad to be able to see Aurora."

Zena smiled. "I think that could be arranged. She is sitting around a campfire with Enoch and Elaine."

"That would be wonderful. I have heard a lot about those two. I would love to get acquainted with them."

~ ~ ~

"Where is Enoch?" Aurora asked as she returned to the campfire, handing Elaine a plate of sausages to roast and took a seat.

Elaine shrugged. "I am not sure. I think he walked over to that lake," she said, gesturing to a nearby body of water. "He seemed to be depressed tonight."

Aurora frowned. "With everything that has happened to all of us, I am not surprised."

Elaine nodded solemnly. "I think he is missing Mother and Father tonight. He has been a wonderful brother. He has been taking so much time taking care of me and my grief, he has not dealt with his."

Aurora nodded. "This war has done nothing but give us grief, and now with Shiva with the eye, I fear things are going to get worse."

Elaine nodded again. "I guess I should go and find him."

Aurora stood up, saying, "Let me."

"Are you sure, Aurora?"

Aurora nodded firmly. "Yes. Your brother is special to me. He has been there for me as well."

Elaine smiled. "I will keep the fire burning, and I will cook the sausages."

Aurora put her hand on Elaine's shoulder as she walked past her and headed to the lake. She found Enoch sitting at the lake's edge. The moonlight rippled on the gentle waves. Enoch was tossing stones into the lake as he whistled and hummed to himself. "May I join you?" Aurora asked.

Enoch turned. "Aurora. You sure can," he said, standing up. He took his jacket off and placed it on the ground. "Please take a seat," he said, indicating his coat. When Aurora chuckled, he asked, "What?"

"Enoch Eclipse, you are ever the gentlemen."

He smiled. "Which would you rather have, Enoch the gentlemen or Enoch the barbarian?"

Aurora put her hand to her chin in thought. "I think a prefer a little of both."

They both laughed as they sat down. She offered her hands, and Enoch placed his hands in hers. "Please talk to me, Enoch."

He looked at her, confused. "Well of course. You are here; it would be kind of rude not to talk."

Aurora squeezed his hands. "I know you are troubled. You have been busy helping Elaine in her sorrow. You've also helped me, so I want to help you. Please let me know what you are feeling."

Enoch frowned. "I miss my mother and father. They gave their lives for us. I know Father accidentally killed Shiva, and I know he and Mother are the most hated people in Apollyon, especially now. Xavier Pulsar is responsible for Shiva becoming a monster, but my father will be blamed. I know that my sister and I will be equally hated. I am afraid for Elaine; I want her to be safe. I am glad to be a part of this fight. I know the odds are against us, but I believe we will overcome. Like you, I am not afraid to die. I will gladly lay my life down for freedom. I feel that if I die, it won't be in vain.

"I am also overwhelmed by all the love you and your family have given us," he told her. "In a lot of ways, I did not blame Zena for not trusting us at first. I feel that Elaine and I do not deserve what you all have given us. I feel terrible, and I cannot help but blame myself for your grandparents' deaths. I still feel responsible. I feel that us coming here brought the wrath of Pirena down upon you."

Aurora gave him a concerned look. "You cannot blame yourself, Enoch. You did what you were expected to do. You had no control over what has happened. Yes, your father accidentally killed Shiva. It was an honest accident.

"Even if he had been successful," she went on, "Pirena still might have found out my grandfather's plan and still would have attacked. We all had no idea that the eye really had this power. I was told by Bethany this was just a legend. It is irrational to blame yourself. You hear me? This is not your fault, and I don't want you to blame yourself."

A tear ran down Enoch's cheek, and he hugged her. "I love you," he whispered in her ear.

Aurora jumped to her feet, looking panicked.

Enoch got to his feet hurriedly. "I am sorry, Aurora, I have said too much."

Aurora looked into his eyes, and before she could think, she wrapped her arms around him and kissed him. Enoch pulled away, his eyes wide, then pulled her to him. They kissed passionately. As her heart felt like it was going to pound out of her chest, Aurora felt a feeling she had never experienced before, terrifying and exciting at the same time. She loved it, drinking it all in.

They kissed for several minutes, Aurora not wanting it to end.

"Ahem," said a voice behind her.

"Mother!" Aurora quickly pulled away from Enoch and turned around. "Grandmother!" she exclaimed when she saw Abigail. Her face turned three shades of red as she tried to think of an explanation. "Um, we were . . . um, we were just . . . um, we were—"

"You were just kissing," Zena said.

Aurora looked down. "Yes, Mother, we were. Well, you know."

"Well, I come looking for you and Enoch. Elaine said you were here. I guess we found you," Zena said.

Abigail looked over to Zena. "I think it is safe to say they are more than just friends," she smirked.

Zena put her hands on her hips. "Well, I should say so." Zena scowled at Enoch.

At first, Enoch backed away from her gaze, but then he stepped forward. "I know you told me to behave myself."

"That you did. What do you have to say for yourself, young man?"

Aurora moved to say something, but Enoch looked at her and shook his head. "This is what I have to say. I love your daughter. She is the best thing to happen to me besides my parents and sister. With all due respect, I am glad I kissed her, and I am not sorry that I did not behave myself."

Zena looked at Enoch, wide-eyed. "Well, you know what, young man?"

Enoch looked at her defiantly. "What?" he asked.

Zena walked up to him and looked at him, face-to-face. Enoch braced himself for a slap or maybe a kick to the groin. Then Zena wrapped her arms around him. "I am happy for you and my daughter." Enoch almost fell over.

Zena kissed him on the cheek. "Aldar and I are fine with you courting our daughter."

Aurora hugged her mother, and Abigail laughed. "I remember my first kiss. Barnabas kissed me under a clothesline—not exactly the most romantic setting. However, I will never forget that moment as long as I live."

Zena smiled. "Our first kiss was under the bridge leading to the palace." The older women laughed, and Aurora turned red again, embarrassed. Seeing her embarrassment, they laughed even harder.

"Enoch, I want you to know we expect you two to wait until this war is over, and if you are still in love, you can ask for her hand."

Enoch and Aurora nodded. "I understand. We will honor and respect what you have decided," Enoch said.

"One more thing. We do expect you two to behave yourselves in public."

Enoch smiled. "Yes, we will behave ourselves in public."

Zena smiled and looked at Abagail, who also smiled. "Young love," they said in unison.

Aurora rolled her eyes. "Well, Mother, those sausages Elaine was cooking smelled good. I think we should get some."

Abagail nodded. "Well, you two, we will meet you at the campfire. Don't take too long." She smiled.

Enoch and Aurora watched Zena and Abagail leave, then looked at each other, smiled, and kissed.

Chapter Fifty-Three

For the Love of Shiva

Daniel looked at his plate of food, and his stomach turned. He could not eat after seeing Shiva kill her mother and sister. Shiva, by contrast, had finished dinner and was finishing an apple pie. She smiled. The day before, she had sobbed and mourned the loss of her mother and sister, and today, she acted as though nothing had happened.

"I cannot wait to meet with the other rulers! By now, they should have broken camp. Praise the almighty eye the war is over and there will be peace!" she squeaked gleefully like a child. Then she frowned. "Daniel, you have not eaten a thing on your plate. Are you all right?"

Daniel tried to smile. "I am not feeling well, my love. I seem to not have an appetite tonight," he replied.

"Is it the food? If the food is not to your liking, I can replace the chef."

"No," Daniel said, more hastily than he had meant to. He certainly did not want the chef to die. "I mean, the food is fine. I am not well."

Shiva eyed his pie. "Well, my love, if you are not hungry, I will take your piece of pie." She took the pie.

As he watched her devour the pie, he wondered, *when will this evening be over?* He and Virion had a plan, and if it worked, Daniel would take the eye away from her and they would kill her. *Oh, Shiva, it pains me so to see you this way. Soon—very soon—your pain and suffering will end, and you will have peace,* he thought. When Shiva eyed him, he felt his throat go dry. So far, he had managed not to make love to her, but she had love in her eyes as she stood from her chair and took his hand.

"Come, my love, let us make a child."

Daniel started to gag and, standing up from his chair, took off. "I am sorry. I'm sick." He ran into the privy and made himself vomit. *That will ruin the mood*, he thought. He hoped it would, anyway. When he walked out, he said, "I am sorry, my love. I am ready," gambling that she would not pursue him for the rest of the night.

Shiva looked away. "No, that is all right. You are obviously sick. It is time for bed; let us rest." Daniel held in a sigh of relief, hoping that after tonight, he would no longer have to deal with this.

Once in their bedchamber, they readied themselves for the night. Shiva did not actually sleep in the bed with him. Instead, she would place the eye on a pedestal and would sit cross-legged on a mat for hours, chanting, making the eye glow dimly. Daniel was not sure if she was in a sleep or a devilish trance; either way, he had to wait for the right moment.

Shiva blew out the last candle. "Good-night, my love," she said.

"See you in the morning, love," Daniel replied.

Daniel lay in bed, trying everything he could to pretend to be asleep without falling asleep—no easy task. After waiting half the night, he noticed the eye starting to dim and Shiva's chants getting quieter. The time had come.

He crawled out of bed and quietly crept across the floor, feeling sweat bead on his forehead and neck and run down his back. As he drew closer, he noticed the glow of the eye ebbing and flowing slightly, in time with Shiva's breathing. Sadness filled his heart as he made it to the eye and looked at Shiva.

Her eyes were closed. She looked so beautiful, and he thought of what could have been. What a tragedy. He forced a smile upon his face. *This is my act of love for you, my love—peace. Wonderful, glorious peace,* he thought. All he had to do was take the eye and command it to kill her, then place the eye on the pedestal that Xavier had made. Then he and Virion would figure out how to destroy the eye. *One thing at a time*, he thought.

He gently picked the eye up. He felt power surge through him. The eye brightened as he raised it over his head. The power was overwhelming.

He screamed as lightning coursed through his body. He crumpled, and the eye clattered across the floor.

Shiva's eyes opened and she let out a curse. "Daniel!" she screamed and ran to his side. His hands had burns on them, and he was trembling and gasping for air. "What in the name of Apollyon were you doing?" Daniel coughed violently as two guards walked in. "Get some water and a healer!" Shiva demanded. As one of the guards bowed and raced out the door, Shiva put Daniel's head on her lap. "I am amazed you are still alive," Shiva said.

"The feeling is mutual," he managed to say between coughs.

When the guard came in with a healer, the healer gave Shiva a cup, and she gave Daniel a drink. After several minutes, the healer had Daniel's hands bandaged. "He will be fine, Your Highness," the healer reassured her.

Once the guard and the healer had walked out, Shiva's eyes glowed brilliantly and narrowed. Daniel managed to crawl into bed, where he looked at her angry face. He managed a nervous smile as she walked up to him, but she snarled. "Were you trying to kill me?" she demanded.

"No, my love. It was mere curiosity—foolish curiosity, you might say," he said with a nervous laugh.

"Don't lie to me. If you were curious, all you had to do was ask, you cretin." She paced the floor. "One thing is for sure; I am glad the eye has protected me. I have made an agreement with the eye. It will shock anyone who touches it but me. Why, Daniel? Why do you betray me? I love you. I have given you a palace to live in, a kingdom to rule. I have given you all this, and this is how you repay me? I should have used the eye and finished you off.

"It's my mother's fault!" she fumed. "You talked to her without me. She influenced you, that cursed witch. She put a spell on you. Well, I am glad she is dead." She returned the eye to its pedestal and crawled into bed with him. She sobbed. "I have failed as an empress, and I have failed as a wife. I promise you we will overcome this. I do not know how to cure you from her spell, but I will do everything to make you love me."

Daniel looked at her, dumbfounded. He had thought for sure she was going to kill him. In some ways, he wished she had. He tried to say something, but she put her finger to his mouth. "say nothing, my love.

You must rest. I will treat you like the emperor you are, and you will love me again."

Then she returned to her mat and crossed her legs. "I love you," she said.

I love you too, Shiva, and I promise you somehow and some way, I am going to release you from your pain, Daniel thought.

Chapter Fifty-Four

Supreme Monarch

Aurora watched with pride as her father, standing on a makeshift platform, addressed all the gathered monarchs and armies. He had just been appointed supreme monarch and was to lead the march into battle against Shiva. All the other monarchs would still lead their armies, but final decisions were to be made by Aldar.

To Aurora's surprise, after her father had addressed the assembly, he walked up to her and hugged her. "I am sorry I have not had much time with you. I feel as though I am a failure at fatherhood."

Aurora frowned. "You are a wonderful father who just so happens to be fighting to save the world. I would say that is a good excuse for being just a tad busy."

Aldar kissed her cheek. "I love you." Aurora smiled as they hugged again, putting her head to his chest and wishing the hug would never end. As Zena approached with a smile, her father said, "Speaking of which, I have not been the greatest husband either." He pulled away from Aurora and caught Zena's arm to pull her to him and kiss her.

Zena's eyes widened as she pulled away. She looked at him, stupefied, and almost lost her balance before regaining her composure. She straightened her skirts, then smiled and jumped into Aldar's arms, kissing him with a passion she had not displayed in a long time.

This was Aldar's turn to be stupefied. He almost dropped Zena as she continued to kiss him. Cheers and whistles abounded around them, and Aurora smiled. Emperor Savage patted Aldar on the back and grinned, pointing over to a tent. "That tent is available. it has a cozy cot." Aldar, with a devious grin, walked toward the tent.

"Put me down, you barbarian!" Zena laughed. He put her down and shrugged.

Everyone around them was laughing. Although slightly embarrassed, Aurora found herself laughing. It felt like all the tension in the air was gone.

Aldar kissed Zena again. "Someday, my love, when this is over . . ." he whispered.

Zena smiled. "Someday, my love, someday," she repeated, and they kissed one more time.

Enoch and Elaine approached them, laughing. "Good," Aldar said. "I need to talk to you two, and you, Aurora."

"Yes, what is it, Aldar?" Enoch asked.

"Tomorrow we are entering the Apollyon border and I am sending out eight units ahead—two units from each nation—basically to scout for any hidden bands of resistance. I do not have anyone to go through the mountains. The path there is too narrow; however, I need you three to lead a group around the mountains near that forest where you encountered that beast."

When looks of concern showed on their faces, he added, "No worries. I am not asking you to go through the forest but around it. I figured Enoch; you were the most familiar with that area. You three will lead two hundred of some of my best soldiers. You should have no fear if that creature appears, if it appears at all.

"All eight groups will be equipped with a portable cystallis. You all will report to me each evening. Obviously if there is an emergency, you can contact us sooner. After we get further into Apollyon, you will rendezvous with us. We are to meet at the abandoned city of Ashtor. From there will be a straight line to Adaliah." He smiled at Aurora. "I know I am putting you, Enoch, and Elaine into a dangerous situation. But as you reminded me, you are not a little girl, nor is Elaine, and neither is Enoch a little boy." He looked at Enoch and Elaine. "Are you up to the task? I know that you had a terrifying experience."

Elaine frowned. "Yes, indeed, Aldar, I am afraid, but that does not mean I am not brave, I am glad to take up this challenge."

"Enoch?" Aldar asked.

"I am with my sister. We entered this war with you to make a difference. In honor of our mother and father, I gladly accept."

"Let us pray this all works and pray Shiva does not kill us before we get there."

"Your Majesty!" cried a soldier who ran up to them.

Aldar held up his hand, stopping the soldier. "It can wait."

"But, sir," the soldier protested.

"Give me five minutes," Aldar barked.

"Yes, Your Majesty," the soldier said as he walked off.

Aldar turned back to Aurora, Enoch, and Elaine. "I have five minutes." He offered them his arms, and they all had a group hug. After their hug was over, Aldar spoke. "In one hour, I will have a meeting with all the groups; then you will leave in the afternoon."

~ ~ ~

Afternoon came quickly. Aurora hugged and kissed her mother and father; then she mounted her horse. Everyone in the small band bowed their heads in respect. "May God protect you and guide your path," Aldar said. Aurora blew him a kiss as she, Enoch, and Elaine turned their horses.

"Let us be off," Enoch commanded.

Aldar put his arm around Zena, who said, "Our little girl is not so little anymore."

"You are right about that, my love," Aldar agreed.

"I am scared," Zena said.

"As am I," Aldar replied.

Zena wanted to say more but did not want to trouble Aldar. She was full of dread, an overwhelming feeling that she was never going to see Aurora again.

Chapter Fifty-Five

Relieving an Old Itch

Sweat trickled down Pirena's face as she wielded her battle staff Four soldiers with swords charged at her from all four sides. She dodged one soldier who took a swipe at her with a sword, and she tripped up another, then hit him in the face with the butt of the staff as another soldier took a swipe at her. She dodged that attack and swiped her staff upward, hitting him in the jaw. He crumpled, and she turned and hit the soldier she had tripped in the back of the head as he was trying to get up.

A look of terror crossed the last soldier's face. Pirena grinned and gestured for him to attack. The soldier dropped his sword. "I yield," he said.

Pirena laughed as she walked up to him casually. She hit him in the groin, and the soldier groaned, falling to the floor. "In war there is no yield, you fool." The soldiers slowly got up, and Pirena announced, "That is all for today." The sound of applause rang in the training room as the soldiers limped away.

"Virion," Pirena said, "what brings you here?"

Virion scowled at her. "You know full well why I am here. We need to talk."

Pirena grabbed a towel and dabbed the sweat from her brow. "Fine. I am all ears."

"Can we talk somewhere more private?" Virion asked.

"We are fine talking here," Pirena said. "You will just have to take your chances." She folded her arms, and Virion narrowed his eyes.

"What in the name of Apollyon do you think you are doing?" Virion demanded.

"I am doing what must be done."

"What does that mean?" Virion hissed.

"I don't like what has happened any more than you, Virion. Unfortunately, stealing the eye did not turn out to be such a good idea. I do not regret killing Victor Talon. I *do* regret stealing the eye, for I had no idea that Uncle's plan was going to fail so miserably. But I must do what Aunt Shiva asks of me. I am her tool, and I will do as I am told. It is foolish to resist. That is why I have spies tailing you; I am doing Aunt Shiva's bidding. Her bidding is my command."

Virion sneered at her. "I am disappointed in you. I have always thought you to be the most brave and fearless woman I know. Obviously, that has changed. You are afraid; you don't want to suffer like Xavier did."

"Admit it," he said, "you are afraid. For the first time in your life, you are afraid to die. Xavier's death shook you to the core. It is all right to admit you are afraid—I am afraid—but to be afraid yet do what is right, that is bravery. You are not weak because of fear; you are weak because you will not stand with us to defeat Shiva. Therefore, you are a coward."

Grabbing her staff, Shiva swiped it under Virion's feet and flipped him onto his back. Then she pulled one of her swords and put it to Virion's throat, rage filling her eyes. "I am not a coward, you decrepit old man. There is also a fine line between bravery and stupidity. Look, you and Daniel can do what you will. I will even applaud you if you can figure out how to destroy the eye. I, however, have chosen a different path. I have my own reasons for doing what I am doing. I will try not to stand in your way as much as I can; however, I will not disobey a direct order from Aunt Shiva." She put her sword away and offered her hand to Virion.

He pushed her hand away and got up on his own, looking at her in disappointment. "All right, you do what you see fit," he said, shaking his head.

A soldier walked in. "General Nebula, I have news from the front." He handed a letter to Virion, who frowned after reading it.

"What is it?" Pirena asked.

"None of your business," Virion snapped. "You can ask your aunt later. I also must do what must be done, Pirena." He scowled at as he turned to leave, making his way to Shiva and Daniel's living quarters.

~ ~ ~

Shiva looked at herself in the mirror and smiled. She was wearing a new crimson dress. "What do you think, Daniel?"

Daniel smiled. "You look stunning, my love."

Shiva walked up to him and kissed him. "Thank you. I want to look my best when I meet all the monarchs." There was a knock on the door, and Shiva said, "Daniel, be a dear and answer the door."

Daniel nodded and walked to the door. He fumbled a bit because of his bandaged hands but finally managed to open the door. "Virion," he said, and Virion looked at Daniel's, disappointed that their plan had not worked.

"Who is here?" Shiva asked. "Oh, Virion, come in."

Virion walked in and bowed. "I have news from the front." He handed her the note, and when she looked at it, her smile disappeared. Her eyes narrowed, then started to glow as anger showed on her face.

She screamed and the note caught fire in her hand. "I told them to go back home, and they betray me?" she screamed. "The fools! Did they think I was not serious? Do they not fear the wrath of the eye of the cyclops? Those traitors will pay! I will make them pray for death and will not give it to them until they can no longer scream."

She raised the eye over her head and chanted, then flew out the window while Virion and Daniel watched helplessly. They walked to the balcony as she shot across the sky like a bolt of lightning.

~ ~ ~

Shiva flew at an unimaginable speed. Her crown flew off her head, and her dress started to tatter. In fewer than five minutes, she had the armies in view. She stopped and floated in the air, pondering what to do. She was still too far away for them to see her; she could shake the earth and cause it to swallow them up. Or she could make rain and hail fall on them.

A devious idea came to her—she was not going to destroy them, at least not yet. She was going to toy with them awhile, make life miserable, and maybe they would run back home. Then she would take away their rights as monarchs so she and Daniel would be the only monarchs left.

She smiled. If they continued, she would wait for them to come all the way to Adaliah, and then she would destroy them all in grand fashion. "This will be fun!" she exclaimed as she flew back to the palace.

~ ~ ~

Virion and Daniel were shocked when Shiva flew back into the room with tattered dress and windswept hair. The devilish grin on her face was so intense that it sent shivers down Virion's spine.

Shiva walked to the door and spoke to one of the guards. "Find General Solaris. I have need for her." The guard bowed his head and left to do her bidding. "I lost my crown," Shiva said with a scowl. "Oh well, I will have another made."

After several minutes, Pirena walked in, her eyes widening as she looked at Shiva, and then she composed herself. "I am sorry, Aunt Shiva, for making you wait. I was taking a bath," she said, glaring at Virion. She then bowed. "I am at your service, Aunt Shiva. I will do what you command of me."

Shiva hugged Pirena, then kissed her cheek. "Pirena, my beloved niece, I am so glad you are so willing to serve. I am putting you on a special assignment. I need you to pack your weapons and your things. Meet me at the stables in one hour. I will have a horse ready with saddlebags with rations and everything you will need." Pirena bowed her head and left the room, and Virion could not help but pray for the souls of the approaching army. Shiva turned to him, saying, "I want you to order all of the armies back to Adaliah."

Virion scratched his head. "Why, Your Majesty? That does not make sense."

Shiva scowled. "It makes sense to me. Now do as you are told," she commanded.

Virion bowed. "It will be done."

~ ~ ~

An hour later, Pirena stood at the stables as Shiva approached. All the stable hands bowed their heads, all looking shocked at the state of Shiva's garments and hair, but Shiva seemed not to care. The stable hands brought a horse to Pirena, and Shiva commanded her to get on the horse. Pirena got on the horse and noticed the blinders on its eyes. "Aunt Shiva, why does-"

Before Pirena could finish her sentence, Shiva was holding the eye over her head, chanting, and she, Pirena, and the horse gently floated into the air. Pirena held on for dear life as they flew.

Two hours later, they had landed. "This is what I need you to do," Shiva said. "Pirena, you are about a day's ride from the army. I did not want us to be seen. I want you to sneak up on the armies and infiltrate the camps. I want you to kill whomever you can, sneak in, kill, sneak out. Create chaos. Go for any royalty you can. I want fear to reign in the camps. You are the best at this, and I am relying on you to give them sorrow."

"I have a question, if I may," Pirena said.

Shiva nodded. "Ask away, my lady of death."

"I am glad to do this; however, could you just destroy these armies all on your own?"

Shiva smiled. "You would be correct, but I want them to pay for defying the eye and defying me. Believe you me I, will play my own part in their suffering. I have plenty of ideas of what I am going to do to them."

"What do you plan to do?" Pirena asked.

"You will see all in due time. Between us two, we will give honor to the eye. Believe you me, they will know sorrow and pain that they would not think possible."

Pirena bowed her head. "What you ask of me will be done. I am the Lady of Death, and that is what I will bring them. It will take a few days. I might have to come in from behind, but believe you me, I will make them pay."

Shiva smiled. "That is my girl. I must leave. I will keep an eye on you from a distance." She raised the eye and chanted. "Good luck," she said as she shot up into the air before flying across the sky.

Pirena smiled. It felt good to have something to do, even if it was wrong. It made her feel alive. Murder and chaos It was like scratching an old itch, and did it ever feel good!

She took the blinders off the horse and nudged it into a trot.

Chapter Fifty-Six

Facing an Old Fear

Aurora, Enoch, and Elaine rode their horses down a dirt road. It was early in the morning, and they had just broken camp. An eerie fog had crept along the path; the farther down the path they went, the thicker the fog became. They were near the forest, and the only sounds were the horses trotting on the path. Enoch felt an old familiar feeling.

"Are you all right, Enoch?" Elaine asked.

"I admit I am a bit nervous. I know we are near the forest. I can feel it. Can you?"

Elaine nodded. "I can smell it as well," Elaine said.

Enoch nodded; the familiar smell of rotting foliage and wood filled the air. Elaine felt a shiver go down her spine as they traveled down the path.

"Stay close to each other," Aurora commanded. They had decided to take turns leading the group, and it had been Aurora's turn today. Trotting up to Enoch and Elaine, she looked at them. It was so dark that she could barely see their expressions. She frowned. "Are you two all right?"

Enoch managed to smile. "Everything is fine; no worries."

Aurora smiled. "I love you, Enoch Eclipse. You are a terrible liar, but I love you all the same."

They all stared at each other then started to chuckle.

Enoch smiled. "I guess you are right, Aurora. We are near the forest where that creature is."

Aurora frowned. "How can you tell?" she asked.

"You can smell it," Elaine said. "The forest is dead and decaying."

Aurora sniffed. "I guess you are right; there is sort of a musty mildew smell in the air. Probably one of you should lead this time."

Elaine looked at Enoch. "Go ahead," Enoch he said, nodding at his sister as they continued.

After another half hour had passed, the fog was slowly starting to lift, and the outline of the forest came into view. Aurora marveled at the trees that lined the path, the fog giving them dark shadows and the gnarled branches looking menacing. Then another smell hit their noses. Aurora coughed. "It smells like death," she said. Everyone there, including the soldiers, started to cough and gag from the rancid smell. The horses started to shuffle nervously as they approached the smell. Aurora looked down and almost fell off her horse. "A skeleton," she said. It was a partial skeleton, but everyone stopped.

As the fog lifted more, they all were shocked at the horror they saw. Skeletons with rotten bits of flesh littered the path. Elaine shivered at the sight. "It looks like it is maybe the century that chased us," she suggested.

Enoch shook his head. "No, it is not. We were deeper into the forest when we were chased. This is a different group of soldiers—and look, there are pieces of what looks like a carriage."

Aurora rode to a damaged wheel. "You are right, Enoch." She looked at other pieces of the carriage. "It looks like it might be the same carriage that Virion and Maximus rode in, but I'm not sure."

Enoch frowned. "I do not like this at all. Not one bit," he said. "I feel bad, for the dead should be buried. Unfortunately, we do not have time to do this. We must continue to move forward. I think it would be wise for us to continue as cautiously and quickly as possible and get out of here. Whatever did this might be nearby." They led the group of soldiers carefully around the carnage.

They traveled a little farther. Most of the fog was gone, except for in the forest itself. Enoch had been holding his hand on the pommel of his sword but raised it and commanded the group to halt. He turned to face them, looking as though he were going to vomit. "What is wrong?" Elaine asked.

"Keep your hands near your weapons."

Elaine looked at him. "What is wrong?" she demanded.

"I have felt a sensation," he said. "The last time I felt that, that creature attacked."

Aurora investigated the woods. Fortunately, the fog was clearing fast, so whatever it was, they would be able to see it ahead of time. She looked at the woods again, seeing them clearly for the first time. The forest looked truly foreboding. There were trees of all shapes and sizes, some small, some large. There was a massive tree not far away. Had it moved? She looked more closely. She had to be imagining it, she told herself.

Finally, the fog was completely gone. Aurora's eyes widened in shock as the tree started to run toward them. "Look out!" she yelled. Everyone looked at Aurora and her horrified expression, then in the direction she was looking.

The ground shook as the creature leaped out of the woods and roared. The horses whinnied in fear. The creature stood right in front of them—the creature from Aurora's nightmares. The creature on the cover of her book, the creature that stood in the palace. The cyclops. It roared menacingly. Its bloodshot eye, thick arms, and barrel chest, and its muscular legs, pointy teeth, and nostrils brought fear into everyone's hearts. The horses reared up in panic, dumping some of the soldiers to the ground.

To her surprise, Aurora found herself charging the creature. She noticed Enoch and Elaine right behind her. The cyclops lifted its hands in the air and brought them crashing them to the ground. Aurora, Enoch, and Elaine dodged the blow as they rode past the creature, and the cyclops turned, reared its head, and roared. That roar was nothing Aurora had heard before—more like a loud shriek.

The soldiers attacked from behind the cyclops, shooting a volley of arrows into its back. Most of the arrows bounced off its hide. The cyclops howled in pain, turning and charging the soldiers. Horses and soldiers both were flung like rag dolls.

Elaine shot an arrow in the cyclops's neck. It reared its ugly head and charged them. Enoch and Aurora rode opposite each other, slashing with their swords, cutting the cyclops's legs, but their swords barely penetrated the skin, which was like iron. The cyclops looked at Elaine and began to charge. "No!" Enoch yelled as he and Aurora chased it. As the cyclops ran toward her, Elaine aimed her bow and loosed the arrow. The arrow hit the cyclops on its upper lip. The beast stopped as it reached up and pulled the arrow out, blood running down its lip.

"Good shot!" Aurora shouted as she and Enoch tried again to cut its legs, with the same results.

"It's skin is too tough!" Enoch yelled. The creature killed several more of the soldiers crushing them with its fists. "That thing is killing everyone!" Enoch yelled, frustrated.

Elaine drew her sword, saying, "Maybe three swords." She charged the cyclops with Aurora and Enoch this time, Enoch standing in his saddle. As they took another pass, he jumped the cyclops, getting on its back and trying to slit the creature's throat. He drew no blood. He yelled in pain as the cyclops grabbed him and tossed him to the ground.

"Enoch!" Aurora yelled. Elaine rode over to him to check if he was all right. She dismounted and kneeled by his side. "Watch out!" Aurora yelled as the cyclops charged the brother and sister. Aurora kicked her horse into a full gallop. She charged directly at the cyclops. The creature's eye burned with rage, and the cyclops looked ready to swipe at her. Aurora anticipated its attack, and as the creature swiped at her, she made the horse jump. She and the horse collided with the cyclops.

Aurora, the horse, and the cyclops went flying. Aurora's eyes widened as she realized they were falling into a canyon. She screamed as she fell into what seemed like a bottomless pit. She was headed for a tree.

Everything went dark.

Elaine screamed as the soldiers charged toward where Aurora had fallen. They barely stopped in time, looking down in shock at the canyon. The woods hid it well.

~ ~ ~

Enoch came to, groaning in pain. He lifted his head to look up at a crying Elaine and yelped in pain. It felt like he had some broken ribs. "Is the creature dead? Where's Aurora?" he asked.

"Oh, Enoch, I think she may be dead."

Enoch bolted up, then grimaced in pain. "What do you mean?" When Elaine explained to him what had happened, he said, "Show me," the desperation clear in his voice. With the help of another soldier, Elaine walked him to the edge of the canyon. "We have got to find her!" he shouted.

"You have been unconscious for a couple of hours now, and they have not been able to find a way down."

"We can use the cystallis and contact others for help," Enoch said. Elaine frowned and looked down. Enoch let out a curse. "The cystallis has been damaged."

Elaine nodded. "Beyond repair. The cyclops stepped on it."

"Well, we need to figure something out. She is down there with that creature."

A soldier approached. "Sir, most likely, Her Highness is, dead along with the creature. The canyon is at least a hundred feet deep."

"I don't care. We must find her."

Elaine grabbed her brother by the arm. "We cannot, Enoch. There is no way down, and we do not have any rope long enough to reach the bottom."

"Aurora!" Enoch yelled, his voice echoing across the canyon. There was no response. He hung his head, then looked at his sister with pain-filled eyes.

She knew that look—the look of pain, sorrow, and suffering. She hugged him as he started to cry, remembering as she did so that awful day when she had found Jonathan dead. Enoch had been there for her; he had been there for every tear, every scream of sorrow. Now it was her turn to be there for him.

Chapter Fifty-Seven

Lost

Aurora awoke with a start. She looked up. Trees loomed above her and the midday sun shone down on her. "How in Tiban Talon's name am I alive?" She asked out loud. She took inventory of her body. She had a bad bump on her head and a lot of scrapes but no broken bones. She looked to her side and started again. Her horse lay beside her, its dead, glazed eyes staring at her. "Poor thing. It must have broken my fall." She made her way to her feet, but dizziness hit her like a wave, and she fell back to the ground.

"I guess I am not ready to get up," she muttered, and waited awhile before trying again. This time she stumbled a bit but was not as dizzy as before. "Enoch, Elaine!" she shouted.

Silence was the only answer.

Then she remembered. That cyclops creature had fallen into the canyon with her. She hoped it had died in the fall. Where had that creature come from? she wondered. Enoch and Elaine had felt its presence as it had attacked that century of soldiers, and that had been long before the eye had been stolen, and she had heard tales even before that of a mysterious spirit of the forest.

The only explanation she could think of was that when Tiban Talon had destroyed the cyclopes all those centuries before, he had missed one. It was around that time that the legend of the forest spirit had been born, and over the centuries, the forest had slowly decayed. That would make sense, she thought, and she decided that if she found the body of the cyclops, she would examine it. If she remembered correctly, the book Bethany had given her had told of each cyclops having the shape of a crown on the bottoms of its feet. "Well, there's no use speculating," she said to herself. "I have to find my way out." She looked at her surroundings. "My sword!" she exclaimed when she saw it lying beside the horse.

When Aurora picked the sword up and returned it to its sheath, a shiver ran down her spine; she thought she heard something. She looked around frantically but saw nothing. With some effort, she then managed with a dagger to cut one of the saddlebags off the horse. Thankfully, it had a full canteen, a pot, and some food. It was a little heavy, but it would do to survive for a while. She figured out a way to strap it to her back, then walked as fast as she could without making a sound.

After an hour of walking, she had made it to a rock face. She smiled; it was not quite straight up. It looked like, if she was careful, she might make it to the top. It was probably good that the horse had died, she reflected, because she probably would have had no choice but to leave the poor creature behind.

Aurora pulled out her canteen and had a drink, then began the long and treacherous climb up the rock face. She made it to the top after an hour, tired but proud of her accomplishment. She drank more from her canteen and ate some jerky then rested for a while. She got up in late afternoon, as far as she could tell, figuring the sun would set in a few hours and then she would have to make camp.

She walked for a few more hours. A little fatigue was setting in, and her bumps and bruises started to ache. She was grateful that she had had no run-ins with the cyclops, and she figured it was either dead or trapped. *Good riddance either way*, she thought.

Aurora's eyes widened when she saw movement in the distance. Narrowing her eyes to try to see better, she saw a shadowy figure stumbling around. Quietly, she walked closer to the figure, drawing her sword and feeling sweat beading on her brow. She got close enough to realize that whatever it was, it was not the cyclops. Drawing closer still, she finally recognized the mysterious figure. "You!" she gasped, then charged.

~ ~ ~

Maximus staggered through the forest. He seemed to have lost his way. One minute, he had been on a path, and the next, he was in the woods. He staggered around aimlessly, then saw a woman in the distance. He must be having another hallucination, he decided as the woman started to run toward him with her sword drawn. He stood still as the woman approached, shouting at him. *Apparently, an angry woman.* By the time Maximus realized he was not hallucinating and turned to run, it was too late. He yelped as the woman tackled him. He managed to roll onto his back and look up into the angry eyes of Aurora Talon.

"You murderous, backstabbing son of a siren!" she screamed as she held the tip of her sword to his throat. Her face turned red. "My grandfather and -grandmother are dead, I lost friends, and several hundred more lost their lives. You are also responsible for *their* deaths. I should kill you now, you bottom-feeding slime."

Maximus looked at her in stunned silence, unsure whether to be frightened or amazed. She was beautiful, and her fierce, murderous expression made her even more beautiful.

"Well, say something," Aurora demanded.

Maximus found it hard to speak, he was so weak from traveling and being ill. "I have not had any drink. It is hard to talk," he said in a scratchy voice.

Aurora rolled her eyes. "I don't know why I am doing this," she said as she put her sword on the ground and pulled out her canteen. She handed it to him, but when he tried to take it from her, she realized he was ill, so she lifted his head and gave him a drink.

Maximus nodded his thanks as she put her canteen away. "I am sorry, Aurora," he managed.

Aurora folded her arms. "So?" she said.

"I am sorry. I had no idea Pirena was going to kill your grandparents."

Aurora picked up her sword again and once again held it to his throat. "You lie," she said, tears streaking her cheeks. "I really want to kill you, for you do not deserve mercy. However, I will not. I am going to take you with me. You are now my prisoner. I will let my father decide your fate."

She helped him to his feet, but then Maximus screamed in terror. Aurora felt a chill go down her spine for there would only be one reason for Maximus to scream. She slowly looked in the direction that Maximus was looking about fifty feet away. The cyclops stood there, looking at them.

The cyclops was bruised and scratched everywhere. It gave out a low, guttural growl that ended in a snarl. Then it roared and charged.

Maximus stared at it in shock while Aurora charged it. Then he watched in amazement; he would have never thought anyone would charge such a creature. It was either the bravest act he had ever seen or the most idiotic.

As Aurora screamed with her sword in the air, the creature swung its fist to hit her. Aurora ducked just in time and slashed at its wrist. Once again, there was hardly any blood. "How does this creature die?" Aurora screamed.

The creature then slammed its fists to the ground, the percussion of the strike sending Aurora flying. She rolled as she landed on the ground, then sprang to her feet. As she flew, the cyclops turned its attention to Maximus and charged him. Maximus cursed and tried to run. The cyclops reached for him and howled, and Maximus turned to see that Aurora had rammed her sword into the creature's ankle with all her might and was trying, in vain, to pull the sword back out.

The creature howled as it turned to face Aurora. It pulled the sword out of its ankle and snapped the weapon in two before throwing it at her. Aurora managed to dodge the pieces of her sword, then pulled out a knife that had been strapped to her ankle. She was not sure what she was going to do with it, but it was the only weapon she had left.

The creature hobbled toward her. The wound she had given the cyclops slowed him significantly. She looked at her ten-inch blade and then at the cyclops coming at her. "How in Tiban Talon's name am I going to kill this beast?" She looked once more at her knife and then at the creature getting closer. She shrugged, then threw the knife at the cyclops. The knife landed deeply in the creature's eye, and the cyclops screamed in agony. Blood gushed out of its eye as it put its hands up to its eye. It stumbled and tripped over a fallen log, then thrashed on the ground, its unholy screams echoing across the forest. After several minutes, the cyclops stopped thrashing and drew its last breath.

Aurora made a mental note that the cyclops's eye was its weak spot. Then she walked up to the dead creature and pulled the knife from its eye. She looked down at her broken sword, which was so special to her because she had earned the right to own it on that special day. A tear ran down her cheek as she remembered her grandfather and grandmother cheering her on.

Aurora next turned her attention to the cyclops, examining the creature for the tell-tale crown on the bottom of its foot. Sure enough, there it was. She was amazed that this creature had wandered this forest for a thousand years. No wonder almost no one came here, with that creature as the evil spirit of the forest. Maybe now that it was dead and the evil gone, the forest would return to its former glory.

Remembering Maximus suddenly, Aurora panicked, but then she saw that he had not run away—he was too weak, she supposed—but was standing where she had left him, on shaking knees. She walked took his sword away from him and then helped him to the ground. He immediately turned his head and vomited, then groaned and lay down, clenching his stomach, saying,. "My stomach hurts so bad."

Aurora found herself touching his forehead. "It looks like you have a fever. Have you had anything to eat or drink lately?" she asked.

"I have been drinking that nasty river water and I have been eating some delicious mushrooms."

Aurora looked at him with narrowed eyes. "What kind of mushrooms?"

He pointed to his pack. "I have some in that pouch." She opened the pouch and looked at the mushrooms, then started to laugh as she dumped them on the ground. "Hey, those are good mushrooms!"

Aurora shook her head. "They are poisonous."

Maximus's eyes widened. "They're poisonous? I am going to die. That is it, I am going to die."

"Calm down. You are not going to die. Have you had any hallucinations, bad dreams, diarrhea? Obviously, you have vomited." When he nodded his head, she smirked. "Well, Maximus, you are not going to die—at least not yet—these are called nightmare mushrooms. They cause nightmares, hallucinations, diarrhea, and vomiting. They will not kill you. However, before you are better, you are going to wish you were dead," she said with great satisfaction. Maximus groaned as she chuckled.

"The hour is late, and I must make us a shelter. Don't go away," she said with laughter in her voice. As she gathered her supplies and firewood, her laughter turned to tears and she prayed. "Lord, guide my path back to the army, and please, Lord, let Enoch and Elaine be safe."

~ ~ ~

Maximus opened his eyes and looked at his surroundings. He was lying by a tree, and his hands and feet were bound. Aurora was sitting at a nearby river and appeared to be drinking from a cup. "Don't drink that water!" he yelled.

She gave him a quizzical look. "Why not?"

"Because that water is contaminated, tastes awful, and will make you sick."

Aurora shook her head. "No, it will not. I boiled this water. It should be clear of anything that will make me sick. It still does not taste that great, but it is certainly safe to drink," she said as she raised her cup to her mouth. "I gave you plenty of it when you had a fever, with no problems . . . or maybe you do not remember."

Maximus was confused. "How did you boil the water?" he asked.

Aurora nodded to the campfire. As he did so, he noticed that in the hand not holding the cup was a stick with an impaled rabbit. "I hope you like rabbit," she told him. "I can't believe it—it pretty much hopped right to me. I am sorry I do not have any salt or seasonings, but it is food."

Maximus was shocked. "You are cooking? You are a princess; you are not supposed to cook."

Aurora laughed. "How would I have survived if I did not know how to cook? You mean you don't know how to cook?"

Maximus shook his head. "Of course not; that is slave's work." Aurora gave him a disgusted look, so he asked, "Don't you have servants and cooks to do your bidding? You are no different from us. You look at me with disgust like you are high and mighty, yet you have slaves; they just go by a different name."

Aurora glared at him. "You got one thing right—we do have servants who answer our beck and call. You should know—you ate plenty of food and drink at my grandfather's table and were served day and night. The difference is your slaves are forced to work against their will. If they make a mistake, well, you can kill them. What is another slave to have to dispose of? If you are not satisfied with the food, you can have the cook beaten. Our servants are there because they want to be. We pay them a fair wage. They can leave if they wish and not worry about being beaten or killed. Our head chef has been with us for forty years and has four children and eight grandchildren. I highly doubt you can say that about any of your slaves that were cooks."

Maximus looked down in shame, unsure how to react. Then he looked at her and nodded. After a moment, he spoke. "Who taught you to cook?"

Aurora frowned as memories flooded her mind. Bethany had taught her how to cook when they had gone camping together. She tried to hide her tears. "A dear old friend taught me. Sadly, she is no longer with us."

"I am sorry to hear that. It sounds like you had a very special friend."

Aurora wiped away a tear. "More than you will ever know."

While Aurora was cooking the rabbit, they told each other stories of what had happened with them and the cyclops. As they shared their stories, a realization dawned on Maximus. "I have been lost for days now. I am sure my father has search parties looking for me. I am sure by now; he has figured out that eye is a worthless rock. He is probably stewing about it and has realized he has brought your wrath upon him."

Aurora looked at Maximus. "You have no idea, do you?"

Maximus looked at her, confused. "Idea about what?"

She told him the story of what had transpired, of Pirena's escape and the legend about the power of the eye being true. She, of course, did not mention Bethany. Then she came to the part that Maximus did not want to hear. "Your mother killed your father. Now she has become a threat to the entire world, and we are here to stop her. Your mother has been looking for you, and seeing that she has not found you, she assumes you are dead."

Maximus's eyes widened in disbelief. "You are a liar! Do you really think I would believe such rubbish?"

Aurora shook her head. "I do not know what to tell you. I may hate you, but I promise you I am not lying."

Maximus looked her in the eyes. When she did not flinch or turn away, he knew she was telling the truth, and he burst into tears. "I hate you, Father! I told you that you should not meddle with powers you should not have. Now Mother is an evil creature, and you are dead! What good did this do you? You are a fool, a selfish, self-centered idiot, and Mother did not deserve this."

He looked at Aurora with determination in his eyes. "I must stop Mother. I must try to convince her to stop this madness. I know you do not believe that I had no idea that Pirena was going to kill your grandparents. Take me to your father. I am willing to face the consequences for my part in this deception. I want to, in whatever way possible, help in stopping my mother and destroying the eye."

Looking into his eyes, Aurora said, "I am not sure if I trust you; however, you will have an opportunity to speak to my father. You can tell him what you have told me, though I am not sure if he will believe you either. He is a tired, determined, angry man right now. You will have your work cut out for you. He will not be easily convinced. "Well, dinner is ready. It isn't much, but it will give you energy." Maximus felt his stomach growl as hunger pangs hit him hard. She got up and pulled out her knife. "I am going to cut your bindings. I do not trust you; however, a part of me thinks you will not run."

As she approached him, Maximus's eyes widened. "I am not going to kill you," she told him. Then she realized he had started to shake, and she had a strange feeling, like they were being watched. "I thought I killed the cyclops," she muttered. She turned, and to her surprise, what she saw was not a cyclops at all. "Who are you?" she asked.

"Your Highness, I am the Lady of Death, Pirena Solaris, and I am your executioner."

Chapter Fifty-Eight

Reconciliation

It was evening, and the crumbling city of Ashtor had a menacing look to it. No one had lived here for decades. It had been a mining town, and when the mines had stopped producing, Xavier Pulsar had abandoned the town, leaving it to rot. The only occupants now were stray cats and plenty of mice. The smell of rot, must, and mold filled the air. Aldar and Zena Talon walked down the main street of the city, enjoying a rare opportunity to be together. Zena looked at the tall buildings, town houses, and what looked like a dried-up canal. She imagined what it had looked like before it had been abandoned, with boats moving in the canal and people talking.

Although it was far from a romantic setting, Zena was happy to spend time alone with her husband. It had been a long time since they had had the chance. Zena reached her hand to him, and he took it and held it as they continued to walk. She smiled at him. "Well, my dear, are you not going to take me out to dinner? I am famished."

Aldar smirked as he pointed to what may have once been a restaurant. "We can eat there."

Zena laughed. "Yes, I hear that they have a delicious filet of mouse with a mold reduction sauce," she said. Aldar looked at her, surprised at her quip, and then they both laughed.

They were a little nervous. Aldar had been in touch with the other groups since they had split up but had not heard from Aurora, Enoch, and Elaine's group. It was not uncommon for the cystallis to fail—it did happen often—but still, the lack of contact was worrisome. "I hope they are all right. I feel like I gave them too hard an assignment," Aldar said.

Zena, knowing who he was talking about, kissed him on the cheek. "I am sure they are fine. They are capable of fending for themselves. After all, dear, you sent some of your best men with them. Even if they find trouble, they are in good hands."

"I know my love; however, all the other teams have arrived, and I hoped they would have arrived by now." As he mused, his thoughts turned elsewhere. "And I find it odd that there have not been any sightings of the Apollyon army. I wonder what game Shiva is playing. She is up to something, and I do not like it at all."

"It is odd, indeed," Zena agreed. "It is almost like she is waiting for us to make the next move." Their conversation was interrupted by galloping horses. Aldar drew his sword, and Zena reached for her pistol. She struggled, pulling up her skirts. "This is so undignified," she complained as she finally pulled it out.

Isaiah and a group of soldiers rode up to them. "Sorry for the interruption, Aldar, but I have some grave news."

Aldar looked at Isaiah, and somehow, he knew. "Aurora!" he shouted.

Isaiah nodded solemnly. "That creature attacked them. It was a cyclops-like creature. It killed half of the soldiers. Enoch took a bad bump to the head, Elaine is fine, and Aurora—well, I am sorry; she and the cyclops fell down a canyon. Her fate is unknown, but it is assumed she probably did not survive the fall. It was at least a hundred feet down."

Zena screamed as she wrapped her arms around Aldar's shoulders. "Our girl, our little girl, is gone."

Aldar and Zena went quickly back to the camp and to the medical tent, where Enoch's head was being bandaged. Elaine, who sat beside him, ran into Zena's arms when she saw her, and they both sobbed. Aldar took Elaine's place sitting next to Enoch. "Tell me what happened, Elaine"

Tears fell from Elaine's eyes as she told the story. "I am sorry, Aldar. She fell a long way down, as did the cyclops. You would have been proud of her. She fought that creature with all her might. I am sorry, but there's little chance she survived."

Zena came over and hugged both Elaine and Enoch, sobbing as Aldar sat in stunned silence as a tear ran down his cheek. "I have lost my mother, my father, and now my daughter. This war has to end; it has cost me too much." Aldar stood. He felt dizzy and did not know how he was going to move on, but he had no choice.

Zena turned to him. "We must look for her. She might still be alive. We can send a search party."

Aldar shook his head. "I am sorry, my love, but we cannot. The other parties have arrived. Tomorrow we must head to Adaliah. We must end this war."

Zena pounded her fist against his chest. "We must go back and find her! She is our daughter." She cursed as she continued to hit him.

Aldar grabbed his wife's fists and wrapped his arms around her. "If our daughter is alive, she will find us. I think Aurora would be disappointed if we waited. She would want us to continue the fight." Zena pulled away and looked at him with grief-stricken eyes, then took off running. Elaine tried running after her, but Aldar stopped her. "She needs some alone time, I think, Elaine, but thank you."

~ ~ ~

Zena ran toward the city. As she ran past them, soldiers and guards cried out, "Your Majesty, it is not safe!" She ignored their cries. After several minutes, she reached the restaurant she and Aldar had stood in front of just a little while before. She sat on the dirty ground and leaned against the stone wall. She put her hands up to her face and screamed, yelled, and sobbed. She cried like she never had before.

A while later, she woke with a start, realizing she had fallen asleep. It was dark. She rubbed her eyes. When she looked up, she saw her father standing nearby holding a torch in his hand and wearing a concerned expression. Tears fell down his cheeks. "I am sorry, Zena," he told her. "I am so terribly sorry your baby is gone. I am so sorry I was not there for you. I let you down, and because of me, Victor, Amber, and Aurora are gone."

Zena got up and wrapped her arms around him. He dropped the torch and let her cry on his shoulder. “I forgive you, Father. You cannot blame yourself. All of this could have happened even with your help.”

“But I am responsible,” he protested.

“Please, Father, hold me. Please just hold me,” she said.

So that was exactly what he did.

Chapter Fifty-Nine

Fight

"Run, Aurora! Run! You have no chance against her; she will kill you," Maximus pleaded as Pirena approached.

Aurora, thankful to have a sword in her hands, replied, "I will not. I am a Talon, and I will not run away from anyone or anything, even if it means my death."

Pirena smiled as she drew her swords. "Your Highness, you had better heed Maximus's words. You had better run—not that it matters. It is too late to run, too late to hide. As far as your death, I will be happy to give that to you. What an amazing turn of events; I go to create fear and chaos in the armies, and I find you two here."

Maximus shouted as he pulled at his bindings. "Why, in the name of Apollyon, are you helping Mother? She will destroy us all! She has become an evil creature. She must be stopped, or she will kill us all."

Pirena snorted. "So, I see Her Highness told you, eh? I see she seems to have captured you easily too." She laughed. "As far as why I am doing this, I am certainly not doing this for Aunt Shiva, but for now I must do her bidding. I want to slice that wretch's head off her shoulders. That day will come, and then I will take the eye and I will rule.

"I am done talking to you, you are a weak, insignificant whelp. I need to address Her Highness before I kill her." She looked at Aurora with a wicked smile. "I love killing royalty, especially royalty that plots to kill the ones I love. Your grandfather hired Levi to kill Uncle Xavier, and you already know what happened to Aunt Shiva. I have a way of figuring things out. It helps to have spies, and I planted the best one. Your loving and trusting teacher Bethany, she told me everything, including you all taking in Enoch and Elaine."

Aurora felt anger rise inside her. She wanted to charge Pirena; she wanted to separate the woman's head from her shoulders. But she knew

Pirena was trying to throw her off by getting her angry. That was one thing her sword instructor, Amanda, had taught her—she needed to keep calm no matter what.

"It was a happy day for me when I killed your grandfather. The shock on his face brought me joy. Then the other spy I hired slashing your grandmother's throat? Priceless. If only the others I hired had killed the rest of you."

Aurora gritted her teeth and started to shake. There was only so much she could take, and she was at the breaking point.

"I see you are angry. I can feel your pain. You need not worry, Your Highness, I will take your pain away. Just give up now. You do not have a chance. I have killed hundreds with these blades. If you fight me, I assure you, you will feel unimaginable pain. Sometimes I like to toy with my victims. However, I am not entirely ruthless; if you give up, I will make your death as painless as possible. A quick decapitation and it will be all over, no pain, no suffering . . . it will be over in a snap."

"Don't do it!" Maximus yelled.

"Quiet, you fool! Stay out of this, or it will be your head that will be taken off your shoulders." She looked intently into Aurora's eyes, expecting to see pain and sorrow but instead finding determination there.

Aurora saluted Pirena with her sword and crouched in a battle stance. "If I am going to die by your hands, Pirena, then I would rather die fighting you."

Pirena sniffed. "So, you want to die the hard and painful way. Well, no matter, this will be very enjoyable for me." Aurora smiled at Pirena, her anger fading into determination, her desire for revenge replaced by a desire for justice. Pirena was taken aback by Aurora's salute. "This is your last chance, Aurora. Put down your sword."

Aurora scowled. "For the last time, I will never give up or give in. Like you said, I choose the hard way."

Pirena smiled. "You have a lot of spunk, Your Highness. I think I will get more enjoyment killing you than your grandfather."

"Your coarse words no longer bother me, Pirena. I've had about enough of your mind games. If I die, it will be doing the right thing, but what about you, Pirena? What do you think is worth dying for?"

"I don't understand your question, Your Highness. Worth dying for? I don't ever plan on dying."

Aurora smiled. "Someday you will. Maybe not now, maybe forty years from now, but someday, you will die."

Pirena frowned. "Where are you going with this? Are you stalling for time? If you are, you are delaying the inevitable."

"I feel sorry for you, Pirena."

"What do you mean by that?" Pirena asked, scowling.

"You feel miserable inside."

Pirena laughed. "I feel no such thing."

Aurora gave her an almost sympathetic look. "Do you ever feel regret? Don't you ever feel guilty or worry about all the death and pain you caused? Are you not afraid for your soul?"

This time it was Pirena's turn to get angry. "Absolutely not."

"That is why I feel sorry for you; you have no remorse. You are lost, and you don't even realize it."

Pirena stiffened as she felt a tear run down her cheek. Then her face turned dark she cursed angrily. She had shown weakness. "Enough! You are wasting my time. Let us fight." She walked toward Aurora. Then she charged. She feigned with one sword, but Aurora blocked the attack. Pirena swung her second sword, and Aurora ducked, the blade just missing her head. Then Aurora swung her sword. Pirena swiped the blade away. They backed away from each other, Pirena nodding her approval. "Very impressive, Your Highness. I feel I have misjudged you a little. No matter, we have just begun."

Aurora nodded back, thankful that Amanda had trained her to fight against two-blade fighters. Before Aurora could realize what was happening, Pirena moved forward and swept a leg out, knocking Aurora to the ground. Pirena swung both of her swords at Aurora, trying to cut her throat, but somehow, Aurora blocked both blades and kicked Pirena in the shin. Pirena grunted as she hobbled backward. Aurora jumped back to her feet, grunting a little herself; she still hurt from falling and from fighting that cyclops.

Pirena was caught off guard as Aurora charged, lunging to stab her in the chest. Pirena barely blocked the attack.

Maximus watched in amazement at the dazzling battle, shocked at how well Aurora was doing.

The women continued to fight for several more minutes, eventually nearing the riverbank. Aurora noticed a look of concern on Pirena's face.

Pirena swiped at Aurora's face. Aurora was not fast enough, and Pirena's sword sliced her cheek. Aurora stumbled backward, but to Pirena's surprise, she recovered in time to block Pirena's blow with her other sword. Then Aurora kicked Pirena in the chest.

Pirena fell into the river, gasping as she landed in the water. The icy water took her breath away. As she stood up in the waist-deep water, she realized she had lost her swords. She climbed out of the water, then, seeing one of her swords, she put her hand in the numbing water to fetch it, shivering as she did so. She stopped as Aurora held her sword to Pirena's throat.

"Well, Your Highness, you fight better than I thought possible," Pirena said with a shaky voice. She crossed her arms and shook uncontrollably in her wet battle dress.

"Turn around," Aurora demanded. Pirena did so, and Aurora put her in an arm lock. Once again, Aurora put her sword to Pirena's throat. "I am going to take you to my father. He will decide your fate," she said, sounding exhausted.

Pirena laughed. "I don't think so." She slammed the back of her head against Aurora's face, and Aurora screamed in pain, dropping her sword and putting her hands to her face. She kicked Aurora in the chest, and this time, it was Aurora who landed in the frigid water.

Aurora gasped as she made her way out of the water. She looked around but did not see or hear Pirena. She staggered, dizzy from the blow to her head. "Watch out!" Maximus yelled, but before Aurora could react, Pirena had kicked her in the face. Aurora was unconscious before she hit the water, landing with a huge splash.

Pirena smiled victoriously as she grabbed Aurora, dragging her to shore and seizing Aurora's sword. She found her own swords and sheathed them, then smiled at Maximus. She bent over with her hands on her knees and breathed heavily, exhaustion setting in. Then she laughed. "I have fought men twice the size of me and women twice as fast as me. I have fought opponents in all shapes and sizes, young and old, but none has fought like her."

Maximus fought against his bonds, and Pirena scoffed at him. "What are your plans if you get free?"

Maximus spoke through gritted teeth. "I plan on stopping you."

Pirena laughed. "You, stop me? You must be drunk."

"I am not drunk!" he yelled. "Someway, somehow, I am going to stop you. Please, Pirena, have mercy."

Pirena shook her head. "Your father would be disgraced by your behavior. I am glad he is not alive to see this."

Blood started to flow down Maximus's wrists as he struggled at his bonds. "Please Pirena—"

"Enough!" she said. "You know, your mother believes you are dead. You are such a spoiled, foolish, rotten brat. Aunt Shiva made you soft." She walked up to Aurora and turned the younger woman onto her back, then picked up Aurora's sword from where she had dropped it. Straddling Aurora, she said to Maximus, "I guess I cannot blame you. She is a pretty girl. It is a shame. I think with my training, she would have been a good ally. Oh well, nothing can be done about that." She pointed the sword at Aurora's chest, looking at Maximus and smiling as she lifted the sword.

Maximus screamed as Pirena thrust the sword toward Aurora's heart.

Chapter Sixty

Training

Alana smiled as the clash of swords echoed in the practice chamber of the palace. She imagined what was happening in front of her as Hunter's and Amanda's swords clashed. It really frustrated her that she could not fight anymore, and she found that ruling Antillean in her brother's stead was rather boring. It did bring joy to her heart that Aurora had been able to join the fight, however, she knew that her niece would do her proud. Alana was also proud of Hunter. She prayed this war would be over before he had to go, although she knew he would also do her proud.

Hunter had been struggling in his training, so Amanda had been giving him some private sessions conducted carefully with real swords. Amanda put her sword away. "I think you did well. I think it is time to call it a day. Remember the moves I taught you today. I want you to practice every day until our next session."

Hunter faced her and bowed. "I will, Amanda. I will not let you down."

"I hope so, young man. I have given up some alone time with my beau to train you, I hope you know." When Hunter's face turned red in embarrassment, Amanda laughed. "No worries. He and I are going to walk the harbor tonight." She then turned to Alana. "Well, Your Excellency, I think you would be much impressed by his progress."

Alana smiled. "I know he has improved. I can hear you two fight. I am very proud."

Amanda smiled back. "If he practices hard this week, he will be ready for even more intense training."

Hunter looked at her in wide-eyed shock. "More intense than today?"

Amanda's smile grew. "Young man, you are far from ready, yet this is only the beginning.

"Oh, I see," he said dejectedly.

"You will survive; your sister did," Amanda said with no sympathy. "Don't give up, Hunter; it takes time to learn all the moves, and a lifetime to master."

"I am ready," Alana said as she reached out her hand and Hunter took it. "Hunter and I are headed to the kitchens for a snack, Amanda. Would you like to join us?"

Amanda bowed her head. "Thank you, no. I have another engagement."

Alana laughed and smiled. "I forgot; you have a date with your beau."

"Yes, Your Excellency, I am sure he is there waiting for me now."

"Before you leave, I have just one question for you."

"Yes, Your Excellency?"

"Is he cute?"

"Aunt Alana!" Hunter said, embarrassed. Alana and Amanda laughed at his discomfort.

"He is very handsome, Your Excellency."

Their merriment was cut off as screams of terror erupted outside.

"What was that?" Alana asked.

"I am not sure, Your Excellency."

When the room started to shake, Alana said, "An earthquake? Here?" Amanda tackled her as a huge piece of the ceiling crashed to the floor, and Hunter jumped out of the way barely in time. The open sky appeared above them, and then a strange orange glow shone down from the opening.

"What is happening?" Alana asked as Amanda helped her up.

A woman holding a reddish-orange orb floated down and touched the ground. Amanda and Hunter gaped at the sight. "Who are you?" Amanda asked.

"I am Empress Shiva Enigma. You might remember me as Shiva Pulsar. Hello, Alana, it has been a while."

Alana frowned. “Shiva, what is the meaning of this?” she demanded.

Shiva smiled. “I have no time to explain everything to you. All I can say is your brother has done something rash. Because of his disobedience, he must pay, so I am going to take you and Hunter prisoner.”

Amanda drew her sword. “Your Majesty, I do not know why you have the eye of the cyclops or why you are doing this,” she said, assuming a battle stance, “but I will not let you take Her Excellency away.”

Shiva laughed with amusement. “I don’t know who you are, nor do I care. you don’t have a chance.”

As Amanda charged, Shiva held the eye up and chanted. A lightning bolt struck Amanda in the chest. “Amanda!” Hunter yelled as he rushed to her side. There was a black hole in Amanda’s chest, and smoke rolled out of it as her dead eyes stared back at him. “Murderer!” he yelled at Shiva.

“What has happened?” Alana demanded.

Hunter cried, “She killed Amanda,” as tears streaked down his cheeks.

Shiva gave him a sympathetic look. “I am sorry. It was her fault, lad. She should have not attacked me.”

Hunter drew his sword. “What are you doing?” Alana asked as she heard his sword being unsheathed.

Shiva looked at Hunter in amusement. “Do you think you can do better than her?” Hunter shook as he held up his sword, and Shiva smiled. “You have a choice, boy: give up and live or attack and die.”

Part Three

Wrath of the Eye

Chapter Sixty-One

Wrath

A little girl awoke with a cough. She looked over in shock at her mother, who lay, lifeless, beside her. "Mother!" the girl cried. She shook her mother, but her mother did not respond. "Wake up, Mother." Tears streamed down the girl's cheeks. After trying this several times, she realized her mother was never going to wake up again, and she began to take in her surroundings.

She and her mother had been in the cellar, getting cooking oil, when it happened. The cellar was now a cluttered mess. Part of the ceiling had collapsed, and the stairs were severely damaged. The girl struggled up the steps, climbing on her hands and knees, which were bleeding when she made it to the top.

She pulled whatever slivers she could out of her hands and knees, then looked at the main floor. She was shocked to see that the kitchen was gone except for the stove. She could see to the street outside where part of the wall was missing. People were running up and down the streets.

She made it to the front door of the house, where the door leaned on just one hinge, and managed to climb through. Her mouth gaped open in shock as she looked down her street. Every house was damaged or had collapsed. It looked as though the entire city that she knew and loved had been damaged or destroyed. As she cried for Antillean City, she looked toward the palace and saw that one of the spires that had stood proud and tall in the distance was gone.

Moans and cries of pain echoed everywhere as people continued to run up and down the streets. "Father! Father, where are you?" she cried, looking around her desperately, hoping her father would come.

"Father!" the girl cried again, as her father, who was a palace guard and had a cut on his forehead, ran to her. The girl embraced him and sobbed.

After several minutes, the girl's father asked, "Where is your mother?"

"Oh, Father, Mother is dead!" the girl exclaimed. "She is in the cellar, and she is dead."

"Are you sure?" he asked. The girl nodded her head, and he said, "I will go check. She might still be alive. Stay here." Then he walked toward the house.

The ground shook again, and the house collapsed completely. Father and daughter looked in shock at the ruins of their home, and then the sky grew dark. They looked up as a flash of lightning lit up the sky and was followed by a booming thunderclap.

A reddish-orange streak flew across the sky and then stopped high above the city. Floating there was a woman holding a reddish-orange orb above her head. Beside her were what appeared to be a woman and a boy, who looked like they might be dead. The ground shook again as the woman spoke in a booming voice. "I am Empress Shiva Enigma. You have your king to thank for all this death, despair, and destruction. He disobeyed the almighty eye and he disobeyed me, and because of his disobedience, you all paid the price.

"I am now your ruler, the ruler of Apollyon, Mirodia, Salonia, Violida, and Antillean, and from now on, you will answer to me. You all must bow down to the almighty eye, and you must bow down to me. Do it now," she demanded. When all the people looked at her in fear and stunned silence but did not move, she scowled. "Do it now!" she screamed.

Everyone quickly went to their knees or bowed.

Shiva smiled. "Good. The eye is pleased. I will spare what is left of the city, and you who are still alive, consider this my mercy." She raised the eye above her head and chanted, and she, Alana, and Hunter flew away, leaving a distraught Antillean City behind.

Chapter Sixty-Two

Determination

Pirena stopped her downward thrust just as the tip of the sword touched Aurora's breastbone. She smiled at Maximus, who looked horrified, then laughed. "You are a pathetic, worthless fool. You really don't want me to kill her even though she is the enemy. You know your father expressed his concerns to me about your ability to lead. Well, his concerns are confirmed. You really are a spineless coward and a traitor." Maximus looked down as her harsh words cut him to the core.

"It does not matter. After I kill Her Highness, I will kill you, and then I will kill your mother and take the eye. I will become Empress Solaris. I will rule the world. I will be treated like a goddess, and Uncle Xavier will be proud. He was more of a father than an uncle. I will take the power of the eye in his honor."

She looked down at Aurora. "I think if our fight had lasted much longer, she would have killed me." She shook her head. "It is a shame. I will always remember this day." She removed Aurora's bracelet and put it on her own wrist. "It fits perfect. I will keep this for myself as a remembrance of this day. I must say, even though she is a Talon, and she is the enemy, she has my respect. Well, I am afraid, Maximus, it is time to say good-bye to your lovely princess, for this time, I am really going to kill her."

She relished his pained face, then raised the sword up. "Good-bye, Your—"

Aurora's eyes popped open. Pirena yelped as Aurora pulled her legs out from under her. She grunted as she hit the ground hard, and the sword clattered to the ground. Aurora scrambled back to her feet, picking up her sword as she did so. She wobbled, trying to keep her balance, while Pirena made her way back to her own feet.

Pirena's eyes met the scornful eyes of Aurora Talon, and she stood in stunned silence, not knowing what to do.

"That bracelet is mine, you evil witch!" Aurora screamed at her. "Give it to me now or I will kill you slowly." Pirena's eyes widened in fear and dread, and she pulled off Aurora's bracelet and put it on the ground. Then she ran to the horse she had hidden in the brush, climbed on, and rode off at a gallop. "Who is the coward now?" Aurora managed to say. Pirena did not reply as she continued to ride away.

Aurora hobbled toward Maximus and collapsed to the ground. She groaned in pain, touching her head. She crawled over to Maximus and used her knife to cut his bindings, then rolled onto her back.

"Are you all right?" Maximus asked, then immediately regretted asking such a stupid question.

Aurora gave him a flat look, then rubbed her head. "Oh, I think I have had better days," she said with a forced smile. She looked at his scratched and bloody wrists. "Pirena is wrong; you certainly are not a coward. You tried everything in your power to save me when you certainly did not have to. I would call that brave. When you face my father, I will let him know you tried to save me. I believe what you said about not knowing about the assassination. However, that does not mean I completely trust you. I know you have a great hatred for Enoch and Elaine Eclipse, and as Pirena said, they were with us when you were there."

When Maximus's face grew dark and his eyes narrowed, she said, "I know you are angry because their father accidentally killed your mother. I know I cannot blame you for being angry at their dad—I feel the same about Pirena—however, as angry as you are, you cannot blame Enoch and Elaine; they are innocent, plain and simple. I appreciate your concern about me, but you also must realize Enoch is my beau. His sister is like a sister to me, and they are part of my family. I am not asking you to love them—after all, that is my job. I am asking you to not blame them. They truly had nothing to do with your mother's death."

Maximus pondered, then replied, "You are right; they are not to blame, so I no longer blame them, but I will not be their friend. Especially Enoch." Aurora looked at him, puzzled, and he added, "The fact he is your beau is most upsetting."

Aurora laughed, then yelped and touched her head. "I am flattered," she managed to say. She caught a whiff of something burning and exclaimed, "The rabbit!" as she saw the charred remains of dinner. She groaned. "I ruined dinner."

Maximus chuckled. "It is quite all right. That is the least of our problems, Aurora."

Aurora managed a laugh. "I guess you are right." Her eyes widened.

"What is wrong?" Maximus asked.

"Oh no! It just dawned on me . . . Pirena said she was pursuing the armies to create fear and chaos. We need to go warn them. Heaven only knows what that woman will do! We must go now." Aurora tried to sit up, but dizziness hit her like a wave, and she groaned, putting her hands to her face.

Maximus looked at her sympathetically. "I am sorry, but there is no way we can warn them in time." Aurora sat up again and tried to make it to her feet but fell and landed on her back. "Aurora, you must stop. You are in no shape to travel, and she has a horse. We do not," Maximus pleaded.

"I don't care." Aurora tried again to stand, but this time, Maximus got up and pushed her down with his foot. Anger burned in her eyes as she struggled against him. "Get off me!" she screamed as she tried to push his foot off.

Maximus looked at her calmly. "I know you hate me right now, but you cannot do this right now. I know this is frustrating. You cannot even stand. You will do no one or yourself any good."

Aurora frowned. "You are right, Maximus." She cursed as tears ran down her cheeks. Maximus gave her a drink of water, pulled off his outer shirt, and put the shirt on her. "Thank you," she said weakly. She wrapped his shirt around her, then met sleep's sweet embrace.

~ ~ ~

Aurora awoke and sat up quickly, slapping a damp towel away from a startled Maximus Pulsar. She looked around, confused.

"It is all right, Aurora. It is I, Maximus. Are you okay?" he asked with concern.

Aurora stared at him blankly for a moment, then started to come back to her senses. She looked at the damp cloth on the ground, then looked at Maximus. "You were taking care of me?"

Maximus smiled. "Just returning the favor. You felt feverish, and I wanted to keep the cut on your cheek cleaned."

Aurora looked over at the fire. "You built a fire well. I must say I am impressed."

"Not a problem," Maximus said, not wanting to admit it was the fire she had built, and he had just kept it going.

"How long was I out?" Aurora asked.

"The rest of the day and through the night. It is morning."

Aurora stood up gingerly and smiled. "Well, the dizziness is gone. I think I will find us breakfast. Then after breakfast, we shall leave."

"Leave?" Maximus asked.

"Well, yeah, we can't stay here forever. We must go warn my father."

Maximus frowned. "We will never catch up. Heaven only knows how far they are."

Aurora scowled. "I do not care if they are on the dark side of the moon; we will catch up to them."

"Are you sure you can? You took that fall in the canyon and Pirena hit you hard."

"I know," Aurora admitted. "My head hurts." She touched her face. "Ow!" she yelled, then realized her face was swollen. She felt her nose. "It is broken!" she yelled, then felt her cut. "Well, I must be a sight." She sighed.

Maximus looked at her sympathetically. "I am sorry. I was hoping the wet cloth would help."

Aurora looked sullen as she looked down and clenched her hands. Then she looked at Maximus and smiled. "Well, I am going to see if I caught anything in my traps, and hopefully fix breakfast." An hour later, after eating a squirrel she snared they were on their way.

"Thank you, Maximus, for taking care of me. I can tell you are a nice man, and I will do what I can for you," Aurora told him as they walked.

Maximus smiled. "You are also a very nice woman. Enoch is a lucky man, and I hope someday I will find a woman like you."

Aurora blushed a little. "Thank you. I am flattered. I know someday you will find that girl."

They continued their trek for several hours, eventually reaching an open plain. Aurora smiled. "Well, Maximus, I think we are going to catch up to the armies sooner than later." Several horses, all wearing battle armor, saddles, and reins, were grazing the plains.

Aurora and Maximus approached the horses carefully to avoid spooking them. "These are from my entourage," Maximus said. They took the armor and equipment off the horses, then chose the healthiest horses and put just the saddles back on.

Aurora looked to the south. "A two-hundred-fifty-thousand-soldier army will move slowly. With horses, we two should catch up quickly if we can find their trail, and that should be easy," she said. Maximus nodded, and they both smiled. "Let's make haste," she said, and they rode off.

Chapter Sixty-Three

The Path of Pain and Suffering

Zena rode on the seat of a wagon next to Enoch and Elaine. She hung her head, her cheeks still red from crying. She looked at Enoch and Elaine and saw that their cheeks were red as well. A fresh stream of tears ran down her cheeks as she looked away, she was so tired.

Enoch spoke. "Please, Zena, you do not have to hide your tears from us."

Zena looked at him. "I am tired," she said. "I am so sorry, Enoch. I hoped to see you two get married. You two would have made a wonderful couple."

Enoch managed a smile. "Aurora was the most beautiful, determined, fearless woman I have ever met. She was as strong as the most hardened blade ever forged, yet she was as soft as the prettiest flower. I loved her so much. I will miss her smile. I will miss her honesty and determination. I cannot believe she is gone."

Elaine chimed in, "You two talk as if she is dead. We do not know that for sure. I am sorry, Zena, if I sound harsh; I do not mean to, but we must hold onto hope. She might have survived. Unless we go back to that canyon and find her body, I am holding out hope that she has survived. She is strong and she is a fighter. If anyone could have survived that fall, it is her, and I am not going to give up hope."

Zena smiled. "You are such a precious girl. You are right—"

Zena was cut off by a sudden rush of wind. The air went from hot and humid too cold in an instant. Zena shivered in the wind.

Shiva flew over the armies, looking like a fireball streaking across the sky, then stopped and hovered several feet in front of the advancing army.

Aldar and the other monarchs cried the armies to a halt.

Shiva raised the eye over her head, chanting. A bolt of fire shot up into the sky, and the sky grew dark as storm clouds swirled around the firebolt. Her voiced boomed and echoed across the plain as she spoke. "Aldar Talon, you have defied the eye of the cyclops and me. There is a price you must pay for your defiance, and now you must be punished."

As she descended to the ground, the clouds rolled away and the sun and the hot, humid air returned. She was within bowshot, so several archers from Violida nocked their arrows. Aldar yelled, "Barnabas what are—"

Before Aldar could finish, Barnabas yelled, "Loose!" Hundreds of arrows flew straight at Shiva. She chanted, and a gust of wind blew the arrows aside. Barnabas stepped back and the archers shuffled nervously as she glared at them.

Then Shiva laughed. "Oh, Barnabas, making up for lost time, I see. You will be the next to suffer for this slight. You will pay dearly." Sweat beaded on King Zanthor's forehead, and his face turned pale. "I will figure out your punishment later," she told him. She then turned her attention to Aldar, who stepped forward to face her. "Unlike you, Barnabas, Aldar is a man." She gave Aldar a pained look. "I know you have been through a lot, but I cannot let this defiance go unpunished."

She untethered a large sack attached to her waist and set it on the ground, then lifted the eye and chanted. She started to float in the air. "Return to your homes or suffer the same fate as Aldar. If you continue this path, the only thing you will find is pain and suffering." She turned away and streaked across the sky, disappearing into the horizon after a few moments.

Aldar approached the bag cautiously, and Isaiah moved up beside him. "Let me; it might be a trap," Isaiah offered.

Aldar shook his head and picked the bag up. He untied it, and as he opened it, Zena ran up to him. Aldar looked at the bag's contents in shock, then dropped it. Zena yelled, "It could be a trap!"

The bag hit the ground, and a decapitated head rolled out, stopping at Zena's feet. She screamed as Amanda's blank stare met her eyes, and she ran away in terror.

Aldar walked over to the head. "Amanda," he said in shock, "that means Shiva was at Antillean." He looked into the bag again. "There's more," he said, reaching into the bag and pulling out a letter.

Zena walked back to him, giving Amanda's head a wide berth. She watched intently as Aldar read the letter. His eyes widened, and then tears ran down his cheeks. "What does it say?" Zena demanded. He handed her the note.

"King Zanthor, King Unidad, and Emperor Savage, please come to me," Aldar commanded.

Dropping the letter, Zena wrapped her arms around Aldar and sobbed.

After several minutes had passed, all the monarchs were gathered, and Zena left the group, going to Enoch and Elaine.

"Gentlemen," Aldar announced, "Antillean City has been destroyed. Several are dead, and several more are wounded." Everyone gaped in shock. "My son and my sister are being held captive by Empress Shiva. She demands we return, and she will forgive our defiance if we go home, and the eye will forgive us. However, if we continue this path, she says, she will kill my son and sister, and all the capital cities will suffer the same fate and she will destroy us all."

Anger and determination filled his eyes. "I will not back down. I will not stop until the eye of the cyclops is destroyed. I believe if we give up, Empress Shiva will eventually destroy us all, no matter what we do. We will never have this chance again to work together as one force to destroy the eye. All that said, it is ultimately up to you, my friends. I will not judge you if you decide not to fight and instead go home. So, I ask, who will join me in this fight? Who will help me defeat Empress Shiva no matter what the cost?"

King Zanthor stepped forward and took a knee. "I am with you, son. I don't know what Shiva has planned for me, but I will not retreat."

King Unidad also stepped forward and kneeled. "You have my undying loyalty. I will fight by your side until the end."

Sweat beaded on Emperor Savage as his eyes met Aldar's, and then he let out a curse. He also stepped forward and kneeled. "Xavier was a good friend, but his mistake has become our problem, so you have my loyalty."

Tears ran down Aldar's cheeks, he was so proud of his fellow monarchs.

The other rulers stood, and all turned to face the combined armies. Aldar explained to the armies what had happened. "If you choose to go home, no judgement will befall you." The army was so massive that messengers had to be sent to spread the word. Aldar looked out at the mass of humanity, watching to see if anyone was leaving.

Then in the distance he heard a noise. It started as a soft buzzing noise, then grew louder, louder, and louder. "We will fight, we will fight, we will fight!" The armies repeated the phrase until it became a deafening roar.

Aldar and the other monarchs raised their swords in the air, and cheers and applause echoed across the plain. Aldar beamed with pride, and before he knew it, he was back on his horse. He waved his sword, and the trumpeters sounded their trumpets, and then he and the armies were marching with more determination than before.

~ ~ ~

After a long day of travel, the army made camp. Even though the armies were determined, there was a somber feeling in the air. Enoch sat next to Elaine on her cot and put a comforting arm around her shoulder as a tear ran down her cheek. "When is the pain and sorrow going to end? When is the death and destruction going to stop?" Elaine asked her brother.

Enoch looked at her. "I wish I knew. All I know, we must not give up."

Elaine shook her head. "I know what I said about not giving up, and I believe it to be true; it is just so hard sometimes. It is hard to have hope when you lose your parents, your lover, and possibly a friend who is like a sister. It is hard when your friends who treat you like family lose their mother, father, grandparents. It is hard to have hope when you see the pain in the eyes of the ones you care about as they worry about their family being captive. I pray that Alana and Hunter are all right; I pray Shiva does not kill them. With the eye in possession of Shiva, I doubt she will let them live; she is incapable of mercy.

"Curse Xavier Pulsar to the lowest part of the underworld It is his fault for bringing us this wrath that the eye has given us. I really miss Aurora; she would know what to say."

Enoch nodded. "As do I," he said.

Tears streamed down their faces as they held each other close, and then Enoch kissed Elaine on the forehead. "The hour is late, and we leave early on the morrow." Elaine nodded as Enoch stood up. "Things will get better; I just know it," Enoch said as he walked to the tent flap, turned, and smiled.

"I love you, Enoch. You are the best brother a sister could ever have."

Enoch blew her a kiss and walked out.

Elaine sighed as she wiped the remaining tears off her cheeks and went to her clothes chest. She took off her uniform and slipped into her nightgown. She undid her hair and looked over at the empty space where Aurora's cot should have been. "I just know you are alive, Aurora; I just know it. I cannot wait to see you again."

She groaned as she stretched her arms in the air. Traveling had taken its toll on her sore body. She needed to get some rest; another long day of travel would face her in the morning as they drew close to Adaliah. She blew out her candle and lay on her cot, keeping her sword nearby just in case. She prayed for Aurora, Alana, and Hunter and hoped she would have sweet dreams. Just as she was drifting off to sleep, she woke up, startled by a noise. When she heard some squeaking, she smiled. *Just a field mouse,* she mused, then went to sleep.

~ ~ ~

Pirena stood quietly outside the tent. She had managed to kill the guards without a sound. As she slipped into the tent and moved across the floor, she walked carefully so as not to trip on anything. She saw the outline of her target lying on the cot, fast asleep, as she drew closer. She smiled as she made it to the side of the cot.

Pirena looked down at the woman on the cot, then covered the woman's mouth and held a knife to her throat. When she saw the shock and horror on the woman's face, she said, "Good-night from the Lady of Death." Pirena slit the woman's throat and kept her hand over the woman's mouth until the woman went limp. "Sweet dreams," she said as she scurried away.

~ ~ ~

Zena yawned as she looked at the morning sun. Her stomach growled at the smell of bacon and eggs cooking. "Good morning, Zena," said Enoch, greeting her with a smile.

"I am famished," she said, touching her stomach.

"Is Elaine not up yet? She is usually up before the sun," Enoch said.

"That is strange; she's not making the morning coffee," Zena realized.

Enoch shook his head. "I will check in on her. I will have to tell her she's slacking."

Despite the stress they were under, both laughed.

Enoch walked to Elaine's tent and called, "Elaine, are you awake?"

No answer.

"Are you decent?"

No answer.

"Are you all right in there?" he asked.

Still no answer.

"I am coming in, decent or not," he announced. He walked in and looked around, then jumped.

"What are you doing in my tent?" Elaine asked.

Enoch turned away. “I was wondering where you were. You are usually up and making coffee by now.”

Elaine stood in front of the tent door and put her hands on her hips. “Well now you are waiting for your coffee, eh?” When Enoch nodded sheepishly, she said, “Well, sometimes a girl must make a trip to the privy, and they keep changing where they put them. I thought I was going to have to squat right in front of a bunch of people. It took me an hour to find them.”

Enoch started to shake his head, then burst out laughing at the thought. Then Elaine started to laugh, but their laughter was cut short when they heard someone screaming. “That sounded like Zena,” Elaine said.

They ran to the campfire and stopped to see Zena hugging her father. “What is wrong?” they asked.

“My mother. Oh, my mother.” Zena was crying so hard that she could not finish her sentence.

King Zanthor looked at Enoch and Elaine somberly. “Shiva said she was going to punish me. Well, she did. My wife, Zena’s mother, Queen Zanthor, is dead. I found her dead. Her throat was slashed. Shiva got her revenge.”

Chapter Sixty-Four

Bittersweet Reunion

Aurora knew they were close to the armies, not as far behind as she had feared. They rode the horses as far as they could, stopping only long enough to feed and water the horses and get some rest. The remains of the campfires they had seen the day before had been fresh, and they were well on their way to finding the armies.

It was early in the morning as Aurora and Maximus rode up to a massive plain. Aurora squinted. In the distance, she could see the armies. She smiled. "We are almost there!" she said gleefully. The army was still far off, so they would have to be persistent, or they still might not catch up. She figured it would be close to evening before they caught up.

~ ~ ~

To Aurora's surprise, they were near the army by midmorning. She wondered why the armies had not moved, and she looked at Maximus, puzzled. "I wonder what is happening?" she said. Maximus just shrugged.

When they finally made it to the rear of the army, two Violidian soldiers pointed guns at them, asking, "Who goes there?"

Aurora smiled. "It is I, Aurora Talon, and I have Maximus Pulsar with me," she announced.

The soldiers' eyes widened with surprise. "I am glad to see you, Your Highness," one of them said. "Everyone feared you had perished in your fall."

"Thank you. I need to find my father and let him know I am alive."

The two soldiers looked at each other hesitantly. "Yes, Your Highness, but your father is doing something important right now." Aurora looked at him, puzzled, and he added, "However, he will certainly be glad you're alive."

"Lead the way," she said and smiled.

Maximus frowned as they rode. The number of soldiers he saw was intimidating. He shivered. He had not been nervous about his fate until now. He hoped and prayed that Aurora could convince her father not to execute him.

Aurora frowned as they approached what appeared to be a large meeting. Several rows of soldiers were at attention on horseback, a wide dirt path running between them. A sense of foreboding filled her heart, and a chill went down her spine as she saw her father. He was standing on top of a rock, with something that appeared to be one large and one small pine box in front of him.

The soldiers, who were at attention, started to mutter as Aurora and Maximus approached, and Aldar scowled. Then his eyes fell upon Aurora, and they widened in shock. "Aurora!" he shouted, and all eyes looked at them in surprise.

"Aurora!" Zena yelled, getting up from her seat and running to her daughter. Aurora dismounted and hugged her mother. "My baby is back from the dead," Zena said, tears falling from her eyes.

Enoch and Elaine followed Zena, and Enoch kissed Aurora on the cheek. "My love! Oh, my love has returned."

Elaine kissed her as well, and said, "I missed you so! I am so glad you are here; I knew you would make it; I just knew."

Aurora looked at her father as he and Barnabas approached. Aldar's arms were open, and Aurora hugged him. Then she hugged Barnabas, but she noticed that there was a sadness in her grandfather that she could not put her finger on. She looked at her grandfather, confused, as he spoke. "Today is the happiest and saddest day of my life, for today my granddaughter has returned and today we say good-bye to the love of my life."

Aurora looked over to her father, not sure what her grandfather meant. "Father, what is going on here?"

Zena put her arm around Aurora's shoulder. "Your grandmother is dead. She was slain by an assassin's hands."

Aurora looked at her, stunned. "I tried to get here as fast as I could to warn you. Pirena Solaris has come." A great muttering came from the troops as word spread about the Lady of Death.

Aldar called for silence. "There is more. Amanda, your trainer, is dead." When Aurora looked baffled, Aldar explained all that had transpired.

Aurora then took her turn to explain all that had happened to her since her fall into the canyon.

"We were just laying your grandmother and Amanda to rest," Aldar explained. He looked over at Maximus. "I appreciate what you did to help our daughter, but that does not make up for what you were a part of. However, this is not the time or place to discuss this matter. You will be held captive until we can decide your fate."

Maximus nodded as he got off his horse and allowed himself to be escorted away.

Aurora watched him being led away, then took a seat to pay her final respects to her grandmother and her trainer.

~ ~ ~

She mourned the loss of her grandmother. She mourned the loss of Amanda. She mourned the destruction of Antillean. And she mourned her aunt and brother's captivity.

Chapter Sixty-Five

A Lucky Man

"Father, I know what Maximus did was wrong. He was part of the deception that led to Grandmother and Grandfather's deaths. I am not saying he should not be punished, but I do ask for some leniency. He had no idea that Pirena was going to execute anyone or about the attack on us and Antillean citizens. He was led to believe that Pirena was going to steal the eye. Pirena confirmed it."

Aldar tapped his finger on the table. Zena, Enoch, and Elaine were sitting alongside him while Aurora pleaded Maximus's case. "Are you sure this was not an act between Pirena and Maximus to try to deceive you into bringing him here?"

Aurora sighed. "I am sure, Father. You should see Maximus's wrists; he cut them while trying to untie his ropes. There is no way this is an act. He was trying to save me. There is no doubt. I am sorry, Father, I am not trying to argue with you. I just know that Maximus had no idea about the assassinations.

"I know he is hated," she continued. "He is the son of the man who is responsible for all this pain and suffering that we are cursed with. He is also not responsible for Grandma Zanthor's death—Pirena is, and we must keep our guard up."

Aldar gave Aurora a look of sympathy. "I understand why you are coming to Maximus's defense. I, of course, believe you; I have never known you to lie to me, and you are passionate when it comes to the truth. However, convincing the other monarchs not to hang Maximus will be difficult to do.

"Pirena killed not only your grandmother Zanthor but also a half dozen guards. Now, I know Maximus did not do it. Unfortunately, that is irrelevant if she continues to kill people—which you say she will—because it will be easy to blame him."

Aurora hung her head. "I feel it is my fault. I fought with Pirena. I was on the cusp of defeating her. In the end, she escaped, and I was not fast enough to stop her. I failed. Now Grandmother is dead." Aurora teared up; it had been a long day. She was clearly exhausted and was very emotional.

Enoch moved to her side and hugged her. "This is certainly not your fault, Aurora. You did the best you could." Enoch looked at Aldar. "I know there is only so much you can do, but like you, I believe what she says."

Aldar stood up, walked over to Aurora, and kissed her on the cheek. "I will do what I can, dear. I am headed over now to talk to the others. I am also going to double the guard patrols for the rest of the march, with Pirena out there. Heaven only knows what the she-devil is capable of doing." He smiled. "I'll at least have Maximus out of the prison cart and riding with an escort, at least until the war is over."

Aurora smiled. "Thank you, Father," she said, still smiling as he walked out of the tent.

Zena walked up to Aurora and told her, "I will have someone get you something to eat and have a healer look at that cut."

Elaine chimed in. "I will have a bath drawn for you as well. I love you, Aurora, but you smell bad." They all started to laugh.

"Hey!" Aurora protested. Then she smelled her armpit and coughed. "I guess you are right." They all roared with laughter, relieving some of the tension.

Enoch kissed Aurora's forehead. "I guess I will leave you alone for now."

Elaine smiled. "You'd better go away; it would not be proper to watch her take a bath."

~ ~ ~

An hour later, Aurora's cheek was stitched, she had had a well-cooked meal, and she had taken her bath. She was still very tired, but she felt good. It seemed an eternity since she had last felt clean, and she enjoyed Elaine brushing her hair. "Thank you," Elaine said.

"For what?" Aurora asked.

"For making it back. I love my brother; he has been there for me during some of the hardest times we have been through. I love you as well; even though we come from different families, you are like a sister to me. When I saw you fall into that canyon, I felt so lost, hoping and praying you survived. It was unbearable. The only thing that kept me going was the belief you were coming back to us, and you did." Elaine paused as she heard two guards talking, She and Aurora sat quietly for a tense moment.

"Hey, you two, is there any way for me to come in?" Enoch asked.

Aurora, in her nightgown and with her hair still down, looked at Elaine. Elaine started to speak, but Aurora waved her to silence and replied, "It is all right; you can come in." As Enoch walked in, Elaine gave Aurora a look that asked if, she was sure.

"I was wondering when you . . . " Enoch trailed off as he caught sight of Aurora. His jaw dropped. He had never seen her hair down. Looking slightly embarrassed, he said, "Aurora, you are not decent," trying to look away, but without success.

Aurora smiled. "Well, someday this will be a common sight for you. Might as well get used to it now."

Enoch smiled at her. "But if your mother sees me here, she will tan my hide."

Aurora rolled her eyes. "You need not worry. If you behave yourself, everything will be all right."

Enoch looked at her, wondering how that was going to be accomplished, but did walk closer. Elaine, smiling, walked over to her brother and punched his shoulder. "Ow! What was that for?"

Elaine put her hands on her hips. "I am going to leave you two alone for a few minutes. Consider this a warning." Enoch scowled at her and rubbed his shoulder as she smiled and walked out the door.

Aurora patted the bench she sat on. There was just enough room for Enoch to sit beside her. Enoch walked over nervously and sat next to her. He felt his throat go dry as she offered her hand. He gave his hand to her, and their hands clasped. "Thank you for backing me up," Aurora told him.

Enoch smiled. "No problem. I know when you are passionate and genuinely believe in something. That is one of the things I love about you. I am glad that Maximus took care of you, but I would hope I would have done a better job."

Aurora grinned. "Of course, you would, my love. No one else would come close to how you take care of me."

"I have a confession to make. I was just a little bit jealous. I know it is silly, but, yes, I was a little jealous."

Aurora smirked. "You are right, it is silly, but I do understand. After all, Maximus is a handsome fellow." Enoch looked at her for a long time, and then Aurora burst into laughter. "The . . . look . . . on your face," she sputtered barely able to speak. Enoch looked at her surprised, then started laughing as well.

"I'll have you know he was a gentleman," Aurora assured him. "The only thing he said is he did not blame you and Elaine for his mother's death but he still did not like you because you are my beau, and you are a lucky man."

"Well, I would say he is right. I *am* a lucky man." His look became serious. "Could you tell me more of what you discovered about the cyclops?"

Aurora frowned. "That statue back at home is frighteningly accurate. It was a remnant of Ivan Albatross's era and somehow survived all these years. That crown symbol was the tell-tale sign. In all honesty, I am surprised Shiva has not released her own cyclops."

Enoch shivered at the thought. "Let us pray that does not happen before we destroy the eye." Wanting to change the subject, he looked at Aurora and said, "You know, you are extremely pretty."

Her eyes widened in surprise as she touched the stitched cut on her cheek and then her nose. "I think you are blind, Enoch. I am far from pretty. I am a mess; that is what I am."

Enoch carefully touched her cheek and nose. "I must say you really are a sight." When Aurora's jaw dropped, Enoch smiled. "Well, just look at you. Your nose is bruised and broken, and you have a cut on your cheek." He paused for a second as Aurora's eyes narrowed, then continued, "Yet you are the most beautiful woman I have ever seen."

Aurora smiled. "Oh, you are good. Nice save. You were about to receive a slap." She wrapped her arms around him and kissed him.

"Hey, what do you two think you're doing?"

They broke apart to look at Elaine, who stood smiling just inside the tent, her hands on her hips. "I leave you for one second . . ."

Aurora kissed Enoch again, more passionately this time, and Elaine protested, "Hey, you two are not married yet!"

Aurora pulled back from their kiss and put her hands on Enoch's cheek. "Thank you," she told him. "I love you."

Chapter Sixty-Six

A Long Night

Zena paced inside her tent; her nerves shot. She checked for the third time to make sure the guards were outside. "Your Majesty, I assure you," one of the guards told her, "You are very safe. My partner and I are here. There are also eight other guards surrounding the tent. You are safe.

Zena nodded at the guard curtly and went back into the tent, where she started to undo her hair. She looked at the cot. It would be hours before Aldar would climb in with her. She worried about him; how he could continue at this pace and not collapse was beyond her.

She sighed in resignation as she changed into her nightgown. "I miss my bed," she complained, scowling at her cot while she rubbed her back. She had constant backaches and could not wait for the war to be over. She stretched her back, then yawned before blowing out the lantern and crawling into her cot. She lay there for a long time, afraid that she was Pirena's next target. Finally, she fell asleep, and the sound of her snores reverberated around the tent.

One guard stationed at the entrance looked at his partner and grinned. "Her Majesty sure complains a lot," he said.

The other chuckled. "I am not sure which is louder, the complaining or the snoring." They tried not to laugh out loud.

"All I know is it is going to be a very long night," the first guard said.

The other chuckled. "For you, this night won't be long at all." The first guard looked confused, but before he could say anything, Pirena had her knife in his throat. She caught him as he fell, then hid him in an abandoned tent before dispatching the other guards quickly and quietly.

Pirena walked into Zena's tent, knowing she needed to be quick, quiet, and precise. *It is too bad Aldar is not here, but you will do*, she thought as she stood beside Zena. *I think I will be doing Aldar a favor.* She kneeled, and as she moved to cover Zena's face, she gasped, realizing this was a decoy. She stood quickly, drawing her swords as a multitude of soldiers charged the tent.

Torches lit the tent, and Pirena thrust and swung her swords in a tempest of death. She stabbed the first soldier who approached her and decapitated the second, then repeated the process on two others.

Another soldier tackled her from behind, and as more and more soldiers entered the tent, Pirena was quickly tied and bound. Pirena looked over at the cot as two soldiers moved it. Zena had been lying under the cot instead of on it. "Clever," Pirena said with a smile as the soldiers helped Zena to her feet.

Zena pulled a pistol from under her nightgown. "You evil, demented witch!" Zena yelled. She cocked the hammer of the gun and pointed it at Pirena's head. "I should kill you now. You killed my father-in-law, you killed my mother-in-law, and you killed my mother. I hope you rot in the underworld."

Pirena smiled. "I must say, Zena, you are far better at insulting me than Isaiah."

"Shut up, you vile wench."

Pirena laughed. "Go ahead, I dare you. Pull the trigger. You are a spoiled, pampered queen. You are soft. You do not have the grit to—"

Zena pulled the trigger.

Pirena looked at Zena in stunned silence as Zena let out a curse. The gun had not fired.

Aldar ran into the tent. "Zena are you—" He cut off as she saw the rage on Zena's face and the horror on Pirena's.

"It didn't fire," Zena said in frustration.

"Don't worry, my love. Justice will be served. Take away all her weapons and put her in the jail wagon," he ordered the guards, who did as he commanded. Once Pirena had been taken away, Aldar put his arm around Zena. "Are you all right?" he asked.

"I am *not* all right. That evil witch lives while your parents, my mother, and thousands of others are dead."

Aldar nodded. "You are right; however, we now have her, and justice will be served," he said, kissing her cheek. "I am sorry to put you through this, but I thought she might target you next.

Zena started to shake violently and then cried as she watched the dead soldiers being carried out of the tent. "These poor soldiers. They died trying to protect me; I feel so bad."

Aldar nodded. "They died with honor. They died capturing Pirena. I will see fit that their deaths were not in vain." He wrapped a blanket around her, saying, "You will sleep with Elaine and Aurora tonight." Then he walked her to the girls' tent and kissed her. "Try to rest, for tomorrow, justice will be served," he told her.

~ ~ ~

Morning came very slowly for Zena, as she was unable to sleep the whole night through. She sat next to Aldar and the other monarchs behind a table as they waited to try Pirena. Isaiah and Maximus were also there, as well as Aurora, Enoch, and Elaine.

"Bring her in," Aldar commanded.

Pirena was escorted in. She scowled as she saw Enoch and Elaine, then smiled when she saw Aurora, and chuckled when she saw Maximus and Isaiah. "I see Aurora must have said something nice about you, Maximus, for you are not up here with me."

Aldar pounded the table in front of him. "You will be silent; you will only speak when asked a question. You will be able to speak later." Pirena sniffed and gave Aldar a smug smile, then nodded and bowed.

Aldar tried to keep his anger in check as he looked at his parents' murderer, his mother-in-law's murderer, the killer of hundreds, the Lady of Death. He could hardly believe they had captured her. He then addressed her as calmly as he could. "Pirena Solaris, you stand here in front of these witnesses. You are charged with the murders of Victor

Talon, Amber Talon, Abigail Zanthor, and countless others. How do you plea?"

"Does it matter what I plea? Why all the formalities? You all know I did what I did, and I will be punished."

Aldar slammed the tabletop again and stood. "Answer the question."

Pirena smiled. "Such angry people."

The veins in Aldar's neck bulged, and his face turned red. "Answer the question," he hissed.

"I plead guilty. Of course, I am guilty of all the death and despair; I am the Lady of Death, after all."

Zena shivered at Pirena's sarcastic and callous response; it was like evil incarnate was in the room.

After several minutes of deliberation with the other monarchs in a separate tent, Aldar and the other monarchs returned to their seats. He looked Pirena in the eye. "Pirena, you have been found guilty and you are to be executed by beheading."

For the first time, Pirena looked scared. Maximus recognized the look as the same one she had worn when running away from Aurora.

"Do you have anything to say?" Aldar asked.

Pirena stood silently for a moment, then spoke. "Yes, I do have something to say." As everyone waited, wondering what sarcastic things she would say, she turned to Zena. "Your Majesty, I know this changes nothing, but I must say your daughter, Aurora, is an incredibly good fighter. You and Aldar should be proud of her. Unlike the rest of you, she has my utmost respect."

Maximus looked at Pirena, shocked that she was being genuinely nice and kind for once.

Pirena laughed. "It is too bad I defeated her, and she was too late in saving her grandmother."

"And she is back," Maximus groaned.

Aldar stood again. "I have heard enough from you, you battle-axe. Take her to the execution area."

Pirena rolled her eyes. "Temper, temper, Your Majesty." She shook her head as she was led out the door and to a stump, the others following to witness her execution. Isaiah walked up carrying an axe, and Pirena was forced to lay her head on the stump.

Pirena laughed. "Isaiah, dear, do you remember that last time I saw you? Perhaps not—you were unconscious."

Isaiah snorted as he walked up beside her. "I must say I will take great pleasure in doing this," he said with a smile.

"I am sure you will, my love. After all, as hard as you tried, you could never defeat me in open battle."

Isaiah's face turned red as he touched the scar on his cheek. Then he tapped his fingernail against the axe's blade. "Well, Pirena, I suggest you stretch your neck; it will make for a clean cut and a less painful death."

Pirena laughed. "Thank you, my love, that is so thoughtful of you."

Isaiah laughed as well. "Well, good night, my love. I hope you enjoy your one-way trip to the underworld," he said, raising the axe.

As he brought the axe down, there was a flash of light and Isaiah was knocked onto his back. Shiva appeared and grabbed Pirena. Then there was another flash of light and the women disappeared.

A rumble of thunder rolled across the land, and Isaiah groaned as he made his way to his feet. Everyone looked at the stump, shocked, and Isaiah shook his fist at the sky in frustration. "No matter what I do, I cannot win!" he shouted.

Chapter Sixty-Seven

A Good Deed

Pirena shivered in the cold morning air as she saw the palace getting closer at their approach. They landed on the balcony of Shiva and Daniel's apartment and walked into the living quarters, where Daniel and Virion were seated.

Both men stood as the women approached. "Your Majesty," Virion said with a bow.

"Not now," Shiva snapped at him, then scowled at Pirena. "What in the name of Apollyon was that? As long as I have known you, I have never seen you in such a precarious situation. If I had not come to see how you had progressed, your severed head would be on the ground."

"Aunt Shiva, they were craftier than I gave them credit for. I tried to kill Zena, but they fooled me; it was a trap."

Shiva laughed. "I do not understand, Pirena. You are supposed to be the Lady of Death, the most feared assassin in all lands. You seem to have lost your touch. Did you manage to kill anyone, or was this a pleasure trip for you?"

Pirena looked down, her professional pride wounded. "I managed to kill Abigail Zanthor I heard from other soldiers you had threatened Barnabas Zanthor with punishment, so there's that."

Shiva smiled thinly. That is well and good. I am glad he was punished, but there was so much more I needed you to accomplish. I wanted you to kill Enoch and Elaine Eclipse, Aurora Talon, and of course Aldar Talon. Now this opportunity is lost."

Pirena looked at Shiva. "About Aurora Talon . . . I have news about her and someone else. You will be shocked." Pirena told Shiva of the encounter with Aurora Talon and about Maximus wanting to join the resistance.

Shiva's eyes widened in shock. "Maximus is alive?" she exclaimed. At first, she just stood there, then she cried tears of joy. Anger followed, and the eye pulsed with Shiva's eyes.

The room turned cold. "That young harlot turned my boy against me. Despite my threats, they will be at our gates within the next couple of days. They do not heed my warning," Shiva said, pacing. Everyone else in the room shivered in the cold even as anger burned inside Shiva's heart. "Now they will really suffer. Tomorrow I will bring forth Alana and Hunter and I will burn them alive in front of Aldar. I will enjoy his tears of sorrow and Zena's cries of suffering. This will break them for sure."

Virion felt his throat go dry. This was getting way out of hand. He did not like the Talons, but this was too much. "Your Majesty, may I speak?" he asked.

Shiva rolled her eyes, and the room's temperature returned to normal.

"With all due respect, do you not feel the Talons have suffered enough?"

Shiva frowned. "I do not understand what you are getting at. What do you mean, they have suffered enough?"

"Pirena has killed Aldar's father and mother and Zena's mother, and you have destroyed Antillean City and kidnapped their son and sister." He went down to one knee. "Why do you not end this war? You can end this. You have the power to wipe them all out. You can kill them quickly and mercifully, yet you torture them. It is like a sick and demented game you are playing. I implore you to just end this war; it has gone long enough."

Shiva smiled. "Oh my. I do not think I have ever seen this side of you—kindness and compassion," she mused. She slapped Virion hard across the face, and he fell to the floor.

As Virion slowly got back to his feet, Shiva raved. "What is going on? First my assassin goes soft, and now my supreme general has as well. Has a spell been cast on you two? How dare you question me and the eye! I am the eye's servant, and disobedience must be punished." Shiva looked at

Virion sternly. "If you question me again, I will kill you. My leniency has ended; no more chances."

Virion bowed his head. "I understand, Your Majesty. I shall not question you again."

Shiva's smile returned. "Pirena, you probably are famished. Breakfast should be ready. Please join us."

Pirena bowed. "Thank you, Aunt Shiva, but I am not hungry. I feel tired, is all."

Shiva smiled. "Suit yourself, deary." As Virion began to move behind Shiva and Daniel as they walked to the door, Shiva scowled at him. "I have seen enough of you for the present. I will meet with you later."

Virion bowed. "Yes, Your Majesty," he said as the emperor and empress left the room. He looked at Pirena as she took a seat on the couch, and then he looked out the door to make sure Shiva and Daniel were gone.

Pirena set her feet on the table in front of her. "You are a fool," Pirena said. "There is no way you can reason with Aunt Shiva. Right now, I am going to do her bidding. As much as it sickens me, it is the only way. When the time is right, I shall kill her, and I will take the eye for myself I will rule and bring peace."

Virion laughed. "You, rule? That would be a sight! Running a division of the army is one thing, but ruling is another. How do you plan on killing her? Are you going to put a stake in her heart like a vampire?"

He went on. "Or how do you plan on getting the eye from her? She has some sort of curse on that eye; only she can touch it. Or have you forgotten that part? You think me a fool, but if anyone here is a fool, it is you."

Pirena's eyes narrowed. "Careful, old man. I could kill you in an instant, and Aunt Shiva would probably approve."

Virion snorted. "You are probably right; however, as volatile as she is, are you willing to take that chance?"

Pirena frowned, then smiled. "If you fought as well as you argued, it would be you doing the assassinations."

"Look, you and I have different approaches to the situation, who the fool is has yet to be determined."

Pirena stood up and walked to the door. "I will not stand in your way. I hope you succeed. However, you had better not stand in my way, either, or unlike Aunt Shiva, I will kill you for real. Either way, I fear time is running out for you, friend, and maybe Aunt Shiva will kill you. If she requests me to kill you, I will do it without regret or hesitation." At the door, she turned and smiled. "Good luck."

Left alone in the room, Virion pondered what Pirena had said. "She is right; time is running out." He let out a curse and left the room.

~ ~ ~

Later that evening, Virion entered the dungeons and approached the guards. "I wish to speak with the prisoners Alana and Hunter Talon."

The guards gave him confused looks. "Her Majesty just talked to them an hour ago, sir."

Virion glared at them. "Are you questioning my authority?" he yelled.

"No, sir. I am sorry, sir," said one guard in a panic.

"Good, take me to them," he demanded.

The guards respectfully escorted him to the cell without another word.

Hunter looked at Virion with scorn in his eyes. "What are you doing here and what do you want? Empress Shiva has already told us her plans to kill us."

"Who is here?" Alana asked.

"Virion Nebula," Hunter replied.

Alana bowed. "What brings you here?" she asked.

Virion smiled. "I have come to set you free."

The two guards looked at Virion, surprise and confusion on their faces. Before they could react, he punched one guard in the face. As that guard crumpled, he punched the other in the stomach , then slammed his knee into the guard's face.

As both guards lay unconscious, Hunter stood in shock. "What has happened?" Alana asked.

Virion grabbed the keys from one of the guards. "I have come to set you free," he repeated.

"He just knocked out the guards and taken keys from them," Hunter explained to his aunt.

"How do you expect us to trust you, Virion?" asked Alana. "You are responsible for my parents' death."

Virion scrambled to find the right key. Finding the right one, he used it to open the door. "Right now, I do not expect you to trust me; however, I am your only hope to live. I realize I have done a great sin against your family—an unforgivable sin—and I do not deserve your forgiveness. I also know right now; Empress Shiva and the eye of the cyclops are a threat to us all. I am willing to risk my life, and even if your father commands my execution," he said, looking at Hunter, "then so be it. I will die knowing I at least did a good deed. I am tired of all the pain and suffering that Empress Shiva is causing." He picked up the torch that one of the soldiers had carried, and he looked again at Hunter. "Please take your aunt's hand and follow me."

Hunter hesitated for a moment, then nodded. He took Alana's hand as Virion led the way.

Chapter Sixty-Eight

Unknown Destiny

Aldar looked out to the horizon. As the morning sun was about to make its appearance, he let out a yawn. He could not remember the last time he had gotten a full night's rest—probably before his mother and father died. He longed for a hot cup of coffee, but unfortunately, it had been announced the night before that the coffee had run out. "Of all the things to run out of, it had to be coffee," he muttered under his breath. He stood up from the log he had been sitting on, lest he fall asleep and fall off, and looked to the south.

In the far distance, he could make out Adaliah. There lay Shiva, the eye, and whatever horrible fate awaited them. He figured at the pace they were going, the armies should arrive at the city by nightfall.

It had been a long trek, for sure. He hung his head, wishing he could rest the army for a couple of days after they arrived. Unfortunately, they would not have such a luxury, for with the eye, who knew for sure what would happen?

The sun finally rose, causing a faint red glow across the plain. He smiled as he looked at the sunrise. Then something he saw out of the corner of his eye caught his attention. In the distance appeared two horses. He put his hand over his eyes, trying to block the sunlight and cursing himself for leaving his telescope in his tent. He shouted for Isaiah.

"Right here," the general called as he approached.

Aldar pointed to the riders. "What do you think?"

"I am not sure, Aldar. Should I call some archers?"

Aldar nodded. "But just have them nock their arrows. Hopefully, this is not some trick of Shiva's." Within a minute, ten archers were on horseback with their arrows nocked.

The riders sped up as they drew closer. "Archers, draw your bows," Aldar commanded as he saw one rider appear to reach for a weapon. As the archers drew their bows, the rider in front pulled out a white flag. "Withdraw!" Aldar commanded.

Then he recognized the rider in front. "Virion?" he said in surprise. Then he saw a young man and a woman were riding the other horse, and he recognized them. "Hunter! Alana!" he yelled.

They reined up their horses, and Virion raised his hands in the air. Aldar ran up to his son and sister. Hunter got off his horse and helped Alana down, and then Aldar wrapped his arms around them both. He cried and cried hard, all the strain and stress and worry about them gone in a flash.

After several minutes, Aldar turned his attention to Virion, his eyes narrowed. Virion got off his horse and again raised his hands in the air. "Bind him," Aldar commanded. Virion put his hands behind his back and allowed them to be shackled together. "So, explain to me why you rescued my son and my sister. I appreciate you returning them, but I must ask why you would risk your career and your life. Why this sudden change in you?"

Virion bowed his head. "Shiva planned on killing them in front of you this morning. That is why I rescued them. I am tired of all the pain and death this war and the eye of the cyclops have caused. I am sorry for the death and despair Pirena has wrought on your family, and I am sorry I took part in the whole thing. I know no number of apologies could right all the wrong I have caused, and I certainly do not expect your forgiveness. I have been dealing with this gut-wrenching guilt for too long.

"I have seen the grievous error of Emperor Pulsar's ways and the consequences of this mistake. As you already know, the eye of the cyclops is a great threat. It has possessed Shiva. A once beautiful, kind, caring person is now a monster and a threat to us all. Daniel, Pirena, and I tried to figure out a way to destroy the eye. Unfortunately, as you all have found out, Pirena has sided with Shiva for the present. She plans on killing Shiva and taking the power for herself and will become a worse monster than she is now."

Virion looked at Aldar directly. "I know this small gesture of saving your sister and your son does not make up for what I have done. I am willing to face whatever punishment you give me." He looked over to Hunter and Alana. "At least if I die, I know at least I did a little something right in my life. I know this does not mean much to you, but I am willing to offer my sword, my knowledge of the palace. I have spent many hours with Shiva. I can give you my insight on what I know of her plans. I want this evil to come to an end, and anything I can do to help defeat it would be wonderful."

Aldar looked at Virion angrily. "I will have to meet with the other monarchs. We will decide your fate. In the meantime, you will spend time in the prison cart. Take him away," Aldar commanded, and the soldiers then took him away.

~ ~ ~

After an hour of deliberation among the other monarchs, Virion was brought into their meeting tent. He looked at their angry faces. Barnabas spat on the ground in front of him. It was then that he saw Aldar held an axe and stood near a stump.

Aldar looked at him sternly. "General Virion Nebula, you stand here accused of deceiving the crown of Antillean. You stand here accused of conspiring in the murder of King Victor Talon and Queen Alana Talon. How do you plea?"

Virion lowered his head. "I plead guilty."

Aldar frowned. "Then, General Virion Nebula, you are hereby sentenced to death by beheading."

Virion nodded. "I accept this sentence. I am sorry for all the death and despair I have caused you."

Aldar gave him a curt nod as two soldiers grabbed him. "No need," Virion told the soldiers as he looked at Aldar.

"Let him be," Aldar commanded.

The soldiers nodded and let go of Virion, who then kneeled and placed his head on the stump. Aldar raised the axe over his head.

Virion flinched as the axe landed on the ground beside him. He looked at the axe, then up at Aldar, confused as the soldiers untied him.

Aldar scowled at him as the soldiers helped Virion to his feet. "As much as I want to do this, I cannot at the present. I am also growing weary of the death and despair, and right now, even though we all hate you, we could also use you. I talked to Hunter and Alana; they told me the whole story of your rescue and convinced us not to kill you. Obviously, I still do not trust you; however, you just showed me you are capable of some honor, so for now, you will ride with Maximus, and you will be escorted presently. You will come to provide your services to help when I request it; this does not mean you will not be punished. Your punishment will depend on how truthful you are and how dependable you are."

Virion bowed his head. "Thank you for this mercy. I will not disappoint."

Aldar nodded. "I hope not."

Virion was escorted into a tent.

"Virion?" a voice called out as he entered. "What in the name of Apollyon are you doing here?" Maximus asked, scowling at him.

Virion explained the events leading up to his being escorted to the tent. "I am sorry, lad, about what has happened to your father and mother. You would not even recognize her; she has become an evil creature and the eye has possessed her. She has become fanatical. She worships the eye of the cyclops like it is a god. She must be stopped, and the eye destroyed, or we will all perish."

"I am sorry for all of this. You were right about this whole thing being unnatural. Your father and I made a terrible mistake, and I am sorry for treating you so badly. You are the heir to the throne, and by rights, you are the emperor of Apollyon. If faith is restored in us, I pledge my loyalty to you, Your Majesty."

Maximus grinned. "You really have changed, Virion. I do accept your apology."

An hour later, they were on horseback, riding toward Adaliah and to an unknown destiny.

Chapter Sixty-Nine

Power of the Eye

Shiva shrieked. Enraged, she picked up a vase and smashed it on the floor. "What do you mean, General Nebula is gone?"

The guard, with a broken nose and black eye, stood shaking. "We brought him to see Alana and Hunter Talon. Then he attacked me and my partner. When our replacements woke us up this morning, they were gone."

Shiva lifted the eye over her head and chanted, and a bolt shot out of the eye, hitting the guard in the chest. The guard went flying across the room and hit the wall, looking at her with a dead stare. "I cannot believe Virion betrayed me. After all I have done for him, he repays me with this? He is a dead man! I will give him no mercy." Her eyes narrowed and she stared at Daniel. "What do you know of this?"

Daniel started to sweat profusely. "I have no idea, my love."

She walked up to him and smiled, then slapped him across the face. "Liar!" she screamed. "You knew he was going to escape with Hunter and Alana. You have betrayed me as well."

Daniel wiped blood from his mouth. "I am not lying, my love. I would never betray you. I am loyal to you, my love, and I am loyal to the eye of the cyclops. Please believe me."

Shiva put her hand on her chin, and then the tears started to flow. She wrapped her arms around him. "I am sorry, my love, I am just so angry. I am sorry I hurt you. Please forgive me"

Daniel let out a breath he had not realized he had been holding. "It is all right, all is forgiven."

Shiva pulled out a kerchief from the pocket of her dress. She dabbed his mouth with it, then kissed his forehead. "Thank you, my love." Instantly, her anger returned. She looked at another guard who was standing at the door. "Find me General Solaris and find someone to cart this trash out of my room," she commanded, pointing to the dead guard.

Several minutes later, Pirena entered the room as two guards were carrying a corpse to the door. Pirena smiled. *Her Majesty is in a foul mood today*, she thought as she looked at Daniel. *Oh, Daniel, you have a dirty secret, don't you? No worries, though, I will keep it from Aunt Shiva for now.*

"There you are," Shiva said to her. "Pirena, I have news that will shock you."

Pirena perked up at that comment. After Shiva had explained to her what had happened, Pirena's jaw dropped in surprise. *I did not think that fool would run to the other side*, she thought. "I can't believe it," she said to Shiva.

Shiva put an arm around Pirena's shoulder. "I would like to go outside for a walk with you. Daniel, you as well." Before either of them could speak, Shiva was chanting and all three were flying out of the balcony door. They landed on the ground below and walked to the battle training grounds adjacent to the palace. As they walked past some slaves dismantling the last statue of Xavier Pulsar, Shiva said, "Good riddance.".

She then looked at Pirena. "I know you have many irons in the fire, Pirena, but I need you now more than ever. The combined armies are almost here, and I need a general who can lead the Apollyon army."

Pirena's eyes widened in shock as she touched her chest with her finger. "You want *me* to command the army?" Shiva nodded. "Aunt Shiva, I have no experience in running an army. Uncle Xavier had me trained to be an assassin and a spy, not run an entire army. I think you need someone else for that job."

Shiva shook her head. "No, I have chosen you. Trust me, you will know what to do, for I have something to give you." When Pirena looked at her, confused, Shiva explained, "I was going to bestow this on Virion, but that sniveling coward ran out on me." She smiled. "Come to me," she demanded. Pirena walked up to her, and Shiva held the eye in front of her. "Put your hand on the eye of the cyclops."

Pirena looked at her, surprised. “Won’t I get shocked?” she asked.

“As long as I hold the eye, nothing will happen.”

As Pirena reluctantly placed her hand on the eye, Daniel grimaced at the sight, remembering what had happened to him.

Shiva chanted for several minutes while Pirena touched the eye. At first, Pirena felt nothing, but then a warm sensation came over her and seemed to grow warmer and warmer. Then she felt she was on fire. She looked at herself, but she was not on fire, and she felt no pain.

Daniel let out a gasp. “Pirena, your eyes! They are changing color and glowing,” he said.

That strange euphoria that Pirena had felt the first time she touched the eye returned. She felt like she was drunk. The power was different than the last time, but it still felt intoxicating as it surged through her body.

When Shiva stopped chanting and pulled the eye away, Pirena was expecting to feel weak like she had the last time she had stopped touching the eye. Surprisingly, however, she did not feel weak at all; she felt powerful—not as powerful as Shiva, but powerful, all the same. Then she felt another sensation—knowledge. She knew things she had never known before.

This is wonderful! The witch has given me this power, and now she has sealed her doom. I just need to find the right time to strike. She bowed. “Thank you, Aunt Shiva, for giving me this power, but I am still not sure in what manner to use it.”

Shiva smiled. “No worries, deary, this is just the beginning.” She lifted the eye into the air, chanting. She rose into the air, and a bolt of lightning shot up into the sky. The sky turned a reddish-orange, and a black cloud swirled overhead. Then hundreds of beams shot out of the sky and hit the ground. There was a blinding light and the ground shook. Pirena and Daniel covered their eyes.

When they heard several strange sounds, they opened their eyes and their jaws dropped in shock.

Chapter Seventy

Certain Death

Aldar Talon looked at the city of Adaliah. He had not slept at all last night, but at this point, sleep did not matter. He would rest when this battle was over, either in his cot or in the ground, he was not sure. The sun had come up, and they were to finish battle plans, then attack the city today.

He enjoyed looking at the rising sun, taking it all in, for this might be the last time he would see the sunrise. "Aldar," a familiar voice said, grabbing his attention.

"Elaine," he said as she walked to him and gave him a hug.

"Thank you," Elaine said.

"For what?" Aldar asked.

"Thank you for taking Enoch and me in. When we came to see your father, Enoch and I were so lost and distraught, and you accepted us. Then when I lost my Jonathan, you gave me a shoulder to cry on. You and Zena are like a mother and father to us."

Enoch walked up to them. "Well, sister, are you ready for this big day?" he asked.

She smiled. "I am more than ready, for today we fight in honor of our mother and father, my Jonathan, Antillean, and the freedom of Apollyon."

Zena, Aurora, Hunter, and Alana joined the group then. "How come we were not invited to this family reunion?" Zena asked. Everyone laughed, and Aurora kissed Enoch on the cheek.

A tear ran down Aldar's cheek, for he knew he looked at his family perhaps for the last time. He was so proud. Aurora, Enoch, and Elaine oversaw their own divisions. He was putting them in a lot of danger; however, he knew it was the right thing to do. As he looked at the three of them, he smiled. Next, he looked at his son, Hunter. Hunter was not quite ready to fight but still was going to help with the back lines. Aldar's sweet sister, Alana—how he wished she could join him in the front line! She was beautiful and fierce. He was not worried about her; even blind, she could still swing a sword. Then he looked at his spirited, beautiful wife; how he missed her—all this time, she had been here, yet they were always apart. He missed spending time with her. He missed her kisses. He missed her touch. He even missed her hot temper.

Looking at them all, he wished someone could have painted their picture. Instead, he put their picture in his mind. If only this moment could last forever. If only they could be home and not fighting a war.

"Your Majesty—"

Aldar sighed. *If only.* He turned to face the soldier who had spoken.

"The other monarchs await your arrival."

His loved ones gave him a resigned look. He opened his arms, and they all wrapped arms around each other.

Aldar kissed each of them on the cheek, then said, "We will overcome, and we will be victorious in the end." He then walked away, and they all went to their positions and awaited the command to attack.

Aldar walked up to Isaiah. "Well, friend, are you ready for this?" he asked the general.

"You'd better believe it," Isaiah responded.

They mounted their horses and rode to the other monarchs, who were on horseback and ready for their final instructions. Virion and Maximus were there as well, no longer with escorts. Aldar did not know why, but he felt he could trust them, and at this point, he had nothing to lose.

Aldar looked again at Adaliah, which was silent. No army surrounded the city to defend it. Was Shiva planning on fighting all of them by herself? Aldar wondered. She was powerful enough—after all, she had destroyed Antillean City. He looked over to Virion and Maximus, who were going to join him in the attack. "Virion, what do you think Shiva is doing? This strategy makes no sense. Why does she not have the army surrounding the city?"

Virion scowled. "I know if was up to me, I would have had the army surround the city. This is a sick game to her. She is doing everything in her power to make you miserable, and she is enjoying every minute. She justifies her behavior because she claims the eye of the cyclops talks to her. Therefore, judgement and punishment are from the eye and are her duty to fulfill. She worships the thing like a god."

As if on cue, the ground shook for a second. All eyes were on Adaliah and saw Shiva float into the sky. The gates of the city opened, and the Apollyon army poured out quickly. Shiva chanted, and a great flame surrounded the city.

After a few minutes, the flames dissipated.

Aldar looked at Virion. "How did the army surround the city so fast? It should have taken hours," he said in surprise.

Virion shook his head. "The eye has powers that are unnatural. She can do just about everything with it."

They could easily see Shiva, who was wearing a reddish-orange dress that shimmered under the light of the eye in a way that made her look like a golden statue. "Aldar Talon, you did not heed my warning. The eye is displeased," Shiva's voice boomed. You and the other monarchs have sealed your doom, and you will suffer greatly.

"That said, she continued, "I wish to speak to my son."

Aldar looked at Maximus, who nodded. "I will go. Maybe I can speak some sense into her."

"Good luck with that, son," Virion said. "She listens to no one except for that cursed eye."

Maximus nodded. "Well, I am going to talk to her anyway," he said.

"Good luck," Aldar said as Maximus rode off. Maximus galloped close to the Apollyon army but out of bowshot. "I am here, Mother."

Shiva floated down to hover in front of him a few feet above the ground. "Are you all, right?" she asked in a motherly voice.

"I am well. I have been treated well. I have been well fed and taken care of. No worries."

"No worries? What do you mean, no worries? You are my son. Of course, I am going to worry. I am so glad they did not hurt you," Shiva said.

"They are good people, Mother; they would not hurt me."

Shiva laughed. "Those traitors, heathens, defilers of the eye, and you think they are good people?"

"Yes, Mother, I do. They are only here to preserve their way of life, and they're afraid the eye is going to destroy us all." A tear ran down his cheek. "This is not who you are, Mother. The mother I knew was kind and caring. The mother I knew protected me when she could when Father was displeased with me. The mother I knew did what she could do to help the downtrodden. The mother I knew stood by Father's side even though he forced you to marry him against your will. The mother I knew would have never hurt our neighbors or killed people without remorse. Cannot you see the eye of the cyclops has possession of you? You must give up this war. Please, Mother, there has been enough death and destruction. Give me the eye; it must be destroyed."

Shiva looked stunned, then strained, as if she were fighting the eye. Bloodred tears streaked her face. "I am sorry, Maximus," she said sorrowfully.

She let out an unholy scream that knocked Maximus off his horse. The horse galloped away. Maximus got up off the ground and watched in horror as Shiva rose higher in the air, her eyes pulsating with the eye of the cyclops.

"I will kill them all! I will purge this world of their unclean and unholy souls."

"Mother," Maximus pleaded.

"You will be silent," she said to Maximus, then glared at Aldar. "You have turned my son against me."

Virion set his jaw and kicked his horse into a gallop.

"Don't go out there," Aldar pleaded, but it was too late. Shiva smiled as she saw Virion ride to Maximus.

"Get on my horse and go," Virion demanded of the prince.

"But Virion—"

"Just do it!" Virion shouted.

Maximus got on the horse and rode back to the amassed armies as Shiva watched. She frowned, but she let him go. Then she looked down at Virion, who unsheathed his sword. "You are wrong, Shiva," he said to her. "The only one who has turned Maximus against you is you."

Shiva's face grew dark, and she landed on the ground mere feet from him. She gestured for him to charge.

Virion smiled as he threw his sword at her. It stuck into her chest. She gasped in surprised, and he pulled out one of the tsundium battle-axes that was strapped to his side. He screamed as he moved to knock the eye out of her hand, but then his eyes widened. He looked down at his chest to see that his sword, which had been in Shiva's chest, was now somehow in his own. "You Finally actually killed me" he said as he coughed up blood, then fell to the ground.

"No!" maximus cried out.

Shiva walked over to Virion and looked at him, a tear running down her cheek. "I am sorry, old friend, but you left me no choice."

His dead, expressionless eyes were the only reply she received. She looked curiously at the battle-axe he had been carrying. The eye started to dim as she got closer to the axe, and she gasped and ran away.

She took to the sky. "What manner of witchcraft is that?" she shrieked, her voice echoing across the plain, then returned to her position above Adaliah. "Very clever trick, Aldar, but you will never destroy the eye. The time for talk is over. I am a patient woman, so when your army is ready, attack."

~ ~ ~

Aldar looked at the other monarchs and a shaking Maximus Aldar, then gave his last instructions. He got off his horse, removed his crown from his head, and bowed his head. The others followed. "Lord," he prayed, "grant us your power and wisdom to defeat this evil that has cursed this land. Receive the souls of the ones who will die today. Thank you for your blessings. Amen."

When the prayer was done, the monarchs put their crowns back on and returned to their horses. Aldar unsheathed his sword. "Gentlemen, it has been an honor being your supreme monarch."

King Barnabas unsheathed his own sword, then King Unidad did the same, as did Emperor Savage, and all four monarchs crossed their swords. "For freedom!" Aldar shouted.

"For freedom!" the other monarchs said.

"Assume your positions," Aldar commanded. For the next several minutes, the monarchs made their way to the front of their armies and awaited the command.

Isaiah rode up beside Aldar. "It is a joy and honor fighting alongside you, Aldar."

Aldar smiled. "Thank you, old friend. Father would be so proud. I know he is watching over us." He then gave Isaiah a somber look. "Are you ready?" he asked, putting his helmet on.

"Ready as ever," Isaiah replied, donning his own helmet.

Aldar nodded and raised his sword, pointing to Adaliah. The trumpeters blew their horns, and they all charged to what might be certain death.

Chapter Seventy-One

War

Aurora felt a rush go through her body as they charged the city. It felt great to finally do something that would make a difference. The gallop of the horses and the footsteps of the marching soldiers made a deafening roar.

A flash of lightning streaked across the sky, and Shiva disappeared. Then the Apollyon army moved. They did not move forward, however, but split apart, revealing the city's massive, closed gate.

Aurora frowned. Where had Shiva gone, and why had they left an opening to the front gate? Dread filled her body, and a chill went down her spine. She gritted her teeth as they drew closer to the city.

Another bolt of lightning shot across the sky with an associated crack of thunder, and another woman appeared floating in the sky above Adaliah. "Who is that?" Aurora yelled as they drew still closer to the city. The woman was wearing a short black silken dress and she appeared to have a big smile on her face, along with reddish-orange glowing eyes, and she started to laugh. Aurora had heard that laugh before but could not place who's laugh it was. Then the woman drew two swords. "Pirena?" Aurora yelled in disbelief.

"Open the gates!" Pirena yelled.

The gates opened suddenly, and Aurora's eyes widened in disbelief as a cyclops army ran through them. The cyclopes poured out of the gates—there had to be hundreds of them, Aurora guessed—their bestial roars echoing across the plane. All of the cyclopes had wooden clubs, and the ground shook as they charged the gathered armies. Aurora felt her blood run cold as her nightmare was revisited, and she felt for Enoch and Elaine, thinking they were probably feeling the same.

The charge of the armies was halted by the terrified horses, which reared, kicking and neighing, and trying to run away.

“Aim for the eye!” Aurora yelled, but her voice was drowned out in the chaos and confusion.

The cyclopes were closing in, roaring and snarling. In mere seconds, they would clash with the armies. Aurora managed to get Aldar’s attention and mouthed, “Go for their eye.” He nodded. Hoped that, somehow, the message would reach the army, she turned her attention to the charging cyclopes, counting down in her mind to when she thought they were going to clash.

Five. The ground was shaking as the cyclopes hastened their pace. *Four.* The combined armies shouted back at the cyclopes. *Three.* The frontline soldiers lowered their spears. *Two.* The soldiers shouted, “Freedom!” *One.* All was silent. It seemed as if time stood still for a moment, and every moment of every person’s life was relived—every hope, every dream, every triumph, every failure, every time of happiness, every moment of sorrow was relived in that one split second.

Zero. All hell broke loose.

The cyclopes swung their clubs. Men and horses screamed as they were knocked aside like rag dolls. Cyclopes screamed in unholy agony as spears and arrows punctured their eyes. Blood flowed like crimson rivers as soldiers were torn apart and cyclopes’ eyes were pierced.

~ ~ ~

After several minutes of battle, a blood-spattered Aldar looked around at the awe and terror of the fight. They had killed many cyclopes, but for every cyclops they killed, it seemed hundreds of soldiers died. He caught a glimpse of the Apollyon army still standing in wait, and he cursed. “They are there to finish us off.”

A messenger from the Violida army ran to Aldar. “King Barnabas requests help. Some of the cyclopes are reaching the back line.”

Aldar shook his head in fear. Zena, Hunter, and Alana were back there. “Elaine!” he yelled. Somehow even in the chaos, he got her attention, and she rode over. "Take your division to the back line," he told her. "See if you can bring other divisions with you. Make haste!"

Elaine gave him a knowing look. She rode off with her sword in the air, shouting commands, and her division followed.

Aldar, with a group of soldiers in tow, charged another cyclops.

~ ~ ~

Elaine, riding in front of her division and two others, found that four cyclopes had made it to the back line. She pointed to the other divisions. "Attack those three. Aim for their eye. We will attack the fourth." With horror, she realized the fourth cyclops was running towards Zena, Hunter, and Alana's direction. "Let us go!" she shouted at her own division and brought her horse into a full gallop, seeing Zena in the distance.

~ ~ ~

Zena watched the fighting in amazement. She had never seen such bloodshed. Seeing the cyclops army, she had been almost unable to believe what she saw. Now she frowned, unable to tell who was winning. She heard a loud noise and turned, her blood running cold. Two hundred feet away stood a cyclops with a spear stuck in its chest.

"Hunter!" Zena yelled.

"Yes, mother?" he asked as he ran up, then stopped in his tracks.

"Get your aunt Alana and get out of here," she commanded.

"But, Mother—" he protested.

"Do it now!" she screamed.

As Hunter ran off to get his aunt away to safety, Zena turned to face the cyclops. The cyclops roared and started to charge. Zena had two pistols at the ready, just two shots to kill the beast.

~ ~ ~

Elaine screamed in frustration. She was not going to make it to Zena on time. She saw the creature charge. "No!" she yelled as she saw Zena standing her ground. "It will kill her!" she yelled helplessly.

~ ~ ~

Zena narrowed her eyes as the creature drew near. "If my daughter can do it, so can I."

She calmly drew her first pistol. As the creature came within fifty feet, she cocked the hammer.

When it was twenty feet away, she fired. Unfortunately, the bullet only grazed the top of the creature's head.

The creature stopped and touched its head and screamed. It looked at Zena and snarled, but Zena was unmoved. She threw the first pistol on the ground and cocked the hammer of the other one.

The cyclops's eye was bloodshot as it roared. Zena's eyes widened as the creature leapt at her. The creature smashed its fists to the ground. Somehow, to Zena's surprise, she dodged the attack. The shock of the blow to the ground, however, knocked her down, and she rolled onto her back as the creature moved toward her.

Zena had dropped her pistol. Looking frantically for it, she saw it had landed a few feet away from her. She got up as the cyclops swung his arm, and she managed to duck. She ran to the pistol and picked it up, then she tripped on a rock and fell to the ground as the creature approached her. His menacing shadow fell over Zena as he raised his hand for the killing blow.

Zena fired her pistol, and the creature howled as blood spurted from its eye. Blood splattered Zena as she scrambled away. The creature fell to the ground, its huge body barely missing her.

Zena wiped blood off her face as Elaine approached.

Elaine got off her horse and ran to Zena, asking, "Are you all right?"

Zena smiled and then laughed. "Well, I never imagined in my life I would kill a cyclops. That certainly is a first." She began to laugh uncontrollably, looking at Elaine. "Funny, don't you think?" Then her eyes rolled back into her head, and she passed out.

Elaine managed to catch her. “Hunter where are you?” she yelled, and Hunter rode up to her. “Bring her to safety,” Elaine cried.

Hunter looked at his mother. “Is she—”

“No,” Elaine said, “she just passed out, and she killed that cyclops.”

Hunter looked at the cyclops in disbelief as Elaine got on her horse and returned to battle.

Chapter Seventy-Two

The Last Stand

Aurora charged forward on her horse. "Loose your arrows at will!" she commanded, and archers shot at the cyclopes. Aurora smiled; they finally were making some progress. They still had a long way to go but were making progress, all the same. She drew close to the walls of Adaliah and saw Pirena's expression.

Pirena's face looked wicked and contorted, and then she screamed, "Time to take matters into my own hands." She swooped down and decapitated a dozen soldiers in one move, their heads rolling like melons on the ground.

Aurora's jaw dropped.

Pirena landed, throwing half a dozen knives at once and killing six more soldiers. More soldiers charged, and she stabbed and sliced and decapitated them without stopping.

She is far more deadly than the cyclopes. Something must be done or she and the cyclopes will have the upper hand, Aurora thought. "Pirena!" she yelled.

Pirena looked over to her and smiled. "Your Highness. Well, we meet again." She flew over to Aurora and landed in front of her.

Aurora's horse bucked in panic, dumping Aurora to the ground, and Aurora quickly stood back up and picked up her sword, then fell into a battle stance.

Pirena laughed. "Aunt Shiva is sharing her power with me. You have no chance, Your Highness."

"Aurora!" Maximus yelled as he and Enoch approached.

"Well, it looks like you have two friends to save the day," Pirena said as Enoch and Maximus moved their mounts to stand beside Aurora, their swords drawn.

"This time you will have to deal with us!" Enoch yelled.

"I shall," she said, then chanted. Suddenly, two cyclopes charged Maximus and Enoch. The cyclopes rammed the men's horses, knocking them to the ground. "Sorry, boys, this battle is between Her Highness and me."

Aurora wanted to help, but she did not dare, for Pirena would kill all three of them if she tried.

"I have the power of the eye. I am invincible, but to be fair, I shall not use my powers fighting you—at least for now." Pirena charged.

Aurora backpedaled at the onslaught as the battle raged on around them. Pirena was clearly still using some of her powers, for she was much faster than the last time they had met. For a moment, Aurora panicked. How was she going to defeat Pirena with this extra power?

Then a calm came over her and Amanda's training took hold of her as Pirena continued to attack like a fierce beast. Pirena's eyes burned with rage, but Aurora was calm and collected. She breathed in and out slowly, then sprang into action, attacking.

Pirena's eyes widened in shock. She backpedaled, then flew into the air, just barely escaping a swipe to the head. She shot down at Aurora, trying to split her in half. Amazingly, Aurora blocked the attack, but she landed on her back. As the air was knocked out of her, she gasped.

Pirena smiled and walked up to Aurora.

"Pirena, what in the name of Apollyon is going on?" Shiva screamed.

Pirena looked around her. To her horror, she realized she had been concentrating so much on Aurora that she had forgot the cyclopes. The creatures were standing still and were being slaughtered by the dozens. She flew back into the air and chanted her commands, and the cyclops that remained started to attack again.

Shiva's eyes burned with anger. "You fool! You almost cost us this fight. Maybe you are not suitable after all."

Pirena shrieked in anger and looked down at the Apollyon army in wait. *I will show that old wench*, she thought. She then commanded, "Attack!"

Aurora looked over to her father and the army. They had lost too many. The Apollyon army had too many soldiers; their own side was going to lose.

"Form up!" her father commanded. What remained of the armies moved into a defensive position. Her father stood with Grandfather Zanthor, King Unidad, and Emperor Savage as all the armies blended.

It looked as though half their own forces were dead and half of the cyclopes as well, but now the Apollyon army was attacking. Aurora was not sure how many Apollyon soldiers there was, as she lined up with Enoch, Elaine, and Maximus.

Pirena landed in front of the Apollyon army with a devilish grin on her face as she led the charge. "Kill them all!" she commanded, floating in the air above to watch the carnage unfold. "What are you doing?" she screamed in unbelief as the Apollyon army started to attack the cyclopes.

Aurora's eyes widened in shock. The Apollyon army looked like ants attacking an invader as they charged the cyclopes.

"Attack!" Aldar yelled, and his troops moved to fight alongside the Apollyon army.

"Stop it right now!" Pirena screamed, but her army ignored her. She flew straight for Aurora to attack, but then suddenly, Pirena felt her power disappear and she landed on the ground. She looked up at Shiva, who shook her head. As she turned her attention back to Aurora, her eyes bulged at a great pain that filled her body. She looked down at the sword in her chest, then at Aurora.

Aurora scowled as she pulled her sword out of Pirena's chest. "This is justice for all the evil you have done." Pirena's eyes rolled back, and she fell to the ground, dead.

"Enough!" Shiva yelled, landing in the middle of the battle. Her eyes pulsed, as did the eye. She chanted, and a small burst of energy shot from the eye.

All soldiers and cyclopes within a hundred feet were knocked off their feet. Everyone stopped fighting.

Shiva eyed Emperor Savage. "Die, traitor!" she screamed as a bolt shot from the eye.

Savage yelled in agony as his body burst into flame. In an instant, he was ash.

Shiva eyed Aldar next. A horrific animalistic snarl filled her face as she raised the eye with her fingertips and chanted. The chant was in an inhuman, ear-piercing voice that reverberated across the land.

All was silent for a moment, and then the ground started to shake violently. A portion of the wall surrounding Adaliah crashed to the ground. Large cracks formed across the plain, swallowing soldiers and cyclopes alike. An orange-reddish beam shot out of the eye, and the sky turned the same color as dark clouds formed. The clouds came together and started to spin in a vortex, and the wind started to pick up.

Lightning shot out of the vortex randomly, killing soldiers, and thunder boomed, shaking the ground even more. Shiva smiled as the terrified soldiers screamed in agony and tried to run away from the onslaught, she was bestowing upon them. "This is the price for defying the eye and defying me, you traitors and infidels. You now face the wrath of the eye of the cyclops, you evildoers. The eye will cleanse the land of your sins. Now you will die!" she screamed. Her eyes and the eye shone in an almost blinding light.

Shiva started to chant.

"Mother, wait!" Maximus cried. "Please, Mother, wait!"

Shiva stopped chanting. The eye dimmed a little, as did her own eyes. She saw her son shaking on the ground with the remaining army and gave him a sympathetic look. "I am sorry, son, but I must purge this land."

"Why, Mother? Why must you obey the eye? Please, Mother, do not do this. It is not right. Please have mercy."

Shiva resumed her chanting, and Maximus braced himself for the worst, but to his surprise, the storm clouds disappeared.

Shiva slowly descended to the ground, then smiled at Maximus and nodded to him. The shaking stopped where he stood. Everyone else was still shaking—not as hard, but enough to keep them off balance. Maximus walked up to Shiva.

"I am sorry," she said to him. "However, you are my son and I love you; you are the true Apollyon and heir to the throne. I will spare you, and the eye of the cyclops will forgive you. You just must denounce the combined armies and bow and swear fealty to the eye. You will be coronated as Emperor Maximus Pulsar, and you, with the eye of the cyclops, will rule the world."

A tear fell down his cheek. "I love you, Mother—the real you, not who you have become. I am sorry, but I will not swear fealty. Mother, please. You must fight this evil that has possessed you. Please. I know you are trapped deep inside."

Shiva's eyes widened in shock, and she looked confused. Then her face became strained, and the glowing of her eyes and the eye of the cyclops dimmed slightly.

"That is, it, Mother. Fight, fight it with all your might. Fight, fight, fight, fight."

Sweat beaded on her brow. Shiva started to shake. Then she screamed and her orange-reddish eyes and the eye started to glow brightly again. She laughed, then sneered at Maximus. "Foolish boy. You are just as evil as the rest of them. How dare you defy the eye. There will be death, death to all of you." She lifted the eye with her fingertips, then yelped.

Out of nowhere, Daniel had tackled her, bringing her to the ground. The eye clattered to the ground beside them. Daniel got up and grabbed the eye, screaming in agony as the shock of it ran through his body. Somehow, he managed to pick it up as his body caught fire. "Destroy the eye," he said as he tossed it toward Maximus. He fell into a smoldering heap, and the ground stopped shaking.

"No!" shiva screamed as Aldar tossed the battle-axe. It landed in front of Maximus. Shiva watched in horror as she felt her power fade with the closeness of the battle-axe to the eye. She screamed, "Please, son, don't!" as Maximus picked the axe up and raised it over his head. In desperation, she lunged at Maximus and plunged a dagger into his chest. As he dropped the axe and crumpled to the ground, she picked the eye up and ran.

"Maximus!" Aurora yelled as she fell beside him and took his head in her lap. A healer ran up and looked at his wound but shook his head—the wound was fatal.

Shiva lifted the eye over her head and ascended once again as she laughed. "You have no chance. Your fate is sealed." Hearing a noise, she looked down at her son, who was gasping for air.

"Mother, why?" he managed to say.

Shiva blinked and suddenly returned to the ground. She started to shake again as tears streamed down her cheeks. This time, normal tears fell, not bloodred ones.

The eye flickered again.

Sweat ran down Shiva's face profusely, and she cried, "I am a murderer, and I just killed my son!"

Maximus was barely hanging on to life, but he looked up at her and smiled. "That is, it. Fight it, Mother."

Shiva's eyes started to glow yet again. "No!" she screamed. "Evil, you have no power over me." Her eyes returned to normal, and she dropped the eye to the ground and picked up the fallen battle-axe. The eye started to pulse and to glow brighter as if to protect itself, but Shiva smiled as she lifted the battle-axe over her head. She slammed the battle-axe into the eye, and she screamed in agony as the eye shattered into a thousand pieces.

A blood-curdling shriek sounded as an orange-red beam shot up into the air. Everyone their covered their ears. A great wind came out of nowhere, scattering the pieces of the eye across the plain in a thousand directions.

Shiva shouted, "I am sorry for what I have done!" Then she clutched her chest and collapsed. She looked at Maximus. "I am sorry, son. I have killed so many, and I have killed you."

Maximus smiled. "No, Mother, that was not you. It was the evil in the eye controlling you."

"Now we will be together in heaven," Shiva said, smiling as Aldar, Zena, Enoch, and Elaine approached. She reached her hands out toward Maximus. "Now I can rest in peace."

She smiled as her eyes finally shut forever.

Despite his mother dying for a second time, Maximus smiled. "Enjoy your rest. See you soon." He started to cough up blood and reached out to Enoch, saying, "Please come here. Aldar, you too."

They quickly called for a scribe, who wrote down what Maximus had decreed. Maximus smiled. "Now there will be peace," he said, and then his eyes closed forever.

Aurora put her hand in Enoch's as they looked at the carnage. "What happens now?" she asked.

"We rebuild one step at a time, Aurora, one step at a time."

Epilogue

A little girl paced the living room floor. It was her fifth birthday, and she was waiting impatiently for guests to arrive. She sighed and looked out the window as she restlessly tapped her fingers on the frame. Then she ran to a couch and pouted. "Mother, when are they going to arrive? When is Father coming? Please don't tell me he is busy; he is always busy. Why is he always busy?"

"Amanda, you are such an impatient one," said a pregnant Queen Aurora Eclipse as she walked into the room.

"Dad says I am five years old. I am not supposed to have any patience."

Aurora burst out laughing. "Oh, your father is a funny man sometimes. I know it is hard for you to understand, but running a kingdom is hard work."

The door opened, and a voice said, "I hear a little girl is having a birthday."

"Aunt Elaine!" Amanda yelled in delight. She ran to her aunt, and Elaine picked her up and twirled her around. Then they hugged.

"Where's your beau?" Aurora asked.

Elaine smiled. "Jacob is on an errand your husband sent him on. Ever since he became liaison for the king, my brother has him running around like a chicken with his head cut off."

Both women laughed when Amanda said, "That is so gross, Aunt Elaine."

Aurora said, "I will have to talk to Enoch about this."

The door opened again. "I hear a big girl is having a birthday."

Amanda ran to Aldar Talon, and he picked her up. Zena and Hunter came in behind Aldar, as did Barnabas. Aurora walked up to them, and Zena put her hand on Aurora's stomach. "My dear child is going to be a mother again. You are going to have a boy; I can feel it in my bones."

"Not a brother. They are so gross," Amanda said with displeasure, and everyone laughed.

Aldar said, "I ran into Enoch in passing, and—"

"He is going to be late," Aurora finished, hands on hips. Aldar nodded. "That man!" she said in frustration.

"Remember, Mother, you said Father is busy running the kingdom," Amanda said.

Aurora smiled broadly as she patted her daughter on the top of her head. "You're right, I did forget."

"Well, then we have presents for you to open," Barnabas announced with a hearty laugh.

They all gathered around and took their seats as Amanda started to open presents. As another person came in, Amanda dropped her present. "Father!" she yelled as King Enoch walked into the room.

"Late as usual," Elaine teased.

"I call it fashionably late." He smiled. All of them laughed.

The afternoon was spent with presents and birthday cake.

~ ~ ~

Aurora walked up to Aldar. "Father, would you like to walk with me? It has been so long since we talked alone with each other."

Aldar smiled. "I would be delighted. However, should you be walking with the baby due soon?"

Aurora smiled. "Yes, Father, the walk will do me good." She offered her arm, and he took it with a smile. "I wish Aunt Alana could have come, but I suppose someone has to rule the kingdom."

"I am sorry," Aldar said. "Hopefully she can come next time. She hopes to be here to help with the little one."

Aurora smiled. "That would be wonderful." After a brief pause, she said, "I would like to take you to the garden. There is something I want to show you."

They made their way to the garden, which had every color of flora and fauna imaginable. "What a glorious garden," Aldar remarked. Then he stopped as he saw a line of headstones in the garden. He walked to the first one. "Daniel Enigma," he read aloud.

"I wanted him buried here," Aurora explained. He was a victim and suffered many years. If he and Virion had not worked together, the Apollyon army might have attacked us. I thought it was a good idea to honor him. He was a good man and did what he could do to save us."

"Shiva Pulsar Enigma," Aldar read next.

"I thought it was a good idea to put them together; they were each other's true love. What Shiva did was beyond her control; whatever evil was in that eye controlled her," Aurora explained. "Xavier Pulsar is buried in an unmarked grave in an undisclosed location, as are Virion Nebula and Pirena Solaris. Even though Virion did help at the end, I did not feel right having him buried here. Xavier Pulsar and Pirena Solaris were evil people. They are in unmarked graves so their graves will not be desecrated by angry citizens."

Aldar walked up to the last grave. "Maximus Pulsar," he read.

"Yes, Father, I wanted to honor him. He was misled by his father. While he despised Enoch and Elaine, he really meant no harm. It was brave and honorable to name Enoch his successor.

"From what I understand," she added, "Xavier belittled him and accused him of being a coward. Well, nothing could be further from the truth. If he had not reasoned with his mother, we all would be dead and this world would be different."

Aldar smiled and kissed Aurora's cheek. "I am so proud of you." He looked around at the palace. "You and Enoch have done a wonderful job turning this nation around."

Aurora smiled. "As you know, it was not easy. At first, many people hated him and Elaine. They were blamed for being the offspring of Levi and Lana Eclipse, the killer of the Rose of Apollyon. He did find more favorability when he announced he was going to be king and denounced the Apollyon. Renaming this nation Avarlon also gave him more popularity, and with hard work, this nation is prosperous again. Father, I am so proud of him. He has been a wonderful husband, father, and ruler."

Aldar kissed her forehead. "I am proud of you, my young, strong daughter, wonderful mother and wife."

"How have things been, Father?"

"I cannot wait for you to visit," he replied. "Antillean City is almost back to normal. The palace is mostly rebuilt. Maybe in another five years, we will have the palace back to normal. We, of course, do not have the cyclops statue anymore. It was crushed in the attack."

Aurora cringed. "I hated that thing anyway."

"There you are," Enoch said, approaching them. "Amanda wishes you both to play games with her."

Aldar smiled. "Well, I guess we cannot say no to that," he chuckled.

Enoch offered his hand to Aurora, and the three of them left the garden behind and entered the palace, where fun and joy awaited them.

~ The End ~

Acknowledgements

Special Thanks

A special thanks to my daughter Maquela Maxwell who has been with me since the beginning of this massive project. Your help with naming most of my characters and developing their personalities have been invaluable. Your enthusiasm for this Novel kept me motivated to carry on. Thank you, Maquela, I love you, Dad.

Beta Readers

A huge thanks to my beta readers they all did an important job making sure my story was readable and made sense. No easy task to say the least, without their input and advice this book would have been a mess.

Roberta Maxwell, Maquela Maxwell, Denise Sutherland, Michelle Pollum and Judy Sweet. Thank you all for the help. Love you all.

Members of my Facebook Author Page Craig Maxwell's author page Facebook.com

I would like to thank all members of my Author page. Unfortunately, I cannot name you all. You know who you are. I appreciate all of you who read my posts and watched my videos even though I rattled on. Your willingness to take time out of your busy lives touched me. Thank you so much for your love and support.

Thank You!

Thanks to all of you who spent your hard-earned money to purchase this novel. I have spent countless hours on this. It has been a long journey from concept to rough draft, to final draft to novel. It wasn't always easy, but this writing journey was amazing, and I wouldn't trade it for the world! I hope you have enjoyed reading this novel as I have had writing it. Thanks for joining me on this amazing journey God bless.

Thank you, Jesus.

Most importantly I want to thank my lord and savior Jesus Christ for giving me this special opportunity. Thank you for giving me, your goofy child, this wild imagination. For if you had not died on the cross and saved me from my sin I certainly would not be here today. THANK YOU, JESUS AMEN

About the Author

Craig Maxwell Lives with his youngest daughter Maquela and family in Michigan's thumb area. At a young age he developed his love of Fantasy, Science Fiction and anything odd and fantastical. He grew up watching and reading classic monster, science fiction and fantasy movies, comics, books and tv shows. He loves writing, fishing, watching movies, grilling, barbequing and spending time with his two daughters Baleigh and Maquela.

Made in the USA
Columbia, SC
10 November 2023

27d4db54-e65f-46c4-b12e-fdab387a5fe0R01